Jane Harper is the author of the Dry, Force of Nature, The Lost Man, books are published in forty territories worldwide, and Jane has won numerous top awards including the Australian Book Industry Awards Book of the Year, the Australian Indie Awards Book of the Year, the CWA Gold Dagger Award for Best Crime Novel, and the British Book Awards Crime and Thriller Book of the Year. The Dry and Force of Nature have been adapted into major motion pictures starring Eric Bana, with The Survivors released as a Netflix series. Jane worked as a print journalist for thirteen years both in Australia and the UK, and now lives in Melbourne with her husband, two children, and two cats.

Also by Jane Harper

The Dry
Force of Nature
The Lost Man
The Survivors
Exiles

JANE HARPER

LAST ONE OUT

MACMILLAN
Pan Macmillan Australia

Pan Macmillan acknowledges the Traditional Custodians of Country throughout Australia and their connections to lands, waters and communities. We pay our respect to Elders past and present and extend that respect to all Aboriginal and Torres Strait Islander peoples today. We honour more than sixty thousand years of storytelling, art and culture.

First published 2025 in Macmillan by Pan Macmillan Australia Pty Ltd
1 Market Street, Sydney, New South Wales, Australia, 2000

A catalogue record for this book is available from the National Library of Australia

Typeset in 12/16 pt by Post Pre-press Group
Printed by IVE

The author and the publisher have made every effort to contact copyright holders for material used in this book. Any person or organisation that may have been overlooked should contact the publisher.

The paper in this book is FSC® certified. FSC® promotes environmentally responsible, socially beneficial and economically viable management of the world's forests.

*For all the wonderful librarians and booksellers
of my childhood and now, with my ongoing
gratitude as both a reader and a writer.*

Prologue

He had been here, that was clear from the marks in the dust. And he had been alone. That, too, was evident in the boot prints at each of the three houses. His movements could be traced with some precision, the scuffs and scrapes showing where he had walked. Along the length of a verandah, up a hallway and then back again, into a kitchen, a bathroom, a bedroom. The dust showed where he had arrived and where he had left. One set of prints in, one set out.

It was almost believable from a distance that someone could still be living in the houses, but up close the illusion quickly crumbled. The truth was revealed in the detail.

The white cottage that looked so postcard-pretty perched at the top of a winding track, with its green coat of ivy reaching up towards the roof, had an odd quality on nearer inspection. The snaking vines smothered the exterior, binding the walls tight and choking the features. Hungry for more space, the growth had wormed its way through the cracks in the windowsills and doorways and was now slowly consuming the rooms inside.

To the west, a kilometre down the hillside, the Hillary farm-house appeared more hospitable, but only at first glance. The broad wooden gate that used to swing open and closed smoothly and often had, for several years now, been wedged permanently ajar with leaves and debris gathering in dunes at the bottom of the posts. The home's weatherboard façade was barely clinging on to its last coat of paint, the cream colour flaking away like a scab to show the raw, grey wood beneath. Three sagging steps led to an empty covered porch. The front door was missing. Where it had once stood firm and solid, painted a warm yellow, there was now a vacant rectangle of space. The home gaped open, its threshold unguarded, vulnerable and exposed to the elements.

The third house, across the paddocks to the east this time, did not look inviting even from a distance. The low sandstone bungalow had been decisively boarded up and was now sealed firm and tight, wooden panels nailed across its windows like a blindfold.

Each of the three houses had its own curving track. All were wide enough for a vehicle and all still carried a vague sugges-tion of having once been welcoming, but the surfaces now lay uneven and rough, overgrown in places with creeping weeds. The three tracks forged their own routes from the front of each home and down through the paddocks, until they met near the southern fence line. There, they converged for a short stretch to form a single access point from a country road. It had always been known as a quiet route, but now the road could often sit wholly undisturbed as a full day slipped away, morning to night.

The monotony had been broken that afternoon, though.

The bright red hatchback that had trundled up to the access

point was small, with compact tyres and a suspension designed for city motoring. It was a rental car, chosen for its affordability above anything else. From inside the vehicle, the chip and ping of small stones bouncing off the paintwork could be heard over the frantic whir of the air conditioner.

The driver, a reluctant owner of the cheapest legal level of motor insurance, had winced from behind the wheel at each sound. It was his birthday; he had turned twenty-one years old that morning. His laptop bag jiggled on the passenger seat as he turned off the asphalted country road and onto the dirt track leading to the three houses. The small car immediately laboured and complained, and in the back he heard his water bottle and a thick notebook branded with the name of his university in Sydney slide from the seat and hit the footwell with a pair of rhythmic thumps. He swore lightly and glanced over his shoulder, only to snap his head back around immediately as the front right tyre hit a pothole, sending the car lurching. His hands gripped the wheel tighter as he frowned through the juddering windshield and efficiently guided the vehicle to the side of the track, where he brought it to a stop.

The grass alongside grew tall and yellow, and it shuddered in the hot wind as he opened the driver's door and stepped out of the cool, contained atmosphere and into the cloying heat of the February afternoon. He paused for a moment, then reached back to grab his broad-brimmed hat from the passenger-side footwell. Of medium height and stocky build, his hair and eyes a matching shade of brown, he slapped his hat on his head before leaning down to check the car. No harm done to the front tyre, he was relieved to see. He licked his thumb and ran it over the metal on the wing panel. A little damage to the paintwork, though. He swore again, silently under his breath, then straightened and turned his attention outwards. He let his eyes wander over each of the three properties in the distance and felt a familiar uneasy prickle of guilt.

When he'd been younger, this view had been pleasant, impressive even. Now the paddocks that used to be a blend of greens were brown and patchy, dotted in places by the odd sparse copse of sickly eucalyptus trees. He adjusted the brim of his hat to shield his eyes as he squinted against the angle of the sun and pushed the car door closed. He hesitated, then clicked the lock on the key fob. He wouldn't have bothered if it hadn't been a rental. In front of him lay empty paddocks; behind was only the deserted road and a dense stretch of bushland. There was no-one else in sight.

The boy turned back to the vehicle track. The long grass obscured sections from where he stood, but he didn't need to see it. He knew this track very well, knew exactly where it divided from one into three, each path leading to a different door. His gaze slid to the end of the trails and once again across the three outlying structures, left to right.

The weatherboard farmhouse, the ivy cottage, the stone bungalow.

The air that afternoon was carrying its strange tang that always seemed to coat his mouth and tongue, and he cleared his throat. The sound felt loud in the stillness. The only noise other than the rustle of the wind was an unnatural droning, distant but constant. The frequency was low enough that at times he could feel it more than he could hear it. Loud or quiet, he could always sense it though, rattling in his head.

He stood for another minute, debating with himself as the air grew hotter, and he felt an unpleasant feathery sensation where the skin of his neck met his hairline. He swatted impatiently at the bead of sweat sliding down and glanced over at the car. It winked back at him, the metallic tint blinding where it caught the sunlight. Somewhere out of sight, the deep murmur continued.

The young man breathed in, sucking in the tainted air, feeling its bitter flavour rolling around his teeth and gums. He exhaled, emptying his lungs. The wind sent the dust at his feet swirling up, dancing and floating in the light as it latched on to his clothes and skin, and only then, at last, did he move.

Above, the sun slowly crawled across the sky.

It was low on the horizon and the light was fading when his parents finally found the small red rental car, more than five hours later, parked near the point where the three tracks converged into one. The car was locked and seemingly undamaged beyond some minor chips to the paintwork. Its metallic sheen appeared dull now as the last of the daylight dwindled. A laptop lay undisturbed on the front seat, a water bottle and notebook in the rear. On the counter of his family's kitchen, six kilometres away on the south-eastern side of town, the young man's twenty-first birthday dinner waited for him, cold and untouched.

His parents stood beside the car, looking first to each other for answers and then out, at the horizon, the houses, the road, the bushland. They called their son's name into the twilight, perhaps a little self-consciously to start with and then, when there was no response, with mounting urgency. Straining their ears for a reply. Beneath the distant low rumbling there was only silence. At the end of the tracks, the three houses stood empty and still as they in turn were swallowed by shadow.

The weatherboard farmhouse. The ivy cottage. The stone bungalow.

Exposed, strangled, blinded, they sat quietly in the growing dark, waiting for whatever would come next.

Chapter 1

Five years later

R o Crowley couldn't say she hadn't been warned, because she had. And by now she shouldn't have been surprised, and yet still she found she was.

The radio crackled in the dashboard, the sound fading in and out as she drove along the deserted country road, choosing her own speed because she could. There were no other cars, no-one else around to inconvenience or endanger when every now and again she would slow to a halt in the middle of the cracked asphalt, engine idling as she stared through the window at something else that made her face go slack with disbelief. Driving through this place was like being administered with a series of small, unpleasant electric shocks.

The Hewetts had gone, and they'd taken the orchard arch.

It was this absence that made Ro jam her foot hard on the

brake, jerking forward against her seatbelt as the car lurched to a stop beside the gravel shoulder.

The Hewetts' place was deep within the town limits, well beyond the road sign that had once clearly welcomed visitors to Carralon Ridge. The same sign now barely whispered its message in paint that had peeled and faded away.

The Hewetts' neat little house with its wrought-iron lacework was set well back on a generous acreage that had once been lush with rows of fruit trees. The home was still in good condition, externally at least, but every window was dark and the driveway empty. They'd left the trampoline, Ro could see from the road. The one that the Hewett grandchildren could be found tussling on most days in summer, the warm air punctuated by the creak of the springs and the muffled yelps of sibling arguments. Dead leaves covered the mat now, and the grass around the base, which Doug Hewett had kept permanently short and stubby so the grandkids wouldn't be bothered by snakes and vice versa, was tall enough to scrape the springs.

Ro peered at the property through the windshield, a stone of disbelief and dismay turning in her chest, as she switched off the engine. She climbed out of her car, leaving it where she'd stopped in the road and walked over to the fence. She put both hands on a post, her gaze sliding past the house, ignoring the vacant windows and the abandoned trampoline, and instead settling on the north-facing orchard, now growing rambling and wild.

An intricate archway made of woven steel had once stood at the entrance to that orchard. And on a spring day, what felt like a long twenty-seven years ago, Ro had helped thread the arch with boughs of native greenery and handfuls of garden flowers and then she'd been married beneath it. Now, though, the archway was gone. In its place stood nothing but tufts of dry grass and sagging trees, groaning under the weight of their unpruned limbs. Ro stared at the void for another minute, then pushed herself away from the fence and went back to her car. She climbed in, restarted the engine and drove away, not looking in the rear-view mirror.

She didn't stop again, instead simply noting any changes as she caught them. There was a padlocked chain on the door of the community hall. That had been added since her last visit twelve months earlier. The windows of the former medical centre were entirely covered with yellowing newspaper pages, but that was not new; the stories printed on the pages were three-and-a-half years out of date. Ro touched the brake gently as she drew near. The paper was peeling in the corner of the farthest window, the one she used to glance out of between patients' visits to her clinic room for close to two decades.

As she approached, she considered pulling over, walking up to the blacked-out window and pressing her eye to the gap. She was tall enough that she'd be able to peek through, but there'd be nothing much to see on the other side. The practice manager had sold most of the furniture and equipment after the centre had closed. No-one worked there anymore. Ro drew level but kept moving, driving by slowly and only tearing her gaze away when the building fell behind her, out of sight.

Something was very different here, though, she sensed as she approached the crossroads that over the years had served as the centre of Carralon. Once the heart and hub of the place, the commercial land on the four corners used to be prime real estate, but now the former bank was boarded up. Its official branding had long since been torn down but had left such a distinct shadow on the hoarding that the name of the branch was still clearly legible from the other end of the street. Diagonally opposite had stood Greeves & Son, where Ro used to buy her children's clothes and school uniforms. Its doors had permanently closed four years ago and twelve months later what remained of the school followed in its wake.

Now, only two of the four corner sites were occupied. On the north-eastern spot, the struggling general store was still limping along, Ro could see. Supplying basics to a handful of residents who barely numbered enough to support the business but also couldn't do without it.

And on the south-western corner stood the pub.

There was an abnormality in the air, though. Ro could feel it as she brought the car to a stop at the crossroads, the junction as quiet in either direction as the long country roads leading up to it. The sun was low, bathing the town in a warm orange light. Ro tapped her fingers against the steering wheel and looked around. The answer was right in front of her, but even then the sheer peculiarity of it meant it took a moment longer to register.

The pub lights were off.

Ro gaped, only dragging her eyes away to check the time on the dashboard. It was just after six o'clock on a Thursday night. A warm, clear evening in summer, on a day that had traditionally been observed by all in Carralon as the gateway to the weekend, and the Black Creek Inn was closed.

Feeling almost light-headed with disorientation, Ro pulled into the deserted pub car park and got out. A crinkled sheet of paper with a handwritten notice had been stuck to the inside of the glass door, the letters faded in the sunlight to the point that the note may as well have been blank. She squinted at it, trying to get a sense of the message. Giving up, she used her thumb to wipe a clear square in the dirty glass then put her face to it, cupping her hands to shield out the daylight as she peered in.

The place hadn't been gutted at least. That surely meant

something. A single fluorescent exit light flickered at the end of the room, illuminating the battered wooden bar top. The familiar collections of old hats and faded postcards were still pinned to the wall above the shelves behind the bar. Ro couldn't imagine Sylvie leaving them behind, and besides, Ro felt absolutely certain she would have heard about it if the woman had gone. A couple of tall circular tables still stood by the window, the odd barstool scattered around. Behind the countertop, though, the glass fridges were almost empty. A few lonely bottles and cans barely filled a single shelf. The Black Creek Inn still looked technically operational, Ro decided, but that was probably the best that could be said for it.

She eased away from the door, her blurred reflection staring back at her from the murky glass. It was both like her and not. Her eyes fell somewhere between grey and green but appeared in the glass as dark hollows in her face, her straight nose and gently rounded face without definition in the mirrored image. Ro's hair had always been a warm golden brown when she'd lived here before, but now it looked flat and colourless, tied back from her face in a way that didn't suit her but felt more comfortable in the heat. Ro had lived in this town for so many years as a younger woman that she almost half-expected on returning that she'd somehow slip back into the more youthful body that had walked these same streets, tap into that less-burdened mind and lighter spirit. She waited a moment, and when once again it didn't happen, Ro simply turned away.

She looked back down the road, her ears straining instinctively for the typical sounds of life. The distant rumbling had stopped, for now, leaving the air so quiet that Ro felt she could be standing alone in a wide, open paddock rather than loitering in a car park in the alleged heart of town. The streets seemed to almost sing their own mournful, lonely song. It was the creak and settle of unused spaces, the sound surprisingly loud when not muffled by movement and bodies and chatter.

Ro walked back to her car and was reaching for the door when she heard something else. She paused, fingers grazing the handle, and tilted her head to listen. A clanging noise, metal on metal. And then again, this time possibly metal on wood, or the other way around. It had an unpredictable rhythm, frequent but irregular. Odd gaps of silence filled the space between the pockets of sound. Ro listened for a moment longer, then let her hand slip from the car. The noise had a different quality to the natural cracks and groans of the derelict buildings, and she wandered out onto the street, turning as she tried to pinpoint the source. It stopped, then started again, and somewhere underneath she caught a different noise. A faint gurgle of laughter.

Ro stopped where she stood. She had once known everyone in town, but things changed. Instead, she stayed where she was, outside the old hairdressers' salon and a storefront that had been dark for so long she couldn't remember what it had ever been, and listened as the banging started again. It was unexpectedly loud at times, but she had the impression the sound was carrying in the warm, still air. Ro could not tell if she was close or far away when all at once it stopped dead. She stood unmoving in the middle of the street, her own breath in her ears now the loudest noise to be heard. The silence stretched long enough that she began to wonder if she'd been mistaken.

Her phone twitched in her jeans pocket, making her jump a little, and she pulled it out. Ro held it in her palm, letting it ring twice, three times, as she looked at her former husband's name on the screen, then tapped the button to answer the call.

'Hi, Griff.'

'Hi.' His voice was flat, the end of the word cut off. She could hear the rustle of him swapping the phone over in his hands. 'I'm up on the ridge. Saw your car.'

Ro pivoted, turning towards the north and shielding her eyes as she looked past the roofline of the town to the hills beyond. It took her longer than it ever had before to find the spot she was looking for. The place where the bushland broke, giving way to a craggy outcrop forming the ridge for which the town had been named. It must have been prominent in the past but the trees had all but swallowed it now. Catching sight of it at last, she scoured the space for a flash of the binoculars that would be trained on her. She couldn't see them, couldn't make out Griff at all, and after a few moments she gave up, dropping her hand and turning to make her way back to her car.

'Found a parking spot at the pub with no problem,' she said drily into her phone as she walked. 'It's closed?'

'Yeah.' The word came down the line heavy with emotion. 'A lot of the time, anyway. Sylvie only opens a few nights a month.'

'Oh.'

Griff allowed the news a moment of respectful silence, then: 'Thought you'd be getting in a bit later.'

'Got lucky with the traffic.' Ro allowed four-and-a-half hours door to door from her place in Sydney to the centre of Carralon, and it sometimes took all that and more. 'Is Della here yet?'

'She wasn't when I left. Probably not far away, though.'

'Yeah, hopefully.'

There was a softening in both their voices at the mention of their daughter, followed by another lengthy pause. Ro had reached her car.

'So –'

'Listen –'

They started and stopped at the same time. In the sharp slice of dead air, the strange clanging started again. It sounded both closer and somehow further away this time, and Ro turned to look once more, rotating in a slow, full circle. The noise bounced off the buildings, the echo disguising the source. She could see no-one else around.

'What are you doing?' Griff's voice in her ear brought her up short, and something in his tone made her picture him frowning behind his binoculars.

'Nothing,' she said, feeling a familiar itch of irritation. 'Thought I heard someone.'

'Oh.' There was a pause and then another rustle of movement on the line, and Ro guessed he was scanning the surrounding streets.

'Anyone?' she asked.

'Not that I can see.' He was quiet for another short stretch, then: 'Listen, I've left the house unlocked, so if you want to head over whenever you're ready I can meet you at . . .'

Home.

He so nearly said it, and they both knew it. Ro could hear the bitten-off exhalation of the 'h', imagine him clamping his lips shut, releasing the aborted word via a breath through his nose instead.

'The house,' he finished.

'Right,' Ro said quickly. Neither of them wanted to let that moment hang. 'Thanks.' She hadn't bothered locking the car and now pulled the driver's door open. She found herself hesitating, though, as she climbed in and reached for her seatbelt, phone still to her ear. 'Hey, look, are you going to be up on the ridge for a while?'

'Bit longer, yeah. High winds on and off today.'

Ro sat in the hot car, debating with herself. She hadn't seen Griff in person for a year. Whatever they may or may not feel the need to say to each other, she suspected she'd rather do it on neutral ground.

'Wait for me. I'll come up.'

If he was surprised, he swallowed it quickly. 'All right. See you in ten.'

Ro paused, hand on the wheel. There was only one route that would get her to the ridge in ten minutes. Along the northern road, past the three houses.

Griff read her reluctance in her silence.

'Or more like fifteen, twenty, then.' He sighed heavily. 'It's fine, Ro. Just go the other way. See you whenever you get up here.'

And with that, he was gone. Ro tossed her phone on the passenger seat and started the engine. She backed out of the empty pub car park and onto the deserted street, wondering if Griff still had his binoculars trained on her as she turned right, then right again. Taking the long way around.

Chapter 2

The long way to the ridge took Ro seventeen minutes in the end. She passed no-one else on the roads as she skirted the town's eastern boundary before turning upwards along a gently winding slope. Dense bushland towered over her on both sides of the road, tall and deep until, nearing the top, she turned a final corner and the trees suddenly parted, opening a window over the valley.

Griff's ancient four-wheel drive was already there, parked on the wide dirt clearing at the shoulder of the road. He was leaning against the passenger door, frowning at his phone. Tall and solid, at fifty-six he was two years older than Ro and at some point his exhaustion had become permanently etched across his face. He was dressed in old jeans and a long-sleeve t-shirt he'd had since they were married. Ro thought she might even have bought it for him as a present one year. It used to be black, she vaguely remembered as she parked her car behind his, but had faded now to a dull grey. His hair and beard were losing their colour too, still thick but more silver than brown, and both could do with a good trim.

Griff straightened as he saw her pull up, stepping away from his battered vehicle and slipping his phone into his pocket.

'G'day,' he said as she turned off her engine and climbed out of the car. He was unsmiling, but Ro didn't take it personally. She couldn't remember the last time he'd looked happy. Around their daughter, she supposed. He still smiled at Della. As Ro observed Griff for the first time in a year, she found herself inevitably contrasting the man in front of her with who he'd once been. It was deeply unfair, Ro was very aware, but she suspected Griff was quietly doing the same as he looked back at her.

They had met at the Black Creek Inn, the pub's doors well and truly open then, the room hot and crammed far past capacity, the music blasting. Ro had known only one person at the wedding, her friend Heather, who was now flushed and laughing helplessly as her new husband tried to spin her in the middle of the crowd, her full white dress blowing out at the hem. Griff had been laughing too as he'd watched from the other side of the bar, leaning with one elbow on the counter, his suit jacket already off in the early evening heat, his hair a touch longer then. In the packed space beside Ro, someone had dropped a glass, the noise cutting through the music as it shattered against the wooden floor. And at that, Griff had turned his head and he had looked Ro's way.

For the rest of the weekend, Ro had assumed Griffith was his surname. And given that she'd felt very sure that, whatever this thing was, it had a shelf life that would expire in exactly two days' time when she returned to Sydney, she hadn't bothered to probe the matter further. It had been a few weeks later when, somewhat to her surprise, she'd found herself having dinner with him in a city restaurant and he'd mentioned that Griffith had been his granddad's name. For reasons best known to themselves, his parents had decided it should also be his.

That had been close to three decades ago and as Ro looked at Griff now, she could see only traces of that time. It felt like catching a glimpse of an important sign from the window of a speeding car. There, then gone immediately, with a hint of regret. Lost behind the years and the trouble.

Ro waited a moment longer to allow the first impressions of this year to settle on both sides, then nodded at the pair of binoculars resting on Griff's car roof.

'How's it looking today?' She turned towards the gap in the trees.

'Yeah, quiet enough so far.' He scratched his neck. 'Wind's let up, so that's something.'

Ro nodded and moved past him, wandering towards the edge of the ridge. She heard him retrieve the binoculars and follow, but while he focused as usual on the west, Ro found herself drawn, as always, first to the east.

The sun was low enough that she had to squint, the rays of late light casting long, flickering shadows over the land. In the distance below, Ro could make out the miniature version of Carralon. From up on the ridge, it looked delicate and beautiful, like something from one of the illustrated books she used to read to the kids when they were young. The fields, so dead and dry up close, had a welcoming warmth in their yellow tones, and the red roofs of the few houses she could spot looked model-railway charming. Ro slid her eyes over the landscape until she found the most obvious landmark, where the roads crossed in the centre of town. Bathed in the evening light, Carralon glowed, peaceful and inviting. A flock of birds took flight from the trees and soared overhead against the pink sky. The town looked beautiful, Ro thought. It looked like somewhere she could see herself living.

She'd actually pondered the idea, fleetingly, whimsically, the very first time she'd been up here. She had been with Griff then, too, late morning, on the day after Heather's wedding. Both still a little hungover but gently so, with the aftermath of the celebrations dissolving like champagne bubbles, leaving them both pleasantly slow and lazy. They'd got into Griff's four-wheel drive, a different one back then, and he'd driven them up to the ridge where they'd wandered to the edge and stood in much the same place as they were now. Probably a little closer then, Ro guessed, although the memory had rusted from disuse over the years. She could picture them, though, shoulder to shoulder, looking in the same direction.

She pulled her eyes away from the town now and walked over to join Griff in looking out to the west. He glanced over his shoulder and held out the binoculars, but she shook her head at the offer. She didn't need to see what lay that way in detail.

The Lentzer coalmine gaped beneath them like a dark stain. Monstrous and vast, it dwarfed the trees and buildings dotted around its perimeter. It had been carved out by layer after layer dug into the ground, oddly reminiscent of a terraced farm, but every level a variant shade of black. There were two distinct quarries, one more than twice the size of the other. At the bottom of each, a lake of water pooled murky and grey.

Ro stared out at the operation. It looked enormous at a casual glance but it was only the movement of the occasional industrial digger that really gave a true sense of scale, the vehicles appearing as small and flimsy as cheap toys as they crawled around the edges of the quarries. She could hear the low rumble of machinery, the constant grinding reverberating in the air even over this distance. She could smell the sulphur.

There would be dozens of people down there right now, Ro knew. The coalmine was a twenty-four-hour operation, fully self-contained and staffed by Lentzer's specialised and vetted workforce who were brought in from elsewhere on rotation. In the very early days, there had been a faint hope around Carralon of a silver lining in the shape of local jobs and a boost to the town's businesses but none of that had materialised in any meaningful way. The mine's workers lived, slept and socialised entirely within the sprawling complex and were given no need or excuse to venture into the sleepy neighbouring community.

Ro turned her focus back from the mine to the town. The boundaries between the two had been blurred badly over the years as houses and land were sold and bought, but the distance from the eastern edge of the Lentzer dig to what used to be the western edge of the Carralon Ridge limits was three kilometres. In reality, though, Ro thought as she stared down, it had always been as good as right next door.

'They've already got going on that southern expansion, have they?' she said, nodding to where the beginning of a third crater was being carved out.

'Yep.' Griff's voice was resigned. 'Started the day after they got the green light.'

He raised his binoculars to his eyes again, and Ro felt rather than heard him sigh. Griff had headed up the region's fire response for two decades until the local station had been permanently closed three years ago, with the trucks and professional equipment and the only paid position relocated more than an hour away to the next nearest station in Blenheim. Now, Griff's job description was written by Lentzer and his wages were paid from one of the mine's bank accounts, and Ro didn't need to be on close terms with her former husband to know exactly how he felt about that.

He was employed by Lentzer to maintain his few remaining neighbours' private fire-fighting equipment as he patrolled the community for hazards and tackled the spot flares that constantly threatened to break out. With just a sprinkling of rain and oxygen, reject coal had a tendency to spontaneously burst into flame, which Ro had never known before but, like everyone else in Carralon, she certainly knew it now. Griff kept an eye on the winds that carried rogue sparks onto dried, abandoned properties, and generally did his best to prevent what remained of the community from being razed to the ground. Lentzer paid him not for the town's sake, Ro knew without a doubt, but because an out-of-control blaze raging right on their doorstep would hamper their own operations.

Still, for all its failings the job allowed Griff to stay in Carralon, working in the community that he'd been part of for his whole life, and Ro understood that was where the value lay for him. Whatever their personal circumstances, whatever the financial offer, he would never have accepted a role that involved setting foot on the grounds of the quarry.

Griff had lowered his binoculars now and was staring down at his employer, his face unreadable. Ro turned away, looking back towards the centre of town. The pub sat small and quiet on the crossroads, the car park still deserted.

'So Sylvie's still here, is she?' Ro asked. 'Who else has gone?'

'Since last time?' Griff's mouth formed a line as he considered. 'Been a few.'

'Easier to say who's still here?'

He gave a small, hard laugh. 'Getting that way.'

Ro glanced over. 'I saw the Hewetts left.'

Doug and Ruth Hewett had been among Griff's mother's closest friends and when Griff was born, they were elevated to the role of godparents.

'Yeah,' was all he said in reply. 'Think that one had been on the cards for a while.'

Ro nodded. *They got rid of the arch, Griff,* she wanted to say, but was reluctant to mention it. She waited to see if he might but he stayed silent, which made her feel immediately and unfairly irritated. After all, he'd got married under it too.

'They left the trampoline,' she said, instead.

'I saw. They moved closer to Danielle and the kids. She's near the city, though. Small block apparently.'

'Did they get anything for the house in the end, or . . .?'

Griff was already shaking his head. 'Lentzer wouldn't make them an offer, and it's not like anyone else is lining up to buy. Just had to close the door behind them and walk away.'

Ro pictured Doug and Ruth coming to that realisation. The tight conversations, drenched first in denial, then distress. Bank statements laid out over the same kitchen table where they'd fed their children and then grandchildren, calculations run again and again in the hope of reaching a different result. Ro wondered which of them had shut the door of the home for the last time and felt a rush of sadness wash over her as she gazed down at Carralon. Still glowing, still golden, still looking so deceptively like somewhere she might herself like to live.

She'd known Griff maybe eighteen hours that first time they'd been up there. Now, nearly thirty years later, they stood in much the same spot, his arms folded across his chest, her hands on her hips as they each slid their eyes over the scene below. Eventually, he cleared his throat and swapped his binoculars from one hand to the other.

'Wind's died off, I reckon. Ready to head down?'

'Yep. Okay.' They both turned back to their cars.

'Right. See you back there.' He didn't nearly say home this time.

'See you there.' Ro opened her car door and climbed in, hearing his own door slam and the sound of the engine start up. Griff reversed, then turned onto the road, his face grim as he passed her with a curt nod and disappeared down the trail. She sat for a minute, hearing the rumble of his wheels fade into the distance. When all was quiet, she waited a moment longer, then undid her seatbelt and opened her door again. Leaving it ajar as if she might need to make a hasty escape, Ro walked back to the edge of the ridge. She ignored the mine completely this time, her attention focused elsewhere.

Ro had not consciously been seeking out the place, but it seemed at least part of her must have been looking, because her eyes now fell on it immediately. Surrounded by paddocks that looked neglected even from that distance, there they were.

The Hillary farmhouse, the ivy cottage, the stone bungalow.

Ro stood alone amid the rumbling, rolling noise and stared down, her eyes moving from one house to another. Three small shapes, each cast into shadow as the sun dipped lower.

*

Sam had been late for dinner on his twenty-first birthday, and Ro had felt only irritation. It had not crossed her mind to be worried. Not then, at least. Sometimes now she tried to pinpoint the moment when she'd first felt that true bead of concern, the early faint shiver of warning that something was wrong. She suspected she could identify it if she really wanted to, if she tried hard enough, but she never did. Instead, Ro allowed her memory to protect her with its small vagaries and gaps because she knew that whenever it was that she had first sensed trouble, it had been far too late.

Perhaps it had been when Ro's call had gone unanswered, clicking straight through to Sam's voicemail without ringing as dinner hovered on the cusp of being overdone. His phone had seemed to be turned off, which was highly unusual. Had it been then that the cold fingers of unease began to creep over her? But batteries only lasted so long without a charge, she would have reasoned. And it was his birthday; he'd probably been texting all day as he finalised plans to meet his friends for a drink. They weren't due to catch up until later, though, after Sam had eaten dinner with his family. Still, Griff had called the only two of Sam's mates who still lived in town. Jacob, and then Darcy. Or perhaps the other way around, Ro wasn't sure. It didn't matter. Their answers were identical. No, they'd both said in turn, sounding surprised. They hadn't seen Sam. Why? What had happened? Was he still coming to the pub later?

Ro had picked up her phone again and she and Griff had begun calling around their remaining neighbours in the town, which even five years ago had not been a long list. Their daughter, Della, eighteen years old, had checked Sam's social media, fired off texts to their few mutual acquaintances, attempted to track his phone with an app on her own. The clock hands crawled onward. Sam's phone continued to go to voicemail and it was at that point that Griff had grabbed his own car keys and then tossed Ro's to her. This action, this decisive response that had seemed like overkill right until that very moment, felt instantly urgent, rushing up on Ro in a way that had made her feel shamefully, dangerously neglectful for not having gone out to search much, much sooner. They'd left Della watching the door at home and parted ways at the end of the drive, Griff turning his wheels left, Ro steering right.

She had been out for twenty minutes, pausing at driveways and at the end of country tracks, peering out into the growing gloom, when Griff had called. Ro's heart had lurched so sharply that the steering wheel jerked in her hands. She'd made herself pull over to answer, alone in the driver's seat beside an untended paddock, the long straws of weeds trembling gently in the warm breeze, the sky turning purple overhead.

'I've found the car,' Griff had said, then just as quickly: 'He's not with it.'

Ro had already restarted the engine. She had driven straight over to join her husband and had reached the turn-off to the three houses still half expecting to see father and son waiting there together. Sam, physically so like a younger version of Griff, would hopefully be merely sheepish rather than injured. Griff would be hiding his relief behind brusque reprimands and an unwanted lecture. During Ro's short journey there, she had embroidered the scene to a point where she'd felt a ripple of confusion when she'd pulled up at the fork of the track to find only Griff. No relief, no lecture, the worry setting his face hard.

'I've rung everyone again,' he'd said. 'No-one's with him, no-one's seen him.'

'We should call the police, Griff.'

'I already did.'

That had startled her. She had expected to have to convince him.

'How long away?' The nearest station was in Blenheim.

'Few hours, they reckon, minimum. No promises. They've got their hands full with a road smash over there.' Griff forced out a breath of frustration. 'And Sam's twenty. Twenty-one,' he'd corrected himself. 'So, I dunno. Low priority, I guess.'

Ro couldn't think of anything to say to that, to a third party's stark assessment of the relative importance of their child, but she had felt the tiny, warm bubble of disbelief that was still desperately trying to shield some part of her rapidly deflating. Needing to do something, she moved over to Sam's rental car and jiggled the handle.

'It's locked,' Griff said. He was looking in a different direction, out over the land.

He was right, but Ro had still walked all the way around the hatchback, trying the boot as well with no success. The car had been parked considerately at the side of the track so as not to block access, she noted vaguely, and was facing the houses in a way that implied arriving rather than leaving. All four tyres were solid, and later it had been confirmed that there was fuel in the tank. Peering through the windows, Ro could see Sam's laptop on the passenger seat, and a university notebook and water bottle in the back.

It had all been sitting there, she remembered, as she stood on the ridge now and looked down at that same spot, allowing herself to examine it through a buffer of time and height and distance. Everything had been there waiting for them, except Sam himself.

On Monday, four days from now, another of Sam's birthdays would pass. He would be five years older, in theory at least, making him twenty-six. Or not. In Ro's bleaker, greyer moments, she felt deep in her core that her boy had never passed twenty-one, that his date of birth and date of death had become one and the same. At other times, she reminded herself she knew nothing for certain and allowed brief shelter to a small, under-nourished seed of hope. But either way, the facts remained. Five long years later, Sam had never been found.

Chapter 3

A clean silver sedan was already parked outside what had once been Ro's family home. So, Della was on the premises, Ro thought, and felt herself smile for the first time that day as she pulled up beside it. She and Griff were both better people around their daughter.

Ro climbed out and retrieved her bag from the boot, pausing to consider the house. She had left Carralon Ridge eighteen difficult months after Sam had vanished, and whatever Griff thought, Ro knew she had tried her best. Either way, she had returned only once a year since, each time for a few days around the anniversary of what she still worked very hard to think of as Sam's birthday.

The feeling of arriving back here at this house only grew more surreal with every visit. It was with a dizzying sense of time travel that Ro found herself following the same route she had driven along a thousand times before, one she could still navigate with her eyes closed. Down along the southern road, through town and out again, the sky large and wide above her as she passed by neighbouring paddocks that had once been the Murphys' and now belonged to the Lentzer mine. Reaching the familiar turn-off, then bumping up the gravel drive and through the wide-open gate to the low-slung weatherboard cottage. At one time, Ro had felt a sense of relief simply at the sight of her home. She did not feel that way now.

The exterior could do with another coat of paint, Ro couldn't stop herself from noticing as she stared up at it, but the large verandah had been swept clean and the mature bougainvillea that she'd planted herself had been neatly trimmed back where it climbed the posts, its leaves lush and green and the late-summer flowers adding a splash of colour. She was tempted to fill up a bucket from the outside tap and throw some water on it, but she didn't. This wasn't her house anymore. Technically, it wasn't even Griff's.

Ro had been six months out of Carralon and leasing a depressing one-bedroom place in North Sydney when Griff had called to tell her that Lentzer had made another offer on their place. The company had long-term expansion plans for the south of the dig, apparently, which would encroach within two kilometres of their back paddock. As a result, the company would be willing to acquire the Crowleys' property in order to facilitate a smooth expansion in the future. However, Lentzer noted, it considered the market value of their house and land to have fallen sharply since the last time the company had made an approach. Ro's breath had caught in her throat when Griff had told her the revised number.

'What do you think?' he had asked, his voice dull.

Ro had let him make the final decision, as the only one still living there. *Made* him make the decision, she'd admitted

to herself later, after the fog of pain had lifted a little. At the
time, she'd convinced herself that she was being considerate, but
now she felt it had simply been cowardly. Griff probably felt the
same, she suspected. Either way, he had fallen quiet for a few
days, and then come back with his answer.

'Sell,' he'd said. 'If you're really not coming back.'

'I'm really not coming back, Griff.'

There had been a very long silence at the other end of the line.

'We should get it over with straight away then,' he'd said,
and even though it was what Ro thought she'd wanted too, the
decision had felt like a body blow.

It had been the right choice, though. They'd got far less than
they would have if they'd caved earlier and sold in that first year
or so, but received more than the literal zero the Hewetts had
apparently found themselves with as a consequence of trying to
hold out. With the southern expansion still some years away at
that point, Lentzer had magnanimously allowed Griff to rent
his own house back from them while he was employed as their
community fire safety officer.

It was painful to see what a psychological difference that
made, Ro thought, even from her safe distance in Sydney. To be
a tenant in the house that they had bought and owned together.
She had been able to spot telltale signs of the change from her
first visit and could see yet more now. The garden was in need
of cutting back and she was surprised the weatherboard was
still waiting for its latest coat of paint. These were all jobs that
Griff, as homeowner, used to do immediately. Prevention and
maintenance, that was his mantra. He appeared much slower to
act when the weatherboard and the grass belonged to someone
else. Griff, as tenant, technically wasn't required to carry out
any repairs at all, Ro supposed, but if he didn't certainly no-one
else would.

Ro slammed the boot now and heard the screen door squeak open. She looked up to see Della silhouetted in the glow from the house. At twenty-three, her smile was warm and broad as she came down the steps towards her mother.

'Finally.' Della hugged her. She was wearing a short linen dress and smelled lovely, something musky with a hint of cinnamon. Ro reminded herself to get the name of it later. 'Dad's been back for ages, we were wondering where you'd got to.'

'Sorry,' Ro said, meaning it. She never wanted Della to worry. 'I was just . . .' She shrugged. 'I'm not sure. Taking things in.'

'God, I know. So grim, isn't it?' Della murmured. 'Worse every time, I reckon.' She pulled back. 'Hey, I like your hair. Take it down so I can see.'

'Do you?' Ro self-consciously pulled the elastic tie free so her hair fell loose. It felt limp and sweaty against her neck. At her last appointment she'd decided it was time to let the grey grow out, trying to blend the roots subtly with the golden-brown she'd carefully kept up for more than a decade. There had been a fair bit more to blend than she'd expected.

'Yeah. It's good. You can pull it off.' Della was lying, Ro could tell, but she appreciated it, nonetheless.

While Sam had always taken after Griff, Della had something of Ro's own mother in her. Particularly in the slightly appraising look she was giving her now. Tall and straight-backed, with a wide, unflinching gaze, Della worked as a junior accountant for a major investment bank in Sydney's city centre. She and Ro saw each other often, or as often as Della's punishing schedule allowed her to show up, always a little frazzled, with stress zipping around her like electricity as she threw herself down into a chair for a quick coffee or late dinner. On those occasions, Ro would try her hardest not to let the GP version of herself take over, and made a conscious effort to leave her professional advice about anxiety management and the importance of incorporating balanced lifestyle practices back at her clinic where they belonged. Instead she would sit opposite her daughter, deliberately calm and softly spoken, locked into listening mode, simply hoping that Della would feel better when she stood up than she had when she'd sat down.

Ro had quietly wished Della had accepted her offer to drive them both over to Carralon together, but she had declined with thanks and some complicated story about leaving from a client meeting on the other side of the city. It was probably true, but Ro suspected Della might also want her own means of transport to escape for a few hours if the atmosphere around the house grew too heavy.

'Dad says you wanted to be in the hut again, but are you sure?' Della was already talking as she reached over to help Ro with her bag and they set off together, not up the steps to the verandah but along the path leading around the side of the house and out into the large back garden. Magnolia trees lined the space on two sides, with a low fence at the rear separating it from the paddocks beyond. At the bottom of the garden was a wooden cabin, the only window dark. 'The air conditioner's so bloody weak in there.'

'Yeah, I know. It'll be all right, it's only a few days.'

'If it gets too bad you can have my room.'

Of the three bedrooms in the house, one had been shared by Ro and Griff, one had been, or technically still was, Della's, and the other had been Sam's. Ro did not want to sleep in any of them.

'Thanks. I'll manage. The hut's good.' That at least was true. They called it the hut, but the name didn't do it justice. Griff had built the small self-contained studio twenty years ago to give Ro's parents some privacy and space when they visited for extended periods.

'All right, well, if you change your mind . . .' Della put Ro's bag on the steps and nodded back towards the house. 'Dad's firing up the barbecue for dinner, by the way.'

Ro followed her daughter's gaze across the expanse of patchy lawn to where Griff stood at the foot of the deck, arms folded and a spatula in one hand as he frowned down at the grill. The lines on his face were rigid in the harsh overhead light of the porch.

'Sounds good.' Ro picked up her bag. 'See you over there.'

The hut wasn't as homely as it had once been, back when Ro put out fresh flowers and scented soaps for her parents, but as she flicked on the main light the place still had a familiar feel to it. There was a bed tucked up against the far wall, made up with patterned sheets that Ro could see were worn but fresh. A sliding door led to a tiny bathroom and beside the bed stood an armchair and a reading lamp. The wooden floor was covered by a colourful round rug that Ro had chosen herself and she could tell Griff had swept out the place ahead of her arrival. If it had been left more than a day or so, every flat surface would be covered in a fine grey layer of coal dust.

Ro put her bag down and washed her face and hands. She started to fill a glass with tap water, then, seeing the colour run not quite clear, realised she'd better ask Griff what the quality was like these days before gulping it down. She slowly poured it away, feeling suddenly, overwhelmingly exhausted. She slumped into the armchair and turned on the lamp, for the first time noticing a large paper envelope on the side table at her elbow.

Rowena, Griff had written on the front, her name under-lined, and as Ro picked it up she could guess from the weight and shape of the contents what was inside. Carefully upending the envelope onto the table, she spread out a collection of photographs.

She had not seen most of these pictures in years, but now she remembered them instantly. Remembered them being taken, in most cases. Nearly all were of her and Sam together. Occasionally Sam appeared on his own, at age two or eight or eleven, but mostly Ro and her son were side by side, celebrating with a birthday cake, or trying on Christmas hats, or messing around in the garden. Ro's image, the younger version of her, the naive version of her, so stupidly unaware of exactly how good she had it in each of those captured moments, smiled out. Happy, and why wouldn't she be? With her arm so casually slung around her child's back, or her hand resting lightly on his shoulder, or her head touching his. Present Ro, the version of her that was sitting alone in this stuffy cabin, clutching a handful of old photos, found it a little hard not to hate that woman.

She focused instead on Sam, watching with uneasy nostalgia as he lost his baby teeth, shed his little boy softness, grew taller, broadened out. Ro's son had been a man when he disappeared, which she sensed at times was expected to make his loss easier to bear somehow. But Sam had also been her little boy – for years and years – and she found it impossible to think of one without the other.

There were about forty photos in all, which had felt like a lot at first glance, but in reality was not nearly enough to accurately capture twenty-one years. Ro reached the end of the stack and immediately went back to the start, looking more carefully this time, allowing herself to tentatively creep through the memories they prompted, some faded but some surprisingly vivid.

Occasionally, Della or Griff would appear in the background and Ro felt an almost physical jolt to see how carefree they'd both looked in those unguarded, candid moments. Griff's grin particularly was relaxed and natural in a way that looked only strange to her now, and he had a sense of calm around his eyes that he'd shed along the way. It was a little unsettling, she thought as she flipped through, how he could look so familiar with his hair and face and clothes, and yet be almost unrecognisable as the same man.

Ro reached the end of the pile again and, checking the time, resisted the temptation to go through once more. Instead, she turned the pictures over in her hands and then slipped them back into the envelope, for now at least. She stood and stretched, readying herself to go, but at the last minute paused. Her bag lay at her feet, still unopened, and after a moment's debate, Ro reached down and hoisted it up onto the chair.

She unzipped it, ignoring her folded clothes, and reached instead for a faded, pocket-sized notebook with the university branding on the front. The cardboard cover was worn now, but that was mainly from Ro herself handling it. Five years ago, it had been new. She opened the book and flicked through the first few pages, running her eyes over Sam's spidery writing as it crawled dense and black across the lines. She did not stop to read; she knew well enough what was written there. Occasionally a neighbour's name would leap out at Ro from the page, or a date or a reference to a local business that had long since closed. Towards the front were two maps of Carralon Ridge, one of the town centre and one of the wider community, both sparse and hastily hand-drawn in Sam's efficient style. Mostly, though, he had written questions, the curly punctuation marks filling the pages. Ro flipped to the middle of the book, to the final page he had used. At the top he had written a date. The day of his birthday, the very last day Ro ever saw him. Below the date was a name, followed by a short list of questions. Beyond that, the rest of the book was blank.

Ro slowly closed the cover, then reached out and picked up the envelope of photos of her and her son. Held together, the notebook and the pictures had an oddly comforting weight to them, and she placed them carefully on the faded floral bedsheets she'd bought herself seven or eight years ago. She stood there for a minute, her fingertips on the photos and the notebook, then gently brought the heels of her hands to her eyelids, pressing them shut. Just tightly enough that she could see stars and for just long enough to be certain that the tears would not come. Only when she was sure did she let herself lower her hands and open her eyes again. She took a breath in, inhaling the traces of grit and sulphur that were now as much a part of the town's fabric as its trees and paddocks, then opened the door of the hut and stepped out to rejoin what was left of her family.

Chapter 4

On the many evenings over the years when the Crowley family had barbecued for dinner, they would sit in outdoor chairs around the blazing fire pit in the garden, eating together and catching up on the day over their food as the sky changed colours above them. The pit lay black and unlit now as Ro made her way past it and up the verandah steps to the kitchen. Inside, Griff dropped a handful of cutlery onto the table with a clatter.

'Hut okay?' he said, glancing up as she came through the door and then back down to the knives and forks.

'Yeah, it's good.' Ro blinked as her eyes adjusted from the evening gloom to the harsh fluorescent light overhead. 'And listen, thanks for those photos.'

'That's all right.' There was a tiny, odd pause and as she watched, a furtive look scurried across Griff's face, vanishing almost instantly. 'I was sorting through some stuff. Thought you'd want them.'

'Yeah. Of course. I –'

Ro stopped and they both turned as Della came into the kitchen, covering her mouth with her palm as she yawned widely.

'God.' She dropped her hand and frowned. 'Has the mine got worse or am I just not used to it? That bloody rattling gets right in your head.' She swatted the air near her ear as though it was the buzz of a trapped fly in the room, close and grating. 'Can I put on some music?'

She didn't wait for an answer before pulling out her phone and turning to fiddle with the small portable speaker on the counter. Something low and mellow and jazzy started up. It would have been pleasant in other circumstances but now Ro found it an extra layer of irritation, like spraying air freshener to mask the stench of rot.

'Food looks good, Dad,' Della said, taking the plates from the counter and putting them on the table. Out of habit, Ro reached up and opened the cabinet door nearest to her, expecting to find glasses but instead coming face to face with an old blender. She opened the next one along and found only pots and pans.

'In here.' Griff opened the cupboard beside the fridge, which frankly made no sense at all because it was all the way on the other side of the room from the sink, and took out three mismatched tumblers. 'Don't drink too much water straight from the tap, by the way. It's okay in small doses but I've filtered the stuff in the fridge.'

Ro just nodded, but she felt on edge. She had the strong sensation of being in a dream where everything appeared normal, but daring to scratch the surface would reveal it as somehow distressing and wrong. She sat down at the table and ran her palm over the grain of the wood. That was the same, at least. Although she was sitting, she remembered, in the seat that Sam had been in himself – ten days before his birthday, ten days before he vanished – as he'd filled them in on his plan for his degree thesis in rural science and development.

'So the thesis is about Carralon itself?' Ro had asked as she'd checked the oven. She'd been only half listening, moving around, taking out plates and glasses, swinging cupboard doors wide open with the brash confidence of a woman who knew she would find the correct kitchen items stored inside.

'Not directly,' Sam had replied. 'But yeah, partly. I'm using it as a case study.'

'Study for what? What's happened with the mine?' Griff had glanced up over the top of his reading glasses, then gone back to squinting at the thin pliers in his hand. He and Sam had been fixing something, a small motor maybe, because Ro had a vague memory of sweeping a tangle of wires aside to make space for the cutlery.

'Kind of. But less about the mine and more about our response to it.' Sam passed Griff the larger set of pliers from beside his elbow. 'It's so shit here now – sorry, Dad, but it is, you can see it too. I want to take a look at how we ended up here. I mean, was there some way we could have saved ourselves after the mine came in? Maybe not, but could we have done anything collectively, as a whole community, that would have made a difference? Because if so, that could be something other places could learn from.'

'It's the money, though, isn't it?' Della had said, and Ro remembered being surprised she'd even been listening. Della was leaning against the doorframe, halfway between the kitchen and the hall, and hadn't bothered to look up from her phone as she spoke. Ploughing through her final year of school, she was openly counting down the days until she could see the back of Carralon.

Ro couldn't blame her. The family of Della's closest friend had left the year before, leaving her as the only girl of her age in town, and she'd recently lost her part-time job when the shoe shop she'd worked in closed its doors. If Ro hadn't been one of just two doctors left at the clinic, she'd have quietly suggested to Griff at that point that they seriously consider taking Della and moving elsewhere themselves. He would have resisted, she suspected, and for Ro's part it would have felt like abandonment to leave some of her more vulnerable patients without local access to medical care. So she hadn't raised it and instead tried to spend as much time as she could with her daughter, encouraging her to come for a run or join her in the vegetable garden, while Griff had attempted to draw her interest in fixing things around the place. Della had resisted all their efforts with teenage malaise and spent most of her days wandering listlessly around the house and studying in her room.

'I dunno.' Sam had frowned at his sister. 'I mean, is it the money? The sense of community's still pretty bloody strong, don't you reckon? And there's the generational history as well, people raising their kids in the houses they grew up in, that kind of stuff. I don't think it's as simple as some outside group coming in and offering cash. It's not like we all shrugged and said "okay" and that was the end of it.'

Sam had been right, it certainly wasn't as simple as that, and Ro had briefly met Griff's eyes across the table, back when they still owned that kitchen, back when Griff was still paid by the government and not the mine to oversee the town's fire safety plan, and back when they were still on the same wavelength about things.

'No, I think that's true, mate.' Griff had frowned at the wire he was trimming. 'And a lot of us have had offers over the years, before the mine even came in. Developers, and there was that tourism group that wanted to turn the Murphys' place into an artists' retreat. You remember that one, Ro?'

She did. She and Griff had been approached by the group too. It had been an easy no, for them at least. But people had come and gone for all kinds of reasons back then. Health, finance, a desire to move closer to family. Reasons easy enough for their neighbours to understand and support.

'And when the developers or whoever came knocking, sometimes people sold, and sometimes they didn't,' Griff was saying. 'But selling to the mine was different because we could all see it was changing the town. Like it or not. You've got the noise, the air quality's a bloody joke. Everyone had friends who were thinking of leaving. So you might not have wanted to leave yourself, but suddenly maybe whatever was keeping you here wasn't here anymore.'

'And it's not like anyone *wanted* to sell to the mine,' Ro had added, rummaging through a drawer for her oven gloves. 'Given the choice, everyone would've sold their house to someone who was going to love it and look after it. Raise their kids there. Those buyers weren't interested in this area anymore, though.'

There had been the immediate stain of distrust too, Ro had thought but not added out loud. Families who had lived side by side for decades began whispering about each other in the street, because they all knew the reality of the situation they faced. Most locals would try to hold out, but some would cave. And it would be them, the first ones to jump, the quickest to shake hands and strike a deal with the mine, who would get the best prices. Everyone else would eventually topple, after months or even years, when life in Carralon Ridge became too lonely or unpleasant or unrecognisable, but by then they'd have to take what they could get.

'Listen, whatever you end up researching or writing about,

mate,' Griff had passed an electrical component to his son to inspect, 'the mine never gave a shit about the houses, or the land. Still don't. They just want us all out so there's no-one left to complain. Just remember that.'

'Yeah.' Sam had looked from one parent to the other, a note of exasperation creeping in. 'I know that. That's exactly why I'm doing it.'

The tile floor screeched, bringing Ro back to the present as Della pulled up a chair beside her. Griff sat down opposite, and between the three of them they managed to make the topic of Della's workplace fill the whole meal, as the music from the speaker competed with the distant industrial rumbling.

Della finally pushed aside her cleared plate. 'So what's every-one's plan for tomorrow?'

'I thought I might go out to the site,' Ro said.

Della glanced over and even Griff looked up. None of them needed to clarify which site Ro meant. When they were talking about the three houses, they all knew it.

'You're going tomorrow?' Della asked.

'Yeah. I think so.' Ro shrugged. She felt caught off guard a little by the decision herself, but the houses had been playing on her mind since she'd glimpsed them from the ridge and she felt a need to face them up close. 'I'll have to go sometime. May as well be soon. Do you want to come?'

The invitation was directed at Della, who paused. 'No. Thanks, though. I don't think I can.'

'That's all right,' Ro said. 'Are you working from home?'

'Yeah. I am. Supposed to be, anyway. But . . .' Della seemed to be briefly wrestling with something. 'Sorry, I didn't expect you'd be going out tomorrow. Maybe I can . . .'

'Della, no, it's fine. I'm just going to stop by.'

'Okay.' Della nodded, and Ro was surprised to detect a slight hint of evasiveness in her tone. For a second, she thought her daughter might elaborate but instead Della simply slid her chair back from the table and stood, stifling another yawn. 'In that case, I might go to bed. Do you need help with the dishes?'

Ro found herself shaking her head along with Griff, and they both rose to give their daughter a hug and watch as she disappeared down the hall.

'I'll sort all this out,' Griff said, nodding at the plates, and Ro hesitated. He looked as tired as she felt.

'You cooked,' she said, turning on the water in the sink. 'I'll give you a hand.'

From somewhere down the hall, Della must have disconnected her phone from the speaker because the music suddenly cut dead. Ro and Griff moved in uncomfortable tandem around the kitchen, stacking the dishwasher, wiping down the table. The shared routine was so familiar that they were able to complete it in near silence, accompanied only by the faraway rattle, which had taken on a new, lower frequency.

'I hope Della's not working too much.' Griff spoke out of the blue, his voice a little muffled as he stacked the leftovers into the fridge. Ro looked over in mild surprise. She'd been thinking exactly the same thing. Although perhaps that wasn't much of a coincidence. She and Griff were both quietly but acutely observant of their remaining child's mental health.

'She's definitely working hard,' Ro said. 'But I think she's handling it okay. I know she's getting out with her friends sometimes, and she's still playing in that social netball team. I think she's seeing someone new, or . . .' Ro thought back to what Della had actually said. 'Maybe just talking to someone, actually. Which is different, I think. They met online but already knew each other from uni, something like that. I'm not quite sure, it sounds a little . . .'

'Complicated?' Griff supplied, closing the fridge.

'Yeah.' Ro smiled despite herself, and as she watched him move across the kitchen she was struck by a vivid flash of crystal-clear, full-colour memory. Griff, making his way across the Black Creek Inn, past the bride and groom who were still merrily attempting to dance in a space barely big enough for standing, both well under the influence but happily so. The music had been loud, the air hot and the floor sticky, as Griff, still name-less to Ro then, edged through the crowd towards her. He had nearly made it when he'd become hopelessly trapped, just metres from her, behind a group of aunts determined to join the couple on the makeshift dance floor. He had scratched his beard, lifting his chin to peer over their heads, and as his eyes met Ro's he'd shrugged good-naturedly and grinned. She had looked at him, standing there with his tie loosened, his face unlined, full of humour and interest. And Ro had smiled back. A silent ques-tion, asked and answered across that busy bar. The opposite of hard work, the opposite of complicated.

And it had stayed that way for most of their marriage, she'd give him that, until one day their son had vanished and the sheer raw trauma of that event had maimed them both in such a deep and permanent way that suddenly every single thing in Ro's life had felt like insurmountably hard work, every movement and action and decision had felt cripplingly complicated. And Griff impossibly, unexpectedly, felt like the most difficult and complicated thing of all. To Ro, he had become unreachably distant, as though they were locked in two different versions of the same horror. The crushing weight of grief and confusion had continued bearing down until more than twenty years on from that shared smile across the bar, and eighteen months after their son had been lost from their lives, Griff had sat on the front porch of their house with his arms folded and watched in granite silence as Ro had packed some boxes of things into her car. She had ignored his judgemental scrutiny until all of a sudden, she couldn't anymore.

'If there's something you want to get off your chest, Griff,' she'd slammed the boot shut so hard it made her palm sting, 'by all means, now's your chance.'

His face, already rigid, had hardened further and for a second it had looked like he might just take her up on that offer. But then he had closed his mouth, run a hand over his chin and nodded at her packed car.

'I've got nothing at all to say to this, Ro.'

She had looked at him, wanting to turn away. But the weight of that many shared years was a solid one and it had kept her where she was. For a minute longer at least. 'Come with me, Griff.'

He had looked at her like he didn't recognise her. 'No.'

The word hit like a blow and with it he'd turned and disappeared into the house, the screen door screeching open and clanging shut behind him. Having spent almost every day together for more than two decades, Ro and Griff had not seen each other again for another six months.

Ro now finished drying the chopping board and put it away in the nearest cupboard, closing the door with a louder bang than she'd intended. 'I think Della's okay.'

'Yeah.' Griff shot a glance down the darkened hall. 'Hope so.'

Ro folded her tea towel and put it on the counter. The kitchen was clean. The routine finished, the awkwardness between them threatened to return.

'Well,' she said before it could take hold. 'Good night.'

'Yeah. Good night. But, hey, listen . . .'

Ro, already turning to leave, looked back.

'I was thinking I'd come with you tomorrow, out to the houses.'

'You don't have to work?'

'I do, but nothing that can't get done later.' Griff leaned against the counter. His face was set, his eyes not quite on hers. 'Or do you want to go alone? No worries if so. I can go any time. I just thought . . .'

Ro waited, genuinely curious to hear what Griff thought, but he didn't continue. She considered the offer, weighing it up back and forth. Part of her did want to go alone, but a larger part of her very much did not.

'Okay,' she decided.

'All right. Good,' he said briskly, and immediately Ro wondered if she would have been better off saying no. 'See you tomorrow, then.'

'Yep. Okay.' She nodded. 'Good night.'

''Night.'

Ro left him in the kitchen and crossed the garden back to the hut. The stars were out and she took a moment to glance up. It could be a beautiful night, if not for the rumbling on the horizon and the faintly unpleasant tang in the air. Letting herself in, she sat down on the bed, taking the notebook and envelope of photos she'd left on the sheets and stacking them on her lap.

She considered opening them in turn, staring at Sam's face, following his handwriting along the page, but the minutes ticked on and in the end, Ro did neither. Instead, she simply sat there and thought about the day that lay ahead.

Ro pictured the rough, uneven track leading the way up to the three old properties, and she imagined viewing the scene not from the safe height of the ridge but up close, right in front of her. Nothing would have changed much, she guessed. It rarely did out there. But still, there would be another year of wear and tear, fine layers and edges and details sandpapered away, day by day.

Ro got up from the bed, still clutching the notebook and photos, and moved to the window. From there she could see their family house, quiet and still on the other side of the yard. The biggest change here each year was Ro's own connection to this place. It felt worn thin to the point of transparency these days, but once it had been strong and robust. This house had been special to her, even if she'd never paused to appreciate it as deeply as she should have. Once, it had been her favourite place in the world.

Ro stood at the window now and watched as lights went off, one by one, until finally the home that used to be hers, used to be Griff's, used to belong to all four of them, was plunged into darkness.

Chapter 5

'We'd better take two cars today,' was Griff's greeting to Ro when she made her way to the kitchen the next morning in search of breakfast. He was eating toast standing up, frowning at the weather report on his phone. 'I might need to drive out, check the fire break on the western boundary later.'

'That's fine,' she replied, because it was fine. Ro was never sure how she would feel at the houses and she'd prefer to be able to leave when she wanted. She flicked the kettle on. 'Della still asleep?'

'No, I heard her up and about early. Think she's already working.'

'Oh.'

And with that they seemed to have already run out of things to say to each other.

Fifteen minutes later, alone in the kitchen, Ro washed her mug and dried it with a faded tea towel that she'd bought at one of the kids' school fundraisers. The house was quiet and, feeling equally entitled and uneasy, Ro wandered up the hallway. She could hear Griff brushing his teeth in the bathroom at the end, accompanied by the groan of the pipes and the splash of running water. Across the hall, Della's door was shut, her name spelled out in peeling glittery stickers. Each letter had been stuck on individually, forming the word with a slight downward slope. Ro was tempted to knock, but from inside she could hear the low murmur of Della's voice, her tone carrying a distinct briskness that Ro associated with a work call.

The next door along stood ajar. The master bedroom. Ro didn't venture closer, but from where she stood, she could see the nearest edge of the bed that had once been hers. The sheets were tucked in and she recognised the quilt cover. Her bedside table was still there, too, but her books were gone, along with her lavender sleep spray and the usual half-finished tube of hand cream. Now the table held only an ancient digital clock and a spare pair of Griff's reading glasses.

Ro heard the water shut off in the bathroom and, feeling like she'd been caught out at something, quickly turned away and moved instead to what she'd really come to see.

The door on the left. Like Della's, it was shut, but there was no name on this one. There had been, at times in the past. Three letters posted in various age-appropriate styles along with the changing décor. Monster truck stickers, a football flag, all long gone now. She turned the handle and swung the door open.

Sam's room was not his anymore. It hadn't been for a while, even before he'd disappeared. It was neat and neutral, the toys and homework desk and car tracks and retro lava lamp replaced by only a chest of drawers and a double bed with a bare mattress. Ro had known the room looked like this, and she'd thought she had braced herself. The barren nature of it still came as a shock.

Sam had cleared out most of his belongings himself over the years, the first big haul leaving with him at eighteen when he'd packed his bags for university. With each visit home, he'd taken a little more away with him. There had been another big clear-out at the end of his first year when he'd moved into a shared rental place in Sydney with some friends from his course. Whatever he hadn't taken with him then had been given away or boxed up to be dealt with later.

Ro had helped Sam on each of these occasions, casually tossing out the memories with the odd sharp pang of nostalgia, but mostly with a lift at the sight of seeing clear drawers and desktops resurface for the first time in years. When Sam had returned for what would be his final visit, the room had already been neutralised to the point that it could be used as another guestroom. Why she'd been happy to do that at the time, Ro really couldn't explain now. They'd rarely had any visitors at all to Carralon by then, let alone frequently enough that they would need extra space in addition to the garden hut. But Sam didn't live there anymore, she supposed she'd reasoned at the time. All of his important belongings, everything he valued, had been taken with him to Sydney. He'd been a guest in this room himself on that last trip, bringing with him only a small backpack of belongings from what had become his real home in the city.

Ro was glad of it in some ways as she looked over the space now. If they hadn't cleared out the room while Sam was with them, she wasn't sure she could ever have done it after he'd gone. It would all still be there, like a ghostly museum, whispering and calling to her and Griff and Della each time they passed. As it was, for better or worse, most traces of Sam had been removed from this house before he'd disappeared himself.

Ro stood in the doorway of his room, and from up the hall

heard Griff come out of the bathroom. There was a pause in his footsteps and then a quiet click. He had shut the door to the master bedroom. Ro didn't turn to look, just stayed where she was as he came closer. She could feel him standing behind her, could hear his quiet breathing as they both gazed over the empty space, saying nothing as the seconds ticked on.

'Ready to go out there?' she said, at last.

She heard him exhale. 'I suppose so.'

★

It was just the two of them on the road for the whole fifteen-minute journey from the end of their driveway to the turn-off, where Griff touched his brakes and slowed.

On the way, they'd passed the piece of land where Griff's own childhood home once stood. It had been nothing but flat paddocks for close to thirty years, the small brick house demolished after Griff's parents sold the property with their children's blessing to their nearest neighbours to help fund their retirement. Griff had been in his early twenties at the time, a few years before Ro would meet him, but from the way he spoke about it, she could tell he'd been both young enough that his sense of nostalgia did not yet run too deep and old enough to actively appreciate the lump sum his parents had sent his way following the sale. His folks had moved to Adelaide to be closer to his older sister and her children, and Griff had eventually taken his windfall and put it with Ro's savings to buy their own house. He'd always seemed fairly pragmatic about the whole business, and only very occasionally had Ro caught him turning his head to glance over as they passed the site. She had privately used to think the loss of his old home was a bit of a shame, but in later years she'd come to see it as a relief. One less place to mourn.

Up ahead, Griff was slowing his four-wheel drive on the

country road and Ro followed as he turned, her wheels jolting against the rough track. He pulled over to the side and she parked behind him, both climbing out and wordlessly walking the short distance to where they'd found Sam's rental car.

There was little to distinguish the spot from any other along that stretch of track, but Ro knew it the moment they reached it. She could remember exactly which sagging fence post she had been standing beside when she'd spun around on that horrendous day, scanning the surroundings, confused and concerned but still hoping that this – whatever it was – could work out okay.

'Hasn't changed since last year,' she said, and Griff shook his head. The paddocks were wild and thick, the grass tall, the track uneven and potholed. The road still lay empty, and beyond it the shadowy bushland was as dense as ever. But so much felt different now, Ro thought, than it had then. It seemed like a lifetime had passed, several full, heavy lifetimes, since they had both been here beside the red car.

Ro lifted her gaze to look at the three houses in turn, quiet and still in the distance. From where she stood, they really did all seem the same as she remembered, but she knew the condition of each would have worsened close up. As she watched, the sun re-emerged from behind a cloud and in its sudden dazzling brightness, she nearly missed the flicker of movement.

It was fast, a twitch of something in the direction of the ivy cottage. There, then instantly gone again. Ro watched closely, her eyes sliding over the house, but all she could see was the thick curtain of leaves shivering in the summer wind. Nothing else stirred; the paddocks on either side were wide and empty.

She drew a breath and turned to ask Griff if he'd spotted it too, but when she saw him she bit back the question. Griff was leaning against one of the sturdier fence posts, his arms folded tightly against his chest and his head down. His eyes were closed, Ro realised, his face like a mask. She used to know Griff so well that she could guess what he was thinking. Now she had no real idea. She didn't know what kept him awake at night, didn't know what happened in his days. Didn't know with any true clarity how he felt about all of this, with the benefit of five years' hindsight.

Unwilling to examine that too closely, not here or now, Ro wandered a few steps away, scuffing her boots against the empty patch of track at her feet.

It had been dark by the time the first police officer had arrived from Blenheim. Their friends and neighbours had already set to work hours earlier, the nearest ones heading over to help Ro and Griff scour the immediate area, while others checked their own paddocks and outbuildings, swapping notes on any unknown people or vehicles that may have come through town in the past week. On that date, five years ago, there had been nearly four hundred residents remaining in Carralon Ridge, ranging in age from three months to eighty-one years, and in the days that had followed, all had been involved in the search for Sam in the best way they could.

'Is he a keen hiker?' the officer had asked that first night, eyeing up the thick band of bushland that lined the other side of the road.

'Yes,' Griff had started confidently, then wavered. 'He definitely used to be, but he lives in Sydney now, so . . .' He pointed towards the trees. 'But we did all these trails when he was growing up. All of them, lots of times. He knows the terrain well.'

'So he would have felt comfortable hiking on his own?'

'Yeah, but he wouldn't have been stupid about it. Might have walked in.' Griff frowned. 'But not far. Not on his own without telling us.'

'Or without water,' Ro had added. She could still make out the cylindrical shape of Sam's aluminium drink bottle through the rear window. 'And we already checked part of the way along the nearest trail. While we were waiting for you.'

'Right.' If the officer had caught the faint note of reproach in her voice, he'd let it go. 'And who lives here?' He'd squinted into the night and used his pen to pick out the houses. One, two, three. They were little more than shadows, every window dark.

'No-one,' Griff had said. 'They're all owned by the mine.'

'And before that?'

'That was Ann-Marie Birstock's.' Ro had heard herself speaking fast, rushing through the information, irritated by these questions and anxious to move on from the talking to the action. *Let's skip ahead*, she'd wanted to say. *Straight to the answers, straight to the part where we find our child.* Instead, she'd pointed to the middle cottage, its cloak of ivy invisible in the dark, and made herself focus. The sooner they got through this, the better for Sam. 'Ann-Marie lost it in her divorce a few years back but she's still around, rents a place in town with her son. That place,' she pointed to the next nearest house, the boarded-up stone bungalow in the east, 'was Bernie Reece's. He lives with his son's family at the hill farm now.'

'The one I passed on the way here?' The officer peered out at an invisible middle distance. He was looking in the wrong direction but Ro knew which one he meant.

'No.' She made herself swallow her frustration. 'It's a few kilometres on the other side of the hill. That one you're thinking of is empty.' *Clearly*, she wanted to add. It wasn't even a house anymore, just a few walls.

'Got it.' The officer from Blenheim had definitely caught her tone that time but once again let it go as he pointed to the third property in sight. The Hillary house. 'And that one?'

There was an odd pause. Ro took a breath, ready to answer for Griff if he wanted her to, but he did it himself.

'That place was my cousin's. Warren Hillary.'

'And he sold it to the mine, when?'

'Three years ago. It was, ah . . .' Griff had hesitated again, cleared his throat. 'Essentially an estate sale. After he died.'

'I'm sorry to hear that. Mind if I ask how?' The officer glanced up from his notebook. 'Wasn't an accident around here, was it? Hazard or something we should be checking?'

'No –' Griff started, then stopped.

The officer waited, his face suddenly curious.

'Warren killed himself,' Griff stated, flatly. 'Over at the quarry.'

There was a brief professional silence. Ro caught the officer flick a glance from the red car to the gloomy farmhouse, then off into the distance, to where the mine lay in the west, hidden over the horizon but still making its presence felt with the low hum filling the night air and the fine dust already settling on the paintwork of the police car. The officer drew an invisible line with his gaze as he looked there and back, from farmhouse to car.

'Your son was how old when this happened?'

'He was seventeen,' Ro said.

'And were they close? Him and his . . .' He stumbled over the relationship. 'Uncle?' he guessed, which wasn't right but was close enough. Ro and Griff were already both nodding.

'Yeah,' Griff said. 'We were all close with Warren.'

'Must have been hard when he died.'

'It definitely was.'

The police officer noted something in his book and made a small sound in the dark. A tiny, suppressed sigh.

'Okay, well, we'll obviously get on to the mine boss anyway, whoever's on duty over there, get them to check the site thoroughly. I know some of these questions are difficult, but given where we've found the car, it's important to cover all possibilities,' he went on, and Ro had known immediately what he would ask next, had felt the question coming since he'd first glanced towards the Hillary house but it was *not*, she told herself fiercely, *not* because she had considered the same thing herself, not even for a moment. And sure enough, as night follows day, the officer had clicked his pen and raised his eyes to look at them both carefully.

'As far as you're aware, how is your son's mental health?'

Back in the broad daylight, five years on, Ro stepped away from the spot where the rental car had been parked, where they'd stood trying to correctly respond to questions to which they didn't know the answers. Griff had opened his eyes and must have been watching her because as Ro turned, he met her gaze. And in that single moment, she found she could, in fact, read his mind once more, and knew with absolute certainty that he had been remembering the same scene.

A sudden whisper of movement in the distance made them both twist their heads around, Ro's eye immediately drawn again to the ivy cottage.

'Is that someone –?'

'Where?'

'There. See? By the . . .' Ro stopped short, realising all at once who it was.

'Bloody hell.' Griff breathed out as the far-off figure stepped further into view, now fully visible on the front verandah. 'Ann-Marie.'

For a moment they all stared at each other over the empty space. Something in the woman's stance – half-frozen with an inwards curve to her shoulders – gave Ro the distinct impression she had not meant to be spotted. But then another beat passed and she seemed to relax. She lifted her hand first in a wave, then in a beckoning motion.

'Jesus.' Griff sighed heavily. 'She knows she's not supposed to be up there.'

'Looks like she's inviting us over.'

'Yeah, I can see she bloody is.' He shook his head, a tight movement, more of disbelief than refusal. 'Shame it's not her house anymore.'

Ro shielded her eyes as she gazed out towards the ivy cottage. The woman was still on the verandah, openly watching them now, posture firmed. Her face was too far away to read.

'I can go up alone if you want, say a quick hello,' Ro offered, but Griff was already straightening, pushing himself away from the fence post.

'I'll come. Warn her off in person. Again.'

Ro could tell from his expression that they both knew it would make no difference. Whatever warnings Ann-Marie had received over the years, and there had been plenty, they were falling on deaf ears. She was still watching them from up there, one hand on the verandah post, the other in her jeans pocket. She waited a moment longer, perhaps to check they were on their way, before turning and strolling towards the back, looking for all the world like she owned the place.

Chapter 6

Ann-Marie had disappeared again by the time Ro and Griff had climbed into his four-wheel drive and driven up the central-most arm of the track, coming to a stop at the front of the ivy cottage. Ro got out and stared, needing a moment to absorb the sheer wall of greenery in front of her. The ivy was in full flush, grasping at every crack and fingerhold as it crawled across the surface, burying the home's features underneath. A hint of a front door and a single window peeped out from beneath the canopy, all but consumed.

A faint clatter sounded from the back of the property and Griff muttered something inaudible to himself as they made their way together around the side of the house.

'Jesus, Ann-Marie,' Griff said, very audible this time, when they saw her. Ro suppressed a smile at his tone, which managed to sound both angry and amused. 'You keep asking for trouble and you're going to find it one of these days. You as well, Jacob. Thought at least you'd know better.'

Ann-Marie's adult son gave a resigned shrug from where he stood, holding the bottom of a very tall ladder which was leaning precariously against the back wall. 'She'd do it anyway.'

'Exactly. He's right,' his mother called from where she was balanced near the top. Her own four-wheel drive was parked a short distance away, the boot open and displaying a slightly alarming collection of sharp garden tools. 'So, you may as well leave him alone and save your breath, Griff. The growth's completely out of hand back here. I needed to do something.' Ann-Marie smiled down. 'And hi, Ro, by the way. Good to see you.'

She was a small, neat woman, in her late forties but could have been a decade younger with her long, dark hair tied back in a ponytail. She clutched a rung of the ladder in one hand and held a pair of garden shears in the other as she looked down at her son, who was steadying the base. Jacob would be twenty-six now, Ro knew exactly, because his birthday fell a month before Sam's. They had been friends all the way through school and beyond, and while Jacob had grown tall and broad as a man, Ro could still picture him as the slight child he'd once been, dragging a faint air of anxiety into every conversation. He was still fairly softly spoken, having failed to inherit his mother's bluntness, and he squinted up at her now as she began hacking away once more.

Tough strands of greenery caught in Ann-Marie's blades as she tugged at the vines swarming around a set of French doors that used to open onto the little patio. The intricate patio paving was still in reasonable condition beneath Ro's feet and a wrought-iron table sat nearby, complete with a couple of chairs, all heavily rusted but so far managing to escape the creepers. As Ro stood there, she felt the sun warming the back of her neck, bathing them all in a golden light and a gentle heat that was still comfortable at that time of the morning. For a moment, the scene felt strangely pleasant, just another social call of the kind she'd made frequently to Ann-Marie's place when the boys were both young.

'Who's going to help you if you fall off that, Ann-Marie?' Griff said, shattering the atmosphere as he stared at her up the ladder. He sounded exhausted. 'Or if part of the brickwork comes away and catches you on the head? It's crumbling all along that south corner there, you know? You've seen that?'

'Yeah, I have seen it, thanks,' she said, ignoring his other questions as she pulled at a loose vine. It jerked away in her hand with a jolt that made them all flinch, trailed by a tail that spooled all the way to the ground. 'But that's exactly why I'm chopping this back, so the damp doesn't set in underneath.'

Griff said nothing.

'And I know how to use a bloody ladder safely, Griff. Plus, Jacob's here.'

'The ladder's not all I'm talking about.' Griff waved a hand towards the long yellow grass creeping up to the rotten fence surrounding her yard. 'I saw you walking out there. The other day. And the week before.'

The tall stalks and blades rippled gently as the breeze crossed the paddock, but Ro knew they concealed things that could cause damage. Deep holes and barbed wire and sharp rusted metal and nails in boards.

'Does Jacob know you've been coming up here alone? Wandering around?' Griff looked at the other man. 'Did you know that, mate?'

Ann-Marie did not reply, but Ro saw her shears pause mid-snip as she glanced down at her son. He gave a small, tight shake of his head, annoyance crossing his face.

Griff's voice softened a little. 'I'm not trying to make things harder for you, Ann. But if something happens here, you know there's no real help coming,' he said. 'Yeah, okay, Jacob's here and can go and get someone, but who? It's only going to be me or Noel or someone. At best.'

Griff wasn't exaggerating, Ro knew. The nearest ambulance was stationed out at the hospital in Blenheim, far enough away as to be next to useless in the face of any real emergency. Carralon Ridge had lost Ro and almost all of her colleagues when the medical centre had been shuttered, and the town's only remaining peripatetic nurse was currently up a ladder with a sharp pair of shears in her hand. Whether Griff's words landed or not, Ro wasn't sure, but Ann-Marie made a final decisive snip at a rope of ivy and pulled the strands clear, dropping them to the ground like streamers, before finally climbing back down the ladder.

'Speaking of safety, or the lack of it,' she nodded at Griff as she put down the shears and wiped her hands on her jeans, 'be careful when you're next over at Warren's place. Couple of those big branches have come down in the winds. Might want to clear them.'

'I'm not clearing anything there.' Griff met her eye squarely. 'It's not my house.'

Ann-Marie shrugged, lightly amused. 'Whatever you say, Griff. Just letting you know. For next time. It's a hazard.' She didn't wait for a response, instead turning to Ro. She reached out and took her hand. 'Anyway, more importantly, how are you?'

'I'm okay, thanks.'

Ann-Marie looked at her, closely enough that Ro could see her nurse's training surface, as though Ro were a patient in the clinic with something more to tell.

'Good to hear.' Whatever Ann-Marie may have thought, she didn't press the matter further. Not then, at least. 'I saw you both arrive down there but didn't want to intrude.'

'Is Della back too?' Jacob asked suddenly, glancing up from the car boot where he was organising the garden tools.

'Yeah, she got in yesterday,' Ro said. 'She's working at home, though.'

'Right.' Jacob frowned a little as he nodded. 'Missed a call from her a bit earlier. Wondered what she wanted.'

Ro saw her own faint surprise echoed in Griff's face. It had been Sam who had been close to Jacob, along with another boy who made up the third in their tight trio. Della had been three years younger, a sensible, studious girl of little interest to her brother's friends, as far as Ro knew. Still, she supposed, that was a while ago now, and people changed.

'Maybe it was about the memorial?' Ann-Marie suggested, turning to Ro. 'Assuming you're planning to do it again.' Her face creased as she silently counted. 'When does his birthday fall this year? Monday?'

'Monday,' Ro confirmed, and glanced at Griff. Memorial was possibly too formal a word for the quiet gathering that had become something of an annual ritual. It had started with only the three of them visiting the site as a family on that first anniversary, taking turns to say out loud something they had loved about Sam. It had helped a little, Ro had felt, but the following year Ann-Marie had driven by and seen them out there, stopped her car in the road and walked over to join them. The next year, Jacob had asked if he could come along too, as well as Sylvie, and then a handful of others. Ro had been mostly touched and if, quietly, she found it all a bit overwhelming, she'd never say as much out loud. The community might be a shadow of itself, but those still in it looked after each other and she was grateful for that.

'Yeah, we'll be doing it,' Griff's voice was subdued. 'Probably more or less all the same as last year. If you're around.'

'We'll be around,' Jacob said firmly then looked to his mother, who was nodding in agreement. 'Anyway. I'd better head off. Are you . . .?' His eyes flicked to the ladder.

'Yeah.' Ann-Marie smiled. 'I've finished. You go. Love you. And thank you.' She gave Jacob a quick hug as he got into his own car, and they watched him drive away before she turned back to Ro. Ann-Marie observed her for a moment, as though assessing something, then waved a hand towards the vines crowding the house.

'Want the latest tour?' She then reached out and grasped one of the smaller tendrils, snapping it clear with a sharp twist of her wrist. It made no difference to the thick coat. 'While you're here?'

'Inside?' Ro asked in surprise. 'I thought they changed the locks last year?'

Ann-Marie gave her a small smile. 'Only the front and back, it turned out. They forgot about the laundry door. Or didn't see it under the ivy, maybe. I don't know. Either way, means we can get in, if you want.'

Ro glanced at Griff, who was listening, his face impassive. He gave a tiny shake of his head, seemingly more to himself than her, then turned his back and wandered away across the patio to look out at the land. Ann-Marie picked up the shears and dropped them in the back of her truck with a clatter. She beckoned for Ro to follow her.

'Is it safe inside?' Ro asked.

'Of course.' Ann-Marie smiled back over her shoulder. 'Safe as it ever was. I do it all the time.'

*

Ro stood back and gave Ann-Marie some space as the other woman scrabbled through the vines for a doorhandle Ro couldn't even see.

'Got it,' she said, exhaling with satisfaction as the door released, swinging inwards in a surprisingly smooth motion. Ann-Marie went first, ducking low to pass through the overgrowth, and as Ro followed she felt the feathery tendrils of the vines stroke her neck and back even as she crouched down.

Inside, she straightened, unable to see anything for a moment as her eyes struggled to adjust in the gloom. It was cool and dark and as Ro blinked, she saw they were in what had been the small laundry room, empty now apart from the in-built sink. A pair of corroded taps and a run of plumbing lines showed where the washing machine once stood. Ann-Marie was already moving deeper into the house, and Ro followed her, emerging into the kitchen. It was a larger room but still felt faintly claustrophobic. Every window was covered by a screen of ivy, muffling any noise from outside and laying a green filter over what little daylight was able to creep through. It gave the space a thick, deep quality, like being underwater.

The countertops were covered in a fine, grainy dust and Ro watched as Ann-Marie walked to the nearest one, scattering the particles as she ran a finger over the surface. She seemed both at home and uneasy in the space. Ro watched her for a minute, then left her staring pensively out of a window that had a view only of leaves.

Ro wandered alone into the short hallway, finding her way to the front door. It was locked, from the inside as well as out, and Ro could see the damage to the wood where a heavy-duty bolt had been roughly drilled into the frame. She turned her back on it so she was facing into the house itself. She didn't move, simply stood in that muted light.

Sam had been there, where she was now, on the day that he vanished. The prints he left had been clear and definitive. His boots, his size. Just him, alone. The few tyre marks visible outside were old and did not match Sam's rental car. He had seemingly left his vehicle parked near the fork of the track and had walked to each of the houses. At the ivy cottage, his footprints became clear as he had stepped up onto the porch.

From there, the marks suggested he had walked from one end of the porch to the other, perhaps pausing to peer through a window or look out at the paddocks or glance back towards his car. He had opened the front door, still unlocked five years ago, and had stepped inside, his boots again marking the very spot where Ro stood now. She had seen the prints herself, some hours later.

How long Sam had stood there, Ro could only guess. He may or may not have shut the front door behind him. The ivy was already beginning to take hold even then, so he might have decided he needed the light. From there, he had walked forward, through the house from room to room, as Ro had done herself later that same day, following his footsteps with mounting urgency as she'd searched for him. She traced the route again now, but slowly.

First, the bedrooms, concealed behind the two nearest doors. She opened them in turn. The smaller room then the larger one, both completely empty, as they had been for years. On to the living room, with its once magnificent view of the hills on the horizon shrouded from the outside. Ro could hear the faint sounds of Ann-Marie moving through her kitchen, opening and shutting drawers and cupboards, the floorboards creaking as she roamed around her old home.

'You okay in there, Ro?' Ann-Marie's voice floated across the hall.

'Fine,' she called back. 'Thanks.'

'I was wondering what you think you'll do next year?' A cupboard squeaked open and then closed. 'Will you still come back if Griff's not here?'

Ro paused exactly where she was, her hand resting on the cracked windowsill. 'Why wouldn't Griff be here next year?'

The cupboards and the floorboards fell instantly quiet and Ro could tell Ann-Marie had gone still too. 'Because his contract hasn't been renewed.'

Ro moved then, stepping away from the window and crossing the hall. She leaned against Ann-Marie's kitchen doorway, as she had many times over many years, and they looked at each other in the pale, green light.

'Is that right?' she said.

Ann-Marie kept her eyes on Ro's face. 'It is.'

Ro couldn't pretend she knew. The information settled heavy in her chest.

Ann-Marie let the quiet sit for a minute before she spoke again. 'Hard being back.' It was a statement rather than a question, but Ro nodded.

'Yeah. Hard staying as well, from what I'm told.'

'It is a bit. But . . .' Ann-Marie shrugged. 'I don't know, I suppose I'm still here by choice. So maybe it's more difficult to leave.'

'Maybe.' Ro ran her fingers over the nearest countertop, leaving traces in the dirt as the silence stretched on.

'You can't be sure, Ro. When it comes to Sam,' Ann-Marie said eventually, her voice soft. 'You never know what's still out there to find.'

'Do you think so?'

'Yeah, I do. Don't you?'

Ro didn't know how to answer that. It was a question that frequently trapped her, dragging her down into a spiral that kept her tangled and struggling in its grip. It was complex and sharp and raw, and left her too exhausted to fight her way out. Ann-Marie was still waiting, so she replied as honestly as she could.

'After this many years? I'm not sure.'

They both turned their heads at a light rustle of movement outside. A shadow crossed the nearest window, blocking what little light there was. Griff, Ro could tell immediately from the shape. All at once, the sickly glow of the room felt suffocating and Ro felt an urgent need to surface, to step out into the open air and fill her lungs. She glanced past Ann-Marie towards the door.

'Had enough?' Ann-Marie caught the look and nodded. 'It can get a bit much in here after a while.'

'Thanks,' Ro said, damping down her relief as she followed the woman through the kitchen and into the tiny laundry room. 'It was interesting to look around again.'

'Any time. Really.' Ann-Marie reached for the door and pulled it open, a rectangle of bright light blazing into the cramped space. She flashed Ro a sad smile as she stepped back to let her out. 'Like Griff said, I'm up here more often than I should be.'

Chapter 7

Ann-Marie stood on the front porch of the ivy cottage and waved them off as though she'd been hosting a party. Griff glanced in the rear-view mirror as they pulled around a corner of the track and both she and the house grew smaller behind them.

'She's going to go right back up that bloody ladder,' he muttered, and Ro nodded.

'I'd think so.'

They trundled in silence the short distance to the three-way fork and there, Griff slowed, as Ro had known he would. He looked out of the window towards the westerly branch of the track and sighed heavily through his nose, before glancing over to Ro.

'Do you mind?' he asked.

She shook her head and he turned the wheel, driving wordlessly along the uneven trail that led to the Hillary house. Outside the front of what used to be his cousin Warren's place,

Griff came to a stop but kept the car running. Ro wondered if he was even going to get out, but after a moment he dropped his hand from the steering wheel and killed the engine. The only sound was the distant mechanical pulsing.

Griff climbed out and slammed the door behind him, and Ro did the same, pausing to look up at the ramshackle farmhouse. She had seen dozens of photos that had been taken of this place over the years, a lot of them printed from negatives, the colours overblown and the focus fuzzy. Elderly couples, new babies, birthday cakes.

One of her favourites had been of Griff himself, captured more than forty years earlier near the spot where they were now. In the picture, he was a young boy, smooth-faced and soft-limbed. The sun was beating down as he stood in a pair of shorts and a t-shirt emblazoned with the logo of a fertiliser brand, squinting out from under a broad-brimmed hat that was a little too big for him. He was flanked by his cousins, Warren and Damien. They looked strikingly similar and were all roughly the same height, despite Warren being a year older than Griff, and his brother being a year younger. The three crowded together shoulder to shoulder, their eyes obediently on the camera for that single moment, but their attention clearly leaning towards each other, grinning at some long-ago joke.

'Better check the back,' Griff said now as he moved towards the overgrown side path, and Ro followed him around to the rear of the house, where a wide covered verandah ran along its full length. Just as Ann-Marie had said, two large branches had come down, clipping the curved roof and catching the front corner, where they had smashed through a wooden paling and come to rest. The impact had cracked the worn floorboards, leaving the largest bough wedged between two broken planks. Griff muttered something to himself as he moved closer, surveying the damage. His frown deepened as he ran a hand over the downed branches.

Ro glanced up at the source of the trouble: a huge gum tree towering over the western edge of the home. If Warren were still living there, that tree would have been lopped long ago. Instead, it grew sprawling, the tall tips swaying carelessly and its leaves rattling. Ro felt a small jolt as she squinted up into the broken daylight and saw dozens of cockatoos staring back down at her from the branches. They were eerily still as they observed her with their bead-like black eyes, their pale feathers looking dirty against the bright light of the sky. Ro dropped her gaze first, a hot prickle of embarrassment running through her at the realisation that she felt strangely unsettled.

She directed her focus back to the house, which seemed even more rundown than she remembered. The glass in each window was long gone, leaving gaping holes which Griff could have boarded up but had chosen not to. Years ago, Ann-Marie had once asked Ro why Griff didn't close them over to keep the house in better condition.

'I don't know,' Ro had replied simply, ignoring the slight note of accusation in Ann-Marie's tone. She did know, though. Griff didn't maintain the Hillary house because he didn't want it to be maintained. As long as it stood, it was a reminder of both Warren and Sam and, given the choice, he wouldn't be sorry to see it razed to the ground. For now, though, the house struggled on, battling through its neglect.

Ro left Griff to examine the damage and wandered around to the front. The wooden weatherboard exterior that Ro still remembered being a warm cream colour was now mostly grey where the paint had curled and begun flaking away. Three steps led up to the porch and she tested the first one experimentally. The board creaked under her foot and sagged badly in the centre, giving the impression the house was slouching inwards, weighed down by itself. She moved back to firm ground and looked up to where the front door should have been. The space now lay wide and open, a thin shaft of daylight illuminating a triangle of grime at the entrance of the hallway.

Eight years earlier, Griff and Sam had been together on the afternoon when they'd pulled up at this house and banged on the yellow front door. Probably both leaning against the porch posts as they waited for an answer, chatting maybe. Possibly sharing a slightly shameful unspoken relief at being home in Carralon and back in familiar territory. Ro wouldn't have blamed them for that; she had felt that way a little herself.

Her father had died just ten days earlier, his passing both abrupt and violent when he was struck by a car as he was leaving the gym. His name had been Sam as well, and his fierce love for his daughter, son-in-law and grandchildren had been returned in kind. The collision had been severe enough that the driver had fractured his own skull and been placed in an induced coma. Ro's father had been thrown across the street, further than Ro would have believed possible, and was dead by the time the ambulance arrived. Dead as he hit the ground, most likely, and his sudden absence had left Ro shaken in a way she had never before experienced. She had forced herself through the necessary actions and decisions for her mother's sake, but the funeral itself had passed in a painful blur.

They had been staying at Ro's parents' house in Berowra for more than a week – Ro, Griff and both of the children – and it had been on their last night that Griff had missed a single call from Warren. His cousin had left a voicemail, which Griff listened to at the time but Ro only heard much later.

'Sorry.' Warren's voice had sounded tired and distracted. 'Forgot where you were. Never mind.'

The week of mourning and stress had made it easier for Griff to take his cousin at his word, and it had not been until the following afternoon, back home in Carralon, that Griff had returned Warren's call. There had been no answer but, unconcerned, he and Sam had driven over to the Hillary farmhouse to drop off some borrowed tools.

There'd also been no response when they'd knocked on the front door. It had been unlocked, though, which usually meant Warren was around so they'd stepped inside, Griff calling out to let him know they were there. At the end of the hall, the back door had been swinging wide open too. Griff had called out again then, a little louder this time, and with Sam following he checked each of the rooms off the hall.

The house was empty. So was the back verandah, with its sweeping view of the paddocks and the sunsets and, more recently, in the distance, the black smudge of the Lentzer mine on the horizon.

There was a single beer can on the outdoor table, still half-full and with the liquid inside now flat and warm. The barbecue had been turned off but its lid was open, displaying the cooked meat on the grill. Three sausages, overdone but untouched other than by the flies that were swarming around.

Griff had stared at that food and then pulled out his phone. He had not bothered trying his cousin again. Instead, he had thought for a minute and then called Warren's younger brother, Damien. Damien would normally have been on the other side of the world in London, where he'd lived permanently for twenty-odd years, but that week he was relatively much closer to home, attending a conference in Sydney. The brothers had made plans to meet up.

But Damien had sounded first busy and then surprised when Griff called him. No, he said as the background bustle and chatter from the bar in his harbour-side hotel floated down the line, he hadn't spoken to Warren that day. Although, Warren had tried to phone him the night before. Damien had missed the call, but not deliberately, the man had stressed. He had hesitated and had the grace to sound a little shamefaced. The brothers had in fact not been in touch since Damien's brief visit to Carralon Ridge three days previously, which had ended prematurely. Damien filled Griff in, on Damien's side of events at least, and Griff had hung up from the call more worried than when he'd started.

Next, he had tried Warren's ex-partner Sylvie, over at the Black Creek Inn. She had picked up straight away and on the other end of the phone, she'd already been crying. Warren had called her, too, the night before, and they had actually spoken. Argued, really, Sylvie admitted. Rehashing old grievances about money and misunderstandings. The conversation had come to a close when she had hung up on him. Several minutes later, Warren had sent Sylvie a text.

I'm sorry, Sylvie. Never wanted to hurt you, it read. *Just want you to know that I love you.*

Sylvie had not replied.

It had been Sam who had called Ro, and she could still remember the odd inflection in her son's voice. 'Mum.' It had barely sounded like him. 'They think Warren's dead.'

She had reached for the right words, for the correct reaction, and found nothing but disbelief. 'Where's your dad?' she'd managed finally.

'On the phone with the police. Sylvie got a call from them, I think.'

In the background she'd heard Griff.

'Is that your mum?' His words were muffled then clear. 'Ro? Yeah, listen, something's happened. Can you come and get Sam? Sylvie got a call from the cops, they've found a body in the quarry and –' He cut himself short, his voice tightening.

'So yeah, I need to go with Sylvie to –' He stopped again, and there was a rustle on the line as though he'd turned his head. 'No, Sam. No way, mate. Ro?' He was back with her. 'I'll wait here with Sam, if you can get over here as soon as you can. He shouldn't be around any of this.'

Sam had been waiting by the front porch, pale and shaken, when Ro had arrived fifteen minutes later. She had loaded him into her car, fastening her seventeen-year-old's seatbelt for him as though he were a child, and then turned back to the house.

The front door had been ajar and she'd walked up to the porch and into the hallway. From there she had been able to see right through the house, to the scene framed by the wide open back door. A slice of bright white sky above and a dark shape hunched below. Ro could hear the gravelly, gasping noise and moved towards it. Stepping through the doorway to the outside again, she had stopped, and there she had kneeled down and put her arms around Griff. She had held him as he sat on the boards of the deck, his face buried in his hands, making a sound of raw anguish that she'd never heard from him before.

More than eight years on, Ro wandered slowly back around to the rear of the house. Griff was where she'd left him, standing on the verandah in much the same place as he'd been on that dreadful afternoon. The deck at his feet was partly concealed by the heavy fallen branches and he was staring down at them with a blankness in his face. As he noticed Ro reappear, he blinked and straightened.

'How bad is it?' she asked, nodding at the damage.

'Hard to say.' Griff's mouth was downturned and he heaved his shoulders in a shrug. 'Suppose it doesn't really matter. Let's just go.' He didn't look at her as he turned his back on the house. 'I'll deal with all this another time.'

Chapter 8

Where the bottom of the track met the country road, Griff pulled his four-wheel drive to a stop beside Ro's parked car.

'Thanks.' She reached for the handle to get out. 'See you later back at –' She nearly did it herself that time. 'Your place,' she finished instead.

'Right.' Griff frowned, drumming his fingers lightly against the steering wheel. 'Are you heading back now? Or are you going to walk the trail?'

'I was going to do the trail. While I'm here. Some of it, anyway.'

He shifted in his seat, looking for a long moment through the windscreen at the thick bushland on the other side of the road. Then he switched off the engine. 'I'll come.'

'What about the fire break?'

Griff glanced up at the sky. It was overcast with a dull, yellow tinge but the wind was staying low. 'I can check it later.'

He slammed the car door shut and together they crossed the empty road, not bothering to look either way. The hiking path had once been well maintained, but now the entrance was as wild and neglected as everything else. Ro could have missed it, if she hadn't known where to look.

She pushed the curtain of overgrown branches aside and stepped in first, Griff close behind, and they moved in single file for the short stretch until the walking trail widened out. The trees flanking the path had been left to grow tall and thick, giving Ro the unwelcome sensation of being tightly enclosed despite being outside. The shade provided some respite from the mounting heat, at least, and she tried to feel grateful for that instead.

Ro had walked this route dozens of times, perhaps even hundreds, both alone and with Griff, and then with Sam and Della as they grew from babies to teenagers. In some ways, the bushland was a familiar constant, the growth and movement so subtle year after year that it appeared never to change. But every time Ro stepped in here she saw something different. The surroundings shifted and evolved, exposing new layers and cloaking others. Ro's memories of walking this trail with her children were always accompanied by a soundtrack of constant birdsong. She wasn't sure now if that was accurate. Today, the dominant noise was the low growl from the mine.

The rumbling was undercut by something else though, suddenly, and Ro slowed her pace. The air carried a faint mechanical buzzing that seemed to draw closer as she listened. Griff's head turned as he caught it too. It was lighter and more variable than the industrial groaning, and they both looked up at the same time.

'There.' Griff pointed. The sky above their heads was a cracked maze of lofty tree branches, but Ro caught a glimpse of something through the gaps as it dashed past. A small drone. 'Did you see it?'

Ro nodded, her neck craned back as she circled around, trying to follow the path of the machine. 'Is that Noel's?'

'Yeah, would be. Looked like his. Probably Darcy flying it, though.' Griff tilted his face towards the sound, squinting up at the sky. 'He seems to be out more often these days.'

They stared up for a minute longer, watching and waiting. Ro could still hear the buzz, but it seemed softer now, and the machine itself was out of sight. She dropped her gaze and met Griff's, and for a moment he appeared on the verge of saying something. He didn't, though, instead simply looking past her to the path ahead. With unspoken agreement, they began walking again, a little slower this time.

Ro wasn't sure if she was surprised or not to find herself still automatically scanning the tree line as she and Griff followed the trail deeper into the bushland. This area had been searched extensively after Sam had disappeared, both formally by the police and more thoroughly by the locals.

Ro's son having become lost somewhere in these trees had been among the stronger theories, and one of the suggestions that she'd clung to in those terrifying early days. Partly because she could imagine that scenario playing out but, even better, it had teased the promise of a good resolution. Sam could conceivably have walked into this bushland, wandering along a trail he knew well or, crucially, used to know well. He had been living away, though, and had perhaps grown more familiar with city parks and short, well-marked reserve tracks, his memory and knowledge of this rugged area fading without him realising. He had misjudged the route, lost the path somehow, and while his car remained parked over the road, he himself was among the thick curtain of trees, dehydrated, disoriented, with a twisted ankle maybe. Alive, though, and waiting to be found.

The police had had another theory about this bushland. One which they had not shared openly with Ro but which she found very easy to infer. An alternative scenario, in which Sam had once again made the decision to walk into the dense, overrun forest, but this time because he really did know the rugged dangers so well. Walking alone, he had left the trail, but in this version of the story, his choice had been a deliberate one. He had hiked deeper, with purpose, not caring if he lost his way because he had no intention of finding it again. He carried on with a determination to do what he'd planned without being discovered. Or not by his parents, at least.

Ro did not believe she had any sixth sense about her son's whereabouts, and she resolutely refused to buy – either emotionally or financially – into any suggestion that some form of psychic intuition would help locate him. Yet, privately, she was aware as she walked through this bushland now that she did not feel any sense of her child being near her. Even at the time, she had joined the searches herself, tramping for kilometres through the overgrown scrub for hours on end, all the while hiding a quietly despairing certainty that the hunt would come to nothing. This bushland was thick, yes, but she struggled to believe it wouldn't have given Sam up eventually. If not dehydrated and nursing a twisted ankle, then otherwise. Griff had continued searching the bushland for a very long time, though, for weeks and months after everyone else had moved on. And that alone made Ro take the possibility seriously.

When the initial searches of the bushland and the town and the surrounding areas yielded no sign of Sam, other possibilities were considered. The mine site was thoroughly explored and the dozens of workers on site questioned. None of them admitted to knowing the boy, none believed they had seen him. Most claimed to have never even driven through Carralon, other than on the first day they had arrived for the job. Whether on shift or off, they worked and lived on site, wholly untroubled by life playing out in the town just a few kilometres away from their staff accommodation. A junior member of Lentzer's public relations team based in Sydney was aware a student named Sam Crowley was doing a research paper on the demographic structure of a community bordering their operations in Carralon Ridge, New South Wales. Sam had submitted some questions via email. The company had not yet responded at the time of his disappearance.

Meanwhile, closer to home, the police chased up a handful of old reports from locals who had raised concerns about outsiders coming to the town to spend the night in one of the abandoned houses. There had been spates of incidents in the years before Sam vanished, causing enough unease that the remaining neighbours had started doing late-night checks from time to time. Griff had discovered a backpacking couple in their twenties camping out in Warren's old front room one evening, and Noel Reece and then later Ann-Marie had on separate occasions both caught a young guy with a camera and a ring light trying to break into the stone bungalow.

Some of the unwanted visitors posted their experiences online under trite titles like 'My night in a haunted house' and Ro knew police had spoken to at least two of them. Ro found herself watching some of the videos, turning down the volume on the shrieks and the badly lit play-acting as the hosts captured shaky handheld footage of themselves wandering through a space that had once been someone's home. She wasn't particularly worried about these idiots; Ro was instead far more troubled by the ones who came and didn't post online. The strange intruders who seemed to have their own private reasons for spending a dark night in an unsafe, lonely building.

Ro wondered at times what Sam would have said had he stumbled across one of those visitors. What kind of discussion might have played out, or what argument, perhaps? The tourist would presumably have had a vehicle, needing a way to get into Carralon and leave again. A van? Ro had wondered. Their desire to poke around abandoned spaces could suggest a tendency to act somewhat irrationally. Someone operating a little outside of society's norms, someone who might overreact to confrontation. Ro could imagine it, when she allowed herself to try. The mutual shock of a discovery, an argument gone badly wrong, a panicked response. Her son's body wrapped in a sleeping bag in the back of a rented van. Driven away, to be dumped in the sea or in a hole or in other bushland far from where she and Griff walked now. She had no real idea, though, she thought, as she gazed over the trees. None of them did.

She and Griff had discovered some things later that they hadn't known at the time. Like the fact that six weeks earlier, Sam had split up with a girl neither of them had been aware he'd been seeing. From text messages still being exchanged until up to four days before he vanished, it appeared Sam was the more upset of the pair at the collapse of the three-month relationship.

Sam's university grades had been fine without being great. Certainly good enough, Ro would have said truthfully if asked, but she was aware those numbers could weigh a lot heavier on the person being assessed.

Sam had been taking antidepressants. Neither Ro nor Griff had known that. His prescription had not been a regular repeat, but it had been active at the time of his disappearance and twice before that. Sam had seemed to briefly return to the medication over the past few years, on and off, beginning with the first course – the only one Ro had actually been aware of – prescribed shortly after Warren's body had been found at the mine. They had all struggled after that, and Ro found herself glancing over at Griff now. His head was bowed and even as he walked, he wore a hint of a frown.

'Della and I can give you a hand clearing those broken branches if you want,' she said. 'While we're here.'

Griff jerked his head in a way that was both a nod and a shake. 'Thanks. That house isn't my problem, though.'

Warren's truck had been discovered before Warren himself on that bad day. The vehicle was spotted by a security patrol along the mine's northern perimeter. It had been left, unlocked, beside the weakest stretch of Lentzer's boundary, where the edge of the site met dense bushland. Access along the overrun track was notoriously tricky and at some point in the past, someone running numbers in a corporate office had decided the heavy growth made it too difficult or expensive to install more than a tall chain-link fence topped with barbed wire. The locals all knew exactly where along the boundary sat the mounted cameras that peered out at their town. There were none on that tract of bushland. The security team found the fence's links had been snipped vertically and then horizontally to create a pocket wide enough to step through. Warren's wire cutters were left abandoned on his passenger seat.

The northern quarry was a secondary pit and a daylight-only operation at the time, as Warren would have known. It was by far the smaller of the two craters, with the steep drop from the fence line to the base roughly the equivalent of falling from a twenty-storey building, as Warren would also have known. After a site search by the security team, the morning crew had dragged the murky grey lake at the bottom of the pit. Warren's body had been snagged by the machine's claws and hauled to the edge. He had suffered extensive injuries consistent with a severe fall, including a broken neck and fractured limbs.

The fence had been replaced at considerable cost – both to the mine and the bushland – with something sheer and industrial. Spotlights had been added and additional cameras put in place. Griff had been given a referral for three phone counselling sessions by Ro's colleague in the GP surgery, and then so had Sam, who had taken the news of Warren's death even harder than Ro might have expected. Both had completed their sessions without argument, taking turns to shut themselves away in the hut at the bottom of the garden for an hour each month.

'Is it helping?' Ro had whispered to Griff as he'd lain awake one night, hand behind his head, staring at the ceiling, his eyes glossy black in the dark.

'Yeah,' he'd said. 'Think so.'

She had not believed him, or Sam, when she'd asked the same question and received much the same answer.

Warren's death, coming so soon after Ro's father's, had damaged something in them all. Ro had known it even at the time, and could self-diagnose trauma as well as anyone. She had been able to see clearly from a professional stance that what they were experiencing needed serious attention, while on a personal level she had found herself barely able to cope with the demands of struggling through a full day.

Her own unprocessed grief had draped itself around her like a chain as she dragged herself between her husband and son and occasionally, when she remembered, her daughter, asking the same question a dozen different ways. *How are you? How are you feeling?* Griff had asked her the same questions too, and they'd lied back and forth to each other. *I'm okay. I'm doing better.*

Eight years on now, Ro trudged along the trail beside Griff and listened to the crunch of his boots against the dirt. She wondered what his answer to that question would be today. What hers would be, for that matter, if they were to ask each other, with interest and honesty? If they were to respond in the same spirit? Perhaps the answer was already plain, she thought. He was staring out into the dense wall of trees in the same way that she had been.

'Ann-Marie told me your contract's ending.' Ro's voice was almost lost under the rustle of the bushland, the words surprising even herself. She had been planning to wait for Griff to bring it up.

He slowed his pace and then stopped completely. 'Yeah. It is.' His shoulders slumped inwards as he turned to face her. 'I'm sorry. I was planning to tell you myself.'

Ro could hear the undertone of despair, and she trod carefully into the conversation. 'It's okay. When did you find out?'

'Few weeks ago.' He glanced back in the direction they'd come. 'I didn't want to tell you over the phone, then I nearly brought it up after dinner last night, but it was getting late and . . .' He sighed. 'I don't know. It felt a bit much to drop on you the minute you arrived.' He stopped again, let the explanation fade away. 'Yeah. But I'm sorry you heard it from Ann-Marie.'

He was treading carefully with her as well, Ro realised all of a sudden, because they both knew what this change would mean. The lease on the house was tied to Griff's contract. The end of the contract meant the end of the house. And even though it hadn't really been theirs for a few years now, it had really been theirs for a long time, and Ro felt her heart push up against her throat.

'So, how long . . .?'

'Just under three months. I've been starting to clear things out, so if there's anything you want, you know,' he shrugged, scowling out at the trees, 'you can probably have it. Or we can discuss it.'

Ro tried to think ahead, to boxes packed up and rubbish in bins and lights switched off for the last time, and the idea of it all made her feel itchy and uncomfortable. She couldn't stand still, she needed to be moving to process this, and began to walk again, a little faster now. Griff fell into step alongside her.

'I suppose,' Ro managed, finally, 'with the southern expansion going ahead . . .'

'Yeah.' He nodded. 'Exactly. Before too long the house is going to be unliveable anyway.'

His tone was brisk, but undercut with something that made her look over. 'You did the right thing, Griff. Making the decision to sell when we did.'

'Thanks.' He kept his eyes on the ground. 'I mean, yeah. I think that's true, too. Just have to remind myself sometimes.'

'It is true.'

'Yeah,' he said again. 'I suppose at the end of the day, we got something for it and if we'd waited, we wouldn't have. It's worthless now.'

Worthless. Ro turned the word over in her head, testing its weight. Without worth. Their house, steeped in memories across every square metre, from the sunny porch to the fire pit to the kids' bedrooms to her defunct veggie patch to the corner of the living room where they'd always put up the Christmas tree. Worthless. It had once had value. Now it did not.

As though able to read her thoughts, Griff glanced over and for a moment, a fine thread of mutual understanding spun itself across the space, bridging the gap between them. The delicate channel quivered in a sad harmony. Ro slowed her pace. The light was changing over the track ahead where the trees grew thicker. They had reached a natural corner, where the trail led deeper into the bushland. She stopped and Griff did too.

'What will you do?' she asked. 'When your contract's up?'

'I'm not sure.' He held her gaze for a moment longer, then broke it, frowning back down the path along which they'd come. 'Do what everyone else had to, I suppose. Leave.'

He managed not to look directly at her as he said the word, but they both knew he'd been tempted to. The delicate thread snapped. The distance between them felt as wide as it had ever been. Ro let the silence hang until finally Griff cleared his throat and nodded to the darkened track ahead.

'Do you want to go on?' he asked, but Ro suddenly felt bone tired. Not from walking, but from everything.

'No.'

In agreement about this at least, they turned and started back, as all around them the bushland whispered and sighed, keeping whatever it had seen and heard all to itself.

Chapter 9

Della's car was not parked in the driveway when Ro pulled up alone outside the house half an hour later. She paused at the verandah steps and glanced at her daughter's bedroom window. The expected rectangular glow of a laptop on the desk was not visible.

With a faint air of foreboding that Ro knew even as it crept over her was fuelled by past trauma rather than a practical need for concern, she hastily let herself inside and went straight up the hallway to Della's room. The door adorned with its five glittery letters stood slightly ajar and inside the room the main light was switched off. Della's laptop lay closed on her desk. Wherever she was, she was not working from home. Feeling deeply paranoid but also unable to stop herself, Ro pulled out her phone and tapped her daughter's number. At the other end of the line, the tinny ring reverberated several times before clicking over to voicemail.

Ro's fingertips began to prickle and immediately her chest tightened. She remembered this sensation well. Her child not where she expected, voicemail answering rather than the voice she wanted to hear, and her fear was in sudden flight, swooping, screaming at her, full-throated and clamouring. *Where is Della? Where is she? Where is she?*

Ro's phone shivered in her hand. A text message. Della's name lit up the screen.

Can't talk, all good, home soon, love you. x

It took a minute for Ro's breathing to return to normal. Back at her apartment in Sydney, she and Della could go for a run of days at a time without communication. It felt so different, though, here in this house. Ro could tell from the speed and tone of Della's reply that she was aware of it too. She reached out and gently closed her child's door, then walked back down the hall, through the kitchen and out into the fresh air.

Ro crossed the patchy lawn, intending to retreat to her hut, but halfway there she found herself slowing as her gaze was drawn right, towards the large storage sheds Griff had built the first spring they'd moved in. There were two sheds, long and low with wide barn doors, big enough to park a car inside at a push. Over the years, though, they'd been used to house everything from spare bits of machinery to the kids' bikes. When Ro had put her head inside last summer, they'd seemed to now mostly contain boxes of old things that no longer had a place in their lives.

It was what lay out of sight beyond the sheds that was pulling at her now, though, with a friendly, familiar tug. Ro resisted, staying where she was in the middle of the lawn, not allowing herself to move any closer.

Behind the sheds had once been a lush little patch of north-facing ground that caught the best of the sunlight all year long. Ro had dug it up during her second winter in the house, Sam watching first from his baby carrier and then as a toddler as she installed planter boxes and borders, dividing it piece by piece into sections. It had been a long, slow project, abandoned for months at a time on more than one occasion, but she'd always returned and eventually been rewarded with a sprawling vegetable garden which she cultivated with mixed success but a lot of enjoyment. Hidden from view from both the house and driveway, it had been the perfect sanctuary when Ro had needed to disappear for twenty minutes of peace and quiet. The sheltered space gave her the privacy to focus on learning rather than planting for aesthetics and every year she'd been quietly thrilled to coax a small amount of food and herbs from the ground. She had occasionally been joined by the children as their interest had waxed and waned, but the hidden garden behind the sheds had generally been Ro's alone and she had loved it.

Ro stared at the sheds now, her heart still pumping a little faster than was entirely comfortable. When she had lived here, at the first small spike of anxiety and stress she would walk around to the back of those sheds to her hidden garden and select a quick and easy task to fulfill. A little weeding, some pruning, a few minutes alone to let her thoughts settle, and by the time she'd finished, she could walk away having improved both the space and her mindset.

Ro felt an almost physical ache to be there, but not as it was now. She'd last ventured to the spot a few visits previously and thought she'd braced herself for the worst. Even then, seeing the beds she'd built and planted with her own hands sitting dead and dry had felt like a body blow. What Ro really wanted was to visit her garden as it had been, green and flourishing and calming. Her own space, with its own sense of peace. But what she wanted didn't exist anymore, she knew, and the sad, pale husk of its memory would only make things worse.

Ro turned away slowly and trudged instead to the hut, where she let herself in. Collapsing into the armchair, her eyes fell on the stack of photos Griff had left her. His contract was ending, and he was clearing out. Their last tentative fingertip hold on the house was slipping away. There would be more things like this to come, Ro thought. More photos, more mementos. Objects from their shared past. Some things they might both want, or perhaps wouldn't want at all but could not bear to throw away. The idea of it made her feel overwhelmed with something she could only describe as grief.

She closed her eyes. The low humming from the mine felt louder, invading her head, and after a few minutes she couldn't stand the darkness and noise anymore. She blinked her eyes open again and reached for her laptop.

The distant sound reminded her now of the small drone she and Griff had seen buzzing above their heads in the bushland. Darcy Reece would have been the one flying it, Griff had thought, and Ro immediately pictured the dark-haired boy. He'd always had a fast pair of legs on him and a quick smile, but her instinctive image was outdated, she knew, drawn too heavily from the days when a teenage Darcy used to hang around their house as part of a tight trio with Sam and Ann-Marie's son, Jacob. It had been at the wedding of Darcy's parents, before he was born, that Ro had met Griff for the first time, the pub around them alive with joy and optimism. Darcy had arrived a year later and Jacob and Sam both the year after that, putting them firmly in each other's pockets practically from birth until the time came for Sam to leave for university.

Neither Jacob nor Darcy had gone to university, although from what Ro could tell, both would have had the ability if they'd wanted to. But they had seemingly not wanted to, particularly Darcy, who was Carralon farming stock through and through.

His family still owned their property, one of the very last few that did, and in the early years Darcy or his father would often head out from their rambling farmhouse and fly the drone as close to the mine as they could, looking for breaches in the permitted work. They'd been buoyed by a wave of community enthusiasm for this, with no perceived violation too small for the town council's working sub-committee to file a complaint or lodge an appeal in an attempt to slow the steady creep of the mine. But the success had been limited at best, and it became clear fairly quickly that the drone's biggest contribution was that it annoyed the staff on site. That in itself was seen by most as enough to justify its continued use.

Darcy and Jacob had been flying the drone on the day that Sam had disappeared. They'd joined the search that evening along with the rest of their families and by the next morning, having thought to watch the day's footage, Darcy had given a copy to both Griff and the police.

Ro opened her laptop. She had watched the recording from that afternoon hundreds of times, if not thousands, but as she sat in the cabin now, she fired up the screen and scrolled through her files until she found it again. She sat alone in the hut, no more than a handful of kilometres from where it had been filmed, and pressed play.

The footage was silent, and opened with a blurry shot of Darcy's jeans and then a dizzying soar as the machine rose swiftly into the air. Both boys appeared as a flash in the bottom right corner of the shot, Darcy with his hands on the controller, Jacob standing a short distance away, his arms folded across his chest. Their faces were turned upwards, eyes rolling backwards and mouths lolling agape as they followed the drone's lift before it flew away.

Ro knew where the boys had been standing but even if

she hadn't, she would have recognised it. They had positioned themselves a short walk beyond the western edge of Warren's property, on ground that had not long before been public land but now belonged to the Lentzer corporation. Ro usually skipped over the first six-and-a-half minutes of footage but today she watched them in full as the drone followed the mine's fence line, capturing the black edge of the quarry as it hovered right on the cusp of where it was permitted.

The drone pulled back and rose up now, and from the high vantage point Ro could clearly see the position of Warren's former land in relation to the mine. His property had been longer than it was broad, running along the mine's eastern perimeter like a front guard for that side of town. Ro could understand why Lentzer had wanted to own it. Warren had the dubious distinction of having been the very first person in Carralon Ridge to have been approached by the land acquisitions team. He had said no in many ways over more than a year: with certainty, with anger, with wavering confidence, with increasing notes of stress in his voice. He had said no as his six-year relationship with Sylvie broke down, as his brother, Damien, pressured him over the phone from London to say yes, then turned up on his doorstep to do the same in person. He had said no as the mine had toyed with him, renewing its offer with a different price every time. Occasionally a little higher, often a lot lower. No. No. No. Warren had done his best to resist, until one night he had grown exhausted with the strain of resisting and killed himself.

Ro leaned a little closer to the screen now as the drone pulled higher still. Her breath was shallow, her finger on the button ready to pause as *there*, for a fleeting moment the view panned out, and she could see what she'd been waiting for.

Sam was a tiny figure on the ground. He was outside the front of Warren's house, walking across the yard. He had almost reached the verandah. He wouldn't look up, no matter how many times Ro silently pleaded for him to do so from the other side of the screen. He didn't appear to react to the drone at all, and possibly wasn't even aware of it. The machine had been high and some distance away, and on that day, the noise from the mine had been loud. A lot of people, including Ro herself, remembered that later.

Ro watched now as this digital spectre of her son climbed the verandah steps and disappeared under the covered porch. As always, she paused the footage there, rewound it, and zoomed in. Watched again as he walked a few paces, up the steps, one foot then the other, and then out of sight. Again. A tighter zoom. Walk, steps, out of sight. Again. Walk, steps, out of sight. There was nothing new to see; there never was. Again. Walk, steps, out of sight. Finally, Ro allowed Sam to disappear for a last time, and let the footage play on.

The drone moved in now, capturing the top of Warren's house before, maddeningly, drifting away. It skirted over the town and then back to the mine for another long stretch tracing the fence line before returning to land. Darcy's dirty jeans appeared in shot once more and then the screen cut to black.

The camera had remained off for forty-four minutes, according to the time stamps that Ro knew the police had checked and found to be accurate. Darcy and Jacob told the officers they had spent twenty minutes of the break recharging the drone from a portable battery before walking south along the boundary to a new location where the trees grew more sparsely around the fence line. They had not seen Sam during that time or, indeed, at all while they had been out flying.

When the camera had been switched back on again and the drone had lifted once more, it had been from the new spot that Darcy had described. Some weeks later, Ro had been driving past the area and spotted Griff out there, a small figure in the distance as he traipsed through the scrubby grass. She had known exactly what he was doing without having to ask. She had done the same herself, walking between the two camera points while not allowing her thoughts to examine too closely why she felt the need to do so. The walk had taken her fourteen minutes at what she deemed to be an average pace, whatever that piece of information told her. At a leisurely stroll, it obviously would have taken more time. Less, at a run.

Regardless, as the camera on the drone had risen into the air for the second time, it had shown the boys to be where they said they'd been. Darcy remained out of shot, but Jacob was caught once more. He was seated on the ground, Darcy's zipped up black backpack beside him. Jacob's elbows were resting on his bent knees and his head was down, his thick hair hiding his face. This time, he did not look up as the drone flew past.

A noise outside the hut brought Ro back to the room. She could hear the faint purr of a car pulling up. Della, she hoped, or possibly Griff. She closed the laptop, blinking and a little grateful for the interruption as she moved to the window where she indeed saw her daughter making her way across the lawn.

'Hey.' Della smiled as Ro opened the door. She wiped her feet on the mat, glancing at the closed laptop on the chair. 'Sorry to interrupt, are you working?'

'No, come on in.'

'Thanks. I'm supposed to be dialling into a meeting but I couldn't face it. Pleaded technology issues.'

'Are you all right?'

'Yeah. Just needed a break.' Della sat on the bed and lifted her arms in a stretch, her shoulder joints cracking softly. 'How was the site?'

Ro leaned back in the chair. 'The same as it always is, to be honest. Hard to be there but . . .' she considered. 'I'm glad I went.'

'Dad stayed out, hey?' It wasn't really a question.

'Yes.'

If Della caught the inflection, and Ro was certain she did, she let it slide past without comment, instead reaching out and picking up the envelope of photos. She glanced at Ro for permission before opening it, and Ro nodded, watching Della's face as she flicked through.

'He called me, just then. Dad did.' Della's eyes moved over the images. 'While I was in the driveway. Told me about the end of the contract and the house.'

'Right.' Ro watched her face. 'What do you think about that?'

Della seemed to be weighing her answer as she continued shuffling through the pictures.

'Well, it's always sad to say goodbye to something you've loved,' she said finally, raising her eyes to glance through the window towards the house in which she'd spent her entire childhood. 'Honestly, though, I think it's time. This isn't the place it used to be, hasn't been for years. I'm not sure what it would take to get Dad to leave but he obviously can't do it without a push so maybe this is what he needs.' She turned to eyeball her mother. 'How do you feel?'

'I think . . .' Ro paused, trying to find an honest answer. The knot of emotions was tight with regret and sorrow and guilt, but as she picked at it she could sense that somewhere in there was a fine thread of relief. 'I think you're right,' she settled on eventually.

Della drew breath to say something more but was cut off as her phone buzzed on the bed beside her. As she checked the screen, Ro was reminded of something.

'Hey, we saw Jacob earlier, out at Ann-Marie's place,' she said. 'He said you'd called.'

'Oh. Yeah.'

Ro waited for her to go on, but Della simply tapped her phone a couple more times before tossing it down again.

'Was Darcy with him?' She looked up.

'No.' Ro shook her head. 'But we saw the drone flying.'

'Oh.' A frown slipped across her face. 'Actually, I saw that too.'

Ro waited a moment more then opened her mouth. 'Were you –?'

'I'm sorry I –'

They both stopped, and Della smiled at her mother.

'I was just saying sorry I couldn't answer when you called earlier. I went for a drive into town and bumped into Sylvie.'

'How is she?'

'She seems the same, but you can ask her yourself if you want to. She's opening the pub tonight,' Della said. 'In honour of our return, I guess, so she wanted to make sure we'd be there.'

'Who else is going?'

'Sounds like most people.'

'Have you already said yes?'

'I didn't commit.' Della shrugged. 'Wasn't sure how you'd feel. I don't mind going along, though. I'm happy enough to sit there for a couple of hours with Dad, show my face. I can make your excuses if you like.' She paused. 'But it might be a good chance to say hello to everyone. You know, rather than run into them for the first time at the memorial.'

Della made a valid point, Ro thought, and although she felt like doing nothing more that evening than crawling into bed, she nodded. 'Okay. I'll come too.'

'Right. Good. I'll let Sylvie know. Anyway,' Della stood and stretched again, 'I'd better get back to work. Unfortunately. Love you.'

'Love you,' Ro said. She sat there alone for a minute, listening to her daughter's footsteps recede. She pictured the pub and tried to think who was still around to come along tonight, silently running through a short list of names. As she did so, her eyes were drawn to Sam's notebook, still where she'd left it on the side table. A lot of those same names were in those pages, scrawled in his own handwriting. Underneath some were notes, and underneath most were questions. Ro was tempted to flip through again, but there was no real need. She'd read it many times, and instead she reached for her laptop, firing it up once more.

The drone footage sprang back to life. Any signs of Darcy and Jacob were long gone from the shot as the camera flew serenely over the empty paddock that butted up against the mine's boundary. Impatient with it now, Ro skipped ahead over the next ten minutes, past the blurry fence line, looking for what she really wanted to see. She stopped in the right place, just before the end, and watched as once again the drone rose, its view growing broad and wide.

Ro knew her son had not died in any of the three houses he had visited before his disappearance. The prints on the dirty floors that led in and then out again made that much clear. And no-one else had been there either, at least not in the houses themselves.

But Sam's mobile signal would stop pinging with the nearest repeater towers within an hour of this footage being captured. His phone was already dead or switched off by the time Ro first tried to call about the spoiling birthday dinner. It had still been in Carralon when it fell silent, they'd learned later, and while the location couldn't be pinpointed more closely than that, the data suggested it had never left the local area. Ro found that fact both horrifying and comforting.

Ro stared at the screen now as the drone panned back even further, taking in a sweeping view of the mine boundary and the town's properties beyond. The shot itself amounted to no more than twelve seconds from start to finish before the drone swooped lower once more, gliding back down to earth.

A few years ago, Ro had taken those twelve seconds to a professional film editor and paid to have them slowed down and the quality improved as much as was possible. She had spent what she knew would add up to hours watching the shot, both the original and the edit, pausing, enlarging, looping the clips together back to back.

She could see a lot in those twelve seconds. She could see Warren's house, Ann-Marie's ivy cottage, the stone bungalow. She could see, small and lonely, the red rental car, parked in the same place where it had later been found. She could see the empty track, the deserted road, the bushland. Ro could see the roof of the pub, the crossroads. For twelve seconds she could see the whole town, but no matter how many times she had tried, she could never see Sam.

Chapter 10

Both Ro and Griff offered to drive to the pub that night, but Della had insisted.

'We'll call it returning the favour for the first eighteen years,' she'd said, jangling her keys and ending the conversation. She slowed now as she turned at the crossroads and pulled into the car park. The pub lights were on this time, and Ro could see movement inside. As Della came to a stop, a man who had been leaning against the shadows of the wall looked their way and straightened, slipping his phone into his jeans pocket. He started across the car park towards them.

'Oh, it's Damien.' Della narrowed her eyes as she peered at the man in the rear-view mirror. 'I wondered who that was loitering around outside.'

'Yeah, it's him.' Griff twisted in the back seat to look at his cousin and reached for the doorhandle. 'He said he might swing by.'

Ro stepped out too and paused in the warm evening air, listening closely to the muted sounds of the still town. Beneath the steady low thump of music seeping out from the pub and the faraway rumbling of the mine, all seemed peaceful in Carralon that night. She could detect nothing like the odd metallic clanging that had echoed through the streets the day before. Ro listened for a moment more then gave up, turning to the tall, clean-shaven man who was raising his hand with a smile as he neared.

Damien had certainly been cut from the same cloth as both Griff and his own brother, Warren, but his time in London's financial district had left him much smoother around the edges than those two had ever been. Even after eight years back in Carralon Ridge, he hadn't entirely lost it. On this quiet evening in a deserted country town, Damien's jeans were dark and well-fitting and his shirt sharply ironed. Despite being only a year younger than Griff, he followed a skincare and workout routine that seemed to make the age gap grow a little larger every time Ro saw them together.

'G'day.' Damien shook Griff's hand then leaned in to graze his lips lightly first against Ro's cheek and then Della's. 'Welcome back to town.'

Ro appreciated his subtle choice to not welcome her 'home'. It would have been deliberate, she knew, because everything was with Damien.

'You coming inside?' Griff nodded towards the door, and Damien shook his head.

'Can't, unfortunately. Got to dial in to the UK in twenty minutes.' He smiled at Ro. 'But I wanted to stop by quickly. Say hello.'

'Thanks. It's good to see you,' Ro said, meaning it.

'You too.' Damien's slight English accent was real enough

but had faded to the point where it sounded a little affected, like someone doing a weak impression. Intelligent and efficient, Damien carried a faintly abrasive air at times that Ro knew might have rubbed her the wrong way if he'd been a colleague. But he was not, so Ro had learned to mostly overlook it. If anything, she usually found herself responding to Damien with a slightly unexpected sense of warmth.

'It's because he reminds you a bit of Sam,' Della had observed once, and Ro had opened her mouth to deny it even as she'd realised with a jolt that it was true. Where Sam differed from Griff, he'd mirrored Damien. Neither was naturally the type to be content to stay in Carralon all their lives, and both had an ambitious streak that had still been developing in Sam but could border on cutthroat in Damien. Damien had been mainly overseas when Sam was younger but they'd inevitably seen a lot more of each other after he'd returned, finding that their conversation style and humour often aligned.

They had been together on Sam's last known day. It was a fact woven through Damien in a way that Ro could never now untangle. For more than an hour after lunch, Sam had visited the man's townhouse and interviewed him for his university research, making Damien the last person to admit to seeing Sam alive.

Later, the police had spoken to Damien, extensively, and from what Ro understood he had been full and frank in his cooperation. Doug Hewett, riding along the main street with his grandkids on their bikes, had seen Sam say goodbye to Damien on the doorstep of his house before crossing the road and unlocking a small red car. Both Doug and Damien put the time as having been shortly after two o'clock. A long-term night worker, Damien had then returned to bed, catching up on his sleep before rising again a little before 6 pm local time. He had switched on his camera and logged in for a live briefing with a colleague in London. The meeting had been recorded, and the police had been able to confirm that Damien's background on the call was indeed his home office. A little more than two hours later, Sam's rental car had been discovered. Damien had left his computer immediately to join the search and, when Sam had not been found, voluntarily identified himself to the police and provided a detailed statement.

The gap in his afternoon had caused a sizeable amount of concern, both for Damien himself, certainly, and for the police, who had been very interested in those few hours when he claimed to be sleeping alone in his empty house. They had found no evidence to suggest otherwise, but they had tried. Griff, by contrast, had insisted repeatedly that he was not concerned at all, shaking his head sharply, back and forth like an angry dog at the barest suggestion that his cousin could be connected in some way to his son's disappearance.

'No,' he'd said, simply, shutting down the discussion before it started. 'Not Damien.'

Ro sometimes wondered who Griff was trying to convince, although, in truth, she found herself inclined to agree with him. Not because of any family loyalty, but because she privately suspected Damien was too clever to leave himself exposed to suspicion around something as serious as this.

Ultimately, Ro had found herself having to make a conscious choice as to whether to trust Damien or not, and she had oscillated back and forth for longer than she would ever have admitted to Griff. Damien's movements that day were not wholly solid and were not fully accounted for, but that was true of nearly every person the police had spoken to. It was true equally of Griff, who had been out for the entire afternoon driving around alone and unobserved, checking the fire hotspots. It was true, for that matter, of Ro herself. She had spent several hours working on her own in her secluded garden while Della went for a run, returning unseen to the house at a time that Ro could not later even guess at.

It had become painfully clear to Ro in that first awful year that she would not survive day-to-day life if she could trust no-one at all and so she had slowly allowed herself to make some cautious choices. She believed Damien, she decided, and as the years crept on her trust in him had come to feel less like a belief and more like a fact.

Now, the knowledge that what appeared to be some of Sam's final few hours had been spent with Damien and not, for example, with Ro herself, mostly filled her with a potent cocktail of both gratitude and resentment towards him. She could still feel it, stirring uneasily as she stood outside the pub and looked up at him. 'How've you been, Damien? Busy?'

'This quarter, yeah, a bit.' He stifled a yawn. 'God, sorry. I was struggling to sleep today.'

Ro suspected no-one had been more surprised than Damien himself by his permanent return to Carralon Ridge. He had left the town at eighteen with barely a backwards glance and after university had moved straight to London. He had still been working there eight years ago, specialising in Commonwealth contract law, when his firm had sent him over to Sydney for ten days for an industry conference and some in-person meetings with key clients.

On the Saturday of that ten-day visit, Damien had hired a car and driven to Carralon to visit his brother, intending to spend the night with him at the house in which they'd both grown up. The Hillary house was technically still half Damien's, the brothers having inherited an equal share of the place when their parents died. The subject of the property's future came up before they'd even opened their first beer, Damien admitted later to

Griff, and it had descended into an argument before the bottles were empty. Having planned to stay overnight, Damien had instead thrown his bag into his rental car and driven all the way to Sydney, checking back into his conference hotel a little after 1 am. He'd had no further contact with his brother until a missed call three days later.

Along with Griff and Warren's estranged partner, Sylvie, Damien had been one of the three people Warren had phoned the night before his body was dragged from the lake at the bottom of the northern quarry. Still in Sydney and still lightly seething, Damien had, like Griff, also failed to answer when Warren's name had flashed up on his phone screen.

Damien had driven to Carralon immediately on learning that Warren's body had been found, pulling up that same afternoon in his rented black sedan and this time he had stayed. For his brother's funeral, of course, and then for the completion of the mine's internal investigation, and then a little longer still, ostensibly to work out the future of the Hillary house.

Warren's half of the property had passed after his death to Sylvie who, deeply shaken, had tried to refuse it. She ignored the estate lawyer's attempts to persuade her that the process would be far quicker and easier on everyone if she could find her way to accepting the gift. But Sylvie had wilfully turned a blind eye to both the legal argument and the house, seemingly unable to bring herself to make the short drive from her flat above the pub to even visit the home she'd shared for six years with her partner. She had never set foot in there again after Warren's death, as far as Ro knew, leaving Damien and Griff to clear the place out.

An uneasy resolution had been reached only when Damien had eventually offered to buy out Sylvie's half. He had stayed in the farmhouse himself for a couple of months and then he, too, had quietly moved out, publicly citing wi-fi difficulties.

Privately, though, alone with Ro and Griff, he had shaken his head.

'Couldn't be there anymore,' he'd said. 'Warren's in every room, you know? The place feels haunted.'

He had stayed local, though, instead renting a townhouse beside a vacant shop in the heart of town. The Hillary house had sat empty for another month until finally Damien, without fanfare, agreed to sell the entire property to Lentzer for what little he could extract from the company by then. Ro did not need to know what the final figure was to be certain it would have been a fraction of the first offer.

With the family house off his hands, Ro had waited for Damien to book a flight back to the UK, but instead he had remained. He had continued to work for his London employer, fully remote and keeping Greenwich Mean Time hours, logging in every night and finishing his workday as the sun rose in New South Wales.

'How long will the guilt last, do you reckon?' Griff had whispered to Ro in bed one night after Damien had stopped by for a meal that had been dinner for them and breakfast for him. He'd left yawning and with his phone already ringing with an international number.

Ro hadn't been able to guess. They had both been there after Warren's funeral, when Damien had sat hunched over in their living room, an untouched drink beside him and his face in his hands.

'For God's sake.' Damien's voice had been strangled as he performed a rolling monologue. 'Why did I push him so hard to sell? Why am I always so – I mean, Jesus. He didn't bloody want to, did he? He didn't want to. But for the past . . . what? Six months? Longer? For *months* I'd been on at him to accept that offer from the mine. I mean, it was a good deal. It was!

It made sense. That money wouldn't come along again. Not from anyone else. No way. Not the way this town's going. And Warren *knew* that. He knew it, but he still said no and that pissed me off so I wouldn't let it drop, would I? Couldn't back off for five minutes and give him some peace.' Damien had lifted his bloodshot eyes to Ro and Griff before dropping them again. 'Did you both know that?'

They had met each other's gaze over the top of Damien's head. Yes, they had both known all about that. Warren had told them at length and in detail of the pressure Damien was applying to convince him to sell their joint property. Warren had spoken of it many, many times. But there had been no benefit by then in sharing that with Damien, and so Ro had simply put a hand on his shoulder while Griff replaced his warm beer with a fresh, cold one.

'I wasn't pushing him for my sake.' Damien had continued, his words laced with a pleading note. 'It was for him! So he could get a decent amount and have a chance to start somewhere else. With Sylvie. Or not, who knows? But at least Warren would have made some money from it. It was in his own interest to get shot of that house.'

They all chose to let it go unsaid that what was in Warren's financial interests was equally in Damien's as co-owner.

'Jesus. He should've taken the money when he had the chance. I mean, this bloody town . . .' Damien had faltered, his head still bowed. Ro had watched as a tear dripped onto the carpet. 'It used to be good here, I remember that as well as he did, but it's not anymore. This whole place is only going one way. And everyone stuck here'll be dragged down with it.'

Perhaps that was what Damien wanted, Ro wondered sometimes. To be swallowed up in the town's misery as a form of self-punishment for letting his brother down. His isolation, his lonely midnight hours, it was all part of his penance and if he suffered enough, perhaps he could return to his old life cleansed and forgiven.

Or maybe, Ro thought at other times, it wasn't just that. Because if Warren was the first reason for Damien's atonement, she could see the second one walking up to the pub now.

They all turned at the sound of footsteps as Ann-Marie approached, her son Jacob by her side. The dusk was creeping in fast now, but the light from the pub windows fell on the young man's face, illuminating his oddly familiar features as they came closer.

Beside Ro, Damien shifted his weight. 'G'day Ann-Marie. Jacob, mate.'

'Hi, Damien,' Ann-Marie replied, neutrally. Beside her, Jacob didn't bother to respond. There had been quiet rumblings at the time of Jacob's birth that Ann-Marie's husband was perhaps not the natural father of their child. Over the next twenty-six years, the private suggestion had become more of a public-facing statement. Ro hadn't seen Damien and Jacob in the same place since the memorial last year, but yet again she was struck by how closely they echoed each other these days.

Ro had professionally seen all sorts of situations play out in her GP rooms, and she had learned not to judge or assume. She could understand it had suited all parties at the time to ignore the rumours and give Ann-Marie and her husband the best possible chance to build a family life together with their new son.

But the evidence grew as Jacob's face took shape, and he had been twelve when his parents' marriage had finally collapsed. There had been an opportunity then, Ro had thought, when Ann-Marie's divorce was in motion and her husband had left Carralon and for a while Jacob had seemed to be simply floating, bewildered and rudderless as he desperately cast about for something to anchor him in this new life. It had been then when Damien might have stepped forward and found that he was the right person to fill an important void. Perhaps the offer would have been welcomed and perhaps not, but Damien had stayed silently in London and let the moment slip by without giving either himself or Jacob the chance to find out. And for that, Ro suspected, Damien had always despised himself a little.

'Why are we all standing around in the car park?' Ann-Marie said with a nod towards the pub door. 'Sylvie only opens the place for five minutes a month these days. We should be inside, thanking and appreciating her.'

'I reckon filling the till is the best form of thanks,' Griff said with a grin.

'Yeah, I think you're right there.' Damien pulled out his phone and glanced at the screen, the stark uplight distorting his features. 'Anyway, enjoy. I'd better head back, so I'll let you all get on. Griff, mate, I'll give you a call tomorrow. There are a couple of fallen branches down at the farmhouse, they've smashed part of the verandah. I've been trying to get to them this week but . . .' He frowned helplessly at his phone, which already had a string of messages and alerts filling the screen.

'Yep. I've seen them.' There was a resigned pause in which Griff determinedly ignored Ann-Marie's knowing gaze. 'Listen, don't worry about it. I'll deal with it.'

'Yeah? Well, thanks mate, only if you have time. Let me know if not. And good to see you, Della, Ro.' Damien raised a hand in farewell. 'Catch you properly before you leave.'

Ann-Marie had already turned towards the bright lights of the pub and as Jacob followed in her wake, he glanced only briefly over his shoulder at Damien's departing back. They had the same gait, Ro thought, the same build. They could almost be the same person going in two different directions.

Griff and Della started towards the pub too and Ro turned to follow, watching for a moment longer as Damien moved away down the empty street.

Sam had used his phone to record their interview on that last day, Damien had told the police, but the record of it had been lost along with him. Damien had tried to recall their discussion in as much detail as he could and had typed it up to add to his statement. He had given a copy to Ro and Griff as well, but Ro had known both Damien and her son well enough to guess what their conversation had centred around.

And she'd been right, she thought as she watched the man's shape disappear into the growing dark, his head bowed a little and his shoulders hunched. According to his own transcript, Damien had talked almost entirely about Damien, and when he hadn't, he'd talked mostly about Warren.

Chapter 11

The pub may have been sparsely filled but the music was still loud and the overhead lights as bright as Ro remembered. Sylvie was there, as ever. Positioned in her customary spot behind the bar, she made it seem as though no time had passed at all as she poured beer smoothly into a glass. Ro had started towards her when she felt a warm hand touch her elbow and paused.

'Heather, hello.' Ro turned to the tall, athletic woman by her side and felt herself smile as they hugged tightly. 'So good to see you. How are you?'

'Yeah, you know. I'm okay. I'm good.' Heather's return smile was wide but didn't hide the signs of strain at the corners of her eyes. 'How about you?'

'Also okay,' Ro replied, and she looked at the woman who was her oldest and possibly closest friend, a pulse of silent understanding passing between them. The bar may have been barely

filled with a handful of punters but it still felt too bright and
exposed to have the kind of conversation she could tell they both
needed.

'Listen, what are you doing tomorrow morning?' Ro said.
'Why don't you come over for coffee? We can catch up properly
in peace and quiet.'

'Yeah. Or . . .' Heather hesitated. 'Could you come to me
instead? Sorry. Do you mind? It'd probably be a bit . . .' She
chose her words. 'Easier. And hey, wow, Della, you're looking
just great.' Her face lifted with warmth as Della joined them. 'I
really love your hair that length.'

'Oh, thanks.' Della smiled as she ran a hand through her
neat chop, but glanced at the door, a little distracted. 'No Darcy
tonight?'

Something in Heather's expression hardened a little as she
shook her head at the mention of her oldest son.

'No. He's not coming. Kyle and Zach have been a bit . . .'
Another careful word choice. 'Difficult.'

There was the tiniest pause, during which Ro quickly ran the
numbers. Heather's youngest two would be fifteen and sixteen,
she decided.

'I mean, God, they're obviously plenty old enough to be left
on their own and they're usually fine but . . .' Heather didn't
finish the thought out loud, waving a hand vaguely to brush
away the small shadow that crossed her face. 'Anyway, Darcy said
he'd stay behind to keep an eye on them, keep them company,
whatever they're willing to call it. I don't care, to be honest, as
long as Noel and I could get here.'

Heather aimed for levity but fell a fair way short, and Ro was
struck by a pang of guilt. The fact their friendship was still intact
was not down to Ro, who was very aware she had contributed
little towards the relationship over the past five years. Looking at

Heather's tight face now, Ro wished she had tried harder to find the energy to make the effort.

The women had first met at university, acquainted only well enough then to nod a polite hello, but a couple of years later while training as a junior doctor in Parramatta, Ro realised she recognised the new occupational therapist working along the hall at the clinic.

Heather had been quiet and contemplative as a student, and as a therapist treated her clients with a thoughtful respect that put her in constant high demand at the medical centre. She was a country girl both in spirit and in practice, disappearing every chance she got to visit her boyfriend back home in some town Ro had never heard of a few hours west of Sydney. She was also a big believer in the restorative power of long walks in the fresh air and, over the next six months, managed to coax Ro into joining her in lacing up their shoes and heading out together under the dawn sky as often as their schedules allowed. They talked a lot as they walked and it was during these early mornings that Heather had announced she was engaged, then later invited Ro to be a bridesmaid at her wedding, and then eventually confided that she would be handing in her notice at the clinic once she was married.

'You're leaving?' Ro had tried to mask her disappointment.

'Yeah. We'll live in Carralon.' Heather had glanced over and smiled. 'What can I tell you? I love him.' She thought for a moment. 'And I really like it there, for myself. It's a great little town, good place for kids eventually.'

Noel, Heather's boyfriend-turned-fiancé, farmed crops alongside his father, Ro had learned during their walks, tending the land that had been in their family for three generations. Noel and Heather had shared their first kiss at their high school's Barbecue Blast fundraising evening and from that moment on, had never looked back.

'So, is there a clinic in Carralon?' Ro asked. 'Will you be able to find work, or . . .?'

'Oh my God, yes.' Heather had nodded and laughed. 'Manual labour and a pretty relaxed attitude to safety everywhere you turn. It's an occupational therapist's dream. Or nightmare, I suppose, from a health professional standpoint.' She had glanced towards the city skyline and back to Ro. 'Look, I know. I can hear myself, and it all sounds ridiculously parochial, but . . .' She'd shrugged and smiled. 'I dunno. I feel a lot happier there.'

'Good. I mean, that's great to hear, Heather.'

The other woman had stopped walking at that and turned to look Ro in the eye, suddenly serious.

'Be honest,' Heather said quietly. 'Do you think I'm making a huge mistake?'

'Be honest,' Ro replied. 'Do you?'

'No.' She had smiled. 'I really don't.'

'Then no.' Ro had smiled back. 'I don't either.'

Ro had, though, privately, right up until the wedding itself when she had arrived in Heather's home town. It had been beautiful. She later held that initial impression responsible for everything she did next, because if Heather's wedding to Noel had been hot and tiresome and drawn-out, Ro would simply have completed her bridesmaid's duties, endured a poor night's sleep in a noisy guestroom, and slipped away from Carralon Ridge the following day without giving the place another thought. As it was, the whole weekend had been absolutely lovely.

Ro had found herself unexpectedly enchanted by the gorgeously low-key wedding, conducted in the lush garden of Noel's parents' quaint sandstone bungalow. She had clutched her homemade bridesmaid's bouquet and soaked up the view over the rolling paddocks. In the distance she could make out a neighbouring weatherboard farmhouse with comfortable-looking chairs on the front porch and a string of washing fluttering on the clothesline. Further along, at the top of a small rise, sat a little cottage naturally decorated with delicate tendrils of ivy that dotted the walls like something from a fairy tale.

After the ceremony, Ro had been ferried along with a buoyant crowd to the town's only pub, where she'd been engulfed by the warmth and love filling the room. A man with a nice smile and a laid-back charm had fought his way through the crowd towards her.

'Griff,' he'd said when he finally reached her. His palm had been warm and coarse as he'd shaken her hand.

'Rowena.' She'd smiled back and from there it had simply flowed, smooth and easy, and hours later she was still smiling as they stood alone in the darkness outside the pub, muffled music and laughter floating out on the night air as he'd leaned over and kissed her long and deep under the thick blanket of stars. When at last they pulled apart, Ro had looked at Griff, with his eyes on hers, and decided in that moment to let herself get swept away, just for now, just while she was there. And so she had, dropping her guard with him, being her true, open self in a way she never was on city dates to sushi restaurants and overpriced cocktail bars. It had all felt so natural and so effortless over those two days with Griff, and Ro had told herself that it was because whatever this was, it was purely fleeting.

The morning after the wedding, she and Griff had stood together up on the ridge, the sun warming her face and her fingers tingling with an unexpected surge of happiness every time he'd touched her hand, and she had gazed down over the sweeping patchwork greens of Carralon.

'It's so beautiful. Different from what I'm used to, though. What's it like living here?'

'It's good,' he said. 'Not for everyone but I reckon you'd like it.'

'Really?'

'Yeah. I could definitely imagine you here.'

She looked over and he'd grinned back, attempting to pass off the comment as a joke. But he had meant it, in that moment, and they both knew it. And suddenly, without warning, Ro could imagine herself there too.

The following week, back in Sydney and back at work, Ro had never known the city to feel quite so grey and drab. Her apartment was suddenly small and cramped in a way she hadn't really noticed before and its view of the wall of the neighbouring block of units only depressed her further. She had plodded through the motions, feeling sorry for herself while mentally revisiting and regretting almost every life choice she'd made to bring her to this point, and then Griff had called. It had felt like the clouds were parting as she held the phone.

'Listen, I know it was all maybe just a weekend-type thing but –' He'd started, then stopped again. 'But I wanted to call, so I got your number from Heather. Hope that's okay.'

'Yes, it's okay.' Ro had been on the verge of plundering Heather's contact book herself.

'What would you reckon about me driving over this weekend? Buy you dinner?'

'Drive over to where?' Ro had been incredulous. 'To Sydney?'

'Yeah.'

'It's five hours away.'

'I know. But that's okay with me. Is it okay with you?'

'Well, yeah. It's okay with me.'

She had heard him smile down the line. 'Great. Guess I'll see you there, then.'

Eighteen months later, they were married under the intricate wrought-iron arch in the Hewetts' orchard and afterwards, their friends and families toasted them at the Black Creek Inn while Griff spun Ro on the scratched wooden dance floor in her white wedding dress.

Chapter 12

Ro looked now across the bar to where she had danced on the day she got married. Physically, nothing much had changed. The same faded photos still hung on the same walls as the fan twirled ineffectually overhead, but it felt like an entirely different place from the room where she'd celebrated her marriage, or Heather's, for that matter. The energy and spirit had belonged to the people, not the space, and as they'd gone, one by one, it had slipped away with them. Ro felt a wave of loss wash over her, and forced it down as she followed Heather to where the woman's husband and father-in-law were sitting at the end of the counter. Griff was already deep in conversation with them both.

'There she is.' Noel looked up as he saw Ro approach. In the past, Heather's husband would have grinned widely and thrown his arms around her. Now, his smile was a little tired and vague as he eased himself off his stool. He was still a large, sturdy

man with shoulders and limbs made for the outdoors, but as Ro
hugged him she could feel that his muscle was starting to run
to fat.

'Thank you very much, Rowena mate, for giving Sylvie a
good reason to throw open the doors and let us all in,' Noel
said as he released her and lifted his beer glass, tilting it her way.
'Now,' he drained the last mouthful and swallowed, 'what are
you drinking?'

'I'll get these,' Noel's father, Bernie, said from the stool beside
him. 'How are you, Ro?'

He didn't try to get up and Ro was glad. Bernie had once
been as solid as his son, but now his skin was baggy on his face,
suggesting recent weight loss, and the whites of his eyes were
tinged yellow. Ro didn't need to see his medical records to make
an educated guess as to the current state of Bernie's health. He
had aged in a way that told her enough.

It felt unfair, Ro thought. After a lifetime of good physical
activity, Bernie should have been able to reap the rewards as he
aged. His working years had been spent in the paddocks, and
he'd been a volunteer firefighter at the local station for more
than three decades, working alongside Griff for half that time.
At weekends, Bernie and later Noel had coached whatever rugby
teams Carralon had been able to field in any given year. There
hadn't been enough players for even a single team for more than
a decade, Ro knew, but for a while afterwards, she had occasionally spotted Bernie with his son and grandsons running a
few exercises between themselves on the town's bald oval. They
all moved well, but there was only so much you could do with
a handful of people.

When the rugby club folded for good, Bernie had set up an
active seniors program which many of Ro's patients enjoyed, as
Bernie led them three times weekly through a brisk walk and

gentle stretch followed by – probably most beneficial of all – a cup of coffee and a chat in the community centre. That had also been forced to end somewhat suddenly after Bernie had woken up one unremarkable morning to discover his car was nowhere to be found. It had turned up quickly, parked in the centre of town. Bernie, though, had no memory of why it was there or how he'd got home so Heather had brought him to the GP clinic, where Ro had carried out a full check-up and ordered a range of tests. The results had cleared him for dementia, somewhat against expectations, but had instead called for further investigation of a different sort, which in turn had revealed a cluster of pre-cancerous cells.

Nearly ten years on, Bernie was still with them, but he was certainly not coaching rugby games or leading brisk walks. Instead, he now sat quietly at the bar between Griff and Noel, sipping what appeared to be nothing stronger than water.

'Sylvie, love,' Bernie called to the bartender, who was pouring a pair of beers for the couple who ran the small grocery shop across the street. 'We'll have another round here when you're ready.'

'Thanks, Bernie.' Ro's smile was returned but she watched him for a moment longer after he dropped his eyes back to his drink.

She always sensed a genuine warmth in both Bernie and his son but also, buried deep, she thought she could detect the finest layer of frost. They both worked hard to hide it, and it was so subtle that Ro would have missed it completely had she not been highly attuned to the complex web of politics that tangled all of Carralon together in its uneven, misshapen form. The divide between those who had left and those who had stayed was real. Between the ones who had taken the mine's money in any way and the ones who had held out. Ro felt her thoughts dart to

Damien, choosing to wait for them that evening in the gloomy car park rather than inside the well-lit pub.

Once Damien had sold Warren's place, it was like a dam had broken on that western side of town. Ann-Marie's ex, long since moved away and sick of squabbling over a home he had no desire still to own, had been able to instruct his lawyer to use the very real threat of diminishing value to successfully force the sale of the ivy cottage to Lentzer.

Bernie, hunkered down in the sandstone bungalow that his father had built with his own hands, could technically have held out for as long as he'd wanted. But Lentzer had simply made it clear that with both the farmhouse and the ivy cottage now in their portfolio, the buy-out price for a small, isolated bungalow would drop every single day that he did so. Bernie had sworn for months that the money was of no consequence, that he would be crowbarred from that place in a coffin. The mine did not argue, but it did exercise its new right to the shared access track and suddenly heavy vehicles were lumbering their way up and down past Bernie's front door, all hours of the day and night. Bernie's nearest neighbour was now the mine, and his new neighbour's expensive lawyers loved to quibble over boundaries that had always been marked by goodwill rather than fences. After more than six decades in the house, Bernie found himself living on shared ground and borrowed time until, eventually, he too could take it no more. He had finally sold, receiving less than anyone in town would have called a fair price. Griff had joined a few of Bernie's friends from the fire station and the rugby club in helping him and Noel to board up the windows and doorways. The father and son had tears in their eyes the whole time, Griff told Ro later.

Ro glanced outside now to the empty dark spot where Damien had been waiting. Damien may well have had a phone call with London that evening, probably did, in fact. But that didn't change the reality that since selling Warren's farmhouse to the mine, Damien moved through town keeping his head down and his profile low.

'I've got a very mediocre pinot in, if you're interested.'

Ro turned at the sound of the voice to see Sylvie smiling at her from behind the bar. The woman turned a bottle of wine so the label was visible. 'It's not much,' she said, 'but it is alcoholic.'

'Thanks, Sylvie.' Ro laughed and pulled up a stool. 'I'm sure that'll be lovely.'

'I'm sure it won't be, but it's the best I can do with the suppliers these days,' Sylvie said as she poured. Mid-fifties, she sported henna-red hair that in the decade Ro had known her varied only in the amount of silver shining through at the roots.

Sylvie had been born and bred in Melbourne, spending her teens in and out of the hip, grungy clubs of Brunswick, and she still wore the essence of it like a perfume. She zipped along the country roads in a vintage red convertible Ford Capri which she'd owned since the nineties and serviced and maintained herself, and whatever the weather, Sylvie's wardrobe was exclusively black from head to toe. She'd spent her twenties behind the counters of bars and clubs, working not drinking, and by her thirties had been manager of a major venue for touring bands. Those had been some crazy years, she'd told Ro once, unpretentiously dropping names like confetti. She'd burned out quickly, though – 'It's not so much the dickheads, because they're mostly all dickheads. It's the ones who also can't sing or play that do me in' – and had been recuperating on a much-needed solo holiday in Bali when her eyes had met Warren's over a tray of mojitos at the beachside resort where they'd both been staying.

Sylvie slid the glass of wine over the counter to Ro, then paused with the open bottle still in her hand, nodding to the far end of the bar. 'One for Della, as well?'

Ro followed Sylvie's gaze and sure enough spotted her daughter in the corner, somewhat unexpectedly sitting with Jacob. They were talking, or Della was at least. She was reclined comfortably in her wooden chair, legs crossed at the knee, speaking calmly and quietly, her attention fully focused on his face as though in some sort of business meeting. Jacob's performance review, or whatever it was, did not appear to be going well, his curly head bowed as he stared intently at his beer bottle on the table, scraping at the label with his fingernail. Della continued to speak, undeterred that she appeared to be leading an entirely one-sided conversation. About what, Ro couldn't begin to guess.

'No, she's driving,' Ro said, dragging her attention away as both Heather and Ann-Marie pulled up stools next to her. 'I'll let her order when she's ready.'

'Well,' Sylvie raised her own glass of iced water, 'welcome, Ro. It's nice to have you back.' Her smiled dimmed a little. 'Despite the occasion. Cheers.'

Ro joined the others in touching her glass to theirs and took a sip of wine. It was far nicer than she'd been promised, to be fair. Sylvie had always had a good eye for what kept the customers happy.

'So you'll let us know the details about Sam's memorial?' Sylvie looked at Ro over the rim of her own water glass.

'Yeah. Of course. I'll talk to Griff. Think it'll be much the same as last year.'

Sylvie nodded slowly, her eyes still on Ro. 'And what's the plan for the rest of your time?'

Ro shrugged, aware of Ann-Marie's and Heather's attention also on her now.

'Not much. Just . . .' She grasped around for the right words. 'Be here, I suppose.'

Sylvie reached out and placed her palm on Ro's hand. Her

skin was warm and the metal of her rings cold against Ro's knuckles. 'Well, we're always happy to have you back.'

She sounded like she meant it, and maybe she did, Ro thought. She had always liked Sylvie, both as Warren's other half and as the woman who ran arguably the town's key institution with a firm and fair touch. But Ro watched now as Sylvie removed her hand with a smile and turned away. Bringing the encounter to an end, Ro thought as she sipped her wine, perhaps a little sooner than strictly necessary in this mostly empty bar. Neither Ann-Marie nor Heather had seemed to notice, though, already talking about the worsening condition of the big pothole on the southern road. But Ro had noticed. She was aware of it in the same way that she knew Sylvie was aware of Ro's eyes still on her as she moved around the bar, wiping already clean tables. Ro watched for a little longer, but Sylvie did not look over again.

Sam had spoken to Sylvie, of course, in the week before he disappeared. It was impossible to get a good read on a place without consulting the person who kept the community lubricated, and Sam had dutifully done just that. Twice, in fact. Later, of all the interviews in his notebook, it was those pages that Ro found herself returning to most frequently. She could picture them now, even as she sat in the bright bar, sipping her chilled wine. Sam's handwriting scratched across the paper that was now a little furry at the corners from Ro's repeated handling. A list of questions written in black ink, and then, later, a short blue-inked addition.

A few extra words – Ro could see them in her mind's eye – scrawled in the margin seemingly in haste. Written below them was Sylvie's name. And beside that, a single question mark, pressed deep into the paper. The curve, the line and the dot of its shape traced into the page, over and over again.

Chapter 13

Ro woke, suddenly and unnaturally. She lay in the dark of the studio hut at the bottom of the garden, her head pounding more than would be warranted by her two small glasses of wine at the pub the night before, and listened to the rumbling from the mine. The sound always seemed to travel further at night, the low-frequency bass note reverberating with an almost physical sensation as it rolled in constant waves that she could feel passing through the floorboards and walls.

She sat up, fumbling for the bedside light switch, her eyes stinging as the bulb blazed to life. Rummaging through her bag, she pulled out her noise-cancelling headphones, fitting them over her ears with some relief. The audible sound was deadened, but she could still sense the frequency quivering all around her. It was better than nothing, though, and Ro simply sat there for a few minutes, blinking as her vision adjusted to the light. She yawned, knowing even as she did so that sleep was some way off, and instead she allowed her mind to wander back through the previous evening.

She, Griff and Della had stayed at the pub until Sylvie had finally rung the bell and announced closing. Ro had, somewhat to her surprise, enjoyed the gathering and had found herself both relieved and sorry when it had come to an end. It felt weirder each time now to be in a place she knew so well, surrounded by such familiar faces, and yet all night experience tiny, disconcerting moments of confusion. Throwaway comments and half-started conversations had left her at sea and scrabbling for understanding, reminding her that she didn't know this place well at all, anymore. Ro had been blithely unaware and unaffected by the worsening pothole on the south road that seemed to trouble most of Carralon on a daily basis. She had not known the windows at the back of the community hall had been smashed. She had not heard that Ann-Marie's ex was getting remarried. The faces around her were all recognisable, but the true closeness that built friendships had been diluted by time and distance.

As Sylvie had begun switching off the lights they had all trickled out into the darkness of the car park, Della clicking the key fob to unlock her silver sedan with a subtle beep while Ro and Griff said their goodbyes. They'd climbed into Della's spotless car and she had reversed carefully, the wheels crunching against the gravel. She had turned the nose towards the exit, the headlights sweeping over Heather and Ann-Marie, who were talking together beside a truck Ro did not recognise. Their heads shot up in unison as the beams flashed over them, momentarily startled, their features harsh in the glare and their eyes wide. Ann-Marie blinked and squinted, raising a hand in farewell and then Heather did the same, their smiles grimace-like under the twin spotlights. Ro lifted her own hand in return, unsure if they could see her through the windscreen. She watched them as the headlights slid sideways and the two women disappeared once more into the gloom.

Della had not spoken as they'd pulled away and left the town behind, her hands at ten and two on the wheel, focused fully on the black night in front of her. From the passenger seat, Ro had leaned back against the headrest and looked over.

'What were you chatting to Jacob about?' she asked softly.

'When?' Della replied, and with that response alone Ro knew she was about to be lied to.

'Earlier. Just after we arrived.'

'Oh.' Della's eyes were glassy and unblinking as she stared hard at the road. 'I don't know. Not much, really. Catching up, I suppose.'

Ro said nothing, but glanced in her own side mirror. She could see Griff in the back seat, his eyes closed and his arms folded across his chest. Awake, though, she could tell. Ro let her daughter drive on in silence and returned her attention to the shadowy landscape flashing past outside the window. She would ask Della again, another time, when it was just the two of them.

Still wearing her headphones, Ro now climbed out of bed and padded the short distance over the wooden floor to the armchair. She pulled her laptop onto her knees, wincing a little at the fresh brightness as she opened the screen and powered it to life. She located the folder she wanted, right there in prime position on the desktop, and clicked it open.

Sam's interviews and research notes.

The police had said repeatedly at the time how lucky it was to have his laptop, recovered in perfect working condition from the passenger seat of his abandoned rental car. It had been Della who had successfully guessed the password, it being the same one Sam had used since school, and Ro had seen the relief on the regional division sergeant's face and suspected they would never have got into it without her. They could learn a lot from the laptop, the same sergeant had promised, its presence alone offering valuable information about the nature of what may or may not have occurred. What, if anything, the police had learned in the days they'd had possession of it, Ro was never quite sure, because eventually it had been only the computer, and not Sam himself, that had quietly been returned to her and Griff.

The anniversary of Sam's disappearance fell on a Monday this year, two days from now. At this exact moment, five years ago, Sam had still been with them. Breathing, living. What had she been doing herself, Ro tried to think, five years ago at – she checked the clock – twenty past one in the morning in those last precious forty-eight hours or so before her son would slip away? Sleeping soundly, probably. She used to sleep well back then.

Sam's birthday had been a good day, right up until it had become the very worst of Ro's life. It had dawned warm and sunny, the breeze a little high perhaps, enough to prompt Griff to wander outside with a frown on his face every now and again. Other than that, they'd all had a leisurely morning. Ro had pottered around in her garden until Sam had emerged from his bedroom at around ten o'clock, a sleepy smile on his face as they'd sat around the kitchen table together to watch him open his gifts. Among them was a new shirt from Ro, and an access code for a freshly released online game, which Sam had ordered himself with his parents' credit card and then handed over to a slightly bewildered Griff to present back to him. Della had given her brother a mug bearing the logo of his favourite football team. Sam had smiled and thanked them all. He'd had a shower and put on his new shirt, drunk a cup of coffee from his new mug. He had never had a chance to play the game and the shirt had gone missing on his back along with him. Ro had taken the coffee mug with her when she'd left Carralon, though.

She still used it most days, the logo on the side now almost fully faded away. Ro could only make it out because she knew what it had once been.

After lunch, Sam had helped Griff repair a loose post on the front fence, and then he'd gathered up his laptop, backpack and water bottle and shouted goodbye from the hallway. He was heading out, he'd said. Going to Damien's place.

Ro had been in the kitchen, and she had stayed there. 'Dinner's at six thirty. I'm doing lasagne,' she'd called. 'If that's all right?'

It would be, she had known, because that had been his favourite.

'Yes,' Sam had shouted back, or something just like that. *Yep* or *yeah* or *okay* or *sounds good* or *thanks, Mum*. Something affirmative, of that Ro was absolutely certain. Something that fully indicated his intention to be eating lasagne with his family for his birthday meal that evening.

'All right, see you later,' she had replied from where she'd been standing beside the table. She had been distracted by something, but later she could not recall what. A hunt for a utensil? A cleaning task? Whatever it was, it had seemed absolutely crucial enough in that moment to prevent Ro from crossing the few paces from kitchen to hallway to say a proper goodbye to her son. What could she possibly have been thinking about when she heard the front door slam? What had stopped her, at the sound of his engine firing up, from running outside and chasing him down, waving for him to stop and pulling the car door open and simply putting her arms around her child and clutching him tight? From looking into his face and telling him what he meant to her? *Sam, my little one, my baby, I love you. I love you so much.* What had been so fascinating and distracting to Ro in her tired, ordinary kitchen that she had not even glanced out of the window to watch him drive away? That she had not stood and waved, spending an extra minute to keep her child in sight as his car trundled away from the house and disappeared down the road? Ro didn't know. She simply hadn't. But at the time, she'd thought she'd see him again.

After that, the events of the day grew hazier. Sam had gone to Damien's, as he'd said, and was seen leaving the townhouse and climbing into his car just after 2 pm by Doug Hewett. Darcy's drone footage captured Sam less than an hour later walking towards Warren's house, for reasons Ro had never understood with any certainty. Most likely, it had simply been part of his research, she had concluded. Or possibly sheer curiosity. Sam wouldn't have been alone in having an interest in the remains of the empty buildings, especially as he'd spent so much time in them growing up, back when they were solid and clean and had lights glowing in the windows.

Whatever Sam's motivation, the trails of his footprints showed he had visited all three properties in the hours between him leaving Damien's house and Ro lifting the lasagne from the oven. Ro had glanced at the clock first with a seed of annoyance and then with mounting concern as the meal grew cold and rubbery. The lasagne had waited on the counter uneaten as Ro and Griff had been calling their son's name into the twilight beside his abandoned car.

Ro sat alone in her hut now, feeling the familiar tightness blooming in her chest, and she shook her head to try to clear the memory. She readjusted her headphones and turned instead to her computer.

Sam had been typically diligent in keeping track of his research and he had transcribed the interviews he'd carried out before he vanished. Ro had later organised the documents and transferred them to her own laptop. The exception, of course, had been his chat with Damien, whose words had been lost on Sam's phone the same day they were recorded. Ro skipped past Sam's own notes for now and instead opened a copy of the statement Damien himself had provided to the police about the interview.

Sam Crowley is my cousin's son and I have known him since he was born. My conversation with him on the day of his disappearance lasted approximately an hour, Damien had written, *and our discussion centred largely around the impact of the Lentzer expansion on Carralon Ridge. Other topics we covered briefly included mental health, local history, a lack of opportunities and entertainment for young people in the town, environmental concerns and my late brother, Warren Hillary.*

Damien may have truly believed he and Sam had spoken mostly of these things, and perhaps in real time they had, Ro would never know. But whether Damien recognised it or not, over the hundreds of words of his statement, the primary focus was on Damien himself.

He had written reams justifying his decision to sell the Hillary farmhouse. He had laid out the case like a legal argument for the defence, drawing on numbers and real estate statistics, referencing formal offers from Lentzer paperwork, dedicating page after page to his own mitigation. Pleading, implicitly but desperately, Ro thought, for forgiveness and understanding. She wondered – if this was really how the conversation had played out – whether Sam had given Damien what he was hoping for. Sam had liked Damien, but Warren had played a present and active role in his life for seventeen years. The only clue came right at the end.

Sam asked me how I felt on a personal level about selling the house I grew up in, Damien continued. *I replied that people sell their child- hood homes all the time. It happens right across the country, thousands of times a year. It was the best decision from a financial standpoint and while I regret the impact the sale of such a significantly positioned property has had on the wider community, I stand by the choice I made. I felt it was the best option available to me under the circumstances.*

The statement continued on the page unbroken, but Ro knew Damien well enough that she was sure she could detect a pause in his thoughts. She could imagine him lifting his hands from the keyboard at that point. Pushing back his desk chair, finding some excuse to stand and step away for a moment – a cup of coffee, checking a noise outside the window – before eventually returning and typing the last paragraph, fast and efficiently, freeing himself from the unpleasant task at hand.

Sam then asked how I felt in light of the fact that Warren had refused to sell the property before his death. I replied that I was very aware that Warren enjoyed living in our family home but I also knew my brother to be an intelligent man with a good eye for business. It was my honestly held belief at the time that Warren would eventually change his mind and agree to a sale.

Ro let her eyes linger on the words for a moment, before closing the document. Did Damien really believe that was true? she wondered. *Was* it true? Possibly. No matter how loud the protests, nearly everyone had sold eventually. Ann-Marie, Bernie, even Griff and Ro themselves. Noel and Heather were among the very few exceptions, and Ro scrolled down the list of Sam's transcripts until she found their joint interview.

Noel's conversation was interesting in that it had been virtually a polar opposite to Damien's. While Damien's focus had been self-reflective, Noel's gaze lay firmly outwards, speaking about Carralon at length and with enthusiasm. Ro had read the interviews many times and she ran her eyes down the page now, picking up the occasional sentence and phrase.

Couldn't ask for a better place for the kids. I love it here, I grew up here, met my wife here, my happiest memories are here. This was a town well worth saving, Noel said, repeatedly and in many different ways. *I want my boys to have the chance to grow up with that same kind of community and support around them. Neighbours look out for each other, that's the beauty of this place. We're all in it together.*

His optimism was unfailing, and Ro had no doubt Noel had believed everything he said, but the unwavering positivity had the effect of coating his answers with a lightly artificial quality. Noel had been talking about Carralon, that was true, but it was certainly not the town as Ro recognised it now, or even as it had been five years earlier when he'd been speaking those words to Sam. Noel was clinging to shadows, whether he accepted that deep down or not.

Heather's response was more measured, and even as she offered words of support to Noel's vision, Ro sensed something circumspect in her replies. Sam should have interviewed her alone, Ro thought. He would have got more out of her.

She scrolled on, glancing through the pages of interviews. Bernie's poor health at the time seeped through in his words. Normally articulate, he had mostly indulged himself in long anecdotes about the community's golden years, peppered with acidic comments about the problems it faced today. After a while, Sam had resorted to reporting much of the exchange in summary sentences. *Bernie criticises changes to road system. Bernie suggests a goods tax for mine workers from which locals are exempt.*

Ro moved on. Ann-Marie had focused with unguarded bitterness on the way her ex-husband had successfully campaigned from a distance to force her out of the ivy cottage. She had recalled an unpleasant series of events which Ro had partly forgotten about, mainly because they'd been superseded not long after by the twin shocks of first her father's death and then Warren's. Ann-Marie had clearly remembered, though, recounting a string of petty thefts in which items of little value disappeared, followed by a series of break-ins to her sheds and culminating in an upsetting incident when she'd travelled to Blenheim one night to see a man she'd met online and returned the next morning to find that someone had been in her house and her bed was missing. She had eventually discovered it dumped in the middle of the back paddock, and Ro could still picture Ann-Marie's shock.

Ann-Marie had phoned her ex-husband and tearfully shouted at him down the line to keep whatever friends he still had in town well away from her place. She was not going to sell, did he understand that? She wanted to stay and he would not bully her into changing her mind. He had denied it, of course, but it had never happened again. Jacob, who had been sleeping over with Sam while his mum was out of town, was white-faced with fury at the sight of his mother's distress. He and Sam had joined Griff in moving the bed back inside for a visibly shaken Ann-Marie. Her ex-husband won in the end, though, Ann-Marie had told Sam in her interview. He had dropped the scare tactics and called in his lawyer instead and eventually he'd achieved what he wanted. He'd got his sale and his money and Ann-Marie had lost her cottage.

Ro scrolled down the computer screen. Sam had also interviewed Jacob and Darcy, all three of them reflecting on the experience of growing up in a tiny town. Noel may have waxed lyrical about the benefits of spending a childhood in the small community, but the boys themselves had been notably less enthused. Not for the first time, Ro wondered if she and Griff had made a poor choice in raising their own children in such an insular place. They had been happy here – all of them – she felt sure, but they could probably have been as content somewhere else, with a larger mix of people and broader horizons.

In some ways, this was what Ro always found most interesting about Sam's interviews. They exposed people, herself included, to their own thoughts on an unintended level. Sam had been respectful in his questioning, she could tell from the nature of the conversations, but in page after page of responses, Ro could sense a reluctant resistance in the answers as he held a mirror up to his neighbours in turn, forcing them to examine their choices and think about what they'd gained or lost.

No-one ever enjoyed that, Ro knew, and as she closed the laptop she thought once more, with the benefit of hindsight, that it had probably been a mistake for Sam to study people he was personally so close to.

She put her laptop to one side, feeling exhausted in a way that wasn't entirely to do with sleep. She should go back to bed, lie down with her headphones on, close her eyes and try to ignore the strange pulse filling the air around her. Instead, Ro reached for Sam's notebook and ran her eyes over the handwritten lines. The stapled spine of the book was weak from repeated handling over the years and if allowed to fall open naturally, it always presented her now with the same page. Sylvie's interview.

'You never know,' Ann-Marie had said to Ro earlier, up at the ivy cottage, 'what's still out there to find.'

Ro wasn't convinced. She had trained herself, slowly and painfully over the years, to manage her hope. From day to day it lay boxed away tightly, stored somewhere half-forgotten and starved of the light and oxygen it would need to thrive. It still lived, though, weak and dormant as it may be. Its heart still beat and occasionally it twitched and stirred in its box, drew a shallow breath and whispered to her the same three words. *Time changes things.*

There was some truth in that, Ro knew as she pictured the pub that very evening. Virtually empty, compared with even five years ago. So many people had left that it was possible whatever little information there had ever been about Sam's disappearance had gone with them. The answers Ro needed might be lost forever, especially if buried in a lonely stretch of bushland or an abandoned paddock. If they were buried in someone's conscience, though, that could be a different matter.

Her eyes fell to the scribbled note Sam had made at the side of Sylvie's interview. The question mark he'd traced over and over.

Re: Warren and Lentzer. Ask Sylvie?

And so Ro had asked Sylvie, three times in fact, over the years. And each time Sylvie had warmly welcomed her up to the bar counter, poured her a drink on the house. Each time she had leaned in, nodding as Ro showed her the page, listening closely as Ro urged her to think back to the interview and try to recall anything specific that the note might refer to. *Anything*, Ro would plead, *even if it feels like nothing*. Each time, Sylvie would furrow her brow, tap her chin, spend several long minutes in deep, silent thought. Then each time, she'd shake her head. *No. I'm so sorry. I don't know. It could be anything.*

Sylvie was certainly right about that. And it was just a single scrawled note in a book full of scrawled notes. And Ro might have dismissed it completely after that very first conversation if she had not, then and each time since, felt bone-sure deep in her gut that Sylvie was lying.

Chapter 14

The morning dawned windy and hot, and Della was waiting on the steps of the hut when Ro returned after breakfast.

'Oh, there you are. I was looking for you.' Della shielded her eyes against the harsh sunlight as she watched Ro cross the lawn with half a piece of cold toast in one hand and a collection of screwdrivers in the other. She nodded at the tools. 'What are they for?'

'Sorry, I was in the small shed,' Ro said, opening the door to the hut to let them both in. 'I thought I'd try to get this loose.' She finished the last of her toast and brushed the crumbs from her hands before stepping over to a small round mirror that was screwed into the wall above the armchair. The mirror was spotted in places with age and was only a little larger than Ro's outstretched palm, but around the circular edge it was framed with tiny stones of coloured glass, which offered a touch of warmth to whatever it reflected. Ro had bought it herself at a second-hand market about a decade ago. It had only cost her a few bucks then and was worth even less now, but she still found it pretty.

'Are you going to take it home when you go?' Della asked, and Ro shook her head. She'd actually considered it, briefly, but her life in Sydney was kept carefully and deliberately separate from Carralon Ridge and she allowed very few remnants to spill over the boundary.

'Thought I'd bring it as a gift to Heather's this morning,' she said. 'She seemed a bit down yesterday, didn't you think?'

'Maybe. I thought most people did, though.'

'Yeah.' Ro considered that for a moment before turning back to the task. 'Well, anyway. I'll take this as a little offering for their saloon.'

'It'd look good in there,' Della said. 'They're still collecting stuff, are they?'

'I assume so. I asked your dad if he was okay to part with it and he said it was fine.' In fact, Griff had simply shrugged and rubbed his eyes.

'Take whatever you want, Ro,' he'd replied vaguely.

Ro heard her daughter's silence now and glanced at her reflection in the mirror. 'Sorry, you didn't want this for yourself, did you?'

'Oh. *No.*' Della's mouth turned downwards involuntarily at the very suggestion of hanging the brightly coloured mirror in her mostly beige apartment.

Ro smiled as she undid the bottom screw. 'That's what I thought.'

'But listen,' Della's voice was oddly light, 'can I come with you to Heather's place?'

Ro let the loose screw drop into her palm before turning to look at her daughter properly. Della and Heather had always got along well but were too far apart in age to have become friends. 'I'm sure you can, but why?' she asked baldly.

Della's face was open and unflinching. 'I think I just need a break from work.'

She was lying again. Ro could feel it instantly and hated it, the swooping unbalanced realisation that her daughter wasn't being honest with her. For the second time in as many days, as well. The faint suspicion that had been bubbling in the back of Ro's mind since last night resurfaced now and she let the silence hang. Only when Della blinked and dropped her eyes did she speak.

'I don't even know if Darcy's going to be there,' Ro said, seeing the touch of surprise cross her daughter's smooth face. 'If that's who you're hoping to see.'

Della weighed up her answer before nodding slowly. 'Yeah. It is.'

'Well, I mean, that's fine, Della. It doesn't matter to me, so why all the secrecy?' Ro couldn't hide the irritation. 'I mean, are you interested in him?'

'What?' Della's eyes widened. 'God, no.'

That felt like the truth at least and Ro turned back to the mirror. Her face was creased with worry in its bright reflection. She removed the top screw and the image disappeared as the mirror came away from the wall in her hands. 'And since when are you so keen to catch up with Darcy? Or Jacob, for that matter.'

'I know. Look –' Della seemed to be considering something. 'I don't think it's anything to worry about. It *is* nothing to worry about,' she corrected herself quickly. 'It's probably nothing at all, to be honest. I just want to ask them about something I heard.'

'About what?' Ro caught the specific note in her tone and her reaction was immediate. 'About Sam?'

'No, but –' Della cut herself off. Ro kept her gaze steady and

Della tried again. 'Not really, is what I mean. Not in the way you're – no, Mum, look, this is why I didn't want to tell you, I can see that you're already –'

'Already what?' Ro protested. 'I'm not doing anything . . .'

'You are. You're –'

'What? I'm not – Della, I don't know what you're –'

'You're getting your hopes up. Okay? That's what you're doing.' The fight had gone out of Della's voice and she just sounded sad.

It was enough to make Ro bite back the denial that sprang to her lips and instead she took a breath and glanced down at the mirror in her hands. There *was* something different in her expression, she could see it herself, the change that Della had picked up on.

'Sorry,' Ro said, not quite sure what she was apologising for.

Della watched her for a moment longer. 'No, it's fine,' she said, at last. 'But this thing I'm chasing Darcy about, it's going to be nothing, Mum. Honestly. It's barely even got anything to do with Sam, but . . .' She held up a hand against Ro's attempt to interrupt. 'But look, give me a chance to talk to Darcy. Get my facts straight or whatever. Then I'll tell you, I promise. For whatever it's worth. Okay?' Della's voice was gentle, every word layered with a concern that made Ro feel almost ashamed.

'Yeah.' Ro made herself nod. Her daughter should not have to worry about her. 'That sounds good. Thank you.'

'All right. Well, great.' Della smiled, her relief tangible. 'Give me a shout when it's time to go.' She waved towards the mirror in Ro's hands as she moved to the door. 'And that's a nice idea for a gift, by the way. Heather'll like it.'

Ro stood in the open doorway and watched Della walk away across the lawn. As she disappeared into the house, Ro glanced down at the mirror again. The daylight played across the lines on her face in a way that made her look brittle, and there was something distorted in her reflection that made it hard for her to meet her own gaze. Della had been right to be wary, Ro thought, but she'd been wrong in her interpretation. It wasn't hope she'd seen in Ro's face, or it didn't feel like it, anyway. To Ro, it looked like cold, tired desperation.

Chapter 15

Heather was running. Ro could see her shape up ahead on the long, gravelled drive. She looked even taller from behind in her leggings and sports top, her trainers flicking up a small cloud of dust each time her heels kicked back. Ro watched her through the windscreen as she and Della drove slowly along the track, paddocks stretching out on both sides. At the end of the drive, still some way off, stood a rambling farmhouse. Heather slowed and turned at the sound of the car engine, waiting with her hands on her hips as they approached. Her face was flushed and damp and her breathing ragged as Ro drew up and wound down the window.

'Hello. Jump in, if you want.' Ro nodded to the back seat.

'No, it's all right, my shoes are filthy.' Heather wiped a forearm across her face, her chest rising up and down. 'Meet you at the front door. I'll be right behind you.'

That would be true, Ro thought, as she edged past and pulled away. Heather had always been a strong runner, lithe and smooth in her stride with her long legs pumping. Even at a slower pace on all those early-morning walks they used to take together, Heather had enjoyed movement for movement's sake. She still ran very well, Ro could see as she glanced in the rear-view mirror, watching her friend pick up speed again, agile as she navigated the uneven track. There was a difference in her gait now, though. The enjoyment seemed to have evaporated some-where along the line and now Heather seemed to be pushing herself along with an air of grim determination.

Ro turned her attention back to the low wide farmhouse as she pulled up outside and came to a stop. The whitewashed stone was bright in the mid-morning sunlight as she and Della climbed out. In the twenty-five years Heather and Noel had called the place home they had infused it with a warmth that was still evident now, from the paved pathway leading to the door, to the fragrant fruit vines growing on trellises between the window frames.

'Hello, hello,' Heather panted as she drew up, checking her watch before brushing a damp strand of hair from her forehead. 'Sorry, thought I'd be back and changed by now but I've been resting my knee for a few days so I was quite slow around the route. Anyway, welcome! And Della, you came too. Good to see you.'

'I hope that's okay? I was at a loose end.'

Della lied so smoothly, Ro noted with something close to disappointment. She watched her daughter's eyes slide over the paddocks and barns visible from the driveway. There was no sign of Darcy.

'Yes, of course. It's so quiet around here, now. God knows, I hear enough about that.' Heather waved a hand down at herself. 'Look, I'm too sweaty to give you both a hug but come on in.'

She fished out a single key from a thin lanyard hanging around her neck and opened the large wooden door to the farmhouse. The house and its land lay to the east of town, on the other side of the hill and several kilometres away from the sandstone bungalow in which first Bernie and then his son, Noel, had grown up. Neither of the pair talked about it much now, the old stories not as much fun to tell these days.

Ro had heard them plenty of times over the years, though. Memories of the place where the family had made their living, with Bernie working in the paddocks, alone at first and then later with his son. Welcomed home to the sandstone bungalow each evening by Bernie's gentle wife Cathy, back when she was still alive. Bernie would reminisce about his three decades of volunteer service at the fire station. Noel used to recall warm evenings and weekends when, as a teenager, he'd cycle along the track to meet up with Warren and Damien at the neighbouring Hillary house. They'd ride off together, usually finding Griff somewhere along the way before carrying on, free and unsupervised to kick a footy or explore the bushland or cool off in the creek or catch up with any of the dozens of other kids living in the town.

Noel, and Heather too, had envisaged raising a gaggle of children in the same country idyll when they'd bought this house, Ro knew, but things had changed faster than any of them had expected and their two teenage boys were now the only children of any age left in town. No raucous football games or group bike rides for Zach and Kyle. Instead, the electronic beep and whine of a video game greeted Ro as she stepped inside, the tones loud and shrill.

Heather frowned at the noise. 'Shit. Bernie was trying to sleep when I left, I'd better –' She vaguely motioned up the hall in the direction of the kitchen. 'Sorry. You go on through. I'll be there in a sec.'

She strode ahead and disappeared through an entrance that Ro knew led to the lounge room. As Ro neared the open doorway she could see Zach and Kyle slumped side by side on the couch. They were a year apart in age but Ro wouldn't have guessed it from looking at them. They shared the same tangled caps of curly hair and both seemed to have grown more in the past twelve months than Ro would have expected. Their limbs looked overly long and their jaws, Zach's in particular, sported faint stubble. They both held game controllers in their hands, their eyes fixed on a screen out of sight, ignoring Heather as she bent over the couch, speaking in a low, pressing tone.

'. . . your grandfather needs his – hey, are you listening . . .?'

The volume of the game continued to blare and as Ro drew level she saw Heather reach over and snatch for the remote control in a move that smacked of desperation. The electronic tones died away at last and in their wake was a grunt of annoyance and a single muttered word.

'Bitch.'

Heather's head snapped up, her mouth thin and the colour in her cheeks high from something other than exertion. Her eyes briefly touched Ro's, and Ro simultaneously felt a sharp rush of both sympathy and embarrassment at having witnessed the exchange. She moved on quickly, catching up with Della, who seemed not to have heard, and followed her into the clean and airy kitchen.

Feeling ill at ease, Ro took a seat at the table, placing the wrapped mirror down carefully as she watched Della move straight to the large window over the sink. She stood there, surveying the paddocks and sheds outside. The electronic music began again, dulled but still audible, and if anything more was being said in the lounge room, Ro couldn't hear it. The only other sound was the loud ticking of the kitchen clock.

At the end of the table lay a loose pile of printouts that Ro instantly recognised as aerial drone shots. Curious, she leaned closer, glancing at the top few. The date on the prints showed they'd been taken the day before, when she and Griff had heard the sound of the machine hovering above them. Flicking through the rest of the images, Ro could see none of the bushland, though. Every shot was of the fringes of the mine, gaping and dark.

'They're both a bloody disgrace, I know.' With a creak of floorboards, Heather appeared in the doorway, her mouth turned down tightly at the corners as she entered the kitchen and moved briskly towards the mugs and coffee. Ro stacked the images in a pile and put them back where she'd found them.

'The boys,' Heather went on by way of explanation, jerking her head towards the living room as Della turned from the window with a look of mild confusion.

'Oh. Right.' Della nodded and joined Ro at the table as Heather pulled a bottle of milk from the fridge and dumped it on the counter with more force than strictly necessary.

'The thing is, there's nothing for them to bloody *do* around here. They've got no friends, no sports, no activities. Trailing all the way to Blenheim for school every day was a disaster, so that's all gone online, which they hate. It's hard to think of a punishment that means anything. I mean, what? Stay at home? Don't see your mates? That's day-to-day life anyway. Limiting screen time is pretty much the only option, but it's literally the only thing they seem to enjoy, so . . .' Heather paused. The video game music had stopped completely, the fresh silence carrying something almost more ominous. Her eyes lingered on the now quiet hallway, and she dragged them back as the kettle reached boiling point. 'I'm so sorry you saw them like that, they're really not –'

'God, Heather, no.' Ro hated seeing her like this. For a pain-fully long time it had seemed that Darcy might be the only child for Heather and Noel, and Ro still remembered their sheer elation when the two longed-for younger boys were born. 'Please don't –'

'No, I know, but still.' Heather concentrated on pouring hot water into three mugs. 'I'm not excusing them, but they're so bloody fed up and lonely. Sometimes it comes out badly. Thank God they at least have each other, I suppose. Anyway,' she handed around the mugs and the milk and nodded at the wrapped package by Ro's elbow, 'on a brighter note, is that for me?'

'Yes. It is.' Ro smiled and passed it over. 'Well, all of you, really. For the saloon, I thought, if you want it.'

'Oh, beautiful, thank you,' Heather said as she opened the paper and ran her fingers over the coloured glass of the mirror. 'I've always loved this. We'll take it out to show Noel when he's back. But are you sure you don't want to keep it?'

Ro thought about the little hut at the back of their own house, several kilometres away and both soon to be empty. Or perhaps not. Perhaps she and Griff and Della would each take only a handful of things that mattered to them and pull the door closed on the rest. Some people had done that, she knew. Either way, Ro simply nodded now.

'Yes, I'm sure. It's yours if you want it.' Keen to change the subject, she moved over to the arrangement of framed photos on a nearby shelf and picked up a picture of a tiny baby. 'Oh, is this your new niece?'

Heather's enthusiasm was infectious and the conversation grew quicker and lighter as they lingered over coffee, naturally falling into their familiar style that made it easy to draw Della in as well. As they chatted, Ro's eyes slid occasionally back to the photo shelf, landing specifically on the large framed black-and-white image that had served as the centrepiece for as long as Ro had been visiting this house.

It was a professional shot of Heather and Noel on their wedding day, caught in a beautifully candid moment as they clutched each other's hands in joy and triumph at the conclusion of their marriage ceremony. Behind the happy couple, the assembled guests had been captured unawares, chatting, hugging, laughing, some rising from seats, some lifting up children. The faces in the background crowd were a little blurred, the photographer's focus firmly on the couple, but Ro had seen this photo many times and, as always, her eyes instantly found herself and Griff.

They had been standing close enough in the image that Ro had been surprised the first time she'd seen it. They were separated from each other in the crowd by only two people and were looking in different directions. Still strangers then, but their lives had been about to converge. Their paths would cross within an hour and from that moment on they would remain inextricably intertwined, even now, despite tragedy and distance. If she had known then, Ro wondered as she looked at her younger, happy self, what lay ahead for them both, would she still have done the same? Beside her, Della sipped her coffee as they chatted, and Ro immediately knew her answer. Of course she would. She would go through it all again, and worse, for Della.

'Hey, while I've got you here,' Heather drained her coffee mug, pursing her lips at the bitterness, 'I actually wanted ask you both –'

She stopped abruptly as the video game music started up again. They all listened for a moment to the rattling jingle floating in from the hall, then Heather's chair squealed against the tiled floor as she shoved it back and stood.

'For God's sake, I'll – oh, Bernie. You're already up.' Heather sighed as her father-in-law appeared in the doorway. He had heavy purple bags under his eyes and had not shaved that morning, his chin covered in fine white stubble. 'God, sorry. Did the boys wake you?'

'No, it's fine. It wasn't them, I couldn't sleep anyway,' Bernie said, a little unconvincingly, as he found a tired smile for the guests. 'G'day Ro, Della. Good to see you both.'

'Do you want some coffee?' Heather reached for a clean mug as Bernie nodded.

'Thanks, Heather, love. Yeah, I'll take it outside, get some fresh air.'

'No worries, I'll carry it for you,' Heather said, pouring the hot water. She looked over to Ro and Della and nodded at the mirror lying on the counter. 'Noel must be back by now. We'll show him what you brought.'

Ro stood as Della gathered up their three empty cups and took them to the sink, pausing at the large window.

'Thanks, Della. Dump them anywhere,' Heather said. 'I'll sort them out later.'

'No worries.' Della obediently placed the cups on the draining board. She gazed out for a moment more then turned back to them, a small smile on her face.

'Listen, you guys go ahead,' she said. 'I'm just going to run over and say hi to Darcy.'

Chapter 16

As the first anniversary of Sam's disappearance had approached, Ro had found herself out at the three houses almost every day. Each evening, she would finish her shift at the medical centre and get into her car, determined that this time she would go straight home. Instead, she would feel herself taking all the wrong turns, pointing the car left rather than right, and inevitably, as she once more trundled along the painfully familiar quiet country road, she would silently promise herself that today she would keep moving. She would not slow down, she would not pull in at the track, she would simply snatch a glimpse of the site as she passed by. She stopped every time.

The brick of the old stone bungalow was blazing golden in the low light on one of these evenings, as Ro sat alone on a small wall in the back garden. She heard the engine purr of a vehicle pulling up at the front and froze, listening hard. Griff and Ann-Marie had both separately seen signs of trespassers in the area recently, and

Ro reached into her bag and pulled out her phone at the sound of
the engine shutting off and a car door opening.

'Ro?'

She relaxed at the voice.

'You back there? It's Bernie. Everything all right?'

'Yes. I'm fine. I'll come around,' Ro called, with a last glance
out to the wide, open land. She used to love this view from the
bungalow. It had been right here that she'd first begun to fall in
love with the town, standing in her bridesmaid's dress as Heather
and Noel were married in his parents' garden, surrounded by the
rich amber of the paddocks and the deep greens of the bushland.
Dappled sunlight had danced over the wedding party and with
every breath, Ro had drawn in the fresh tang of eucalyptus in
the air. The gum trees had swayed gently overhead, kookaburras
calling down from the branches, their good-natured laughs
competing with the vows. Ro could picture that day so well,
but at times it felt almost as though it had never really happened.
Everything felt different; it was like remembering a fever dream.

Ro could hear Bernie now rattling around at the front of the
bungalow and she pushed herself up from the low wall where
she'd been sitting. The top surface of the brickwork was gritty
and it crumbled a little under her fingertips as she rose to her feet.
The wall had once marked out a winding path that led through
a charming native garden, but now it went nowhere and the
ground was flat and barren in some spots, wildly overgrown in
others. Ro turned towards the bungalow. Its windows had been
freshly washed on the morning of the wedding, she remembered.
She'd been able to see herself and her blue bridesmaid's gown in
the shine of the glass as it had reflected the happy gathering.

Wooden boards nailed to the window frames stared back
blankly at her now as she made her way along the paved patio
that encircled the house. It was covered all the way around by

a generous awning and in the past, visitors popping in to see Bernie or Cathy were usually ushered to one of several comfortable outdoor chairs that faced the views. The seats had been flanked by large, lush plants in decorative pots and side tables that were perfectly placed for a glass of wine or a cold beer. The patio was now as bare and featureless as the rest of the property and Ro's footsteps left a trail in the dust as she followed the paving stones around to the front.

'Hi, Bernie,' she said as she rounded the corner and saw his truck parked next to her car. He was crouched on the front verandah, rummaging through a toolbox by his feet, and glanced up as Ro joined him.

'G'day. Thought I'd swing by and take a quick look at this.' Bernie stood and ran his hand over some minor damage to the board that covered what had once been the dining room window. The top right corner was loose and the wood slightly splintered, as though someone had attempted to pry it off. 'Saw your car parked. You having a little wander around?'

'Yeah. Sorry.' Ro felt the faint heat of embarrassment, as though her secret ritual of grief was about to be dragged into the light. 'Hope that's okay?'

'Course it's okay.' Bernie replied, his face sombre. 'It always is.' He turned to the house, a small frown settling as he pressed a callused finger against the damaged edge of the board. 'Keep an eye out, though, if you're going to come here alone. Been a few people messing about lately, have you heard?'

Ro nodded. 'Griff said.'

'Yeah, Darcy reckons there was someone the other day as well. Spotted them on the drone footage. Came over to check and found this.' Bernie pulled at the corner of the wood. It was loose enough that it could be wrenched away if someone felt keen. 'Have you noticed anyone hanging around?'

'No. Sorry.' But a couple of times Ro had sensed that someone else had been there in between her own visits. Trampled weeds, once. Another time nothing more than a faint, subtle feeling in the air. 'I'll let you know if I do, though.'

'Yeah, thanks. Hopefully they've had their fill and moved on, any luck.'

Ro watched Bernie as he bent down and pulled a hammer and small bag of nails from his toolbox before standing again and assessing the wood. As his GP, Ro might at times in the past have been concerned about him being out here alone, but Bernie had currently been enjoying one of his better windows of health, responding well to his latest cocktail of medication and treatment. There was something else bene-ficial though, Ro reflected, about Bernie being here at the house that he'd loved so much. As though the muscle memory of simply being in the space where he'd grown up allowed him to move better and left him able to focus on his actions and thoughts more clearly. It made him seem a little younger, even. As she looked on, Ro wondered if Bernie's treatment over the years might have been easier on him and gone a little more smoothly if he'd been able to complete it in the comfort of his own home, rather than as a guest – however welcome – at his son's place. Perhaps, but equally, perhaps not. They'd never know.

'Anyway,' Ro said as Bernie lined up a nail against the window frame. 'I'll leave you to it.'

'Stay if you want,' he replied, but she shook her head. She preferred to visit the past alone, and guessed Bernie was the same. As if reading her mind, he lowered his hammer and regarded her across the patio.

'Anniversaries are bloody awful.' He didn't need to specify what he was talking about. 'Especially first ones.'

Ro swallowed, hoping her voice would sound close to normal. 'It's still a couple of weeks away.'

'Yeah,' Bernie said, quietly. 'We all know when it is, Ro. No-one's forgotten.' He glanced out in the direction of the mine. 'And I know it's technically not my place to offer anymore, but as far as I'm concerned, you're free to come by here any time you want. Griff as well. Della. If it helps.'

'Thanks, Bernie.'

He nodded, then hesitated for a beat, his eyes still on her. 'He was a good lad, your Sam. I know you and Griff don't need me to tell you that, but he was. Great mate to Darcy, always polite whenever those boys were hanging around here as kids. And then last year, even after he'd been away for a while, you know? Sometimes people go off somewhere and come back . . . I dunno –'

Bernie shrugged and looked down at his toolbox. Ro braced herself for the rub, but it didn't come.

'Come back with a different mindset, I suppose. Think that they've seen the whole world and we've seen none of it,' Bernie went on. 'But Sam wasn't like that, not from what I could tell, anyway. When he went around to us all, asking his questions for his studies, it didn't feel like he was coming at you with an agenda, he was . . .' Bernie considered. 'Interested, I suppose. Made you feel like your story was worth telling, and that he had the patience to listen.'

Ro felt a dangerous weight bloom behind her eyes and blinked hard. 'I'm glad.'

'Yeah, well, it's true.' Bernie gave a small shrug. 'And he was very patient with me, which was good of him, because I know I wasn't at my best. I mean, you'd remember, all those appointments you and I had. I was pretty bloody grumpy chatting with Sam. Felt a bit bad about it afterwards, to tell you the truth.'

'Please, Bernie,' Ro said quickly, 'don't worry about that. He was grateful to you for doing what you could.'

That was mostly, if not entirely, true. Sam had felt Bernie's views would be valuable, but Ro had cautioned at the time that he might not be an easy interview subject. He'd been struggling with a new treatment regime and some worrying test results had been hanging over him. Bernie had insisted he'd wanted to take part in the project and was eager to go on the record with his thoughts about the mine's impact on his community, but Ro had been able to tell from Sam's notes later that the older man had been tired and brusque throughout, bordering on rude. He had improved a lot since, though. The next round of tests had come back relatively positive, and adjusting the dosage of the medication had made a difference. Standing outside his old home now, ready to repair a broken board, the colour was back in his face.

'Well,' Bernie said. 'For whatever it was worth in the end, I appreciated Sam giving me a chance to say my piece. All of us, really. You and Griff can be proud of him. He was respectful to people who haven't had a lot of respect around this business – from the mine, from each other.' Bernie turned back to the house, lining up a nail and testing its size before speaking again. 'I wanted to make sure you knew that.'

'Thank you.'

'No worries.'

They looked at each other for a moment more, before he turned back to the house. Ro took a step to leave when his quiet voice stopped her.

'I still wonder sometimes why Sam came here that day.' Bernie sounded almost as though he was asking himself. Again, Ro didn't need him to specify what he meant. 'Why to this house? To any of the three, I suppose, but . . .'

Bernie ran a hand gently over the stone of his old home, as if it were an animal caught up in a moment of confusion and distress.

'I think about it too,' Ro replied. 'Probably something to do with his research, is my best guess. That seems most likely.'

Bernie moved his gaze to look beyond Ro, out to the vacant neighbouring properties. His palm still rested on the damaged board, one of many he'd helped install himself, and Ro wondered if he was ever tempted to tear them down, indulge himself like Ann-Marie and simply walk the old floorboards, soaking up the air in the familiar rooms. She watched Bernie's face, and felt certain that yes, of course he had.

'I sometimes think we should have demolished all three when we still had the chance.' Bernie's voice broke a little. 'I couldn't face it back then, wouldn't even consider it. But it might've been best. They're a dangerous draw, sitting here empty.'

Ro wondered who exactly Bernie was thinking of when he said that. Curious locals like Sam, unknown trespassers from elsewhere? Himself? Ro? Probably all of the above, she guessed.

'Maybe we still should,' she said.

'Tear them down?' Bernie had nodded slowly. 'Missed our chance though, haven't we? Not ours anymore. Not our decision to make.'

Four years on, and Ro watched Bernie now as he wandered slowly out onto the deck of his son's house. The healthy colour in his cheeks was long gone and his movements were unsteady. He took his coffee carefully from Heather with thanks and leaned his elbows on the wooden railing for support, mug clasped in both hands as he stared out at the land. He grimaced a little, shifting his weight from one foot to the other as he tried to get comfortable, bony and hunched in a way that made him look starkly vulnerable, as though he were preparing to shield himself from an invisible blow.

'Noel! Hey!' Heather shouted across the wide back garden, raising her arm in a wave.

Ro followed Heather's gaze to the far end of the yard, where Noel stood with a shovel poised over what remained of an old stump. He looked up at her call and took his hat off, running a hand across his forehead before heading over.

'G'day,' Noel called as he approached. He was carrying the shovel with him but had left a can of what Ro suspected was beer beside the stump. Heather's eyes touched on it quickly before bouncing away and she said nothing, her jaw tightening.

Della did not wait for Noel to reach them, instead throwing a cheery wave in his direction before peeling off towards the large barn, where Ro could see that another figure was also watching them.

Darcy had been crouched on the ground in front of the barn doors, a vast array of tools laid out around him as he worked on an old motorbike that appeared more a collection of spare parts than a driveable vehicle. At twenty-seven, he had cropped dark hair and was tall when he stood, taking after his mother with her wiry athletic build and pale eyes. He had been working on that same bike when Ro visited last year, she was fairly sure. She thought she recognised the distinctive paintwork on the body. When there was nothing much to do, you took your time with things, she supposed. Darcy slowly wiped his hands on an oil cloth as he watched Della approach. Ro did not know what her daughter wanted from him, but she had the distinct impression that Darcy had some idea.

Heather was gazing in the same direction, and whatever she made of the scene gave her pause for a moment.

'Everything okay?' Ro asked.

'Yeah.' Heather shook her head. 'Just didn't realise Darcy and Della kept in touch.'

Ro considered her response for a beat, then simply replied: 'I don't think they do.'

'No. Well, anyway.' Heather frowned a little as she turned back to her husband. 'Put the shovel down, Noel, and take a look at this. Ro brought it for the saloon.'

'Yeah? Thanks, Ro. You didn't have to bring us anything.' Noel's eye caught Ro's in the reflection as he took the mirror to examine it. 'How are you this morning, after a night back at Sylvie's?' His own face looked slack with fatigue.

Ro gave him a small smile as she shrugged. 'Always good to be back at Sylvie's.'

'Yeah.' Noel nodded, a little wistful. 'Don't get the chance so much now.'

Della had reached Darcy at the barn now. He said something that Ro couldn't make out over that distance and Della nodded. The pair stepped back into the shade of the doorway and were immediately swallowed by the shadows. Heather's gaze lingered on the large empty door for a moment longer, but there was nothing more to see.

'I was thinking we should take Ro over to the saloon, Noel.' Heather dragged her attention back and nodded at the mirror. 'Find a good spot for this.'

'Right now?' Noel squinted over at the stump he'd been set to tackle.

'Well, yeah, ideally now.' Heather's voice was laced with impatience. 'The stump can wait. And the mirror's fragile. It'd be good to get it hung up properly before the bloody boys manage to break it.'

'You honestly don't have to –' Ro started, but Heather cut her short.

'Yes. I want to.' Her voice softened, and she turned between her friend and her husband. 'Sorry. I'm sorry. I'm just a bit stressed. But yeah, it would be nice to do it now. Okay?'

Heather looked up at Noel, who gazed back at her for a long moment. An invisible thread of what Ro could only describe as sadness seemed to pass briefly between them, then Noel nodded.

'Yeah, all right. No worries. I'll grab my tools,' he said. 'Meet you over there.'

He turned away and Ro fell into step beside Heather as they headed together around to the eastern side of the house, Heather carrying the mirror under her arm.

'Are you okay?' Ro asked gently, and Heather pressed a finger to the corner of her eyes in turn before nodding.

'Yeah. Thanks. I mean, not really, but it feels like there's not too much that we can do.'

'About what exactly?'

'The boys. Life here now, with the town as dead as it is. Bernie. His health, I mean. Noel's not happy either, about a few things, but you can probably tell that.' Heather looked over. 'I was going to ask you before – in the kitchen, when Bernie came in – you must be relieved to be gone, are you? Happier to be somewhere else?'

'Well . . .' Ro felt her answer should be clear-cut by now, but the reality remained a little murky. It was true that she enjoyed many things about her new life. Her work at a clinic just a short drive from her home was reasonably rewarding; her patients kept her busy and her colleagues were kind and professional. She felt a benefit from her weekly yoga class and weekend swim and the occasional light run. She liked cooking meals she had planned and shopped for, and was always happy to meet Della for a drink, before returning to the quiet hum of her tidy apartment to read in bed. It was a cocooned existence, but one Ro had worked very hard to construct and maintain. Carefully neutral and designed to be largely unpainful, it was short on highs but also on lows, and after the massive emotional upheavals she associated with Carralon Ridge, yes, to Ro that felt like happiness. An approximation perhaps, she was aware. A decent replica. But that was the thing about quality replicas, as anyone who has ever bought one knew: unless you looked very, very closely, it could be almost as convincing as the real thing.

'I'm better off overall for moving to Sydney.' Ro chose her response carefully as she shot a sideways glance at Heather. 'That'd be fair to say. Why do you ask, though? Are you and Noel thinking of leaving?'

'No.' Heather let the word hang as they walked, and for a moment it seemed like she wasn't going to say any more. 'No, we're not.'

'You could, you know. No-one would blame you.'

It was true, and they would be far from the first. Although Ro found herself struggling to imagine Carralon Ridge without her friend living there. Heather had been her introduction to the town all those years ago, and rightly or wrongly, Ro still mentally entwined her tightly with the fabric of the place.

'Look, between us, I would consider leaving at this point. But it's Bernie.' Heather lowered her voice, although they were out of easy earshot of the deck. 'I mean, you can see for yourself, he's gone downhill a lot. Probably hasn't got too long left with us, realistically, but whatever time he still has he's desperate to spend it here. In the town, I mean. Says he was born here and wants to see out his life here. Die at home, he reckons. And, Ro, he's absolutely bloody set on it, which is –' Heather made a noise of frustration in her throat. 'I mean, the sheer practicalities of that . . . I don't know where to start, honestly. And Noel won't try to convince – I mean, he won't even consider it. No discussion, nothing, he just always –' She cut herself off sharply, looking guilty. 'And, okay, I understand. I do. I love Bernie.

God knows, I don't want him to be unhappy in his final days, either. And he doesn't have forever left, I'm well aware of that. But . . . the boys. It's their life too. And it feels like things with them are getting worse by the month. So I worry, you know?'

'Yeah.' Ro nodded. 'Of course you would. Anyone would, Heather, so don't be hard on yourself about that. It's tricky at the boys' age wherever you are, but it must be tough out here now.' She reached over and touched her friend's arm. 'For them and you.'

'Thank you. For saying that.' Heather's eyes had been trained on the ground as they walked, but she looked up at Ro now. 'I'm glad you still come back. I'm so sorry it's for the reason it is, but it really is good to see you.'

'I am too,' Ro said. 'I do sort of dread it, to be honest, in the lead-up. Still find it really hard. But then once I'm here, it feels like the right thing to have come. For lots of reasons, not just Sam.'

They rounded the corner of the house, and up ahead, Ro saw the saloon slip into view for the first time. It stood at the near edge of the eastern paddock, strange and wonderful in all its sprawling, ramshackle glory.

'Still.' Heather barely even glanced at the structure, her eyes looking beyond it, out to the horizon. 'Bet you're bloody glad when the time comes to leave.'

Chapter 17

'Here we are.'
Heather traipsed up the few steps to the deck of the saloon, but Ro paused at the base, taking a moment to absorb the unusual structure.

It fell somewhere between a cabin and a cubby house, but neither of those labels began to do it justice. Noel had begun building it . . . when? Ro counted back. Twenty years ago, at least. A little more, probably. Darcy had been old enough to pretend to help, she remembered, with Sam often joining in during those frequent visits to Heather's place in the early years. Della had still been a toddler clutching Ro's hand as she'd watched Sam run out to join Darcy and Noel in wielding a small hammer or fixing together a join.

The structure had started life as a modest playhouse, but its scope had ballooned over the years, with Noel and his sons adding windows and features and decking, expanding the space

158

from kid-friendly to adult-sized as it became a teenage hide-away. And then again, as more and more houses in Carralon Ridge fell quiet and empty, the retreat took on an unexpected new identity.

Noel and his sons had begun visiting newly abandoned homes, salvaging viable remnants and installing them in the ever-growing structure in their backyard. Within that first year of their recovery project, the clubhouse boasted a fully fitted working kitchen that Ro knew had once been in the Sorrells' place, and a vintage clawfoot bathroom set complete with brass taps that Noel had rescued from the Eastmans' farmhouse before it was bulldozed. An antique dinner bell with a rope hung inside the entrance and the rough wooden walls were decorated with dozens of donated local paintings and photographs, many showing the town in its better days. The blue full-sized front door that looked out onto the decking used to be Bernie's own. A large group of his friends, gathered from Bernie's many years with the rugby club and the town council, had carefully removed it from his sandstone bungalow after they'd helped him board the place up and had transported it here for him. Above the door now dangled a neat, hand-painted sign that read:

Last Chance Saloon.

If Noel and Heather had lived in an affluent Sydney suburb, the saloon would have been photographed from every angle for glossy feature pages in the weekend magazines, but as it was, it simply sat in their east paddock, quietly sheltering mementos and relics from a dying town.

Heather retrieved a key from under a little ceramic frog that Ro knew had been handmade a decade earlier by her friend Jenny Logue in the pottery workshops she'd run at the now defunct nursing home and unlocked Bernie's old front door. She hesitated a little on the threshold, peering into the gloom.

'Sorry,' Heather said as she stepped back to allow Ro in first. 'It's been a while since this was last opened up. Needs a good clean-out.'

She wasn't wrong, Ro thought, although she'd never have said so out loud. The large cabin was mostly as she remembered, with the Sorrells' kitchen fittings and the pair of hand-carved rocking chairs and the upholstered floral sofa crowded around the coffee table that had been rescued from the Winfield farm-house. Ro had loved this place. Wandering through had always been like exploring an antiques shop crammed with quirky curiosities.

Now, though, it felt more like a stale attic room. The pieces were crammed together with the unloved air of a forgotten museum and as Ro picked her way through the space, she felt her neck prickle with the sensation she was being watched. She turned around and had to laugh as her gaze caught that of a solemn lady in a bonnet, eyeballing her from a painting of a stagecoach.

'Not what it used to be, is it?' said a voice from the door, and Ro turned to see Noel at the threshold. He shook his head sadly. 'The kids aren't interested anymore.'

He pulled a clean rag from the toolbox in his hand and dragged the cloth over the dull surface of a nearby side table. It left a wide, clear streak and he looked at it for a moment before giving up, balling the rag in his hand. 'I dunno. They thought it was fun for a while.'

'They will do again, Noel,' Heather said, not sounding fully convinced. 'They're . . . I don't know. They're teenagers, aren't they? It's that age. And Darcy's got his hands full fixing up his bikes for now.'

Noel nodded in reply. He stayed where he was in the doorway, surveying the various old cabinets and counters that he'd installed with his children, back when they were still keen to be involved. Ro moved to one of the windows and looked outside at the rough decking. A low outdoor seat had been added since she was last there, reclaimed from where she didn't know, and a small collection of wind chimes.

'I passed the Hewetts' place on the way into town,' Ro said as she peered out. 'I was sorry to see the orchard arch gone. I was kind of hoping you might have brought it here.'

'No, unfortunately. Would've been good,' Noel said. 'Thought Doug'd probably leave it because it was built in, but they must've wanted it in the end. It's always interesting what people take when they go.'

'This was from their place, wasn't it?' Heather said, pointing to a sculpted stone cat sitting by the wall not far from her feet. 'Do you remember her, Ro? Used to be at the edge of the –'

She stopped, her expression instantly hardening as a distant crash sounded from the main house, followed swiftly by the faint but unmistakable noise of something smashing against a hard floor. The noise nudged a memory in a corner of Ro's mind, but before she could reach for it a cry of anger rang out, chased by a shout in reply.

'Shit.' Heather put a hand out to her husband, who was already turning towards the deck. 'I'll go, *no*, Noel, let me. Let me try. I'll just –' She shot Ro an apologetic look. 'Sorry, I'll be back in a minute.'

Noel stepped aside as his wife brushed past him in the doorway, everything about her tense as she strode down the deck and across the grass towards the house. He watched her leave, seemingly lost in his own thoughts, and only turned back to Ro at the creak of the floorboards as she moved across the room.

'Sorry about that.' He sounded oddly detached. 'Heather's probably told you . . .'

Ro nodded. 'She mentioned things are a bit tough.'

A bleak smile flitted across Noel's face. 'Yeah. That's one way to put it.'

He stayed in the doorway, keeping a little distance between them, but it was no use. Even through the fresh breeze from outside and the stale air of the saloon, Ro could smell the booze on him. It was quite faint, weak enough that he could get away with it in the pub last night, but unmissable here in the daylight, before noon.

'How are you going yourself, these days, Noel?' Ro asked, keeping her voice neutral. She ran a hand over the back of an old armchair, the velvet both rough and soft against her fingers.

'Yeah, I'm all right. Just run off my feet, you know? Can't get any workers out here, obviously, and the boys are no real help so . . .' The commotion from the house had died down at least, and Noel held her gaze for a moment more before he dropped his eyes. He nodded at the mirror lying face-up on a sideboard. 'Anyway. Let's get this on the wall before Heather comes back.'

'Listen, Noel, really, I'm sorry about – I don't know, this . . .' Ro glanced at the mirror, feeling ridiculous. 'I hadn't quite realised what was going on and that the saloon was –'

Abandoned was the word on her lips and she swallowed it back down.

'That you weren't really adding to it anymore,' she said instead.

'No, it's fine, Ro, seriously. God, you don't have anything to apologise for. It's nice that you brought us something. I'd love for this place to be back to how it was, it just all sort of . . .' Noel grasped around for the word. 'Fell away.'

'How long ago?'

'I dunno. A while now. Few years, I reckon.' He sounded vague but Ro suspected he could remember more exactly. 'It used to be a lot of fun, but . . .' Noel lifted his shoulders and dropped them again in a heavy shrug as he stepped inside. He seemed unhappy in the space that he had hand-built and as he moved in deeper, his foot caught something and sent it rattling across the floor with a clatter. It was an empty beer can. They both followed it with their eyes as it rolled beneath a couch.

'It has been difficult with the kids,' Noel said, when the can had settled. 'Darcy as well as the other two. And sometimes the memories feel a bit much, you know?'

'Yeah. I can understand that.' Ro went to pick up the mirror. 'But listen, please don't worry about hanging this. Not today, anyway. I can take it back with me if Heather's worried about damage, give it to her some other –'

'No, it's all good. Really. It'll take two minutes.' Noel tried for a lighter tone. 'Heather'll never let me hear the end of it if I let you take it away.' He picked up his toolbox, then looked around. 'Where do you reckon?'

'I don't know. Maybe there?' Ro gestured half-heartedly to the only corner that still had some bare space, but Noel was already shaking his head.

'It's a bit structurally unsound there, need to get underneath and take a proper look before this whole thing ends up collapsing like everything else around here,' he said, moving instead to the wall opposite the door. 'What do you reckon about here?' He found a spot next to a decent watercolour of the town's crossroads. 'Reflect the light?'

'Sounds good,' Ro said. 'Whatever you think.'

Noel rummaged for his screwdriver, both of them listening to the distant angry shouts that were rising once more from the house.

'Griff seemed a bit flat in the pub last night,' Noel said as the cries ebbed away again.

'Did you think so?' Ro frowned. Griff was certainly not happy, she knew that, but perhaps he was worse than she'd realised if Noel had sensed a difference. He saw much more of Griff than she did. 'It's always a hard time of year, you know?'

'Yeah, I know. Of course.' Noel was quiet for a minute as he focused on the chosen spot on the wall. 'Heard about the contract, too. I suppose he'll be leaving before long, will he?'

Ro blinked in surprise. 'I'm honestly not sure, Noel. You'd probably know better than me.'

'He said he hadn't decided, last time I asked. Don't think his options around here would be great, though, without the contract. Wondered if he'd told you.'

'I think he'd be more likely to tell you. If he knew.'

That was true, even if Ro had always suspected Noel was privately conflicted about Griff's decision to take the job with the mine. Griff must be aware of it, too, she thought, even if he never acknowledged it. For the past few years, Ro had detected a light fracture between the two men that, as far as she was aware, neither had addressed. Perhaps they simply felt they didn't need to. To Noel's credit he had kept whatever reservations he had to himself.

Ro remembered watching in shock, just days before the second anniversary of Sam's disappearance, as two former friends of Griff's had cornered him in the pub. The fire station had closed since she had left Carralon and Griff was reluctantly finding his feet in his new role as the mine's community safety officer.

'You sleeping all right at night, are you? Choice you've made?' one of the men had said, his elbow on the counter right beside Griff's beer as he leaned in, upset and unsteady. He had been a volunteer firefighter himself who had worked alongside Griff for years. The other was an assistant coach who had overseen Sam's junior team at the now defunct rugby club. Both men had been several drinks deep as they'd crowded around Griff, which Ro thought perhaps explained their aggression but didn't begin to excuse it.

'Take a look outside, Griff mate. Remind yourself what Lentzer's done to this place, if you want to know where they're getting the money to pay you.'

Griff had not responded other than to move his glass and had simply sat, brooding and introspective, as they launched into their rant. It had been Noel who had pushed his chair back with a screech, rising to his full height before showing the two men in no uncertain way to the door. The next morning, Noel had come over to the house and Ro had made coffee while he and Griff had sat together outside on the porch.

'They're not wrong, though, are they?' she'd heard Griff say. 'But if I don't take the bloody mine's money, I can't afford to stay. And we need someone doing this job.' He'd sounded more upset than Ro had realised. 'There are spot fires out here every week, mate. No-one else is coming out to help us if they get loose. Those two think I should've refused to work with Lentzer, that's fine, I get it. But then who's going to come and help them if a spark lands on their bloody houses? They'll be burning for an hour before anyone even thinks of getting here.'

'Yeah,' Noel had said, his voice quiet. 'And they know that. They're angry. At the mine, the whole situation. Nothing to do with you. You're only doing what you need to do to look after your family. We all are.'

By the end of that year, the same two guys had sold their properties to the mine and left, and Noel and Griff were still there.

'I know Griff'd be sorry to go,' Ro said now as Noel lined up his electric drill against the wall. They both winced a little as the whining filled the saloon, echoing off the walls.

'Yeah.' Noel finished the second hole, then put the drill down to check his work. 'Be sorry to see him go. Won't be the same.'

He lifted the mirror and Ro reached over and helped hold it in place against the wall. Noel fitted the top screw and tightened it, before doing the same with the bottom one. They stepped back and stood side by side to admire the result.

'Looks good there,' Ro said.

'Yeah. Thanks again for bringing it.'

'No worries.' She hesitated, wary of overstepping the line as she looked at Noel's reflection in the coloured glass. 'You know that you could always leave, too.'

Noel made a small noise in his throat, like a hard, brittle laugh. 'No.' He met his own eyes in the mirror as he shook his head. 'We're not going anywhere.'

'Is it your dad? Because from a health perspective, I could have a word if you wanted and –'

'Thanks Ro, really, but it's not only that.' Noel turned away and bent down to pick up his toolbox. 'I can guess what Heather's told you, but there's a lot more to it.' He straightened and with his free hand gestured vaguely around the space that housed the town's treasures. 'I mean, look at all this. I've lived around here for my whole life. Dad, too. And Heather, mostly, even if she seems to forget that sometimes. We've given it so much, how could we walk away?' He sounded almost like he was convincing himself. 'It's not that –'

A movement on the deck outside made them both turn, and a second later Heather appeared in the doorway. Noel looked mildly worried that she might have overheard him, but she was already glancing distractedly back at the house.

'Shit, Heather.' Noel's expression collapsed as he noticed the angry tears in her eyes. He moved across the room towards her. 'Are you –?'

'It's fine. Sorry. I just – you'll have to come and sort them out.' She swiped a hand across her face impatiently. 'I can't deal with them when they're like this.'

Through the open doorway, Ro suddenly spotted Della standing on the grass a short way away. Her eyes found her mother's across the distance, her mouth pressed into a firm line. She gave a tiny shake of her head.

Ro looked from her daughter back to a teary Heather and a defeated Noel.

'Ro, I'm so sor–' Heather started, but Ro reached out and squeezed her hand.

'It's honestly all right. It was lovely to see you both. But yeah, it's time to go.'

Chapter 18

Della glanced back over her shoulder as they pulled out of the driveway. 'Jesus, poor Heather. Those boys seem . . .' She frowned as she searched for the word.

'Tricky?'

'I was going to say bloody awful.'

'Apparently they're bored.'

'Yeah, we were all *bored* at that age.' Della's voice was scathing. 'It's not a licence to speak to your mum like that. I could hear them shouting at her when I was coming back from the barn. Not good. Anyway,' she turned her head to look at Ro, 'Darcy.'

'Yes. Darcy.' Ro strove to keep her tone neutral. 'How was he?'

Della gave a small, dry smile. 'Reserved, I'd say. Not exactly keen for a chat.'

'So, are you still thinking whatever it was is nothing?'

'Actually,' Della frowned, 'no.'

Ro glanced across in surprise.

'I was totally prepared to believe it was nothing,' Della went on. 'Until both Darcy and Jacob started giving me the run-around. The fact they're so cagey makes me feel like it means *something*, you know? Neither of them reckons they have a clue what I'm talking about, but I can tell they do.' Della shifted in her seat to better see her mother. 'Okay, so here it is. A few months ago, I ran into Meaghan Austin. Do you remember her? A couple of years above me in school?'

'Yeah, Sophie and Greg's daughter.'

'Right, well, in her last year at school she went out with Darcy for a while.'

Ro nodded slowly. She had forgotten but could now dredge up a memory of spotting the pair around town together. Sophie had not been overly pleased by her daughter's budding local romance, Ro seemed to remember. Meaghan had received an offer to study law at university in Melbourne after graduation.

'So it turns out Meaghan's now an associate in the legal team for one of my clients,' Della went on. 'We had to get some documents notarised and ended up going for a drink afterwards, talking about Carralon, old times, that kind of thing, and Darcy came up. She brought him up, actually. Asked how he was, but obviously I didn't really know. Anyway, eventually she tells me that part of the reason they broke up was because they had this big fight about Warren.'

'About Warren?' Ro raised her eyebrows. 'Really?'

'Yeah, apparently one night they'd gone drinking down at the creek, Meaghan and her sister,' Della counted them off on her fingers, 'Darcy, and Jacob was there too. And they were all getting drunk and messing around and scaring each other. And either Meaghan or her sister made some throwaway joke about Jacob not having any luck getting girls to go home with him because he and his mum lived in a creepy house, I guess because of all the ivy, and also because that whole area was haunted by Warren's ghost.'

'Okay.' Ro felt the wheels bump over a pothole, jerking them both against their seatbelts.

'Well, Meaghan reckons it was just one more dumb, drunk comment in a night full of dumb, drunk comments, but suddenly Darcy turned on her. Really riled up, telling her that she shouldn't be laughing about a dead man when she had no idea what he'd been through with the mine and everything. And Meaghan says she was a bit pissed off by this because she *did* know about that stuff because her dad had essentially lost half his land after Lentzer acquired the access road –'

Ro nodded. She remembered the anguish when Greg had been forced to give up those paddocks.

'But Meaghan says Darcy wouldn't let up, kept going on at her about showing some respect until eventually Jacob waded in, trying to drag Darcy aside and calm him down. But Darcy's beyond it at this point, and he turns on Jacob and whacks him and storms off.'

'He hit him?'

'Yeah, apparently. So Meaghan said she and her sister are standing there shocked, and Jacob's nose is streaming blood, and they're all still off-their-faces drunk, and Meaghan attempts to laugh the whole thing off and says something like: "God, someone's got a guilty conscience." But then –' Della leaned in. 'Jacob doesn't laugh it off. He nods, all bleeding and drunk and pissed off but kind of serious as well, and says that yeah, actually, Darcy *should* feel guilty because a while ago he did something stupid and then . . .' Della sat back and let her gaze wander out to the horizon. She sighed. 'And then Warren killed himself.'

The only sound for a long moment was the rumble of the tyres against the uneven road.

'Darcy did something stupid and then Warren killed himself?' Ro repeated eventually.

'Yeah, that's how Meaghan remembers it, anyway.'

'What kind of thing?'

'She doesn't know. The night had obviously hit a brick wall. Jacob staggered off to clean up his blood, and the next time Darcy spoke to Meaghan it was to break up. She tried asking Jacob about it but he claimed he'd been too drunk to remember much, which she thought could've been true. Either way, he reckoned he didn't know what he'd said or why he'd said it.'

'Darcy did something,' Ro stared ahead through the grimy windshield, 'and Jacob knew about it.' She turned that over in her mind. 'What are the chances that Jacob knew but Sam didn't? Low, don't you think? They were all close.'

'Well,' Della considered. 'Not necessarily, but I wondered about that too. I mean, Sam's name wasn't mentioned. And look, Meaghan's remembering a drunken conversation from, what? Eight years ago? I think we can assume the details are hazy at best.'

'But Warren . . .' Ro tried to think back to that time. 'I mean, he had so much going on, with the mine pressuring him to sell, and then him and Sylvie splitting up. Obviously none of us expected him to do what he did, but looking at it later, we all knew he wasn't happy. So why would Darcy think he had anything to do with it? Meaghan didn't have a theory?'

'No,' Della said. 'I think she was hoping I might know. With Warren being Dad's cousin and everything. But . . .' She trailed off.

'Did you hear anything over the years? Gossip or rumours or anything? From other kids at the time?'

'I didn't.' Della fiddled idly with a strand of hair as she mulled it over. 'Not that I can remember. But there weren't that many of us around by then. I mean, it wasn't a huge social scene or anything, was it? Sam hung out with Darcy and Jacob, I was kind of on my own a lot, so . . .' Her eyes flicked back to the trees and fences flashing past outside the car. 'Anyway, that's what I've been trying to ask Darcy and Jacob about.'

'Right.' Ro's mind was running to the past, chasing down that surreal year when the town seemed to shift every day with fresh uncertainty. What had people been talking about then, when they ran into each other on the emptying streets? What had the other few remaining parents been saying about their teenagers? Had Warren been trying to tell her and Griff something, if only they'd listened more closely? Anything about Sam's friend, or Sam himself? Ro tried to concentrate. Every single conversation she could recall was about the mine. 'So how exactly did Darcy and Jacob respond when you asked them?'

'Completely clammed up. Don't know what I mean. Don't remember anything like that. I think Darcy would have even claimed he didn't remember Meaghan if he thought he could get away with it.' Della breathed out. 'Like I said, it could be absolutely nothing. But I don't know why they wouldn't just tell me in that case. After all this time, as well. And I'm not even convinced Sam was involved, there's nothing to say he was, really. I . . .'

Della fell quiet for long enough that Ro took her hand off the wheel and reached over, putting her palm on her daughter's arm.

'There are so few answers,' Della said finally. 'About Sam. I thought it might be good to have that one at least. I never bought any of those theories around –' her voice dropped a little on the word, '– suicide. Not with Sam. I know the families often say they didn't see it coming, but . . .' She stared out of the window, chewing her lip. 'I don't know. Maybe I'm just one more person who didn't see it coming. And with his car having turned up so close to Warren's place, I thought finding out what Darcy was feeling bad about might give us a clue to Sam's state of mind in those last few years.'

Ro paused at a junction. There were no other cars in sight and as she turned the wheel, she looked over at Della, who was still staring into the distance, her face clouded.

'What do you think happened to Sam, Della?' Ro realised she wasn't sure she'd ever asked her daughter directly.

'Accident. Something quick.'

'Like what?'

'Jesus, I don't know, Mum. I don't like to think about it too closely.'

'No, okay. Of course. Sorry, sweetheart.'

There was a long pause, then Della exhaled sharply. 'Sorry.'

'You don't need to be,' Ro said, meaning it. 'I shouldn't have asked.'

They lapsed into silence again, and only when they reached the next turning did Della draw a breath.

'I've wondered if maybe it was something that needed medical attention. But whoever he was with didn't call because they knew it would probably be you or Ann-Marie attending.'

Ro kept her eyes straight ahead, allowing that thought to settle.

'So, I don't know.' Della shrugged, sounding resigned. 'Perhaps that brings us back to Darcy and Jacob.'

Ro looked over. 'That's what you think might have happened?'

'It's one of the things I've thought about, yeah. Based on nothing, though.' Della's voice was hard to hear over the rumble of the wheels. 'Whatever happened, I hope it was quick. I hope it was over before he knew it.' She blinked a few times fast. 'I guess at least Sam's not here to see us lose the house. I know it felt like he couldn't wait to get shot of here, but I think he'd be sad about that.'

'Oh, Della.' Ro fished in her pocket and handed her daughter a clean but crumpled tissue. 'I know it's hard.'

'Yeah, it actually is.' Della blew her nose and flashed Ro a watery smile. 'I thought I didn't mind, but I do. More than I expected, honestly. It's a bit silly.'

'No, it's not. Really.'

'It is, though. Because I already felt like we lost the house when it was sold.' She shrugged. 'But this feels very final now.' She sniffed again, gathering herself, then looked over. 'Has Dad told you what he'll do?'

'No.' Ro shook her head. 'Has he mentioned any plans to you?'

'Nothing concrete.' Della hesitated. 'But I got the sense he was thinking about moving to Sydney.'

'Really?' Ro was surprised, but she supposed it made some sense. 'I guess it would be good for him to be closer to you.'

'And you.'

Ro said nothing for a minute. She slowed as they approached the turn leading towards town. 'Della, I –'

'No, I know –'

'I mean, if I wanted to be with my ex-husband I would be here with him.'

'Yeah, and that's fine. Although he's not actually your ex-husband, is he? So it could also be argued that if you two wanted to *be* exes, you know, for real, legally, one of you would get around to filling in the paperwork.' She matched Ro's light eye roll with her own. 'Or you could both stop tiptoeing around each other and talk. Properly. Honestly. You both need to forgive each other for handling your grief differently, that's what you need to do.'

Ro looked over at her daughter and had to laugh. 'Well, Della, I'm sure we'd both be keen for your expert advice when you finish your psychology degree.'

'I'm an accountant.'

'Yeah, exactly.' Ro had meant it as a joke but it sounded a little accusatory. 'I'm sorry,' she added quickly. 'I do know you're trying to help.' She paused, considering. 'As it happens, I actually had a real professional therapist tell me something similar. About needing to accept that Griff and I dealt with what happened to Sam in different ways.'

'Really?'

'Yeah, pretty much.'

Della watched her. 'And what did you think about that?'

'I think she was probably right,' Ro said, her eyes not meeting her daughter's. 'But you can be right about something and still not really solve the problem, you know?'

Della nodded. 'Well, maybe think about it. I mean, I'm not saying this as some kid who wants her mummy and daddy back together, I just think you both miss each other.'

Ro didn't know what to say to that, so she said nothing. As they flashed past the turn-off that led to the three houses, to Warren's place, to the spot where Sam's car was found, Ro and Della twisted their heads and looked over, then wordlessly turned back to the road ahead. They drove the rest of the way home in silence.

Chapter 19

Ro was halfway across the lawn when she heard the soft shuffle of movement from the sheds. Griff's truck had been parked in the driveway when she and Della had returned, but the house had felt empty as they'd let themselves inside. Della had stopped in the hallway, reaching over and pulling Ro into a long hug before releasing her and disappearing into her old bedroom.

Ro stood now on the patchy grass, listening for a moment more to the thumps and clatters before making her own way over to the sheds. The door to the largest one was open, tiny particles floating in the slice of sunlight that reached the entrance. Ro paused in the doorway, spotting Griff inside a minute before he saw her. He was deep among the contents of the space, flanked by a cobweb-covered old lawnmower and a stack of spare tiles for the roof. A set of battered cricket stumps lay by his feet as he crouched beside a collection of cardboard boxes. One was open on the concrete floor in front of him, and at his elbow lay a black bin bag.

'Clearing things out?'

Griff looked up at Ro's voice. His face was set and he had a stripe of grey across his forehead where he'd wiped his brow.

'Yeah.' He stood, careful of the objects scattered around his boots. 'Try to tackle a box or two whenever I can face it.'

There would be years' worth of their belongings – joint belongings – to work through here, Ro knew as she looked around, and she felt a pang of guilt.

'I'll give you a hand. Do you have a system, or . . .?'

'Not really.' Griff shrugged but sounded grateful. He waved a hand towards the rubbish bag. 'Bin the junk, I suppose. That other pile over there is anything maybe worth keeping so I dunno, if you see anything you want, feel free to grab it.'

'Right. Thanks.' Ro reached towards the nearest of the boxes but was immediately distracted by a paint-spattered old tarp draped over an item that stood almost as tall as she did.

'Oh my God.' She pulled the tarp aside to reveal their vintage pinball machine. It was a full-size working model that Griff had bought second-hand when the youth club closed, back before their own kids were old enough to have ever set foot through its door.

The electronic display was dark and when Ro experimentally tapped the familiar buttons, the levers didn't move. She could see the plug trailing loose from the back.

'Does this still switch on?'

'I don't know.' Griff glanced up from the box he was rifling through, then back down again.

He and Sam had often played on it together over the years, wandering out here to the shed after dinner with their iced water or soft drinks when Sam was a kid, and a pair of chilled beers when he was older. They had, in fact, done just that on Sam's

second-last day with them, Ro remembered now. His birthday
eve. Sam had stood out here in the twilight with his dad, the
glow from the machine attracting the mosquitos, and they'd
sipped beer and slapped at their skin as Griff had comprehen-
sively beaten the high score Sam had set on the machine three
years earlier. Sam had laughed and lobbed accusations of secret
practice sessions. Griff had denied any such claims even as he
made Sam snap a photo to mark the occasion. Griff had posed
next to the machine, victory on his face and a beer in his hand.
GRF on the screen where SAM had been.

Ro looked down at the loose plug. GRF would still be there
if she plugged it in, she knew. Sam had not had a chance to
reclaim the top spot. Slowly, she dragged the tarp back over.

As she turned away, her foot caught the rim of a training
wheel of a child's green bike partially buried behind a jumble of
plastic lawn chairs.

'I didn't know we still had this,' she said as she bent down
and hauled the bike free, assailed by yet another memory, older
this time. She ran a hand over the seat and handlebars, her palm
coming away thick with a layer of grime and cobwebs. 'I don't
think I've seen it for – I don't know, what?'

'Twenty years?' Griff suggested, half a smile sliding across his
face as he saw it. 'Whose was that? Both of theirs, probably.'

'Yeah, it was.' Ro grabbed a cleaning cloth from the top of
a chest of drawers and rubbed it over the paintwork, letting the
memories resurface. Wobbly turns up and down the driveway,
scraped limbs and shouts of fear and joy. Ro stared down at the
bike, a little cleaner now and still in decent condition, and was
suddenly unsure what exactly to do with it. She hesitated, then
wheeled it out and put it in the clear space near the open door.
Griff was watching her, and she glanced back towards him, their
eyes meeting.

'I have to warn you.' He jerked his head at the pinball machine and then the bike, his voice quiet. 'It's all a bit like that.'

Ro looked at him, hunched over one box of many.

'I'm sorry, Griff.' She hadn't known she was going to say it until she did. 'You shouldn't be having to deal with all this yourself. You could've called me.'

'Could I?' He was still watching her. 'Would you have come?'

'Yes,' Ro said, but it was she who looked away first. Turning her back on him, she picked up the closest box. Oh God, it was full of Christmas decorations. At the very top lay a painted ceramic oval with imprints of Sam's and Della's small finger-prints fashioned into the shape of a Christmas tree. No way. Ro shut the lid immediately and avoided Griff's eye as she carried the box of decorations to the door and carefully placed it beside the green bike.

Aware of Griff still watching, she grabbed the next box at random, hoping the contents of this one would be more straight-forward to deal with. She opened the lid. Gardening tools. Ro breathed out. A little better, but still not easy, as immediately her thoughts set off at pace, scrambling and tumbling over each other in their haste to reach her own beloved little garden. So near in one sense, its abandoned site just on the far side of the ridged metal wall near to where she now stood, but completely lost in another. Ro lowered herself carefully to the concrete floor and sat for a moment, willing herself not to flip the lid closed on this box, too.

Slowly, as though defusing a bomb, she began to sift through the empty seedling pots and old pairs of gloves stained with ancient dirt. She found and managed to discard a rusted pair of pruning shears that had once been her favourites and a musty planting guide now missing its cover. She stopped only as her hands closed around a small trowel, sized for a child, and pulled it out, half knowing and half fearing what she would see. Sure enough, three wobbly letters were scrawled in thick black pen on the wooden handle.

S-A-M

Ro ran her thumb over the writing, thinking. About her little boy, whose own small hand had once clutched this same handle; about her garden, where they used to plant and dig and talk and laugh. Ro slowly turned the trowel over in her hand so she could no longer see the letters, then placed it aside. Feeling the urgent need to be rid of this box now, to have it gone from her sight, she rattled through the rest of the contents, skimming over rusted metal and worn labels. She was about to declare it closed when at the very bottom she spotted a small plain paper envelope.

Ro reached down through the tools, her fingers grasping around until she felt it. Seeds, she could tell as soon as she pulled it out. Sunflowers, apparently, according to the letters spelled out in faded ballpoint across the front. The handwriting had become more confident, showing a few more years of schooling and experience since the letters S-A-M had been marked on the trowel.

Ro unsealed the envelope and peered inside, gently shaking the contents apart. Ten black sunflower seeds nestled in the crease at the bottom. Had Sam counted each of them out before he'd put them in here, running his tongue along the edge, sealing it with spit that was probably flavoured with chocolate or cheese squares or Vegemite, before finding a pen and carefully spelling out the word? Or had he carelessly flung in a random pinch of seeds before handing it to Ro herself to seal, reluctantly labelling it only at her insistence? Ro looked at her son's childish writing. She couldn't even begin to remember. Sighing, she folded the top over carefully and slipped the envelope into her pocket before getting to her feet.

'This is all pretty much junk,' she said, picking up the rest of the box of tools. 'Nothing really worth saving.'

'Okay. Thanks.' Griff was frowning down at something in his hand. 'Dump it with that other stuff.' He barely glanced up as he waved towards a collection piled against the opposite wall. His attention fell back to the object he was holding and Ro stepped closer, curious.

'What have you got there?'

'Just these.' Griff held out his palm. He was holding four small running medals. The fabric of the ribbons was a little faded and the metal designs could all have done with a good polish but despite the tarnish, they looked cared for. Ro reached over and took one from his hand. She couldn't remember ever having owned these.

'Are they ours?' she asked, and Griff shook his head.

'No, not ours.' He turned the top medal over and held it up to his face. 'They look like Warren's, actually. Or his dad's, technically. He was a pretty decent runner when he was younger.'

'I remember Damien saying.' Ro nodded at the collection in Griff's palm. 'So he won these?'

'Yeah, I think so. And a fair few more. Kept them in that velvet display case on the wall. Do you remember seeing it at Warren's place, behind the door in his study? He left them up when his dad died.'

Ro shook her head. Most of her visits to the Hillary house had been spent around the barbecue on the back deck.

'So why do we have them?' she asked, leaning over to see what else was inside the box at Griff's feet. She rummaged through old board games and school textbooks. It appeared to be mostly junk that Sam had left behind when he went to uni. 'They were in with Sam's stuff?'

'Yeah, wrapped up in a tea towel in here.' Griff held out an old tin in the shape of a phone box. 'Maybe Warren gave them to him? Not sure why he would, though. Or why Sam'd have any use for them, to be honest.'

'Are they valuable? Beyond sentimental, I mean.' Ro held up the medal in her hand. The light glinted off the metal surface. 'This has got to be gold-plated at best. Sam would know that wasn't worth anything, wouldn't he?'

Griff stared at her. 'Why would you even ask that?'

Ro hesitated. Reluctant to raise yet more questions without answers, she had been wondering since the drive home whether to share what Della had told her with Griff. She looked at him now, surrounded by these boxes of their shared history.

'Before Warren died, did he talk to you at all about Sam and Jacob and Darcy? Or maybe even just Darcy?'

Confusion crossed Griff's face as he thought back. 'I don't think so. Nothing specific, at least. Why?'

He folded his arms and listened without interruption as Ro filled him in on her conversation with Della. When she'd finished, he stood very still, considering.

'And Darcy and Jacob both reckon they know nothing?'

Ro nodded. 'And whatever it is, it might not have had anything to do with Sam.'

Griff made a sceptical noise in the back of his throat. 'If Jacob knew, Sam knew. Those three didn't scratch themselves without the other two hearing about it. Don't you think?'

Ro nodded. She did.

Griff fell quiet again, then reached out and took the medal from Ro, running his eyes over the small collection once more before wrapping them back up in the tea towel.

'Sam wasn't a thief.' His voice was low. 'I know that much.'

Ro wasn't sure if he was asking the question, but she shook her head in confirmation. 'No. He wasn't.'

'It wouldn't even make sense.' Griff sounded a little upset. 'There was plenty of stuff that'd be worth a few bucks just lying around Warren's place. Or around here for that matter.'

'Yeah, exactly. He wasn't a thief, Griff. I don't know why he has those medals, but you're right about that.'

Griff nodded, his expression hard. He bent down to the box he'd been working on, but his hands rested on the cardboard edges. Ro recognised the tension in his shoulders. He was weighing up whether to say something. She waited.

'Those two boys were together on that night,' he said, at last. His head was still down, the words almost swallowed by the contents of the box.

'Who, Darcy and Jacob?' Ro didn't need to ask which night. For Griff, like her, it felt as though there was only a single night in their whole lives of any consequence.

'Yeah.' He nodded without looking up. 'When I called from here after Sam didn't come home for dinner, asking if he was with them, I rang Jacob first, then Darcy. But I could hear the turbine in the background both times. They were somewhere near the quarry.'

Ro frowned, remembering the drone footage Darcy had captured hours earlier that day. The two boys had been out near the quarry then, too. Griff shrugged, and she could tell he was thinking the same thing.

'Feels like a long time to hang out in one day, seeing as they were together earlier and then due to meet Sam later at the pub. Or, I dunno. Maybe not.' Griff shook his head. 'Darcy and Jacob are good mates, I suppose. And there's not too much else to do around here.'

'Did they say that they weren't together?'

'No, to be fair.' Griff's forehead creased. 'At least, not later. When I asked them.' The lines on his face deepened, his hands heavy on the box. It shifted a fraction, leaving a ghostly imprint against the dusty floor. 'But neither of them mentioned it that night when I called. Both let me ring them separately without saying the other was right there beside them.'

'I guess they didn't know at that point that anything urgent was going on. I mean, we hadn't even realised ourselves Sam was properly missing by then,' Ro said. 'Maybe they felt embarrassed to be hanging out without him. On his birthday as well.'

'Yeah. Maybe.'

'You don't think so?'

'I really don't know, Ro.' Griff straightened and squinted out of the gloomy shed into the bright afternoon haze. 'I find myself thinking all kinds of things these days.'

Neither spoke, the click and hum of the insects outside loud in their ears until eventually Griff breathed out a long sigh. He glanced over to see Ro still watching him, and a flash of something like irritation flickered in his eyes as they slid from her to the pinball machine and then the small green bike and finally the box of Christmas decorations with which she'd failed to make any progress at all.

'Listen.' Griff turned to a shelf crammed with old sports equipment, his voice clipped. 'You don't have to do this, Ro.'

'What?' she asked, knowing full well what he meant.

'Deal with this.' He waved a hand around the cluttered shed. 'If it's all too bloody hard. Just leave it. I'll work through it myself.'

'It's not too hard,' she snapped back, pushing down the instinctive rush of relief at being offered a release from the task. 'I mean, it's hard, obviously, but it's got to be done.'

'Yeah.' A note in Griff's voice made something unpleasant bloom in Ro's chest.

'What's that supposed to mean?'

'Nothing. I'm agreeing with you.'

'Are you?'

'Aren't I?' He wouldn't look at her. 'I'm saying yes. Yes, it's got to get done. Yes, someone's got to do it. Yes, I'll sort it out. So if you can't face it, feel free to head off.'

Ro stared at him, stung. The stuffy air suddenly felt cloying and she could feel a horribly familiar weight descending. For a moment everything was still as they eyed each other in silence. But Ro could feel it building, the space between them growing thick and distorted with invisible friction. She took a breath as words that went against her better judgement pushed against her lips, begging to be spoken. She clenched her teeth together to keep them contained.

'If you're going, leave the door open.' He wouldn't look at her. 'It's too hot in here.'

Ro loosened her jaw, parted her lips. 'I'd lost my job, Griff. You know that.'

'For God's sake.' He made a noise of contempt in his throat. 'I'm not even talking about that, Ro.'

'No?'

'No. Jesus. You're the one bringing it up.'

Seventeen months after Sam had vanished, the director of the medical centre had gathered the small handful of remaining staff in the break room and told them the facility would be closing in thirty days. Patient records would need to be transferred to the nearest clinic in Blenheim. Ro had stood beside the coffee machine, listening to the director detail the shutdown plan for the next month and feeling, not devastated as she might have expected had she been asked about the scenario hypothetically, but instead experiencing a cool, clear wash of relief. Beneath the appropriate words of regret and disappointment, one long-awaited realisation kept fighting its way to the forefront of Ro's mind. No-one would expect her to stay in Carralon Ridge now.

Griff did, apparently.

'It's an excuse,' he'd said, when the conversation they'd been dancing around had finally come to a head, three weeks later. He'd been sitting at the kitchen table, the remains of their dinner still on two plates, the overhead light harsh as his eyes followed her around the room. 'If you want to leave, be honest about it at least.'

'It's not an excuse, Griff!' Ro had thrown the dishcloth into the sink and turned to stare at him, stunned. 'I don't have a job anymore.'

'Ann-Marie's worked something out with the health department. Staying on, freelance provider or whatever. I asked her, she said you could've as well.'

'It's a peripatetic posting, Griff, and it's not avail–'

'Okay, well, whatever the terminology is.'

'– not available for everyone, okay? It's not –'

'It would have been for you, though. Wouldn't it?' His eyes had fixed on hers. 'They would have made it available for you. Ann-Marie told me.'

Ro had opened her mouth but said nothing, struck dumb by the sense of betrayal from both of them. She had stuck it out here in Carralon, without Sam, without answers, for a year and a half. Hadn't she? *Hadn't she?* Plodding along, dragging herself through the motions day after day after day in this miserable, *dying* town, long – *long* – after she'd felt able to bear it.

Ro had stood in their kitchen, feeling the anger rise and rise as Griff's words had sunk in, and she had had to force herself to look at her husband of more than two decades and push it back down, at least a little. She had taken a breath.

'It's not . . .' she'd started, then stopped. 'It's not only about the clinic, Griff. I mean, you know it's not.' He did know, she'd felt certain. He must do. How could he not? But she'd waited and he'd said nothing and so she'd said it herself, out loud. 'Griff. I can't stay here any longer.'

Still, he had remained silent for what felt like a cruel length of time. Then: 'What about Sam?'

'Exactly. Sam.' Ro had sat down opposite him. She had not reached across the table for his hand, and he had not reached for hers. 'That's what I'm telling you, I cannot live here, in this place. I can't be here anymore.'

He had gazed at her, almost curious beneath his anger, like he was seeing her for the first time. 'How can you leave?'

'Griff.' It was like looking back at a stranger. 'How can you stay?'

They stood across from each other now, surrounded by their own boxed and broken relics, haunted by their loss. The echo of the old argument floated in the hot stale air of the shed and Ro thought to herself: *This is where Della's wrong.* You can miss what you once had, but if it's gone, it's gone. She did miss Griff, deeply and often, but what she really missed was how they used to be, and that wasn't who they were now.

The fracture that separated them ran too deep. They had parted at that moment, over the kitchen table, or maybe even before that. Maybe on the day they had stood by the red rental car wondering for the first of what would prove to be thousands of times where their son was. Or maybe in the days when they'd come to the realisation, separately, that they might never see him again and might never know why. Whenever the parting of ways had happened, it had split them in two, sending them along different paths that occasionally ran parallel but no longer intertwined.

Griff was the first to move. 'Take whatever you want.' He shook his head as he stepped past Ro and the piles of old belongings and headed out towards the door and the light. 'I'm not doing this again.'

Chapter 20

She did remember the medal collection now she thought about it, Ro realised as she sat on the bed in the hut, her back uncomfortable where it leaned against the wood panelling of the wall. She had returned there, climbed on the bed and stayed, unmoving, for – how long? She wasn't sure – just staring into the middle distance, her fingers tracing the faded floral pattern of the bedsheets, feeling nothing but sad. For a while, she had heard the faint angry clatter and thump of boxes and belongings being shifted and stacked – Griff must have gone back to the sheds – but after a short time that had stopped too and the only sound was the distant rumbling from the mine.

Ro could picture the collection of Warren's dad's sports medals, though, at least. The image floated to her, plucked from some memory she hadn't known she'd kept, and as she sat on the bed in the stuffy room, she could visualise them. Exactly as Griff had described, mounted behind the door in the room that had become Warren's makeshift study. Warren hadn't spent more time in there than necessary, and right up until his death it had still retained signs of being his late parents' formal sitting room, with the polished oak side table and matching bar cart rubbing shoulders with Warren's battered pine desk and rattling computer. From behind the keyboard, as Warren trawled through the various paperwork generated by his property, he would have been able to see his mother's good couch still nestled against the far wall, beneath an imposing but decent oil painting of a bushland scene. And behind the door, still proudly hung on the wall, had been the blue velvet case displaying what Ro guessed from memory were perhaps two dozen sports medals.

Warren's entire home had been a bit like that – a collection of mismatched styles. As his parents' health had begun to fade, he'd spent more and more time at the Hillary house before eventually in his late twenties giving up the lease on his North Road cottage and shifting his belongings back into the farmhouse permanently. Warren and his parents had got along well, the three of them creating space and room for them all, his cheap bachelor-style furniture sitting cheerfully alongside their higher quality pieces in a harmony that may have been jarring visually, but suited them all practically and emotionally.

After their deaths, his dad first, his mother ten months later, Warren had changed little to nothing. Women of a different mindset to Sylvie might have been tempted to put their own stamp on the place when she and Warren had moved in together nearly a decade later, but Sylvie had just shrugged her black-clad shoulders and happily put up her stockinged feet beside Warren's socks on his mum's old coffee table.

Damien had cleared it all out though, later, after Warren died. Not all at once but eventually, piece by piece, and by the time the house itself was sold to the mine, he had auctioned, donated or dumped every item of furniture inside, handing Lentzer nothing more than an empty shell.

He had made some money from selling the contents, Ro knew, because somewhat unexpectedly, he'd offered a percentage of the proceeds to Griff as Warren's next nearest relative. Griff had thanked him, surprised and touched, but declined. Damien had simply shrugged and told Griff to let him know if he changed his mind.

'Wouldn't have thought Damien'd bother finding buyers for all those random bits and pieces,' Sam had remarked one night over dinner. 'Whatever he's getting for the stuff must be barely worth the time for him.'

Ro had said nothing but she had also found it a little curious that Damien had made the effort to sell the individual items rather than offload it all to a dealer willing to take the lot for a fixed price. Damien had suggested he was driven by nostalgia, but Ro had caught herself wondering. Outwardly, Damien presented as a man permanently unbothered by money, but she knew enough of the world to recognise that in reality that was true for very few people. Damien had always invested a percentage of what he earned, Warren had told Ro once, but in what exactly she'd never been entirely sure. New businesses and online start-ups rather than the stock market, from what she could tell, and while Ro knew she was naturally more risk averse than some, she'd been glad Damien had never asked or offered to invest on behalf of herself and Griff. Still, Damien's expenses in Carralon Ridge would be next to nothing – his rent was dirt cheap, his social life virtually zero – but when Ro had quietly mused to Griff about whether the low cost of living was partly what kept Damien in town, he had frowned.

'I dunno.' Griff had looked a little troubled by the suggestion.

'He offered me that money from the contents sale, so he can't be too strapped for cash.'

That was true, Ro had agreed, Damien had indeed offered. But, she had chosen not to add out loud, the gesture was a very safe bet on Damien's part. Damien could have put almost any amount of money on the table, secure in the knowledge that Griff would not accept a single dollar from that house.

Griff had been right in what he'd said earlier, though, out in the shed, Ro thought now as she shifted from her spot on the bed. There had been things of value in that house. There had been some jewellery and at least one milk jug that Ro knew for a fact was real silver because no-one ever once used it, not to mention Warren's own tools, and copper wiring and electrical equipment in the sheds outside the house. If Ro's son had wanted to steal something – and, even being as frank and unbiased with herself as she could be, she still couldn't reconcile that with the teenage boy she remembered – there had been plenty of lower hanging fruit.

Ro reached over to the side table next to the bed and dragged across her laptop, opening it on her knees. She found Sam's interview files and clicked through until she came to what she was looking for. A section he had titled: *Young People in Carralon Ridge.*

Sam had interviewed Zach and Kyle, Ro was reminded now as she opened the file. They had been ten and eleven at the time, and of all the interviews Sam had conducted, these were the ones Ro had spent the least time perusing. Picturing the two surly teenagers slouched on the couch at Heather's place, casually abusing their mother, Ro skim-read the lines again now, remembering why she had given the interviews little attention at the time. The boys were bored. They were fed up with the emptying town and frustrated with their quiet, lonely days. Zach and Kyle had said that to Sam a dozen times in a dozen different ways, but that was really the singular message of their interview. They had few friends, they had no fun, they wanted to leave, but their family wanted to stay. The boys had hoped that eventually their parents would change their minds. Ro reached the end of their interview and felt an unexpected pang of sympathy for the young brothers. If they'd already felt that way five years ago, nothing had improved for them since then. And five years was a long time at that age, at any age, to be unhappy with the day-to-day fundamentals of life.

Ro clicked instead on another file. Sam's interview with Darcy and Jacob. He had spoken to them together and the conversation had been relatively short, especially compared with some of the other lengthy monologues. Damien's, seemingly, for one example, Bernie's for another. But Sam's chat with his two closest friends had been short and focused. Perhaps, Ro suspected, he'd felt their experiences growing up overlapped to such a degree that they couldn't tell him much he didn't already know.

Ro had read this interview before, a number of times, but she leaned back and ran through it again, in closer detail than she had previously.

Both Darcy and Jacob referenced their parents surprisingly often for such a short interview and, for the most part, with an implied but undeniable fondness. Jacob said Ann-Marie hadn't had it easy after his dad had left, but she'd always been there for him, working hard and balancing her responsibilities as a nurse and a mum. He didn't mention Damien at all, and Sam had not asked. The omission seemed deliberate to Ro as she read the transcript of the conversation now, years later, suggesting Sam had been aware Jacob would not want to discuss the man on record.

Darcy had touched on several areas of his family's contri-
butions: the work with the local rugby teams, and the fitness
sessions for the elderly, volunteering at the fire station and the
community centre. He had mentioned in passing that he'd
enjoyed building the Last Chance Saloon with his dad, and Ro
made a mental note to tell Noel.

Reading the comments now, she was struck by how conscious
both boys seemed to be of their families' connections to Carralon
Ridge and the amount of stress wreaked by the upheaval of the
town.

My parents fought for the future of this place, Darcy said at one
point. *My granddad too. They hate what's happened here.*

And Jacob: *My mum told me she'll never leave. She said she couldn't
abandon it all like a lot of the others did.*

It was hard to capture nuance in the printed word, Ro knew,
but she got the sense that both the boys were proud of their
parents' commitment, while also quietly frustrated by it.

The conversation on the page moved on to briefly cover the
boys' schooling – *a bit shit* was the consensus – to the retail and
entertainment offerings in town – once again, *shit* – and, finally,
the opportunities for work. On this, Darcy had become reflective. *I wish we had more here,* he had said. *It'd be better for everyone if
Carralon was still as good as our parents reckon it was.*

And that was the end. Ro reached the bottom of the document, then went back to the start and re-read it from the
beginning. It was all there, just the same. Families, a hint of
frustration, lack of offerings, few opportunities. The discussion
was unsurprising and touched on the expected topics in an efficient, box-ticking way.

And yet . . . Ro went back to the beginning and scanned the
interview for a third time. She tried to imagine it spoken out
loud and in person, complete with all the elements that remained

uncaptured in a report – emphasis and eye contact and pauses and the implicit shorthand that existed between friends. She could not recreate it accurately enough to be sure she wasn't simply projecting, but still, Ro could sense something there, buried between the written words. A faint hint of a shared secret in the transcript. She could feel it in the casual exchange between the three young men who had known each other all their lives. Something they had no need to allude to directly, because they were all aware of it. Ro could tell. Or could she? Was there actually anything buried there, or was she just desperate to see something? She read the words again, and then again, trying to peer through the layers of the years and catch a deeper meaning in the light whispers, but it was no good. Whatever may or may not have been there – if anything at all – it had been left too far in the past.

Chapter 21

The afternoon light had moved on, lower and fuller, when Della came to the hut.

'Sorry to interrupt.' Della was frowning as she knocked lightly and peered around the door. 'Do you know if Dad's okay?'

'Why?'

'I just saw him go out. He didn't look okay.'

'No?'

'No.' Della shook her head. 'He looked sad.'

Ro got up.

Griff had not told Della where he was going, but Ro could make the obvious educated guess. She climbed into her car and drove along the familiar roads almost without seeing them, not thinking, not reflecting, simply feeling mostly numb as she moved once again towards the one place that always drew the pair of them back. As she turned off the country road and trundled up the shared track, she could see immediately that

Griff was not at the fork where Sam's car had been found, which would have been her second guess, but no matter because, sure enough, he was at her first.

The sharp whine of the chainsaw cut through the low rumbling from the mine, reaching Ro's ears a full minute before Griff's four-wheel drive came into view. She parked beside it at the front of the Hillary house and got out, the tall eucalyptus trees shivering and whispering overhead as she made her way around to the back in time to see Griff slice the whirring blade into one of the thick boughs of the branch that had crashed through Warren's porch.

He saw her too, mid-chop, so didn't pause, instead continuing smoothly with the motion. Ro watched, shielding her eyes from the low afternoon light as Griff wielded the lethal equipment on the verandah of his dead cousin's rotting house, minutes away from where his only son's car had been left abandoned. He would be out here doing equally dangerous maintenance work probably half-a-dozen times a year, she knew. And he'd be alone then too, on all those occasions when Ro was obviously not around. Ro didn't have to like it, though, if only for Della's sake. And she was around now.

'I thought you weren't going to bother with this,' she called as part of the branch he'd been tackling fell away with a crack.

'Yeah. I dunno.' Griff stopped the machine, lifting his safety glasses as the running blade in his hand came to a stop. He raised a boot and lightly kicked one of the lower boughs with his toe. 'It's a hazard, I suppose. And I can use the firewood.'

Ro stood at the foot of the crumbling steps and looked up at him. They regarded each other with mostly weariness.

'I'm sorry, Griff.'

'Yeah. I'm sorry, too.'

If nothing else, that was what twenty-odd years of marriage

bought you, Ro thought. A genuine apology both ways – not for everything, but for today – and a willingness to simply draw a line and move on. Again, if only for today.

'Listen, I know I was a bit crap with the stuff in the shed.' Ro nodded at the branches. 'But I really will help you with this.'

'Okay. Thanks.' He didn't contradict her, but a half-smile crossed his face as he lowered his safety glasses again. 'If you don't mind giving me a hand to shift the pieces, that would be good, actually. Let me make a few more cuts, be five minutes or so. I'll shout out when I'm ready.'

'No worries.' Ro stepped back from the sagging porch as he fired up the chainsaw and, chased by the whine of the metal against wood, she wandered along the length of the back verandah, the paddocks stretching out into the distance. The long grass swayed and above its yellow tips, she could make out the dark smudge of the Lentzer mine on the horizon. She didn't want to look at it and so she didn't, turning her attention instead back to the house as she walked on. At the southern aspect, she rounded the corner, trailing her hand lightly along the wooden weatherboard, feeling the old paint flake off against her fingers.

She followed the side of the house, keeping to the spots where the grass was bald rather than long. The garden had always been lush under Warren's stewardship. He'd had a natural green thumb and had been patient in helping Ro develop hers. They used to swap plant cuttings and he'd come over and shown her how to install an irrigation system in her veggie patch. Ro had in turn swung by to water Warren's rosebushes and tomato plants whenever he and Sylvie had gone on holiday.

The evidence of all his hard work was long gone now, as Ro turned the second corner and moved along the front of the home. There were no climbing roses working their way up the sun-drenched posts of the porch anymore, and occasionally under her feet she could feel the gnarled twists of stunted tree roots.

Ro stopped as she drew level with the empty rectangle where the front door used to be, and stood for a moment, staring deep into the darkened house. She could see all the way through the belly of the place, down the hall and out of the open back door to where the fallen branch was shivering and shaking under Griff's chainsaw. He kept shifting his position within the framed box of light, appearing and then disappearing from sight as Ro watched.

She remained where she was for a minute more, then glanced up. The sky was blue enough to make her eyes water, and all of a sudden she could picture Sam, as clear in her mind as in the video on her laptop, captured from above by Darcy's drone as he crossed the front yard on that last afternoon, brushing past where she stood now, then up the stairs, his footsteps echoing against the exposed boards as he entered the house.

Ro felt her own feet follow him, tracing his ghostly trail up the three sagging steps to the porch and stopping at the open threshold. There had been no front door in place that day either. A shaft of daylight illuminated only a small patch at the entrance of the hall, leaving the rest shrouded in gloom. Ro looked at it and wondered if Sam had hesitated as well.

The dust lay thick and still but surged to life as she stepped through the vacant doorway, lifting into the air like it was drawing breath. It floated around her and she could feel it sweep over her skin, feather-light, as she moved deeper into the house. Ro let her eyes wander over the dim hallway. She didn't know exactly what Sam had done once inside, but she'd been able to tell from his footprints that he had passed through here, that he had been where she was now.

She raised an arm, placing her fingertips on the wall. The floral
paper was rough and dry as she found a curled edge and peeled
it back, splaying her hands flat against the crumbling plaster and
exposed brick. She pressed lightly. The wall felt thick under her
palm, as though it was burdened with stories, the bones of the
house having absorbed them all. What had it seen and heard? Ro
moved her hands over the wall, skin to stone, willing it to share.
Tell me. She pressed a little harder, more insistent, leaning in, her
forehead touching and her eyes closed, feeling the house return
the pressure. *Tell me. Please. I'd love to know.*

Outside, the creak and sudden sharp crack of a bough
tumbling loose ricocheted through the empty rooms, and slowly
Ro dropped her hands, wiping them on her jeans as she stepped
back. She took a deep breath in and let it out, the air heavy and
unpleasant in her mouth, then turned away.

To Ro's immediate right was an open door leading to what
had been Warren's bedroom, now devoid of furniture other
than a grimy mattress propped against the wall. To her left had
been his lounge room, a relaxed, slightly cluttered space when
he'd been alive, welcoming in its shabby warmth. The carpet
had been ripped back and was now slumped in a sagging roll
in the far corner. The exposed floorboards were dirty, and old
puncture wounds from nails and screws marred the walls, paler
squares in the paint marking where pictures had hung.

Ro ignored both rooms, instead moving further down the
hall. As she drew closer to the rear of the house, she caught a
glimpse of what was left of the kitchen, with its cracked tiles
on the floor and crooked cabinet doors. She could see the dull
metal edge of the sink and a single mug sitting upside down on
the draining board, despite the water having been disconnected
from the property several years ago.

Ro stared at the mug for a long moment, her thoughts creeping in unwelcome directions. Towards those loud trespassers, with their cameras and light rings and shrieks and hunger for audience clicks, and towards those quieter ones, who came seemingly with only their warped fascinations and unsettling anonymity. She felt a cold finger of unease slide down the skin of her neck, and turned quickly away, allowing herself to be comforted by the faint purr of Griff's chainsaw outside.

Ro moved on, passing a full-length cupboard in which a ratty purple rain jacket that she didn't recognise dangled from the sole remaining hook. Next to it was the room she realised she had really come inside to see. Its door remained closed and she peered at it in the dim light.

Ro reached for the handle, wondering even as she did so if the room could possibly be locked, but the tarnished brass knob turned easily in her hand, offering no resistance. The door seemed to almost sag inwards rather than swing open and Ro stepped inside, gazing around what had been Warren's study. The glass in the large picture windows had been smashed long ago and replaced by a sheet of plastic nailed to the frames. It flapped loose at the corners, grimy and old to the point of being virtually opaque, and what light trickled in cast a sickly yellow tint over the space.

Ro had passed by this room many times, usually on her way to the gatherings on the back verandah, or to the kitchen to drop off some plant cuttings for Warren or return a set of birthday party lights lent by Sylvie. She'd never had any real need to go into the study and could only recall setting foot in there on a handful of occasions, mostly to retrieve the kids when they were younger and liked to mess around in places they shouldn't.

But Ro found that being in here now she could picture the layout with some clarity. Her memory was jogged by the scrapes against the wooden floor that advertised the exact former position of the desk and where an office chair had frequently been shuffled in and out. The walls in here, too, were pockmarked with the scars of decoration, and as Ro moved to the door, closing it behind her, she could see the bullet holes of anchored screws and the sun-faded outline where Warren's father's medal collection had been displayed in its velvet case.

It wasn't exactly in pride of place, Ro noted, as she experimentally swung the door gently through its axis. It was only really visible from inside the room when the door was shut, which was perhaps why Warren had never bothered to take it down after both his parents passed away. Or maybe he just liked it, Ro thought. Maybe it served as a small reminder of his dad's achievements and he enjoyed catching a glimpse of it when he sat down to tackle his paperwork.

'Hey, Ro?' Griff's voice floated in from the back, and she heard the creak of boards as he shifted his weight with a grunt. 'Are your hands free?'

'Yep. Coming.'

She stepped back into the hallway and followed the light outside to the verandah, careful where she put her feet among the stray branches strewn across the deck. The thickest part of the largest bough had crashed through the floorboards, she could see, and was jammed in place where it had fallen. Griff had cut it back, his gloved hands wrapped around the raw edge that he was now trying to heave out.

'It's wedged.' He nodded at a spare pair of gloves lying near his toolbox. 'If you grab them and could maybe pull back that bit of decking . . .'

'Where's it —? Oh yeah, it's caught here. I can see.' Ro pulled on the gloves as she crouched, reaching into the gap and wrapping her fingers around the exposed edge of a plank. She pulled back, using her weight as leverage to free the bough.

Both the branch and the board resisted, clinging tight to each other before all of a sudden giving way with a sharp crack. The plank came free in Ro's hand and as the sudden release sent her toppling backwards, she saw a tiny flash, a glimpse of something catching the light, before it was gone and she landed hard on her rear against the boards. She looked up to see Griff staggering under the weight of the cleared bough, stumbling back another step or two before he regained control. When firmly on his feet once more, he dumped the branch behind him on a clear section of verandah before pulling off his right glove and wiping the damp from his face. He saw Ro sitting where she'd fallen with the plank still in her clutches. She put it down and shook off her gloves.

'Christ,' Griff said. 'That one really didn't want to come out, did it? You all right?' He stretched out a hand to help her up and she automatically took it, and suddenly the rough skin of his palm was against hers for the first time in years. The shape and curve of his hand was both shockingly familiar and unsettlingly alien, and she could immediately tell without looking at his face that he felt the same way.

'Yeah, I'm fine. Just a bit of a bump.' They released each other as she got to her feet, her palm still tingling a little in the air. She briskly brushed the dirt off her jeans as they both turned to assess the damage. The bough had taken two boards with it, and left a third hanging loose, creating a long black hole in the porch.

Griff sighed. 'I'll find something to patch that. Listen, you want some water?' He squinted towards the sun then nodded back in the direction of their cars. 'I've got some in the boot.'

'Thanks, yeah, that'd be good,' Ro said, a little distracted. She gazed at the hole before finally stepping forward and crouching again, leaning in towards the hollow.

Jane Harper

'All okay?' Griff stepped closer, his shadow falling over the space, and she waved for him to move out of the light.

'Something fell, I think. When the boards came away.'

Through the hole in the decking, Ro could see the dry, bare earth below, perhaps a little deeper than an arm's length down. Or perhaps more. It was hard to judge. The ground lay mostly in darkness beyond the rectangle of light where the boards used to be. Ro could hear the scurry of mice underneath.

'What went down there?' Griff stepped around the other side and crouched as well. 'A tool?'

'No. Smaller. Much smaller, like . . . I don't know. It might have been a screw or something. It could be nothing, I just –' Ro stopped as her eye snagged at a point where the light met the dark, and she leaned in closer. Amid the dirt was a glint of metal. She pointed. 'Do you see that?'

Griff didn't answer this time, and Ro glanced up. He was still there, frowning into the hole, but his attention wasn't on where she was pointing to the dirt below, but instead fixed on the cracked board by her knees. She glanced down at the worn plank, unclear what he was staring at.

'Something wrong?' She looked again but still couldn't see.

'I'm not sure.' Griff reached out and took the loose board, bringing it closer and turning it in his hands until one of the long thin edges was facing him. He squinted at it, tracing his thumb slowly over the wood. He put it down carefully and reached instead for the other broken board, again turning it to look at the thin edge, before leaning over the hole and checking the same spot on the loose plank.

'Ro.' At last, Griff straightened, his face clouded and his voice oddly tight. He picked up the first board once again, holding it towards her this time. 'What do you reckon this is?'

She could see it immediately, now that the angle was right.

Oil, she thought at first, as she saw the dark stain stretching along the board's thin edge, marking the hidden face where the fitted floorboards would have met. Or maybe some sort of paint, she considered, knowing even as she reached out to take it that that wasn't right, because Ro may not have known a lot about outdoor floor finishings, but she had been a GP her whole professional life and she certainly knew old blood when she saw it. And she was seeing it now.

She stared at the board for a long time then glanced up at Griff. He looked back and neither said anything as Ro dropped her eyes again, running her gaze along the full length of the stain.

'You said something fell in here?' Griff's voice had a forced calmness.

Ro placed the plank down with care and lowered herself to the deck to look into the gap. 'It's all the way down there. Let me,' she added as Griff began leaning over. 'I can see it.'

Ro shuffled her legs around and lay on her front, the dust catching in her nostrils as she inhaled. She rubbed her nose roughly with her free hand, then with the other she stretched down, far into the hole. Her fingers scrabbled against the dirt and she could sense rather than hear the soft glide of something moving deeper in the shadows. She hesitated, then touched the ground, quickly and lightly, trying very hard not to disturb anything or bury whatever she was reaching for before she'd even found it.

Where was it?

She could feel only the grainy earth. She withdrew her arm and edged forward, dipping her head in a little way so she could see better, and for a moment she thought she'd lost it . . . but no – *there*. A dull glint in the dirt. Thank God. Ro fixed the spot in her mind and reached down once more into the blackness,

ignoring a fast scurry of hidden movement this time as she felt
nothing, nothing, noth–

'Ah.'

'You've got it? Good work.'

'Yeah.' She exhaled into the dust as her fingers closed around
the small object, drawing it easily into her hand. She could tell
immediately from the shape and size and curve and edges what
she was holding as she pulled it up from the dark, clambering
back to her knees and holding out her fist.

'What is it?' Griff moved closer as Ro opened her palm and
exposed what she held to the daylight.

'It's a key.'

Chapter 22

The low flames in the fire pit radiated a gentle heat onto the four silent figures seated around it, as the night air cooled above them. Griff had finished cleaning the remains of dinner from the barbecue before pulling up a chair by the fire between Della and Ro. Across the pit, Damien was staring into the flames, the beer in his hand gathering beads of condensation as the flickering light cast their faces with an orange glow. In the distance, the mine groaned at such a deep frequency that Ro could feel it in her back and chest. No-one had spoken for some time.

She and Griff had stood side by side in the glare of the low afternoon sun earlier, looking at the hole in Warren's deck and debating what to do next. Finally, Ro had knelt and dipped her head into the space, using a torch from Griff's toolkit to sweep a light underneath. She could see nothing but dirt and the telltale signs of mice, so Griff grabbed his claw hammer. Together, they carefully prised loose the surrounding boards of decking one at a time. The same black stain had been visible on the edges of two more boards on either side of the hole.

'So if we reckon this is blood –' Griff started, breaking off as he saw Ro nod. She tilted the edge of the board towards the sunlight, turning it one way then the other. The light did not transform the discoloured mark into anything else.

'I'm as sure as I can be that it is.'

'All right, so I mean, how much . . .?'

'Yeah, it feels like a lot.' The size of the stain had been troubling Ro too, and she used her hands to estimate the spread as best she could. 'Some injuries can bleed a fair bit. Head wounds, or if you hit an artery, obviously. Nothing you'd want. If this was all from one person, I'd expect them to need serious medical attention.'

Griff looked up at that. 'Jesus, I hadn't even thought it could be two people. Maybe that's . . . better somehow?' He didn't sound convinced. 'I don't know. We would've heard about this. Don't you think? If Warren or Sylvie had had an accident?'

'Something like this, yeah.' Ro's eyes traced the size of the stain. 'I'd expect us to have heard. Because I'd be thinking it'd involve a hospital trip at least.' She glanced at Griff's phone in his pocket. 'Still nothing from Sylvie?'

Griff checked the screen, shaking his head. 'What's today, though? Saturday? She goes to Blenheim to see her mum in the care home most weekends. She could be driving, low signal. Or busy, I suppose. Think her mum's not too good at the moment.'

'Right,' Ro replied, sorry to hear that. Sylvie's mother had not lived locally, never been Ro's patient, but she knew Sylvie had been concerned about her health on and off for the best part of a decade. That said, she really wished that Sylvie would call back and put their minds at ease with a straightforward explanation. Crouching once again, Ro tried to think what that explanation could be.

'It might not be human,' she suggested. 'Warren was always running the barbecue out here, would he have slaughtered someth–?'

'No.' Griff was already shaking his head. 'He didn't know how. I mean, maybe in theory but not in real terms. Didn't have the stomach for it. He farmed arable out here for a reason.' He stood and rested a hand on the verandah post, contemplating Warren's bright, dead paddocks, the mine hunched low and dark on the horizon. He was quiet for a long time, then drew a breath. 'Listen, Sam –'

'No. Griff.' Ro cut him off. The thought had occurred to her too, rearing up, monstrous, but she kept her voice calm, forcing the idea to settle and slip back into its dark place. 'Whatever happened, Sam didn't die in this house. This isn't his blood.'

'No.' Griff repeated, more firmly this time. He nodded, reassuring himself of something they already knew. 'No.'

'It's not.' Ro felt the need to reassure herself now. 'It can't be, because we could see where he'd walked. There was no blood there. It's not his.'

'Whose then?' Griff stared down at the black hole at their feet. 'Warren's?'

Ro caught a note of fresh distress as he said his cousin's name. 'I don't know. The inquest . . .' She stopped. Warren's body had been as broken as would be expected when found submerged in water at the base of a sheer drop. The inquest had recorded a verdict of misadventure.

She kneeled down beside the two broken boards, running a finger along the stain of the first one, stopping when she reached a small gap in the discolouration. She had noticed it earlier, but now she leaned in to look more closely. It was only a tiny space, about the length of her thumbnail, where the old wood was still visible, grey and worn. In this small space, the wood was not stained, the blackened mark stretching out on either side of it.

A whispered thought taking shape, Ro put the first board down and reached for its partner, running her eyes along its edge until she found a similar clear space in the bloodstain. Carefully, she placed both boards side by side on the porch, lining them up as they would have been when fixed in place. The small gaps in the stain aligned and, reaching into her pocket, Ro took out the key and looked at it once again. It was a standard silver Yale key, a little grimy around its edges but otherwise unremarkable. She bent and gently slotted it edgeways between the two planks of wood. The round bow of the metal matched up well with the size and shape of the clear space. Ro looked at it for a minute longer, thinking about what that might mean, then stood back and motioned for Griff to see for himself.

He did much the same as she had, running his finger over the markings, over the shape of the key, pulling the boards apart and gently pushing them back together.

'So the key got wedged there before the blood soaked in?' He straightened at last, a frown creasing his face.

'Looks that way,' Ro said. 'Doesn't it?'

'Yeah. I suppose it wouldn't have to have happened at the same time, though.'

'No. The key could have got stuck at any point. Maybe they've got nothing to do with each other.'

'Maybe.' Griff sounded uncertain as he bent and retrieved the key. He ran his thumb over the jagged ridges, then looked up at Ro. 'We'd better find out what this opens.'

They had tried. The back door felt like the obvious choice,

but Griff was already shaking his head even as they lifted the key to the lock to compare.

'I've still got the original key for this, and it's not the same. I can tell by looking.'

They had tested it anyway, just in case, but Griff had been right and they'd moved on quickly, finding nothing left inside the house that even invited an attempt. The front door long gone, they had walked instead over to the padlocks still hanging from the side doors of the big barn, and then tried the battered storage box in the smaller shed.

An hour later, with no luck and still no word from Sylvie, they had at last returned to the verandah. Ro had captured some photos on her phone of each board before Griff had replaced them and then they had covered the whole area with a tarp and weighed it down with bricks. Then they had left, Ro taking the key with her.

★

Griff called Damien on the way home and his cousin appeared in their driveway within the hour, his face set and a slim key ring dangling from his fist.

'These are all I still have from the property.' Damien put the keys on the kitchen table with a clatter, his voice terse. 'All I could find, anyway. There used to be a lot more, for the sheds and things, but after the sale . . .'

He stopped as Della came in from the laundry, an old tin rattling in her hand. A faded 'W' had been scrawled on the side and she put the tin down on the table beside Ro. They'd brought through the desk lamp from Della's room and plugged it in, and Ro was holding two keys under the bulb as she examined the pattern.

Ro had been fairly sure this pair was not a match but felt

herself hesitate under Damien's scrutiny, and took the time to compare them again. The rise here and the dip there. Yes, she had been right the first time, and discarded the spare to join the others in the growing pile by her elbow.

'That's the one you found between the boards?' Damien pointed at the key still in Ro's hand and she nodded, offering it to him. As unrealistic as it might be, part of her hoped Damien would seize it immediately with a cry of recognition.

Instead he stared at it lying in her palm for a long moment, before finally reaching out to take it. To help identify it among the many others now scattered across the table, Ro had attached it to a key ring in the shape of a cockatoo engraved with the words *Carralon Ridge Primary School*, and it was by this that Damien picked it up. He turned the key over in his clean fingers, saying nothing as he examined it. Eventually, he shook his head.

'No. Sorry.' He sounded deflated. 'I don't know what it's for off the top of my head. Not that that means anything. They all bloody look the same, don't they?' He put the key down carefully, then lifted his eyes to meet Ro's. 'You'd better show me the photos of these boards.'

It was dark by the time they admitted defeat. Ro sat with Damien in the living room for more than half an hour as he scrolled slowly through the photos she had snapped at the house.

'Send them over to me,' he said at last, his voice flat. 'Thanks, Ro. Hey –' He frowned suddenly. 'There was a lock on the old meter box, out by –'

'Yeah, I know the one,' Ro said. 'We tried it. And the padlock on that western gate. We tested all the ones we could find.'

'Right.' Damien fell quiet again, his brow furrowed. 'What about the other two houses? It'd be worth –' He stopped as he saw Ro nodding.

She and Griff had driven to both of the neighbouring

properties after leaving Warren's house, taking one fork in the track and then the other. The visits had been thorough but brief; there was very little left to check. The stone bungalow's entrances were still boarded up as they had been since Bernie left, and the only lock they could find was on the empty wood-shed. The padlock was badly rusted and Ro had been able to tell that it was the wrong size anyway.

At the ivy cottage, the industrial locks Lentzer had put on the front and back doors in an attempt to keep Ann-Marie out were a completely different make, and both looked far too new. The key had not fitted in the only original keyhole left on the property, hidden behind the curtain of vines covering the laundry door.

Damien exhaled deeply as he stood beside Ro in the living room, scrolling through the photos one more time before handing back her phone and following her through to the kitchen. The four of them sat at the table under the harsh main light, moving the desk lamp between them as they compared every key in the tin of spares collected from the Hillary house over the years. An hour later, they had resorted to scouring shelves and cupboards for any others they might have missed, trying old sets and unmarked singles almost at random.

It was hard to be completely confident where a key would or wouldn't fit without being able to slide it into a lock, Ro found, and she felt the others growing frustrated as well. Between them, they had twice stumbled across spares that at a quick glance looked promising. The first was for a padlock Griff had bought only eight weeks earlier to replace the old one on his side gate. The other, which Ro had identified herself, had been among a small bunch of keys for Sam's old shared student house four hours away in Sydney. Ro had held that one for a very long time, staring at the similar shapes, until Griff had reached over and lightly covered her hand with his. He'd left it there for a moment, its weight warm against her skin, before taking the key from her.

'It's not right,' he'd said softly, holding it up. 'Look. Here, Ro. Look at this. The bump at the end is a double not a single. Yeah? It's not the same.'

She'd looked where he'd pointed and sure enough, what he said was true, and Ro had felt a wave of both relief and disappointment wash over her as she'd put the key aside with the other rejects. She had no idea what she would have made of them being a match.

At some point, Della had gone to fire up the barbecue and, worn down and exhausted, they had allowed themselves to be drawn outside for something to eat.

'We should call the police.' Damien was gazing now into the fire pit, an untouched beer still in his hand. His frown had faded, replaced by an unsettled, faraway look. His faint English accent became more pronounced when he was under stress. 'I know we said we'd wait to hear back from Sylvie but . . .' He trailed off, putting down his beer to pull out his phone again. The blue light was reflected in his glassy stare as he drew his finger and thumb over the screen, enlarging and shrinking each photo of the boards in turn before flicking to the next image.

'I'll do it if you want,' Griff said. 'I mean, yeah. I'm wondering the same. Maybe we should.'

'No.' Della's voice was quiet from across the fire pit and they all looked at her. She had not said much for most of the evening. 'We should call, definitely, but not now. Not on a Saturday night. Whoever picks up that phone at Blenheim station is already going to be flat out and we'll lose nothing by waiting another day. It's an abandoned property in a dead town. It's going to be hard enough to get anyone to take an interest as it is, without admitting we haven't even asked the woman who lived there if she knows what happened.' Della nodded to the tin of old keys that Ro was listlessly working her way through for a third time. 'That key you found could be for Sylvie's flat or for the pub or for anything.'

'What about the blood?' Damien's eyes moved to hers.

'Injured wildlife? Aggressive stray dog they had to deal with?' Della suggested. 'I don't know, but we should at least ask the question. I could see Warren, or Sylvie for that matter, handling something like that without feeling the need to tell everyone.'

Ro nodded. She could see it too, actually. She looked to Griff to gauge his reaction but he didn't respond. He seemed a little distracted, glancing back towards the house, his gaze coming to rest on the cooled barbecue.

'I turned it off properly, Dad.' Della had noticed too. She lifted a hand to her mouth, stifling a yawn, then stretched and stood. 'Listen, if no-one minds, I'm going to call it a night.'

Ro leaned in to give her a kiss, then watched as she disappeared up the steps and into the kitchen. She saw Griff's focus again drift to the verandah, a faintly uneasy air about him that seemed to go beyond the collection of old keys in Ro's lap.

'What's wrong?' she asked, and he pulled his attention back to her.

'Nothing,' he said, but he frowned as he lifted his beer bottle, taking a deep swallow. He shook his head. 'Probably just all this talk about Warren.'

'Yeah.' Damien rubbed his forehead as he stared down at his phone, his face tight in the glow from the images. 'Brings it all back.'

The night breeze rattled in the trees around them, whipping the embers from the low fire into the sky until finally Griff nodded at the pit.

'I should probably put this out,' he said. 'Going to be high winds tomorrow morning. Don't need to be starting anything myself.'

'Yeah, I'll make a move.' Damien put his hands on his knees and hauled himself up with a deep sigh. He slipped his phone into his back pocket, and glanced at Griff and Ro. 'You'll let me know straight away if you hear from Sylvie.'

It wasn't a question but Griff nodded as he stood, too. 'Yeah. Of course.'

Ro saw Damien's eyes slide downwards to the key in her hand dangling from its little metal cockatoo. She could tell he was considering asking to take it with him but the moment passed and he didn't. She was glad because she would have said no. Instead, she dropped it into her own pocket as she pulled herself up from her seat.

''Night, Damien,' she said, but gently. It had been a troubling evening for them all. 'Thanks for bringing those spares over. We'll chat to you tomorrow, no doubt.'

Damien nodded, but didn't turn to leave, instead simply shifting his weight. He glanced in the direction of the driveway, but stayed where he was, lips parted as though about to say something. In the dying light of the fire, Ro could see him silently debating with himself.

'Look, strictly between us,' he said, finally, his voice so quiet that Ro had to take a small step closer to hear him over the wind and she saw Griff do the same. Damien hesitated again then, seemingly decided, took a breath, his eyes flicking from Griff to Ro and back again. 'I wouldn't say this to anyone else, but I'll say it to you two. I don't trust Sylvie.'

Ro fought to keep her expression neutral as she absorbed his words, but her thoughts were already ahead of her, dashing across the grass to the hut and the side table where Sam's notebook lay.

She mentally rifled through the pages to the one she so often turned to. The one with Sylvie's name, and Sam's heavy question mark scored right next to it. She pressed her lips together and waited as Damien chose his words.

'It's nothing new,' he began in mitigation, 'but Sylvie was . . .' He felt around for the right phrase. 'Very *difficult*, I'd say, about selling the Hillary house when she inherited Warren's half. Not in the way I'd expected, she never tried to stop me. Or not exactly, anyway. Almost the opposite, in fact. The whole thing was quite weird. I know she was . . .' He paused. 'Grieving, I suppose, but we all were. Eventually, it became pretty clear that she wouldn't admit it directly, but she wanted to sell that place as much as I did, or –' he corrected himself, 'she wanted *me* to sell the place for us, more accurately, but she wouldn't openly do anything to help it along. Wouldn't actively engage with the lawyers or paperwork, but privately she did nothing to prevent it either. And she could have. Could've put a block on the whole thing for months, or years even. She didn't help, but I could tell that she wanted it to happen.'

Griff glanced at Ro. 'A lot of people found selling their places hard, though, mate,' he said. 'Just because you should, it doesn't mean you want to.'

'I suppose.' Damien looked a little disappointed by the response. 'But this seemed . . .' He breathed out, considering. 'I'll tell you how it felt, it felt familiar. Because I see this all the time at work, albeit on a different scale. People want the money, they want the deal to happen, but they don't want to be seen getting their hands dirty for it. And that was Sylvie, in my opinion. She left all that to me, let me take the heat for offloading my family's place to the mine, which, you know . . .' he shrugged, 'maybe I deserved for pushing Warren so hard to sell when he was alive, but still. Something about it –' He stopped and shook his head. 'I dunno. Keep an eye on her, is all I'm saying. Anyway.' He sighed, and this time turned towards the path leading to the driveway. 'On that not-so-cheery note . . .'

'All right. Thanks, mate.' Griff nodded slowly as Damien raised a hand in farewell. 'Good to bear in mind.'

Ro and Griff stood side by side and watched as Damien left, listening to his footsteps trudge around the side of the house before being lost under the rustle of the wind. A minute later the sound of a car engine cut through, firing up loud and then fading away. She turned back to Griff, who was watching her, his eyes black in the night. He nodded at Damien's empty chair.

'What are your thoughts on that?' His voice was low.

'I don't know. To be honest with you, Griff, I hear Sylvie mentioned and straight away I'm thinking about Sam's notes,' Ro replied. 'Her interview page.'

Griff didn't reply as he walked to the outside tap and unwound the hose, stretching the cable through his hands. He had read all the way through Sam's research notes himself, at least twice, but while Ro had found herself obsessively drawn back to them over the years, she got the impression that for Griff they were simply a distressing and painful reminder.

To Ro's frustration, the few times she had raised any question around Sylvie's integrity, Griff had come to the woman's defence.

'Jesus, Ro. Sam wrote all kinds of things in that book. If she says she doesn't know what it was about, she probably doesn't know,' he'd once said in response, instantly exhausted by the conversation. 'I mean, Warren trusted her. I reckon we should too.'

Now, though, Griff was pensive as he directed the hose onto the pit, dousing the flames with water until the ashes were black. A thin column of grey smoke wound its way up from the remains and disappeared into the sky. He shut off the water and stared at the charred embers for a long minute, checking for sparks. When he said nothing more, Ro glanced across the lawn towards her hut, feeling worn out.

'All right.' She stifled a yawn. 'Well, I'm going to –'

'It's Warren's bloody barbecue.' Griff spoke quietly and Ro stopped where she was. A fresh wave of confusion lapped at her tired mind.

'What about it?' She remembered Griff's distracted glances towards his own grill on the porch. 'That's what was bothering you before?'

'Yeah. I keep thinking how the –' he started, then broke off as they both looked up, a sharp gust of wind catching the treetops and sending their limbs creaking and swaying alarmingly. The forecast for tomorrow was hot and blustery. Griff would have his work cut out for him, Ro thought. For now, he dropped his eyes back to the fire pit as the breeze waned a little.

'I keep thinking how the sausages on his barbecue were burned,' he said. 'That day Sam and I found Warren's house empty.'

'Right,' Ro replied, grasping for her own memories of that day, trying to find the significance.

'But how often did Warren cook up sausages on that thing?' Griff said, immediately answering his own question. 'All the time. Few times a week at least?'

'Yeah.'

'So he knew his way around that grill, didn't he?' Griff went on, again not waiting for an answer. 'He knew how to use it. Didn't burn stuff.'

'No,' Ro agreed. They had been for barbecues at Warren's place many times and the food had always been cooked well.

'When Sam and I went over, we could see Warren'd been outside cooking the night before,' Griff went on. 'That was actually one of the first warning signs for me, even before I was really worried, because I was surprised he'd left all his stuff lying around. It was all there getting dirty in the wind, his cooking tongs, plate, sauce bottle, things like that.'

'He'd been making his dinner, though, hadn't he?' Ro remembered that detail from the inquest. Three sausages. Overdone, the report had said. A single opened beer, half-empty. It had sounded lonely to her at the time and she'd felt sad. Wished they'd invited Warren over more often. 'The coroner said that the food was overcooked.'

'Yeah, but . . .' Griff wound the hose a few times around his fist. 'It's hard to explain but the whole thing felt a bit wrong. The grill was definitely off when we arrived, I know that because I checked the gas. But the food had obviously been out for hours. Covered with flies, because I remember –' A tiny pause. 'I remember Sam swatting them away.'

He stepped forward and ground his boot down on a single ember glowing amid the blackened remains of the fire.

'So, yeah, the sausages had been on too long, I guess that's accurate to say.' He frowned. 'But the thing is, overall they hadn't been done too badly. Mostly they looked fine, just like he'd normally do them. The burned areas were only on the bottom, where they were touching the grill when Sam and I found them. Those bits were ruined, completely charred. Like he was cooking away as usual, then suddenly forgot to turn them for ages.'

As Ro stood there in the moonlight, she found herself trying to imagine Warren's last evening. Preparing his solo meal, alone in the house where he'd lived with his late parents and shared until recently with Sylvie, surrounded by land under threat from the mine that was chuntering away in his line of sight.

'Maybe he got distracted,' Ro said quietly. 'If he'd had a lot on his mind . . .'

'Yeah.' Griff exhaled heavily. 'I mean, that's pretty much what I thought at the time. He's upset, he burns his dinner, turns the gas off, looks around and everything feels a whole lot worse.' A pause. 'Goes and does what he does.' He stared at the dark embers for a minute longer. 'It's just that normally . . .'

Ro nodded. He didn't have to finish. Normally Warren cooked well. She had never known him to ruin a meal either.

'I suppose it wasn't your average night, though.' Griff's voice was pensive.

'No. That's very true.'

'Warren was probably distracted, like you say. Or . . .' He glanced at the tin of keys by her chair. 'I don't know. I keep wondering if maybe something else was going on. Something happened that meant he wasn't concentrating on cooking anymore.' His eyes were anxious as they met Ro's. 'It's just all of this stuff together. Makes you think.'

Ro reached into her pocket and felt the small, jagged shape of the key there, and was glad she had kept it close.

'How did the deck look that day?' she asked. 'Had it been cleaned?'

The wind picked up again, slicing hot and gritty through the night as Griff frowned into the dark.

'It was like everything else around here,' he said finally. 'Five minutes outside and it's covered in dust.'

Chapter 23

Ro lay awake for what felt like hours in her hut, listening to the howl of the wind and the low moan of the mine. She must have fallen asleep eventually because when she next jolted alert, morning was filtering through the cracks in the blinds. She felt uneasy, the remnants of a disturbing dream skittering away in the daylight before she could properly examine them. Outside, the wind was wailing.

Griff had already gone by the time Ro fought her way over to the house, eyes scratchy with fatigue and the hot breeze grabbing at her hair and clothes. A note was propped next to the tin of spare keys on the kitchen table. Griff would be on the ridge all morning, he'd written, watching for spot fires. Ro and Della should call him if they needed to. Stepping quietly along the hall to Della's room, Ro heard soft snoring coming from behind the door for once, rather than brisk corporate chatter. She crept away, leaving her daughter to sleep in the Sunday morning light, and ate a quick breakfast alone, arranging the spare keys into vague patterns on the tabletop as she planned her own task for the day.

Braving the wind once more to gather what she needed from the hut, Ro climbed into her car and drove without stopping to the centre of town. On reaching the crossroads, she pulled into the empty pub car park, just as she had on Thursday evening. Only three days earlier, she thought with some surprise as she looked at the pub, its lights off again. This already felt like a long visit to Carralon.

Ro killed the engine and walked over to the pub. The building had a distinct stillness about it and she knew instinctively that it was empty inside, even as she put her face to the glass door. Sylvie was definitely not there. Ro checked her phone and, wondering for the first time if she should feel worried, hesitated before reaching into her pocket. She pulled out the key with the cockatoo key ring and lifted it to the lock. She'd had some practice at this over the past afternoon and sensed before she even tried that this lock was not a match. She checked anyway, unsure as the key refused to slip in whether she had expected it to or not.

Ro dropped her hand and walked around the side of the building to the back entrance, picking her way past the bins and flattened cardboard boxes. There was no sign of Sylvie's vintage convertible Capri parked in the disused loading dock, but Ro could see the space where it was normally kept. She went up to the door that led to a small flat where Sylvie had lived since she and Warren separated. Ro didn't know how old the lock on the door was or when it had last been changed, but it was clearly the wrong type for the key she held in her hand.

Both relieved and disappointed, she returned to the street and walked out to the centre of the crossroads, looking in every direction. She set off almost at random, choosing south only because it meant the wind was at her back rather than rushing into her face. Ro stopped at the first building she came to, the former bank. The door had been boarded up but still she worked her way around the space methodically, checking both the lock that secured the chain-link fence and the one on the back window shutter. She made sure there were no more to be tested before moving on.

Ro continued in this manner down the road. In some ways the exercise felt so incomplete as to be pointless, she thought as she scoured the silent buildings, looking through broken windows and splintered doors. There was so much missing, but it felt better to be doing this than sitting outside the closed pub all morning waiting for a woman who may or may not turn up. She had no luck at the former Italian restaurant, either on the front and back doors themselves or the padlocks that chained them shut. The strip of small deserted terraced cottages yielded nothing, nor did the old pharmacy with its empty shelves and cracked glass.

Ro simply carried on along the lifeless street, ignoring the groans and creaks all around until, eventually, she reached Damien's townhouse.

There she stopped, looking up at the ugly brick structure. It was one of the very few occupied residences in the centre of town, and just as Ro had been able to tell that Sylvie was not inside the pub, she could sense with the same certainty that Damien was at home. She stepped back and looked at the blinds drawn across the only window that faced the street. No Sunday morning sounds floated out from inside the place; Ro could hear no television or music or coffee grinder, and she wondered if he was sleeping. Keeping mainly European working hours, Damien's day-to-day existence was largely at odds with the rest of his neighbours.

Ro stood beside the front door and hesitated. Damien had not even lived here when Warren had died; he had been based in London full time, staying at a conference hotel in Sydney during his short visit, but – Ro's train of thought reliably followed the well-worn tracks to its most frequent destination – on the day of Sam's disappearance, that had not been the case. Damien had certainly been living here then. Sam had spent nearly two of those last precious hours here, until Doug Hewett had passed by and seen them part ways.

Ro remained still for a long minute, surrounded by emptiness. She trusted Damien. She had made the decision years ago to trust him. Another minute ticked on and then, without letting herself think too hard about it, Ro took the key from her pocket and lifted it to the lock.

It slipped right in, and the shock of the unexpected smooth settling of three centimetres of metal into the groove almost sent her off balance. She had expected the key and the lock to rattle against each other, rejecting an unacceptable, impossible match. Ro stared, struggling to acknowledge what was in front of her. Blood pounded in her ears as she reached up to turn the key.

It wouldn't budge.

Ro twisted it right and then left, her sweating hands slipping against the metal as she tried to rotate it, leaning her weight into the movement so forcefully that in the end she made herself stop for fear of damaging the lock or key or both. She needn't have worried. The key remained stubbornly unmoved.

Heart still racing, it took Ro several deep breaths to recalibrate her knee-jerk response with the facts. She pulled the key out and clutched it tightly in her hand, the metal edges cutting into the skin of her palm. This was not the right door and it was not the right lock. Wherever this key led, it was not to Damien's townhouse.

With a rush of guilt and relief, Ro quickly stepped back into the street, furtively checking to see if anyone had noticed her. There was no-one around, of course, the pavement on either side stretching out as quiet as ever while the blind in Damien's window thankfully remained closed. Ro glanced up at the ridge though, wondering if Griff was still up there, his binoculars trained on the town. If he was, if he had seen her test his own cousin's door, he kept his reaction to himself. Ro's phone in her pocket remained silent.

She was still standing on the doorstep, debating what to do next, when she heard it. The rumble of a car engine in the direction from which she'd come. Ro listened for a moment more, staring down the wide street towards the distant crossroads until she saw it. A flash of red, east to west.

Ro was already walking, her pace faster now. She'd recognise that vintage Ford Capri anywhere, but especially here. Sylvie was back.

★

The woman had been crying. Ro could tell that from a distance, even before she could make out Sylvie's face in detail. The slope of her shoulders and a deliberate delicacy in her movements as she climbed out of the driver's seat gave it away.

Sylvie had parked outside the pub beside Ro's car and she stood with one hand resting on the roof as she scanned the surrounding streets. When she saw Ro approaching she went still for a moment, the wind lifting the ends of her long red hair and snatching at her skirt.

Ro said nothing as she drew closer, taking in the overnight bag at Sylvie's feet and her swollen, bloodshot eyes. She had cried off all her eyeliner, and Ro realised she had never seen Sylvie without it before, even when Warren died. It made her look naked and vulnerable and Ro, who had been intending to tackle this conversation one way, decided in that second to go another.

'How's your mum?' she asked, when the pair were close enough that she could keep her voice at a respectful volume. 'I heard she's not been well.'

'Mini stroke.' Sylvie's face crumpled. 'Happened overnight on Friday, they think.'

'Oh, Sylvie. I'm sorry,' Ro said, her doctor's instincts stirring. 'Do you need anything? Do you want to talk through . . .?'

'It's all right.' Sylvie wiped a hand across her cheeks. 'Thanks, though. Feel like I've had back-to-back nurses and doctors and physios and everyone else talking to me all weekend. They think she'll be okay but she's in her late eighties, so . . .' She blinked hard. 'Anyway. I got your messages.' There was a breath of a pause filled with what – reluctance? Fatigue? Ro couldn't tell – but then Sylvie nodded at the pub. 'Come inside. We'll talk.'

Ro watched as Sylvie drew out her own keys, a huge, clanking bunch, and opened the pub door. She let them both in, flicking on lights and hitting the switch for the overhead fan. It was an instant relief to be out of the rising wind and Sylvie dumped her bag down with a heavy sigh. She waved for Ro to take a seat at the counter before moving through the hatch to her usual spot behind the bar. Her eyes lingered fleetingly on the modest spirits shelf before settling further down the countertop.

'Coffee?' she asked.

'Thanks.'

Outside, the breeze rattled the doorhandle as it flew past, whistling all the way down the empty street. Through the streaked window, Ro could see the trees rocking and bending. She pictured Griff on the ridge in this weather, high and exposed, and hoped he had come down. Although, he'd be safer up there than tackling a spot fire on the ground, she supposed.

Ro dragged her focus back to the present as a cup of coffee was slid in front of her.

'Sylvie, I'm sorry to have called so many times yesterday . . .' she started, but the other woman shook her head as she raised her own coffee, grimacing a little as she took a sip.

'It's all right.' Sylvie blew gently on the liquid. 'I would've answered, if I'd had a minute to breathe.' She replaced the cup and regarded Ro over the counter, a touch of defiance creeping over her face. 'I loved Warren, you know? Even at the end, when I moved into the flat here for a little while, I still . . .' She cut herself short and held out her hand. 'Let me see this key you found.'

Ro listened to the wailing outside as Sylvie rummaged in her tote bag for her glasses, slipping them on before lifting the small piece of metal to her eyeline. She frowned as she inspected it, just as Damien had done, running her fingers over the points and turning it over in her hands. Finally, she placed it down on the wooden bar top with a soft click before reaching out and taking Ro's offered phone. She swiped very slowly through the photos of the stained decking, examining the different angles Ro had captured of the scene.

'What is all this?' she said finally, her voice tight.

'I don't know for sure,' Ro replied. 'But we thought it looked like blood.'

'Blood?' Sylvie's distress seemed genuine, Ro thought, and her hands were unsteady as she went back to the start of the photos and began scrolling through once more. 'Why would there be blood on the deck?'

'I was hoping you'd know.'

'No. Jesus, I've no idea. And I can't tell you what this is for.' She swapped the phone for the key, running her finger again over the ridges.

Ro said nothing, waiting.

'I'm sorry.' Sylvie's voice wavered. 'I wish I did know. I'd say if I did, for Warren. I'd tell you.'

The windows shuddered in their frames as leaves and debris swirled outside. Rather than being menacing, it created an oddly intimate feeling inside the pub. It could almost be cosy, Ro thought as she looked at Sylvie across their twin cups of cooling coffee. As though they were sheltering together from a sudden summer downpour or confiding over a drink on a chilly winter's day, rather than hiding inside a failing business from the hot, coarse gusts raging outside. The closeness was artificial, though, and Ro could tell the other woman felt it too. Ro was there because she wanted something from Sylvie and they both knew it. They watched each other for a moment more, neither speaking, then Ro reached down and took Sam's notebook from her bag. She slid it over the counter, opened to the correct page. The change in Sylvie was instant.

'Ro. For God's sake.' She looked away, draining her coffee in two large gulps. 'My mum's just had a stroke.'

Sylvie wouldn't meet her eye now, so Ro pushed the notebook a little closer, slipping it next to her empty cup and right into her field of vision, before tapping a finger against Sam's scribbled note.

Re: Warren and Lentzer. Ask Sylvie?

The deep punctuation mark at the end glared up at them both, traced over and over again, as though Sam had considered the question for some time.

'I know you can tell me what this means, Sylvie.'

There was no response, and in the silence, Ro felt an unexpected spark of hope. She had been braced for yet another denial.

'This is the last time I'll ask you.' Ro concentrated on keeping her voice steady, trying to damp down the note of desperation she could hear in herself. 'Not for your sake but because it's probably my last chance. Griff's lost his contract, I'm sure you know that. We'll lose the house for good in a few months. So I think this is it.' She felt the sting of tears in her own eyes, sudden and overwhelming, and it was her turn to blink hard as she fought to regain control. Sylvie made no move to comfort her, simply turning the key over and over in her hand.

'And listen, you can tell me or not, Sylvie. I can't make you. It's always been up to you, and nothing's changed now. Except that I won't ask again because most likely I won't be here next year. That makes me wonder, though.' Ro cleared her throat and pushed her empty coffee cup aside. It scraped against the counter. 'Will you?'

The edge in her tone made Sylvie's eyes harden, and Ro saw something wary scuttle behind them.

'Will you still be here? I mean, your mum's an hour away in Blenheim, very unwell, spending time with nursing staff every day rather than her own daughter. You could be there too, living five minutes away, being with her whenever you want, but instead you're here in Carralon Ridge, Sylvie. I can just about understand it for some of the others. For Griff, for Bernie, Ann-Marie even, but why are you still around? Loyalty?' Ro let the question hover. 'Guilt?'

'No,' Sylvie shot back, her answer quick.

'Are you sure? Because you don't have to have done something to feel guilty. Could just as easily be what you haven't done. Something you should've. Look around –' Ro waved a hand towards the rest of the room and she knew they could both see it for what it was: an empty vessel now, missing the people and music and laughter that had placed it right at the heart of the community. Sylvie continued fiddling with the key but her eyes dropped to the page of notes on the counter.

'Sylvie, please. This is all coming to an end, I know you can see that too. So whatever you're carrying, now's your chance to put it down. Because this time next year there might not be anyone left to tell. Leave it here. Make it right.'

The overhead fan lifted the worn corner of the page. Ro saw Sylvie's hand fall still, the key in her fingers.

'Okay.'

Sylvie raised her eyes to meet Ro's. Something in her expression shifted and then settled.

'Okay?' Ro felt like she could barely breathe.

'For Warren. All right? For him, not for me.' Sylvie put the key down with a light tap against the wood, then she reached out and closed the notebook. 'For him, I'll tell you.'

Chapter 24

'I know why Warren killed himself.' Sylvie was very still on her side of the bar. 'I hadn't seen it coming, but when it happened, I knew why.'

Ro waited as Sylvie ducked her head and turned away, taking her time in pouring them both a fresh cup of coffee. Her hands shook a little as she placed the drinks on the counter, and it took her some effort to meet Ro's eyes.

'Go on, then.' Ro couldn't hide her impatience.

'It was partly my fault. Not entirely,' Sylvie added quickly, 'I'm not taking the whole blame, but some of it.' She watched the trees rattling outside the window for a long minute before she spoke again.

'Look, Ro, the thing is, I'd put a lot of pressure on Warren to sell the Hillary house,' she said finally, her tone confessional. 'I'm not proud of it, but I did. Right from the start, back when the mine made their first offer. It was really good money. Excellent money actually, and I thought he should take it.' She gave a small, humourless laugh. 'No. More than that. I thought he was being a bloody fool for not taking it.'

Sylvie studied Ro's face, as though searching for judgement. Whether she found it or not, Ro was unsure.

'My mum's not well now, but her health hasn't been good for a long time.' Sylvie dropped her attention back to the counter and picked up the key again. She closed her fist around it, gripping it in such a way that the metal must have been biting into her palm. 'I'd finally convinced her to sell her place in Melbourne and move up here, which took some doing, I can tell you. But she'd agreed, in the end. She was going to come to Carralon, be closer to me and Warren, but five minutes after the sale was finalised, she had a fall and ended up in hospital, caught pneumonia and that was pretty much it. Health's been downhill ever since. By the time she got up here she wasn't well enough to live with us, and the care home in Blenheim was the closest place I could find with the facilities to take her.' Sylvie's face creased. 'Financially it was a bit of a strain, but emotionally it was worse, for me and her. I'd dragged her up here to be close, but now she was stuck out there all on her own. Without me, without her friends or anyone she knew. But Warren and I both had all our property and income and finances kind of tied up here in town, so it wasn't that easy to untangle it. And then, suddenly –'

Ro knew what was coming. She'd seen that conflicted relief in many other faces.

'Lentzer offered to buy Warren's place.' Sylvie made a small noise of disbelief. 'For so much, Ro. Way more than it was worth. Back when they were making those silly money offers, you remember? Well, he got one. They wanted all that land on the western side and with him positioned where he was, I think they saw his place as the first domino to knock down.'

'But Warren wouldn't sell,' Ro said quietly.

'No. He wouldn't.' Sylvie's expression grew harder as she thought back. A lifeline, tossed out and then yanked away. 'My mum was in a care home an hour away, alone, chronically unwell, and we'd been given this chance and Warren wouldn't bloody take it. I wanted us to sell all our assets – both of us, right? Not just him – and pile it together, move to Blenheim. Buy somewhere really nice, maybe with a little annex or something so people could visit and stay over for a night or two. Mum, obviously, I hoped, but also his family. You and Griff, Damien, whoever. His mates. And we'd have some security knowing we could help Mum cover the costs of staying in that decent nursing home if we had to. So it was peace of mind as well.'

'Warren said no to that?' Ro was familiar with Warren's stubbornness, and she felt a pang of sympathy for the woman opposite. Sylvie had presented Warren with a decent offer for the future.

'Wouldn't consider it. Wouldn't even discuss it. And honestly, Ro, that hurt. Warren liked my mum, and he loved me. I know he did. But it felt like he was *always* putting this bloody town first.' Sylvie slapped her palm on the counter, old frustrations ringing out against the scratched woodwork. 'As though some bricks and mortar and grass and dirt were more important to him than what we had together.'

Tears sprang to her eyes and she swiped at them angrily.

'And I know it wasn't an easy choice for him, I understood that. Really. But I wanted the new start for him as well as me. Set up our future together. I liked it here in Carralon myself, a lot. I could see why it was all so important to him, but it was also really bloody clear that it was crumbling away, month on month, and I told him that, you know? I said: "You can't cling on to something that's . . ."' Sylvie made an empty grasping motion, clutching thin air. 'What we could have had in Blenheim wouldn't be exactly the same, but it would have been good and it would have been real and it would have been us facing forward instead of looking back and I still believe that. Warren always said it was loyalty keeping him here but to me it felt so *selfish*. Or . . .' Sylvie considered, frowning. 'Maybe that's not quite right.'

'Misplaced?' Ro offered, and she nodded.

'That's probably closer. It was like this loyalty he kept going on about was to concrete and wood. Not to me, or our relationship, which actually meant something. He was so determined to stand by his neighbours, but those people weren't his partner of six years. They liked him, but they didn't love him like I did. I said that I thought a lot of them would sell to Lentzer eventually, and I ended up being right about that, too. I told him that at the time, but he said I hadn't grown up here, didn't have the ties he had so I wouldn't understand.'

Ro thought about Ann-Marie clearing ivy from windows she could barely see through, and Noel gathering mementos like a magpie for the Last Chance Saloon, and even Griff, toiling away in a watered-down version of the job he used to relish while he lived in a house he'd once owned.

'The ties here are very tight,' Ro murmured, and she could tell from Sylvie's expression that they understood each other on that point at least.

'Yeah, they are. We never argued much, me and Warren. We were never that kind of couple. We got along well,' Sylvie said, a cloud crossing her face. 'But I'll be honest, Ro, we argued a lot about whether to sell or not. He told me not to talk about it to anyone else, not to tell them I was even willing to consider it.' She fell silent for a moment. 'I agreed with him about that, actually. I felt very strongly that we – he, really – should take the money, but to be honest I was also a bit scared what everyone would think of me if they knew that's what I wanted to do.'

She tapped the key gently against the countertop as she looked up at Ro.

'It all seems silly now,' Sylvie said. 'Don't you think? I mean, everyone has sold now, haven't they? Ann-Marie. Or her ex, I suppose. The Murphys. The Hewetts. All these people you thought never would. Not Heather and Noel, obviously, but Bernie, who used to sit in here and cry into his beer and swear he'd hold out. In the end, even you and Griff –' She caught herself. 'Sorry, I didn't mean . . .'

'It's all right,' Ro said, truthfully. 'I never thought we'd sell either. Things change, I suppose.'

'Yeah, they do. It didn't seem like they would back then, though, did it? The atmosphere around here was so bad. Felt like a real witch-hunt. Everyone whispering about each other, accusing them of talking to the mine, or secretly planning to sell. You remember what it was like.'

It wasn't a question but Sylvie looked to Ro for confirmation and seemed relieved when she nodded.

'It was a bad time,' Ro agreed. 'Everyone was under pressure.'

'And I wasn't the only one who quietly wanted to sell.' Sylvie leaned in, suddenly insistent. 'I know that for a fact, because I was in here every night, listening to the chatter and the gossip, hearing who was saying what. Watching the looks on their faces. There were plenty of people tempted, not just me.'

Ro knew that was also true. The temptation had been there and it had been strong. She and Griff had had their own covert discussions in the privacy of their kitchen after the kids had gone to bed. It had simply been fortunate that as a couple they'd been on the same page, at that time at least.

'Anyway.' Sylvie sighed. 'For a long time, I was so angry with

Warren. Hurt as well. Looking back, I can see he was under a lot of stress. I'm sure he was depressed . . .'

Ro nodded, as much to herself as anything. Warren hadn't been in a good place, and he'd been far from the only one struggling that year.

'But I couldn't make him sell.' Sylvie's voice was flat. 'We weren't married on paper, it wasn't legally my property, so I couldn't force him. And I didn't want to. I wanted him to realise himself how important it was to me, and what it would mean for us both. I hoped he'd eventually reach that decision on his own. So when I moved out of the Hillary house,' a faint look of disbelief crossed her face, 'I really thought it would only be temporary. It was my stupid way of trying to show him, you know? He chose the house and the neighbours and the town over me, so fine, how did he like it? But it was petty and I regret it.' Her mouth pressed into a tight, thin line. 'I was upset with him and I felt let down, but I really thought that we'd probably work it out. And I thought he knew that too. That we were just giving each other some space.'

Sylvie hesitated for so long that Ro was afraid she wouldn't go on. Outside, the wind had tired, falling quiet enough that she could hear the cracks as the building shifted and settled around them.

'On Warren's last day, that afternoon, he stopped by to see me here at the pub.' Sylvie's eyes remained down. 'I'd had a bad morning, had another worrying call from the nurses about Mum, so I wasn't feeling too happy with Warren at all. Especially showing up unannounced.' She fiddled with her rings, sliding the largest one up over the knuckle and back. 'I wouldn't talk to him. Told him I was too busy. And look, I probably was, but if he'd caught me on another day I might've made the time. He asked if he could call later and I said no, because I'd be working, but he reckoned it was important. In the end, I told him he could give me a call on my break that night, which he did. But . . .' Sylvie fell silent once again, for far longer this time. 'Look, I told the police when they asked that we'd had words about the house and finances and things, but it was worse than that. We argued, quite badly. Left things on a really unpleasant note. And, yeah . . .' She jammed the ring she'd been turning back onto her finger. 'That was the last time we spoke to each other, and then that night he killed himself.'

She reached over the counter, turning Sam's notebook to face her. She opened it and flicked through the pages until she found the right place, then stared at her name for a long time.

'I never told anyone the details of that last conversation with Warren. Mostly because I was ashamed of myself, and how I spoke to him. But also because I thought he'd probably rather people didn't know.'

Ro watched as Sylvie ran a finger over the handwritten words, lightly tracing the question mark before she spoke again.

'Then Sam came along three years later.' Sylvie raised her eyes at last and met Ro's. 'Chatting to me about all kinds of things for his project. My work here, the town, the changes I'd seen.' There was a long pause, then she drew breath. 'The thing is, Ro, he knew. Sam knew what Warren and I had talked about on that last night.'

'Sorry?' Ro suddenly found herself scrambling to catch up. 'Sam knew?'

'Yeah. Somehow. When I'd thought no-one did.'

Ro felt like she could hardly breathe. 'What exactly did Sam know, Sylvie?'

'That Warren had changed his mind. That he'd told me he'd sell the house for me.'

Chapter 25

'Is Sylvie even telling the truth?'

Ro could hear Griff's confusion down the phone line mirroring her own. She was outside in the street, the weak tail end of the morning's wind breathing its last over her skin. She leaned against the wall of the old bank, near to where the cash-point used to be, and watched the pub on the other side of the crossroads. No movement was visible inside but she knew Sylvie was still in there. Ro had sat at the bar talking with her for a further forty minutes until the other woman's phone had rung, chiming shrilly from her bag.

Sylvie had checked the screen. 'Sorry, Ro. I have to get this. It's one of Mum's nurses.'

Ro's thoughts already clamouring, she'd gathered her things and let herself out, certain she could sense Sylvie's gaze following her through the window. Ro had ignored her car and instead crossed the road, feeling the need to put some distance between herself and the pub before she called Griff.

'For what it's worth,' Ro said. 'It seemed like she was being honest.'

'About Warren deciding to sell? Or Sam knowing about it?'

'Both, actually.' Beneath Griff's silence on the other end of the line Ro could hear the creak and rustle of the trees and the distant whirring of the mine. It was probably louder for him, high up on the ridge, than for her surrounded by empty buildings on the ground.

'Warren hadn't said anything to you about changing his mind, I'm guessing,' she said, but she already knew he wouldn't have. Back then, Griff would have confided in her immediately.

'No.' He hesitated. 'But I'd been so busy in that last week before Warren died. You as well. Helping organise your dad's funeral, getting the kids ready to go to Sydney. I'd hardly spoken to Warren.' He paused. 'I know he really missed Sylvie, though. He had since she moved out. Was keen to make things up with her, he'd told me that. So . . .' Griff was quiet again for a minute. 'If he'd decided selling the place was what it would take to put things right between them, I could believe he might do it for her, yeah.'

Ro turned to look up at the distant ridge. 'I keep thinking about how he tried to call you and Damien on that last night, before he got hold of Sylvie.' Her eyes moved over the bushland until she found the break in the trees. Once again, she could see no sign of Griff. 'I'd always thought he'd wanted to speak to you three because he was feeling low and you were his family. But if he'd changed his mind about selling, you're also the three people he would call first.'

Griff said nothing, then drew a breath. 'Tell me again what Sylvie reckons Warren said.'

Ro had sat across the bar from Sylvie for a long stretch, both staring at each other in silence as they listened to the wind's dying gasps. Ro's head had been physically aching, mimicking the early onset of a migraine as she tried in vain to slot strange new pieces of information into memories that had long since been set firm and rigid. There was no give left in them after so many years, and Ro sensed they couldn't be bent without breaking. The old and the new crowded uneasily together in her head, their mismatched edges clashing.

'So Warren was really willing to sell the Hillary house?' she'd said finally, and from the other side of the counter, Sylvie had nodded.

'Yes. He called me on my break, like he'd said he would.' Sylvie had not looked away this time. 'I asked what he wanted and he said he missed me. And he'd been thinking, and he'd decided he'd rather be with me and without the house, than be in the house without me.'

Sylvie had paused, a funny look on her face. 'That's exactly what he said, those words. Because I've thought about them a lot, since. And hearing them back, it sounds quite lovely and romantic but at the time . . .' She shook her head, and the look darkened. 'I was really pissed off with him. Furious, actually, because I'd felt that way about him all along. I'd always known our relationship was worth more than some house, even if he hadn't. So finally – *months* later – he reaches this conclusion himself and, I mean, what did he expect me to say? I wasn't *grateful*. The whole thing felt a day late, a dollar short. The damage between us was already done. And it wasn't even about the money.' Sylvie tapped a finger firmly on the bar as she said the last word, emphasising the point. 'Whatever anyone might think, it really wasn't. But I also knew that in the time he'd taken to decide, Lentzer had dropped its offer by a lot. The silly money was well off the table by then and they'd gone back to offering people what the places were actually worth, or a lot less, usually. A fraction of what he could've got for it at the start, anyway.'

'So what did you say to him?' Ro asked.

'I was so angry, you know? And frustrated. I definitely wasn't relieved or happy, or whatever he'd bloody expected me to be. I'd been telling him all this for ages, and then I'd had that upsetting call from the nurse about my mum that morning, so I was absolutely fed up with the whole thing. It felt like it had taken so bloody long for him to come around, I couldn't celebrate him suddenly changing his mind. So we argued.' Sylvie reached under the counter and grabbed a bottle of cleaning fluid. She dampened a cloth and swiped at an invisible stain on the wood. 'Or *I* did, anyway. Told him it was too late, I didn't care what he did anymore. He said he was going to sell anyway, because he'd realised I was right, and I told him not to bother me with promises. I had enough on my plate trying to look after Mum, I'd believe him when it was done, that kind of thing.

'We went on a bit like that, and Warren —' She ran the cloth slowly along the counter. 'He didn't say much, actually. Didn't push back, kept saying he understood, that he was sorry. He was disappointed, I could tell. But I was disappointed in him too.' Sylvie stopped cleaning at that, her eyes moving to the windows as she thought back. 'I woke up the next morning feeling different, though. A bit better about the idea, I suppose. Decided I'd go and see him later, after the bottle deliveries, so we could talk properly, in person. But . . .' She tossed the cloth down and dragged both hands over her face. 'The police called before I had a chance. Told me he'd been found in the quarry.'

Outside now in the late-morning sun, Ro shifted against the wall of the bank, her eyes still on the pub as she listened to Griff's silence on the other end of the phone. Finally, he spoke.

'Sylvie told me that when Warren called her on that last night,' he said, 'they'd talked a bit about their joint finances, a bit about her mum's care arrangements.' He sounded sad as much as anything. 'The usual stuff they disagreed about.'

Ro nodded. 'She told the police the same, she says. Felt ashamed that she was so hard on him.'

'She never said anything to me about Warren offering to sell though, definitely not.' Griff sounded upset at the thought.

'No.' Ro kept her eyes on the pub. She could see Sylvie's shadow moving behind the glass of the windows. 'Well, apparently she never told anyone.'

'You believe her on that?'

'I think I do,' Ro said, somewhat to her own surprise. 'Not just covering herself for the argument, but for Warren's sake. Things were so tense back then, we were all turning on each other. I can believe that she'd want to protect him from that. The idea of telling everyone that Warren had decided to sell out, when he wasn't here to defend himself or explain . . .' She pictured that for a minute and could sense Griff doing the same. 'I can see why she'd think in the moment that it was better to hide it.'

'I can too. But . . .' Griff's voice was incredulous. 'She reckons Sam knew?'

'Well, she says he asked her about it. Which isn't –' Ro stopped. Spun her head around.

'Isn't what?' Griff said, but Ro didn't answer because all of a sudden she was listening hard.

She stayed quiet, hearing nothing but her own light breathing, then – *there*. She held the air in her lungs, alert. There it was again. She straightened against the wall and took a few steps into the street. A distant metallic clang rang out, echoing through the still air, and then another one. The sound took her right back to the evening she had arrived.

'Ro?' Griff's voice was concerned down the phone. 'You okay?'

Another clang. The noises were closer than they had been a few days earlier, Ro could tell immediately. She could pinpoint the direction at least, and turned to the east, staring down the deserted street.

'Ro?'

'Sorry.' She dragged her thoughts back. 'Yeah, ah, I was just saying that Sam *asked* Sylvie about it, which isn't quite the same thing as knowing.'

'In what sense did he ask her, though? For his report?'

'No, I don't think so. He'd already done his main interview with her, which we knew.' Ro and Griff had over the years pieced together almost everything about Sam's movements in his final days. She kept her eyes on the empty street. 'Then he went back to see her, which we also knew, five days later –'

'Which was, when, the day before . . .?'

'Yeah, exactly, the afternoon of the day before he disappeared.'

Griff didn't reply to that, so she carried on.

'He'd interviewed her at lunchtime the first time around, when the bar was still open, and apparently he told Sylvie some of her answers had been drowned out on the recording,' Ro said. 'Which tallies with what I can see in his notes, actually, there are a few small gaps. So second time around, he's checking some general things with her, like staffing figures, footfall, and then at the end, as he's about to leave, Sylvie said he suddenly seemed a bit – well, *embarrassed* was her word; *worried* was another – and said he was sorry, but could he ask her something about Warren. She says okay. And then Sam asked her if there was any truth in the idea that Warren had told Sylvie that he'd decided to sell, so was possibly feeling guilty about that when he died.'

Griff exhaled sharply. 'Did Sylvie ask where he'd heard that?'

'Yeah, of course. And Sam said he wasn't sure, he'd spoken to so many people that week, that kind of thing –'

'She didn't believe him?'

'No, not really. But he seemed happy enough to take her word for it when she denied it. Was mainly relieved to hear it wasn't true, she told me, like he wanted to believe her over whatever else he'd heard. Sylvie said she told him that she and Warren had barely spoken in his final weeks – which was true – and Warren didn't mention anything about selling the house during their last conversation on the night he died – which wasn't true. But Sam seemed to accept that, apologised for asking, said he hoped he hadn't upset her.'

'And that was it?'

'Yeah, seems to be. He left, and then we know what happened. He came home, did some work in his room, had dinner. You two played pinball in the shed. We had his birthday the next morning, after lunch he went off to speak to Damien, and then . . . yeah. Out to the houses.'

Ro fell silent as she tried to sift through the information. She felt like a drawer in her mind had been upended, exposing all sorts of strange and unpleasant items she didn't recognise and hadn't even known were lurking in there. She could feel Griff doing the same.

'The thing is . . .' he started at last, but Ro lost his thought as she abruptly pulled the phone away from her ear, once more listening intently. The banging had started again, even louder this time. It had a different timbre from the first day, but the same quality. Frequent but uneven. A cluster of noise, then a pocket of silence. Nothing in her eyeline moved.

'Sorry, Griff.' She lifted the phone to her ear again. 'I missed that.'

'Oh, right, I was saying the thing is that whatever Sam

believed, the information itself was right. So if we're taking what Sylvie's told you at face value, how would someone else know that Warren had decided to sell?'

'The easiest answer is that he told someone himself, I suppose,' Ro said. 'But selling the Hillary house was such a big decision. He'd held out for more than a year. Who would he talk to about it before you and Damien? And Sylvie, obviously.'

'Honestly, I don't think anyone,' Griff replied. 'If it were me making that decision, besides you I'd have told him and Damien first, no question. I can't imagine Warren talking to anyone else before us. Especially as he'd only seen Damien a few days earlier and they'd had their big bust-up over that exact issue.' He fell quiet at the thought.

'It could just be gossip.' Ro shielded her eyes against the sunlight, harsh overhead now that the wind had died down and the clouds had cleared. Around her, all seemed quiet and still. She realised she'd lowered her voice a little. 'People around here love to talk about each other.'

'They do.' Griff didn't sound fully convinced and in the silence she could sense him working through something else. When he spoke again, there was a deep note of distress in his voice. 'Ro, what if – tell me if this is too paranoid.' He stopped.

'Okay,' she said, softly.

'It's just with those stains on the deck and the key and . . .' He made a noise of frustration. 'I don't know if I'm thinking straight.'

She waited. Somewhere to the east she heard another round of clanging but this time she ignored it.

'What if someone was out there that night and overheard what Warren said to Sylvie?'

Ro breathed out, her lungs tight. 'At the house with him?'

'Maybe or – I don't know.' Griff's voice was so low it was hard to hear. 'Somewhere on the property even, poking around in the dark for some reason. We know he was cooking outside, so he was probably talking on the phone outside too. Would've been easy enough for someone to hear, especially if he and Sylvie were arguing. Things getting a bit loud and heated.'

'And then . . .' Ro trailed off, unsure which long, slippery avenue of thought to follow.

'Yeah. I don't know. Then, what?' Griff paused. 'I mean, maybe nothing. Warren's had a fight with Sylvie and someone overhears, but so what? His idea to win her back hasn't worked, he's upset, Lentzer's still digging away on the other side of his fence, breathing down his neck, so he gets in his car. The rest we know.'

The line crackled between them as they both let their thoughts gather and swirl.

'Anyway,' Griff sighed. 'I should probably tell Damien all this. Do you think? As his brother.'

He tried but failed to hide the faintest note of reluctance. For reasons Ro couldn't quite crystallise, she felt inclined to agree with him. She caught herself. A long time ago, she had made the decision to trust Damien; she should trust him now.

'Yes,' she said, pushing down the memory of herself slipping the key into his door that morning. 'He deserves to –'

A voice this time. Faint beneath the banging, but she felt sure.

'Shit. Griff,' she said into the phone. 'Can you see anyone else down here?'

There was a long pause and the line went muffled, then clear again, as she heard him move high up on the ridge, bringing his binoculars to his eyes.

'No,' he said eventually. 'Can't see anyone but you.'

'What about earlier?'

'It's been pretty quiet.' He considered. 'There was Darcy's car, about half an hour ago. Probably while you were in the pub.'

'Darcy.' The young man seemed to be hovering on the periphery everywhere Ro turned these days. 'Where did he go?'

'Not too sure, he dropped out of view behind the roofline –'

'On the east road?'

'Yeah. Ro, why?' Griff sounded worried now.

'I can hear something.' She listened again but was rewarded with nothing but the creak of the old bank behind her. 'What did he do while he was here? Could you see?'

'No, but can't have been much. I lost sight of him for two minutes, maybe, if that. Next time he came into view, he was headed towards home again.'

Ro looked up towards the ridge, and this time she saw the flash of Griff's binoculars as the lenses caught the sun. He must have stepped closer to the edge, and she felt a rush of comfort at the sight.

'You can see me, can't you?' She raised a hand. 'Now?'

'Yeah, Ro. I can see you.'

'Okay, I'm going to start walking along the east road. I'm going to hang up because I need to listen, but I want you to watch me, okay? Follow me and if I drop out of sight, or you lose me, call me until I get back into view.'

'What for, though?'

'I can hear something. A banging sound. I heard it the other day as well.'

'I'll come down now and help.' The line rustled and the lens flashed; Griff was already moving.

'No.' The idea was tempting but Ro shook her head. 'It'll take you ten minutes to get here. It might have stopped by then.'

'Are you sure?' He sounded anxious. 'I can come down.'
'It's all right. Just keep me in sight, make sure I'm okay.'
A pause. 'Okay, Ro. I'm here. I'll watch out for you.'

Chapter 26

The noise continued, here then gone again, carrying Ro along the eastern arm of the crossroads until she found herself outside the medical centre where she used to work. She hung back out of sight behind the large faded signboard advising of opening hours and services that were no longer on offer, and listened. Through the papered-up windows that faced the street floated a muttered voice, followed by a snatch of a reply and a low laugh. A drumbeat of footfall. Whoever was inside was on the move.

Ro stayed where she was, picturing the familiar interior layout of the now-darkened building, and felt her phone buzzing silently in her pocket. She glanced down at the screen – Griff – then up in the direction of the ridge. She couldn't see it from where she stood, the rising bushland concealed behind the sloped angle of the roof. She was out of his sight.

Medical centre, Ro texted as the phone fell still. *Someone's inside.*

A moment passed and then the phone immediately began buzzing again, the screen lighting up with renewed urgency in her hand. She hesitated, then pressed a button to make it fall still before stepping out from behind the sign. She crept over the stretch of dead ground that formed the nature strip and moved quietly up to the window of the office that had once been her own.

Keeping low, Ro put her eye to the corner where the newspaper was peeling and waited. The gloomy room was mostly empty but Ro was instantly struck by memories. It was the small details – the position of the light switch by the door, the pattern of the faded linoleum on the floor – that sent her thoughts reeling back, and she felt an intense wave of loss. She had loved working there, she realised. She had liked her colleagues and had enjoyed the connections she'd built with her patients. Her new clinic in Sydney was fine, but she saw different faces every week. Her patients didn't know her and she rarely knew them. If asked, she'd say the work was fulfilling, and it was. But – she surveyed the familiar space – it wasn't the same.

She was so deep in thought that the flicker of a shadow in the hallway made her jump. She watched as a figure appeared in the doorway, followed a beat later by a second one. Ro peered at them both, then closed her eyes and rested her forehead on the glass for a long moment. She sighed deeply, her breath clouding the dirty pane, then straightened and pushed herself away, not bothering to keep quiet or low anymore as she pulled out her phone which was once again buzzing hot. She tapped out a second text to Griff and this time the phone fell still.

Ro considered her next move as she listened to the sounds inside and then, decided, she turned and walked around the corner of the building, searching for a way in. It didn't take long. The back door to the centre had been locked last time Ro had seen it some years earlier, but the handle now lay smashed and the door swung open freely. Ro stepped into the musty darkness of what had been the staff kitchen, the instant rush of memories so powerful she almost swayed on her feet. Most of the furniture had been sold and only a handful of fixtures remained, but as Ro looked around the miserable space, the source of the sounds she'd heard was obvious.

Loud clangs and thuds were still reverberating from deeper inside the centre and Ro followed them again, the noise masking her footsteps as she moved down the stuffy hall that felt thick with an eerie sense of déjà vu. At what had been her own clinic room, she stopped. She stayed a few paces back from the doorway, shrouded in the dim light of the hall, and watched.

Inside the room, Heather and Noel's youngest son drew a cricket bat high over his head and slammed it down with force on what used to be Ro's filing cabinet. The crash bounced off the empty walls as Kyle handed the bat to his older brother and stood back. Zach wound up for his swing and sent the bat whistling through the air, connecting hard enough to send the metal box screeching across the floor. It was Kyle's turn again, and as he primed himself to strike, Ro searched the boys' faces for any sign of exhilaration. They seemed to be tackling the destruction not with enjoyment so much as a kind of bleak determination. Kyle's second blow sent the box skittering towards the door, and they both looked up as Ro chose that as her cue to step in.

The boys' faces mirrored each other, shock morphing into something close to shame, before bravado tried and failed to kick in. The bat hung limply in Kyle's hand. Neither said a word.

'Your mum used to work out of these rooms sometimes,' Ro said, partly to herself. 'With the physio outpatient clinic.'

The boys watched her warily as she moved further into the room, examining the damage to the filing cabinet as well as the empty medicine cupboard fixed to the wall. A single plastic chair lay scattered in shards across the floor and something about its pointless destruction made her feel almost on the verge of tears.

'Do your parents know you come into town and smash up the buildings they fought for years to keep open?' she asked.

Zach looked mutinous for a moment, but then shook his head. 'No.'

Kyle stared at his feet.

'No?' Ro pictured Heather's face, lined with worry as she sat in her kitchen, and remembered Noel's quiet disappointment. They knew, to some degree, Ro felt sure. Suspected at the very least.

'What about Darcy?' she asked. 'Does he join in?'

'No,' Zach said, with more conviction this time. 'He has no idea.'

'Really? What did you tell him you needed a lift into town for?'

Kyle dropped a sheepish glance down at the bat in his hand, then to an unzipped duffel bag in the corner in which Ro could see a rugby ball.

'Darcy doesn't know,' he echoed. 'We told him we were going to the oval.'

The sports oval was now nothing more than a vast dry patch of uneven ground with broken goalposts at each end. Picturing it, Ro could almost understand why the two boys were here instead. She shook her head.

'My car's outside the pub,' she said, finally. 'Come with me. I'll drive you home.'

She saw them exchange a look and wondered fleetingly what she would do if they refused, but to her relief they sullenly picked up their sports bag and bat and trailed out after her. All the fight seemed to have deserted them. They followed Ro down the street to her car, where they meekly folded their long limbs into the passenger and back seats. The town had fallen behind them before anyone spoke again.

'Rowena? Don't tell Mum and Dad.' Zach's voice was quiet from the passenger seat. He was staring out of the window. 'Please. It'll only upset them. Dad's already not good.'

'No?' Ro glanced over, but the boy's face was turned towards the empty land flashing by.

'No. We hear him and Mum arguing about it all the time. Her telling him to see a doctor and stuff. Stop drinking.'

In the mirror, Ro could see Kyle slumped in the back seat, looking strangely young as he chewed his nails. She suspected she was being lightly manipulated but it didn't mean what Zach said wasn't true.

'And we're sorry about the damage,' Kyle muttered and then, seemingly unable to help himself, added: 'But there's nothing else to do around here.'

'I'm not disagreeing, Kyle.' Ro met his eyes in the mirror. 'But if you want to tear things apart, why don't you go out with your dad and salvage stuff for the saloon? Build something new in there. At least that's constructive.'

'Ask Dad. It's him who can't be bothered anymore.' Zach sounded aggrieved. 'When he first built that place, it was supposed to be for Darcy, and then for us as well. Mum told me. And at least Darcy got to hang out and build stuff back at the start, but now Dad can't even be bothered opening it up. Forget about working on it.'

'Well, maybe he'd get back into it if he knew you were interested,' Ro suggested but Zach shook his head.

'I doubt it. It's him who lost interest. So now it just sits there like a . . .' He hesitated. 'What's that thing called? A tribute?'

'Shrine?'

'Yeah. That's the one.'

He fell silent again and no-one spoke until they were past the hill. As the farmhouse driveway came into sight, Kyle shifted in the back seat.

'So are you going to tell Mum and Dad?'

'I don't know,' Ro said, truthfully. 'Maybe you two should, though. If you're that unhappy.'

'We have told them,' Kyle replied at the same time as Zach said: 'They already know.'

'Right.' Ro turned into the driveway. 'And what do they say?'

'Not much.' Zach gave a half-hearted shrug. 'I reckon Mum wants to get out of here too but Granddad won't leave, and Dad says we can't make him. Even though Dad probably could, if he wanted to. But it's obvious he's using it as an excuse because he doesn't really want to leave either.'

Ro wasn't sure it was obvious, but it could be true, she thought, as she pulled up outside their farmhouse. Ties within this community were complex and deep, perhaps even more so than she'd realised herself. Not that that was much help to Zach and Kyle.

The farmhouse looked quiet as Ro turned off the engine and she could sense the boys keeping a lid on their relief, wondering if they might get away with it yet. Their faces fell as she undid her seatbelt and climbed out with them.

'You can both go inside,' she said briskly, leaving them to watch as she crossed the driveway and headed around to the back of the house. She hadn't yet decided what, if anything, she would say to Heather and Noel, but as she was here she wouldn't mind having a word or two with Darcy about a few pressing matters. The shed where he'd been fixing his motorbike last time now stood open but empty so Ro carried on, scanning the surrounding grounds. She could see no sign of him.

'Heather's out with Noel. Checking the rear fence,' a distant voice called, and Ro shielded her eyes against the sun as she turned towards the east paddock. Bernie was sitting on the steps of the Last Chance Saloon, and as Ro made her way over she could see a mug of coffee on the deck and several lengths of electrical wire spooled beside his boots. He was using a lighter to strip the wire, his hands shaking a little as he heated the insulation with the flame before pulling it free with his thick, callused fingers.

'Are you okay to be doing that?' Ro couldn't help herself as she drew closer. The saloon was constructed almost entirely from wood.

Bernie gave a ghost of a smile as he glanced up, squinting into bright daylight.

'Sometimes no, but today I am. Promise. Appreciate the concern, though.'

She nodded at the wires in his hands. 'What are you working on?'

'Just preparing these for Noel. I try to help them out where I can, which isn't too much these days.' Bernie waved vaguely out towards the back of the property. 'Wind smashed something against the automatic gate, damaged the electrics. Not that having a gate really matters these days,' he added.

He motioned for her to join him and so she did, climbing the steps to the deck as he shifted along the top one to make space for her. She sat down and leaned back against the neat carved railings that Noel had installed with Darcy and Sam when they'd been – Ro tried to work it out – about ten or eleven, she guessed. The saloon door was wide open and someone looked to have swept the floor. She could see her mirror inside, winking out at them as it caught the light.

'Heather said to let some air in.' Bernie held the flame to his wire. 'Feel free to have a wander around, if you like.'

Ro shook her head. 'I'd better get going in a minute.'

'She'll be back soon, I reckon, if you want to wait.'

'It's all right.' Ro hesitated. The rumbling from the mine was softer on this side of the hill but it was now undercut by a faint pounding bass of music floating from the farmhouse. 'I was just giving the boys a lift home from town.'

Bernie's eyes flicked up at that, and he and Ro regarded each other for a moment, assessing what the other knew.

'Where were they this time?' he asked, at last.

'Medical centre.'

He nodded, resigned. 'Your old workplace.'

'Yeah.'

'I'm sorry.'

'Not your fault.'

Bernie didn't answer immediately, placing his wires in a neat pile on the deck of the saloon beside the lighter. 'Heather reckons if we lived somewhere else, the boys'd have something better to do. Maybe she's right, who knows?'

He seemed to be inviting a response but Ro weighed up the benefits before eventually opening her mouth.

'Listen, I know I'm probably speaking out of turn here, Bernie,' she said. 'But if I were still your GP, you and I would be having some serious discussions about the realities of end-of-life care. I'm not trying to put any pressure on you, but I am saying, from a medical standpoint, dying at home isn't as romantic as it sounds. It can be complicated and stressful. It can be painful, without ready access to professionals, which realistically you won't have all the way out here. I'm not trying to tell you what to do, honestly. But I would encourage you to have a clear-eyed understanding of what it involves and what you'll be asking of your family.'

'What I'm asking of them?'

'Yes.'

'Well, I haven't asked them to stay for me.' Bernie frowned down at his hands. They were still shaking slightly and he pressed his palms together until they stopped. 'If that's what you're getting at.'

'Maybe not directly, but . . .'

'You think I'm the only reason we're still here?' Bernie lifted his eyes to meet Ro's, an expression she couldn't read on his face. 'Think I wield that much power?'

'Yeah,' she held his gaze, 'I do, actually. Because your family loves you, so they'll do what they can to look after you. Because that's what families like yours do for each other. As you well know.'

'I'm not about to argue that,' he said, looking away. 'But if you think it's that simple, I reckon you're underestimating my son. Noel knows his own mind. Wouldn't you say?'

Bernie was echoing his grandsons, Ro thought. She wondered if the youngest and oldest generations in that house were more aligned than perhaps they realised.

'Noel obviously grew up here, too, same as I did,' Bernie carried on. 'And Heather. Chose to live here, work here. Get married here, buy a house here. Their connections are as strong as mine. I couldn't make them stay here if he didn't want to. Noel makes his own choices, and I reckon he'd tell you that himself.'

Bernie's words had a slight tremor and Ro wondered which of them he was trying to convince as he looked over at her. 'I've lived in Carralon Ridge my whole life.'

'I know.'

'Served the community. Loved this place. Tried my best to save it.'

'That's very true, Bernie.'

'So after everything,' a sad note crept into his voice, 'I'd say I deserve to be here at the end, wouldn't you?'

Ro took in his yellowing eyes, his unsteady hands, his sallow skin. She nodded. 'Yes. I suppose so. If it's really what you want.'

'It is.' Bernie watched her for a moment more. 'You know, I've never judged you for leaving, Ro. Some people choose to go, I understand that. Because they have their reasons. And some people choose to stay. And I think that you can understand that, too.'

The rumbling from the mine and the rhythmic thud from the house filled the air between them.

Ro nodded slowly. 'Yeah. I can understand that.' She breathed out. 'All right, well,' she pushed herself up, 'I've said my bit, so I'll leave you in peace. See you, Bernie.'

'Tomorrow, yes? At Sam's memorial,' he added, seeing her flash of confusion.

'Oh.' Ro felt herself soften a little. 'Yes. That's right. See you then.'

'And listen,' he said, 'thanks for dropping the boys back. You can leave it with me, I'll tell Noel and Heather.'

Bernie raised a hand as she turned away, leaving him alone on the steps of his family's forgotten museum. Ro was accompanied by the music pounding from the house as she made her way back around. She'd almost reached her car when she saw the two men with a motorbike beside the long gravel driveway.

Darcy must have finally got the thing working because he was sitting astride the bike with the engine idling, fiddling with a lever on the handlebars as Jacob looked on. Chatting between themselves, they didn't notice Ro and as she drew nearer, Darcy pointed to one of the dials and said something that made Jacob laugh.

Ro stopped mid-stride. The innocent exchange was absolutely nothing to concern her, she knew. She hadn't even heard
what Darcy had said and her son's old friends were fully entitled
to enjoy themselves, but the sight of them joking together sent
something bright and painful flaring in her chest. She stared
at the pair, no longer little boys or silly teenagers or awkward
young men. They were adults now. They had grown up, but just
the two of them, where there had once been three. A toxic wave
formed and rose and broke, crashing down over Ro, bathing her
in a broiling potion of fury and sharp-edged jealously and tired
suspicion and a dozen other burning elements that set her feet
moving, carrying her forward as she marched towards them.

'Hey! You two!'

Both faces turned at her voice and she caught the surprise in
their eyes. There was something else as well, though. Something
neither of them was quick enough to hide. Evasiveness, in Jacob's
case, as he immediately dropped his gaze to the ground. Darcy's
expression was different, though, carrying a hint of calculation
as he watched her approach.

It took Ro perhaps thirty steps to reach the spot where the
two men stood, and it wasn't until the final one that the words
she needed came to her. She stopped in front of them. They both
looked so *old*, with their stubble and fine lines at the corners of
their eyes, and for a briefest moment Ro allowed herself the luxury
of imagining Sam there too, ageing gradually alongside them.

'You both know what Della's been asking about.' Ro had
expected to sound angry, but the words seemed sad to her own
ears. She looked from Darcy to Jacob and back again. 'And you
also know that for either of you, Sam would tell the truth.'

They waited, clearly expecting more, but Ro could think of
nothing else she wanted to say. She couldn't tell them anything
that they didn't already know. Instead, she turned, leaving them

standing in silence. Only when she reached her car did she stop and then, in full view of the two men and not caring if they saw or knew what she was doing, she fished the key from Warren's porch out of her pocket and went straight up to the front door of Darcy's family home and put it to the lock. The metal clashed. No match. *Fine*.

Ro spun back around and pocketed the key once more before climbing into her car and starting the engine. As she sped off down the drive in a cloud of gravel and dust, she glanced in her rear-view mirror. Sam's old friends watched her the whole way.

Chapter 27

Ro found herself, without intention but also without surprise, back at the three houses.

She pulled up along the shared track, stopping exactly where Sam's car had been found, and climbed out.

She felt deflated as she leaned against her own driver's door, the last of the adrenalin that had pushed her through the morning draining away. Ro lifted her head and let her gaze wander listlessly over each of the houses in turn. All was still but even so, she thought she could sense Ann-Marie's presence. She watched the ivy cottage for a little longer, but if the woman was in there, she chose not to show herself. Eventually, Ro turned away, closing her eyes and resting against the car as the daylight filtered bright and red through her eyelids and she listened to the groaning from the mine.

It was a new rumbling – different, nearer – that made her blink alert again, and she straightened. A vehicle was thundering along the country road. Ro heard it before she could see it and as she watched, it crested the rise and came into view. A service truck from the mine, she could tell. It was still some distance away and as it drew closer, she was suddenly struck by how much time she had to make a decision about what, if anything, to do. If it had been a friend, she could have walked down to the road and waved. If it had been someone she'd wanted to avoid, she had time to conceal herself along one of the paths.

Could Sam have heard a vehicle approach that day, Ro wondered, when he was out here, where she stood now? Someone he knew, or someone he didn't? Strangers' vehicles in Carralon always tended to be a little unnerving, more and more so as the population had thinned out. Everyone knew who should be there, and quickly recognised those who perhaps shouldn't. Who might have troubled Sam? Ro tried to think. He was a young man, strong and fit. The list would be short. An aggressive mine worker, perhaps? An odd visitor with a campervan and an interest in abandoned properties? If Sam had felt at all worried or threatened, Ro thought as she watched the service truck grow nearer, he would have had plenty of time to act on it. Pull out his phone and make a call, or hide somewhere among the overgrown paddocks, or lock himself in his own car, or return to one of the houses. There was nothing to suggest he'd done any of those things, nothing to say he'd even had to consider it. The road was usually a lonely one.

The truck grew in size as it came closer and closer until it was roaring past in a rush of speed and sound that left the bushland swaying and gasping in its wake. Ro watched the vehicle with its distinctive Lentzer branding rattle away, becoming smaller again until it was out of sight, the noise fading and the quiet settling once more.

Ro turned from the road and looked back to the houses,

trying to make sense of all that she'd learned over the past
few days.

Warren had been willing to sell. According to Sylvie, at
least, if she was to be believed. Ro hadn't seen Warren at all
in the couple of weeks leading up to his death. At first she'd
been mundanely busy with work and the kids and then she had
been suddenly and wholly consumed by her father's unexpected
death. Her thoughts had not strayed to Warren even once in that
time, but Ro now made herself picture the final short stretch of
the man's life.

He had been living alone in a house he loved but with pressure mounting on him from at least three sides. Lentzer was
breathing down his neck. His brother Damien was openly telling
him to sell, while Sylvie was privately pushing for the same. Ro
wondered how many more of those all-out arguments and clan-
destine conversations had taken place in homes up and down
Carralon Ridge that year, and found her gaze drawn back to the
ivy cottage. Still no sign of Ann-Marie, but Ro remembered
her distress as her ex-husband had waged an underhand war on
the property from afar. They had disagreed about whether or
not to sell, and as a result he'd chosen to make her life difficult,
enlisting old mates to break into her sheds, move her bed while
she was on a date, hide her equipment.

Sam had interviewed a lot of different people and they had
said a lot of different things, Ro thought now, but a recur-
ring theme had been an appreciation for the way people in this
town supported each other. And that was true in some ways,
she knew. She'd experienced it herself many times; a warm,
golden glow in the form of friendship and grassroots sports for
the kids, and community fundraisers and neighbourly chats
in the streets and the comfort of recognising a friendly face in
the shop or the pub. When Ro herself was tucked up in its

embrace, she'd felt like she was part of something that made life better for everyone.

But that embrace could only ever stretch so far and its reach had never been limitless. Because a community wasn't a single living, breathing organism that thought and acted as one. It was made up of flawed individuals, Ro knew as she pushed herself away from her car now and opened the driver's door. Individuals with their own hopes and beliefs and bank balances and family structures, all trying to do the best they could when faced with a difficult situation.

The fact that Sylvie had never been honest about her desire to sell the Hillary house may feel a little shameful on her part but it was far more damning of them all, Ro thought as she climbed behind the wheel. Neighbourly understanding that was only offered to those willing to toe the line wasn't real understanding at all. It was easy to be supportive when your goals aligned exactly; the challenge came when the differences emerged. In Carralon Ridge they had eventually and collectively reached a point where no-one had felt able to admit they were tempted to sell, even if it was clearly the right thing for them to do. The issue had become so black and white, so ingrained with a sense of honour – sell out or stay – that people felt they couldn't be honest with each other. And that was everyone's fault, Ro thought angrily; both those who had sold and those who had stayed. The divisions it created had caused trouble for them all.

Look at Zach and Kyle, Ro thought as she fired up the engine with an unexpected surge of pity for the two boys. Stuck out here, alone and isolated, with no friends and nothing to do, while their parents and grandfather grappled with their principles. It had been bad enough for teenagers in the town when Sam and Della were that age, let alone now. It was no wonder those two teenage boys were so bored that they were –

Ro stopped, her hands still on the steering wheel. She sat where she was, listening to the engine ticking over as she followed the thought, and to her surprise she found it connected to another. The ideas wound together loosely, inviting her to consider two things she'd assumed were separate as one. Ro stared through the streaked windshield, looking at the three houses as her thoughts wandered towards them all, through the interiors and out again, then moving over the paddocks and all the way across town, back to Ro and Griff's own house and their sheds packed full of stuff.

Ro didn't move for a drawn-out minute, letting a realisation spike and settle before at last taking the wheel once more. Slowly, she turned the car around on the track and drove back to the road. Deep in thought, she edged the nose of the car out, checking along the deserted stretch before being jerked forward suddenly against her seatbelt as she slammed her foot hard on the brake. She had sensed the movement before fully registering it, and with her heart thumping loud and heavy in her chest, she peered properly through the passenger window to see what had caught her eye.

The bicycle had stopped some distance away. Thin and silent in its movement, she had not heard it approach. The cyclist stared back, looking both surprised and at the same time not to see Ro there. Her fingers found the button to wind down the window.

'Jacob.'

Astride his bike, the young man shifted his weight. 'I was on my way to see you.'

'Were you?'

He nodded, his gaze sliding away from hers to touch the houses before slinking back again.

'Yeah,' he said. 'Because I was thinking about it and you're right. Sam would've told. If it was my mum asking.' He glanced again to the ivy cottage, his expression unreadable.

'Darcy not with you?'

Jacob gave a shrug, small but strangely loaded. 'I've never been able to tell Darcy what to do. But I can explain, if you want.'

Ro regarded him for a moment. 'Does all this have anything to do with a collection of running medals?'

The look on Jacob's face was almost amusing.

'Lucky guess,' she said, getting out of the car. She opened the boot. 'Here. Put your bike in the back. We'll go to my place. Griff will want to hear this too.'

Chapter 28

Damien's car was parked outside the house when Ro pulled up, and she sensed Jacob hesitate in the passenger seat. She waited, bracing herself for an excuse, but after a moment he simply undid his seatbelt and got out, helping Ro lift his bike from the boot before following her up the porch steps and inside.

Damien was sitting with Griff at the kitchen table, both brooding silently, and with a small collection of keys scattered across the surface between them.

'Oh, Ro. You're back.' Damien's chair screeched against the floor as he made to stand when he saw her in the hall. He seemed slightly dazed and Ro glanced at Griff through the doorway, who gave her a subtle nod. He had told Damien about Sylvie's claim that Warren had offered to sell the house.

'I had another look for keys last night and found a few more to –' Damien started, stopping short as he noticed Jacob behind

268

her. He and the younger man regarded each other a little warily, so much about them echoing the other. Their noses and their chins, their heights, the spans of their shoulders, the lines their mouths formed as Jacob shifted awkwardly.

'Jacob has something he'd like to tell us,' Ro said simply, as she led the way into the kitchen, pulling out a chair for him. 'Where's Della?'

'Out the back.' Griff got up. 'I'll grab her.'

As he disappeared, Ro took a jug of water from the fridge and poured for them all, sliding a glass each in front of Damien and Jacob, who were stealing glances at each other like a pair of shy children. Damien drew a breath and Ro could tell he was still rattled by Griff's news but was doing his best to hide it.

'I –'

'Hey, listen –'

They both cut themselves short.

'Sorry.' Damien sat back in his chair. 'You go, Jacob. Please.'

'Ah. Okay.' Jacob rubbed a hand over his chin, his stubble rasping. 'I was going to say that I got your messages. And yeah. Thanks. I was planning to get back to you, I just hadn't . . .' He gave an uncertain shrug. 'Yet, I guess. I was going to, though.'

'No worries, it's all good.' Damien was effusive. 'That's totally fine. Just wanted to put the offer out there, you know. Open-ended. So, any time, if you did want to . . .' It was his turn to trail off. 'I don't know, pretty much what I said in the message, really. Coffee or a beer or whatever.'

'Yeah, no. I do. That would probably be good. Maybe we should talk after . . .' Jacob gestured towards Della as she appeared in the doorway, followed by Griff.

'Yeah.' Damien nodded. 'Afterwards.'

'All right.' Griff lowered himself into a kitchen chair. 'Go ahead, Jacob. Floor's yours, mate.'

Jacob straightened in his seat uneasily, his eyes flicking around the faces at the table before finally settling on Della.

'Sorry about the pub the other night,' he said. 'I did know what you were talking about. I just hadn't thought about any of it for ages and I hadn't expected it to come up again. Ever, really, I suppose, so . . . yeah.' He shrugged. 'You kind of caught me off guard.'

He fell silent once more and seemed to be struggling as to where to go from there. After a minute, Ro leaned in.

'Jacob, listen. Sam's not here to tell us anything, and it looks like Darcy's decided he'd rather not. But you're here, so you can believe me when I say that we appreciate it. We just want to know what you can tell us. You're not here on a playdate with Sam after school, no-one's getting into any trouble. We're all adults and we've all –' She gestured around the table. 'All of us have done things when we were younger that we wouldn't do today. So we get it, and we're grateful to you for being willing to help us understand a bit better what's happened. That's all.'

Jacob took a nervous swallow of his water then carefully placed the glass back on the table.

'All right,' he said, a note of determination creeping into his voice. 'So I know a lot of people really love Carralon, but when me and Darcy and Sam were, like, sixteen or seventeen or whatever, it honestly felt like the most bloody boring place on Earth. Okay?' He straightened in his seat. 'You all have to get that, first off. There was absolutely nothing to do here. There was hardly anyone our age around. Footy and cricket training were crap because we didn't have enough players. There were no parties, no-one else to hang out with. There were no girls, you know? Like, maybe a few, but they weren't interested in us. So it was just the three of us pretty much every day, and we were really bloody bored, all right? I need you to understand what that was like.'

Griff and Damien exchanged a knowing glance laced with sympathy.

'Well, yeah, Jacob mate, we both grew up here too,' Damien said. 'It's quiet, we all know that. Don't worry.'

'Worse, though, for me and Jacob,' Della said out of the blue, and even Jacob blinked in surprise. 'For the kids around our age, I mean. I'm not trying to compete or anything, but when you grew up here – Dad, Damien – it obviously *was* different. More people around, a lot more going on. You have enough happy memories of this place that you were willing to fight to save it. Same with Ann-Marie and Darcy's folks and the Hewetts and all those others.' She shrugged and looked to Jacob. 'I'd be surprised if anyone our age felt that way. With the mine causing so much stress and people constantly leaving and everything shutting down, they weren't exactly golden days for us, you know?'

'Yes.' Jacob was nodding, relieved to have found an unexpected ally. 'Exactly. Della's exactly right.'

Having said her piece, Della sat back and waved for Jacob to continue.

'So, okay, when we were about sixteen, Darcy – I mean, look, it was Darcy's idea, but to be fair it was all of us, me and Sam as well – we started doing these stupid . . .' Jacob sighed. 'I don't know. Jokes on people. Dares. Whatever you want to call them. It was only small stuff at first. Like if someone had left a bit of equipment out, we'd move it. Maybe hide it. Not so they wouldn't find it, but enough to be annoying. For fun, I suppose.' He said it without humour, a faint frown on his face as he thought back.

'And you did this to Warren?' Ro prompted.

'Yeah, but not so much at first. At the start, we were doing it to anyone. People in town. Darcy's parents.' Jacob gestured across the table. 'Sometimes you guys, actually.'

'Wait. That thing with all the wheelbarrows?' Griff inter-jected suddenly, and Jacob nodded a little nervously.

'Hmm.' Griff sat back and said nothing more, simply stroking his chin thoughtfully, clearly replaying some past incident in light of this fresh knowledge.

'Anyway . . .' Jacob paused a moment to see if anything more was to be said about alleged wheelbarrow infringements, but Griff made a *carry-on* gesture. 'So we got away with the small stuff, and then – look, it was Darcy again, but we all went along with it – we ramped things up a bit. And a lot of it ended up happening at my mum's cottage and Warren's place and Bernie's, because those three houses were pretty isolated but also close to each other and we all had an excuse to be out there, so we could get away with stuff. Like, it was Darcy who took his granddad's car keys and drove his truck into town one night. But then in the morning, Bernie thought he'd gone mad and that he'd left it parked there the day before or something –'

Jacob didn't laugh, and Ro was very glad, because she had never forgotten that incident as she'd perceived it. The worried phone call from Heather, asking for her professional medical opinion. Bernie had brought himself in to the clinic not long after and they'd run a few tests, then had a downcast conversa-tion about age-related mental decline while the older man had listened, alert but anxious throughout. Not dementia, the tests had revealed, but cancer instead. The diagnosis had probably saved his life, to be fair, but those three stupid boys weren't to know that at the time. All they had done was upset an old man who didn't deserve it, and Ro felt suddenly incensed by their silly games that had had real-world consequences.

'Your mum's bed, too, no?' She fixed her eyes on Jacob, and from the look that skittered across his face she could tell he hadn't been planning to mention that one.

'Yeah.' He at least had the grace to look ashamed. 'That was us, too. She'd started seeing this bloke. I dunno, he was probably okay but I'd decided I didn't like him for whatever reason. I was pissed off with her and –' His eyes flitted towards Damien and then immediately away. 'I wasn't too happy with my dad for a few years there, for leaving us and being a bit of a dickhead in general. So, yeah, when Mum went out with this bloke for a night, I was sleeping over here at Sam's . . .' He tried to meet Ro's firm gaze but failed. 'And after everyone had gone to bed, me and Sam rode our bikes back to my place, met Darcy. And we carried Mum's bed and mattress and everything out into the paddock, just dumped it there.'

'But what was the point?' Griff was staring at Jacob like he was struggling to understand. 'What was she supposed to think?'

'That my dad had got some of his mates to do it and blame him.' Jacob looked down at the scratched surface of the table. 'Which she did. But when Mum first saw her stuff all out there on the ground, she was so upset. She cried.' He fell silent again, for longer this time. 'And I hadn't really thought that far ahead, weirdly. To how she'd feel herself. And then she was so angry with Dad, which was what I'd thought I wanted but I actually just felt bad for making things worse between them. They were calling each other liars, talking about getting lawyers involved and things and honestly, I felt really sorry for my mum. She was so sad about it, and all she'd been trying to do was go out and have a nice night, so . . .' He gave an almost imperceptible shake of his head. 'Anyway, I told Sam and Darcy we had to stop doing stuff to her. That had to be the last time.'

Ro looked at him. 'And what did they say?'

'Yeah, they agreed, actually. But then we all kind of wanted to leave Bernie alone as well, obviously, because it felt like that had gone a bit too far with the whole car thing and we'd found out by then that he really wasn't very well. So, the smart thing to do would have been to stop completely, but . . .' He reached for his water glass and took a gulp, his throat moving as he swallowed. 'We were dumb and bored. So we carried on but Warren ended up bearing the brunt of it, kind of by default. We dropped the big stuff, though,' he said with a hint of desperation. 'Went back to the silly things.'

'Making his tools go missing?' Griff said sharply, once again seeming to have a specific incident in mind.

'Yeah, that, and there was some other stuff too. We'd move things around a bit, not much, but enough that he might not notice but would feel something was wrong. I realised I had the same kind of TV remote as him, so we'd hide outside and turn his TV on and off while he was watching, or sometimes go over and switch it on loudly in the night.'

'What about the old sports medals?' Ro asked.

'Whose medals?' cut in Damien, who had been listening quietly from across the table. 'Do you mean Dad's?'

Ro nodded. 'From his collection. We found a few of them in a box of Sam's things in the shed. That was part of it, wasn't it?' She turned back to Jacob.

'Yeah, but look, that really was Darcy. He was taking them one at a time, seeing how many he could get before it was noticed. We didn't even know he was doing it and Sam was pissed off when he found out. He and Darcy had words, Sam saying the medals meant a lot to Warren because they'd belonged to his dad. He told Darcy to hand them over, which Darcy did, to be fair. Sam was going to put them back, but he didn't get a chance before . . .' Jacob's face tightened. 'I swear, none of us knew Warren was finding things so hard. If we'd had any idea he might kill himself, any at all, we'd *never* . . .' He couldn't look at them as he shook his head. 'I mean, we knew Warren was a bit stressed, about the mine and everything, but everyone around here was. Everyone was on edge. We targeted Warren because we honestly thought he could handle it, see it all for the stupid joke it was supposed to be. He didn't seem any more unhappy than my mum, or Darcy's parents, or you guys.' Jacob gestured again towards Griff and Ro. 'But obviously he was, and we'd made it worse for him. We could all see that afterwards. And for what it's worth, which I realise isn't much, we all felt really shit about it. And that was the end of it, completely. We never did any of that kind of stuff again, to anyone.'

Depleted from the confession, Jacob fell quiet and for a minute the only sound was the ticking of the kitchen clock. Ro glanced at Griff. He was sitting very still, his face almost a mask, but she could see him battling internally, unable to settle on a reaction. Della simply seemed disgusted. Across the table, Damien was watching Jacob closely.

'You know,' Damien finally broke the silence and they all looked over. His voice was unexpectedly mild. 'Warren used to do stuff like that.' He nodded as Jacob frowned in surprise. 'When he was younger. I did too. Him as well.' He gestured to Griff, who didn't leap to deny it.

Jacob looked from one to the other. 'Yeah?' he said, at last.

'Yeah. Not quite the same, but in a similar vein, I'd say. There was . . .' Damien drummed his fingers against the table and looked to Griff for help. 'God. I can't think. That thing with what's-his-name.'

'I don't know,' Griff said, slightly unconvincingly.

'You do, mate. The one with the tractor.'

'Kevin Kingley.'

'*Yes*.' Damien pointed at Griff, who gave a small smile despite himself. 'That's him.'

'Yeah.'

'And there was that other one we used to do with the washing lines. Yeah?' There was a hint of amusement in Damien's face now. 'And all the clothes. I know you remember that one.'

Griff leaned back in his chair. 'I do seem to remember that one.'

Damien turned to Jacob, who was watching the exchange as though unsure what he should be making of it.

'I think what I'm saying, mate –' Damien's voice had a new note. Tentatively parental. '– is that Warren knew what it was like to grow up out here. How it felt to be fed up, at a loose end and ready to make a bit of trouble. He might've been a bit pissed off to be at the receiving end this time, but you weren't wrong to think that he could take a joke for what it was. Whatever was going on with him back then, there are other people – me, for one – who have to shoulder more of the blame for that. It was a complex situation, but I know he wasn't driven to what he did by a handful of pranks because he'd been there, done that himself. Kingley's tractor was all his idea, for the record. And a lot of the other stuff too. For a while he had this habit of carving these little faces around the place, like a calling card. The mouth was a weird kind of "W" –'

'Oh,' Jacob said in surprise. 'Yeah. They're Warren's?'

He seemed to know exactly what Damien was talking about, and Ro looked at them both in mild confusion. Della also seemed mystified, but at the end of the table Ro saw something ripple through Griff. He shifted sharply in his seat, the faint nostalgic smile gone. His gaze was suddenly far away and his body unnaturally still. Ro stared, trying to read him.

'Sorry, what was Warren doing?' Della asked Damien, but Griff cut in.

'Those bloody carvings,' he said, almost as though talking to himself. 'Jesus, I haven't thought about them in *years*.'

'No.' Damien shrugged. 'Well, me neither. Probably not since –'

'You told Sam about them, though,' Griff said and then immediately stopped. He stayed silent for a beat, thinking. 'Did you?'

'I . . .? Sorry.' Damien faltered. 'What, mate?'

'Did you? Tell him?' Griff sounded unsure, then more certain. 'Yes. You did –'

'Wait. I told Sam about Warren's carvings?' Damien broke in, then paused. His face clouded with confusion. 'I'm not sure. I mean, maybe. Why?'

'You did.' Griff leaned forward, everything in him now alert. 'When Sam interviewed you on that last day,' he said with urgency. 'Damien, yes. Please, mate. Try to remember. I think you must have.'

Ro dragged her eyes away to glance at Della and Jacob. Both were watching the two men intently, seemingly as lost as she was.

'I think . . . hang on a sec.' Damien tilted his head back towards the ceiling. He covered his face with his hands as he thought for a long stretch, then lowered them again. 'Yeah, okay. So, I think Sam was asking how things used to be around here and we were talking for a fair while about my memories of growing up. What it was like being young here, the place being short on entertainment . . .' He glanced at Jacob, then back to Griff. 'We'd talked about Warren quite a bit and I knew Sam was upset about his death, of course, so I was trying to think of some lighter –'

'But nothing about this – this carving or whatever this is – was in your report,' Ro heard herself snap. She didn't know quite what they were talking about, but she knew every word of the statement that Damien had filed with the police.

'Wasn't it?' He looked across at her. It seemed like a genuine question, his face creasing as Ro shook her head. 'I mean, maybe not. It was a – God, I don't know, a throwaway comment at the time.' Damien's eyes flicked from Ro to Griff and back again. 'Sam and I were talking for, what? An hour and a half?'

He sounded worried. Whatever Griff was alluding to appeared to be dawning on Damien in real time. Ro spun her head from one to the other.

'But . . . oh my God, look,' Damien went on. 'If it's not there in the report, then I'm so sorry. Really. Griff, Ro. I tried to remember everything that seemed important, I know what you've both been through and . . .'

'It's all right, Damien.' Griff's voice was deliberately quiet and Ro could feel him keeping himself in check.

'Is it, though?' Damien sounded anxious.

'Yeah, mate. It's okay.' Griff was very still, the urgency that had been flowing through him now channelled into something else. A strange sense of calm. 'You and Sam had a long conversation. You remembered what you could. Did your best under difficult circumstances.' Griff glanced at Ro. 'We all did.'

She recognised that brand of calmness now. It was the one she utilised herself when she knew she had to share some potentially troubling news with a patient. She stared back at Griff, trying to slot together fractured pieces from the conversation in a way that made some sort of sense.

'What did these marks of Warren's look like?' she asked, desperate now for an answer.

Griff was moving, putting his palms on the table and rising to his feet.

'Come on.' He reached a hand out to Ro, then nodded to Della. 'Both of you. I'll show you.'

Chapter 29

They took Griff's truck, leaving Damien and Jacob talking quietly together at the foot of the porch. As they bumped down the driveway, Ro watched the pair in the mirror and saw Damien reach out and put a tentative hand on the younger man's shoulder. Jacob didn't pull away, and Ro turned her attention back to the road. Neither she nor Della, who was slumped in the back seat, needed to ask where they were going. They could both guess.

When they reached the fork where the track split and led to each of the three houses, Griff turned first to the right, rattling the short way along the uneven surface until they pulled up outside the stone bungalow. Bernie's place was sealed up as tight as it had been since he left, the boards still screwed firmly over the windows and doorways. As they climbed out of the car, Griff ignored the closed-off entrances and instead silently led Ro and Della along the large paving slabs that circled the outside of the house. Sam had been at the bungalow on that final day and every time Ro had been here since, she'd been able to picture the trail his boots had left in the dust, circling the exterior of the home.

'Around here,' Griff said, gesturing for Ro and Della to follow. Their own shoes marked the patio as they moved to the back of the house, past the small brick wall and the barren garden that had once offered a view so beautiful that Ro had fallen head-over-heels for this town and everything in it. When Griff reached the wooden posts that supported the rear awning, he stopped.

'I know there was one somewhere –' Griff crouched at the base of the nearest post. 'Yeah, you can see it. There.'

Ro bent to look where he was pointing, Della by her side. She could see nothing of note until all at once, right near the very bottom, she spotted it. A small circle carved into the wood. It was on the side of the post that faced neither the house nor the garden, the chosen position making it less likely to be seen by a casual glance, but it was fairly well hidden anyway. Ro would have missed it without Griff pointing it out – had missed it, clearly, all the many times she'd been here – but she could see it now, the etched lines old and dark against the greying wood. The carving was an uneven circle with two dots inside, like eyes. Below them, a mouth was created by a zigzag in the shape of a 'W'.

'Warren did this?' Ro straightened.

Griff nodded. 'Yeah, went through a phase when he was fifteen, sixteen, something like that. They're all over the place.' He nodded towards the farmhouse and then the ivy cottage. 'Now you know what to look for, you'll probably see them yourselves.'

'I've seen them.' Della ran a finger across the shape. 'Over at the Hillary house.' She glanced up at her dad for confirmation. 'There're two in the kitchen. Inside the cupboards. I never knew Warren did them, though.'

'Yep. That would've been him.' Griff moved closer to the bungalow, examining the board covering the nearest window. 'There was one on the window frame here, I'm pretty sure. Can't see it now with the board, but there's at least a couple more . . .'

They continued on around the outside, pausing for Griff to locate a carving near the drainpipe, before Della spotted one herself on the inside of the handrail by the laundry door. As they rounded the final side of the house, returning to the front of the bungalow, Griff came to a halt. Ro waited for him to pick out another carving, but when he said nothing she followed his eyes to the tracks they had left themselves along the paving stones.

'It's the same, isn't it?' Griff said flatly. 'More or less?'

Ro stood beside him and pictured the marks Sam's boots had left on those paving stones five years earlier. Their own collective trail was wider, the three sets of scuff marks creating more disturbance than just the one, but the pattern of the movement was the same. A simple circle following the outside of the house.

Ro nodded. 'Yeah. It's the same.'

They drove to the ivy cottage next. Ro could see no sign of Ann-Marie now, if she had been there at all that morning. The laundry room seemed undisturbed as Griff fumbled around for the door latch and let them in. The interior of the house was cool and pond-green as the filtered daylight flickered lazily through the vines at the windows. Ro's feet guided her across the kitchen and down the hall to the front door. Five years earlier, Sam had been able to let himself in through that door, before Ann-Marie's constant trespassing had forced the mine to change the locks. He had stood inside the entrance and, as at the stone bungalow, Ro could easily picture the pattern of his footsteps now. They showed him roaming the rooms, one at a time, seemingly wandering aimlessly through the empty home.

Griff joined Ro in the hall, and without speaking she let him guide her through the house – to a carving on a windowsill, a skirting board, a doorjamb, a cupboard – and this time she could feel it straight away. They were following Sam's trail, perhaps not exactly, but in essence. In the kitchen, she could hear Della opening and closing cupboard doors, and waited until finally, that too fell silent.

The Hillary house was crawling with carvings. They were hidden in every corner, peering out from every cranny. It seemed like suddenly there were so many that Ro could barely believe she hadn't noticed them before. She certainly couldn't unsee them now, their distinctive faces grinning out at her from their odd little hiding places.

'I don't like them,' she murmured to Griff as they wandered around the bare lounge room, their footprints once again scuffing the floorboards in a strange dance of déjà vu.

'They're a bit weirder than I remember, I have to say,' Griff admitted. 'Aged badly, probably. I don't mind them, though.' He ran a thumb over a small face looking out from the edge of the mantelpiece. 'They remind me a bit of Warren, I suppose.'

Quarter of an hour later, Ro was desperate to get back out into the fresh air, as stifling and gritty as it may be. Griff followed her onto the back verandah, where Ro was both relieved and unsettled to see that the tarp they'd used to cover the hole the day before was still in place. Its edges had curled up from the morning's high winds, and together she and Griff found a couple of extra bricks to weigh down the corners. Della had taken one look at the covered hole and turned away, walking briskly alone across the barren yard to the back fence. She stood there now, hand on a rotting post and her back to them as she stared out at the black industrial smudge in the distance.

Ro sat on the sagging top step and heard the boards creak as Griff came over. He hesitated only briefly, then lowered himself down to join her. They stayed there, side by side in silence, listening to the rumbling from the horizon and watching Della.

'Is this really all it ever was?' Ro said, and Griff glanced over. 'Sam came here that day looking for Warren's carvings? That's all?'

'I think if Damien mentioned Warren's marks to Sam while they were chatting . . .' Griff's voice was heavy. 'I mean, it sounds like Sam and the boys had all seen them around over the years – Jacob knew exactly what we were talking about, even if he didn't know they were Warren's. So Sam probably knew where to look.' He leaned forward and propped his elbows on his knees, his eyes fixed on the middle distance. 'Say Sam was still feeling guilty about what they did to Warren years earlier, and then he suddenly finds out that Warren did his own stupid stuff back in the day. Would have come as a relief, I reckon, to know that.'

Ro nodded. 'I can see him driving out here after hearing that. To the houses.'

'I can too. Take a look for himself. Make some sort of peace, or whatever.'

At the fence, Della had started walking slowly along the edge of the paddock, picking her way carefully through the long grass, the breeze whipping at the ends of her hair.

'I always thought it would mean something more than this,' Ro said. 'If we ever found out why he'd come here. Much more. I thought it would give us an answer.'

The mundanity of it infuriated her. The knowledge she had expected to be poignant and heavy with consequence felt almost unbearably cheap and flimsy. She wanted to crush it in her fist.

'We could be wrong, I suppose.' Griff sounded deflated.

'I suppose.' But a settling sensation had come over Ro as they had walked through each of the houses. Not comfortable, but not wrong. 'It feels like it fits, though.'

'Yeah, it does.'

They sat in silence for a while longer, the wind catching the edges of the tarp and snapping them softly against the boards behind them.

'So Sam came here, and then what?' Griff said, at last. 'What happened next?'

Ro shook her head. She didn't have an answer, and he'd asked the question like a man who no longer expected one. Griff leaned back heavily against the step, then glanced sideways at her.

'How are you doing over there? Are you all right?'

'I don't know.' Ro considered. 'No. I don't think so, actually. You?'

'No. Same.'

They fell quiet again, for longer this time, watching Della make her way steadily through the overgrowth, tracing the line of the property. Beyond her, there were no signs of life.

'I hate the thought of Sam being out there somewhere alone.' Griff's voice was quiet, his eyes settled on the horizon. 'I'm not all right and I don't like anything about what Carralon has become, but before – ages ago – when you asked why I still wanted to be here and how I could stay? That's why.'

Griff turned to Ro, holding her gaze.

'I was really struggling with everything, after we lost him.' He shook his head. 'And I know you were too – I do really know that – but it seemed at the time like you were coping so much better –'

'Me?' Ro was stunned.

'Yeah.' Griff was looking at her intently. 'Yes, Ro. Absolutely it seemed like that. You were so focused and efficient and very, I don't know . . .' He took his hat off and rubbed a hand through his hair. '*Useful*. Everything we needed to be doing to help Sam, you were across it. Going through all his uni notes and reading his interviews and talking to the police. You were actually doing things for him, while I was over there feeling like I was climbing a mountain just to open my eyes every morning. I was . . .' Griff's frown deepened and the silence dragged out. 'Honestly, I was ashamed, Ro. You were doing things every day to try to find out what happened to our son and I was struggling just to hold a sensible thought in my head. It was like I was stuck in a pit and I couldn't get a foothold to drag myself up.'

'Griff, I –' Ro didn't know where to begin, because that was not how she remembered it at all. When she looked back at herself at that time, she remembered a highly strung woman flitting maniacally from one pointless task to the next, cramming her days with ultimately meaningless activity in order to feel busy. Fooling herself that she was moving forward when in reality she was spinning her wheels, achieving nothing more than exhausting herself and snapping at her husband and ignoring their daughter. And the worst thing was that Ro had been aware of it at the time. She had known she was doing it and yet couldn't seem to stop, spiralling deeper and deeper, blind to herself and Griff and Della, unable to focus on anything but Sam as she scrabbled on her knees, groping at the most worthless, time-wasting busywork in the hope that that would help distract from the bone-deep pain that he was gone.

And always there, at the kitchen table or in the corner of the living room or the bed beside her, had been Griff, dark and brooding and unnervingly still. He had seemed to Ro to be much more conscious in his grief. While Ro had dashed around, barely pausing for breath, he had treated the new hole in their lives with a respect and reverence. She had envied him that. She had rushed past him every day, embarrassed by her fruitless activity, resenting his stoicism. Griff made her feel guilty for her own ineptitude and with her guilt already right at the brim, lapping over the edges, Ro had watched his behaviour and relabelled it. Griff was lazy, she had decided, and he was cold, and he lacked basic understanding and empathy. Griff could not have loved Sam the way she had, Ro had told herself fiercely. His love for Sam was inferior to her own.

She had been very wrong about that, of course, as she had realised eventually, and now Ro reached across the step and put a hand on his arm.

'I'm so sorry, Griff.'

He shifted and rested his own palm against the back of her hand.

'I'm sorry, too. I should never have given you a hard time about wanting to leave after the medical centre closed. It made sense to go then, for both of us, really.' He exhaled heavily through this nose. 'I knew it. At the time. But I couldn't do it. Because I hadn't done any of those things you did for Sam, all that work, with his notes and the police. I hadn't done enough for him, but I felt like I could do this.' He nodded out towards the silent paddocks. 'I could stay here in town. Be around, so he wouldn't be left here all on his own.'

Ro's eyes felt hot and scratchy, and she blinked hard. 'Thank you. For doing that for him. I wanted to as well. I just couldn't.'

'Jesus, Ro, no.' He rubbed her thumb with his own. 'You did plenty. More than enough.'

Griff's gaze left her and moved out towards Della, who had stopped walking and was standing at the edge of the paddock, her hands shoved in her pockets, her face turned away from the sun. A tiny smile flitted across his face as he looked at his daughter.

'Della was treating me to one of her free therapy sessions the other day,' he said. 'Telling me about how we'd just handled things differently. You and me.' He glanced at Ro. 'How no-one was right or wrong, we were both doing our best to cope with a terrible situation.'

'Yeah.' Ro felt the corners of her mouth lift slightly. 'I think I got that session too.'

Griff shifted on the step. 'I know she's unlicensed,' his face was close enough that Ro could see the flecks of gold in his eyes, 'but I thought this time she could be right.'

'Did you?'

'Yeah. I did.' He was watching her intently now, gauging her response. 'She quite often is.'

There was something in his voice that Ro had not heard in years. She opened her mouth and took a breath, still not sure what she was going to say when a rustle of movement across the yard made them both turn. Della was making her way back.

'Can we go?' Della called, her voice floating to them across the dried, dead space.

'Yes.' Ro's hand slid from Griff's as they both stood. 'Are you all right?'

'Yeah.' Della was lifting her feet high, wading through the grass. The sunlight caught the damp streak on her cheek. She had been crying. 'I just hate it here.'

Chapter 30

This time five years earlier, Ro had been asleep, but she was awake now. She sat on the bed in the hut, leaning against the headboard and watching the glowing green numbers on the digital clock edge closer to midnight. It was only minutes away and then the day would turn and it would be Sam's birthday once again.

She had been awake at this time twenty-six years earlier, as well. Lying in an anonymous hospital room in Blenheim, seven centimetres dilated and sweatily thankful for the sweet relief of the epidural, Ro had felt the vulnerability of a patient rather than the confidence of a doctor. She'd been almost tearfully grateful for the kindness of the birthing unit professionals with their scrubbed hands and squeaky shoes and reassuring comments. 'You'll be parents before the sun's up!' they'd said as Griff had hovered and tried not to get in the way, smiling obediently, if unnaturally, whenever they addressed him as 'Dad'. The professionals had known their stuff. By the time dawn broke on that day, twenty-six years ago, Sam was in Ro's arms. Small and soft and wrinkled and just over two hours old.

The green numbers on the clock flickered and rearranged themselves.

0:00

Ro got up from the bed. For want of a better destination, she went to the window, drawing up the blind so she could see out into the night. The house was dark, but in the far corner Griff's bedroom light was still on. Was he watching the clock too? she wondered.

The three of them had scattered upon returning from Warren's place that afternoon, Della disappearing into her bedroom, the five sparkling stickers spelling out her name catching the light as she closed her door. Ro had wandered over to the hut, where she'd sat, listlessly flipping through Sam's notebook before opening her computer. She wondered once again how Sam might have known about Warren's apparent intention to sell, but the answer wasn't in his notes, she felt gloomily certain as she scrolled through the familiar files. She knew what was in those pages too well. At some point as the day slipped away, she'd heard Griff venture out to the sheds and had listened to the sliding and soft thuds of boxes being rearranged. She had not got up, hadn't gone to join him.

Ro's phone had rung three times over the course of the afternoon, flashing silently from the bed. It had been Heather twice and Sylvie once. Ro had let them all go to voicemail, had not checked the messages. A little more time had passed and then Heather had texted. Ro could see the apology and her sons' names in the first line and had read no more. She would deal with it all another time. She couldn't bring herself to face it now.

Instead, she had stayed where she was and watched a harsh

slice of sunlight creep slowly across the floor. Rather than being invigorated by her new knowledge from the day, she found herself feeling disembodied and ungrounded. What few certainties she had clung to for the past few years seemed to be dissolving between her fingers and when she opened her hands to check, it was like there had never been anything solid there at all, just smoke and water. And so she had continued to sit there alone, turning pages in Sam's notebook, scrolling through yet another typed interview. Sam was gone, that was real. Ro knew that much.

She and Della and Griff had emerged from their various hiding spots for dinner. Ro and Della had boiled up an insipid pasta using sauce from a forgotten jar in the pantry, while Griff had lit the fire pit. They sat around it to eat their functional meal from bowls clutched in their hands, letting the crackle of the flames fill the lengthy gaps in conversation.

Ro looked out of the window of the hut now, her face reflected in the darkened glass. She knew she should try to sleep. It was the memorial tomorrow, and she would have to talk and raise the occasional smile and thank the handful of people for coming along. She would have to put aside her own private grief for the sake of being polite to her old friends and neighbours and the thought of that prompted a sudden surge of hot anger towards them for hijacking what had only ever been intended as a small family acknowledgement. But that was unreasonable, Ro told herself, the resentment fading almost as quickly as it had arrived. She wanted people to remember Sam, and in finding the time and will to attend their makeshift memorial, that's what the few people left in Carralon Ridge were doing.

She turned away from the window and reached once more for Sam's notebook. Ro automatically opened the cover but then clapped it closed again, dropping the book back on the bed. She simply couldn't bear the thought of being trapped in those pages for another minute and instead looked around, restless. Her eyes fell on a folded paper envelope on the bedside table, and after a moment she picked it up, turning it over in her fingers.

Sunflowers

She looked at the ten letters spelled out in Sam's childish handwriting and suddenly knew exactly what she wanted to do.

The moon was full and bright as Ro stepped out of the cabin. She had pulled on some clothes, ignoring the gently reasonable voice that advised her to wait until morning, and walked out into the night air. The garden and house lay before her, awash with a pale blue light that illuminated everything she needed to see.

Ro crept across the lawn in the direction of the sheds, stopping at the first one and easing the large door open as quietly as she could. The heavy metal hinges groaned against themselves as the door swung aside to let her in. No moonlight followed her as Ro stepped inside and she blinked against the darkness, pulling out her phone and fumbling to turn on the torch. It sprang to life and she swept the thin beam over the forgotten objects, looking for something specific.

Griff had indeed moved some things around during the day and Ro was worried for a moment she wouldn't find what she'd come for but no, wait, *there*. The box was more or less where she'd left it the other day, and now she crouched beside it and opened the cardboard lid. She held the light over the jumble of old gardening tools as she reached in, her hand closing first around Sam's small trowel. She considered it, tempted by the emotional pull, but knowing she'd likely need something more practical she put it to one side, diving back into the box until she pulled out another trowel, adult-sized this time. She gathered both tools up. Sentimentality was all well and good, but the disused ground would be tough and Ro wanted to be able to break through it at the very least.

Picking her way out of the shed, she managed to avoid the tall stacks of boxes, and quietly eased the door closed behind her. Outside, she stood for a moment under the night sky, bathed once more in the blue moonlight. So close now, Ro felt herself hesitate, and she reached into her pocket and pulled out the packet of seeds.

Her vegetable patch at the rear of the sheds had gone the way of so many other once-loved but now neglected things in Carralon Ridge. Ro knew that and she had accepted years earlier that it was long gone. It would never again be the same garden where she had pottered about with Sam and Della as children, but maybe it didn't have to be. It was still the same ground where they'd planted all those things together, putting their hands in the soil and trying to leave the space a little better than they'd found it. Ro could put her hands in that same soil now, in a place where she had been happy.

Ro shook the packet and re-counted the seeds. Ten. She would plant five in the remains of the garden here and take the other five home with her to plant in Sydney. The seeds were old and it was the wrong season, so she had no expectations for them. But Sam had collected them, and he'd labelled the enve-lope as Ro had probably instructed him to, years ago in some long-forgotten conversation. They had intended to plant them then, and so she would put them in the ground now.

Trowels in one hand and seeds in the other, Ro stepped away from the door of the shed and made her way around to the side, the moon illuminating her path. As she turned the corner and what had been her former veggie patch at last came into view, she slowed her feet and then stopped altogether, her eyes running over the space.

Ro had felt heartsick when she'd last braced herself to go and look at the plots a few years earlier, her distress acute at the sight of her raised boxes sitting dried and barren, the ground around them overgrown with weeds. The bamboo stakes that had once supported her tomato plants had blown over and the trellis for the long-gone sugar snap peas lay sagging. Ro had remembered all that vividly as she'd made her way through the dark to the garden tonight and she'd thought she'd prepared herself for whatever she would find. Seemingly not.

She stood very still in the soft glow of the moon, letting the night air flow warm and thick all around her as she stared, disbelieving.

The weeds had been cleared. The raised boxes that had stood so desolate and bare had been refilled with dense, dark earth and now overflowed with hardy native plants and succulents. They were full and healthy, Ro could see as she moved at last, wandering through the well-established greenery. This was no recent planting; spread out in front of her was at least two summers' worth of growth. The plants had been carefully chosen as well, Ro noticed for the first time as she reached out, feeling the leaves cool and soft under her fingers. They were beautiful but also tough and resilient, designed to survive and thrive all on their own. They would continue to grow here, even after everyone else had gone.

Ro walked slowly through the small garden until she reached the very centre, where she stopped again. She looked up at what she knew had to be a more recent addition. Climbing jasmine had threaded its way through the wrought iron, transforming the metal into something soft and lush, just as Ro remembered it being on that bright spring day, twenty-seven years ago at the entrance to the Hewetts' orchard. It had been beautiful then and it was beautiful now, as Ro stood in the renewed garden beneath a star-filled sky and thought about Griff as she gazed up at their wedding arch.

★

The house was settled and sleeping as Ro crossed the lawn, the light gone now from Griff's room. Still, she climbed the steps to the porch, letting herself in and stepping silently through the darkened kitchen. In the hall, she avoided the floorboards that creaked outside Della's room, careful not to wake her as she crept past, along to the next bedroom on the right. There she stopped.

Griff was awake. Ro saw him turn to her, his eyes catching the sliver of light as she opened the door and then shut it again, plunging the bedroom back into darkness. It didn't matter. She didn't need to be able to see, she knew the way. She shed her clothes as she went, leaving them in a heap on the floor as she crossed the space that was so familiar, and as she moved closer she felt like she was finding herself again, here in this room in the dark. As though the ghost of her old self, the part of Ro that remembered how to be happy, the part that had been cleaved from her in the sharpness of her grief, was right here and had been here for years, wandering through the house, desolate and frail, waiting and hoping she would come back and reclaim herself.

Ro felt it now, the past and the present colliding, together again as one as she pulled back the sheets she had chosen and climbed into the bed that was hers and felt her husband slip his arms around her. His body was so familiar it felt like her own as he drew her close.

'I'm sorry.' He was whispering. 'I'm sorry that I stayed.'

'I'm sorry that I left.' She was whispering back, reaching for him. 'You saved our arch.'

'Of course.' He put his mouth on hers and his beard was soft and he was warm and she could smell his skin, and in that moment it was like everything was once again how it had ever been. 'Yeah, Ro, of course I did.'

Chapter 31

Light was streaming through the windows when Ro woke and for a moment it could almost have been twenty years ago. She rolled over in bed towards Griff, who was staring at the ceiling with his arm behind his head. He turned to look at her.

'Hello.'

'Hello.'

He smiled, his eyes running over her face. 'Hey, I like what you've done to your hair, by the way. I've been wanting to tell you since you arrived.'

'Yeah?' Ro laughed and pushed a hand through her blended greys. 'Thanks. I can tell Della's not too keen on it. Thinks it makes me look my age.'

'Well. She's still young enough to think that's a bad thing.' Griff reached over and used his finger and thumb to gently sweep a strand away from her cheek. 'Getting older. We should all be so lucky.'

The morning light dimmed a little outside and his smile faded. Ro felt a heaviness resettle over them both.

'Jesus.' He let her hair fall from his hand. 'I hate this day.'

Ro nodded against the pillow. The anniversary that marked their son coming into their lives and leaving it again. She hated it too.

The morning passed slowly. The wind picked up and Griff left to check the view from the ridge, while Della stayed mostly in her room, venturing out only for coffee between online meetings. Ro moved aimlessly through the house, trying and failing to find something to occupy herself. She took out the small collection of extra keys Damien had brought with him the day before and compared them with the one from Warren's house, wholly unsurprised to find no match, the disappointment barely registering. She tried to avoid checking the time but found she couldn't stop herself, her eyes moving to the clock obsessively. Eventually, she took off her watch and wandered out to the revitalised garden behind the sheds, where she sat under her wedding arch and soaked up the beauty of Griff's hard work in daylight.

As the hour approached when Ro knew she had last seen Sam — when she had murmured a distracted goodbye to him, issued a vague instruction about dinner, barely turned her head as he'd walked away from her for the final time — she picked up his small childhood trowel and counted out half the sunflower seeds as she'd planned last night. She made a series of small holes in the newly rich earth and planted the seeds in a prime spot right beside the arch. Whether they grew or not, and Ro was certain they wouldn't, they could at least enjoy the warmth and the fresh air and the light.

Back in the house, she found Della floating listlessly around the kitchen. It was still a little early in the day, but they got started anyway, pulling ingredients from the cupboards and eggs from the fridge. Working mostly in silence, they beat the butter and sugar together, adding the flour and the cocoa, mixing until the batter was ready to go in the oven. It was the same chocolate cake Ro had made five years ago, the same one she and Della had somehow found themselves making on this day every year since. Ro was not entirely sure why they had started, but the gentle ritual was familiar and soothing and so they had continued.

They let the cake cool and then iced it, by which time Griff was home. He dug out the birthday candles from somewhere. They were the ones they always used but most were now half the size they'd once been, the melted wax frozen in drips down the sides. The three of them stood together in the afternoon light, watching the glow of the tiny flames. And it was only as Ro gazed at them, her thoughts deep in the past, that somewhere in a corner of her mind she felt a faint shift. She looked at the candles. Something flickered softly in response.

She waited for the thought to emerge naturally and when it didn't, she reached for it. It stayed elusive, refusing to rise to the surface. What was beckoning to her? Some sort of flame? Or light? Ro tried to coax it out. Was it a memory, something she'd seen? Or perhaps just dreamed, she couldn't be sure. Whatever it was remained beyond her, before slipping away as Della spoke.

'After three?' she said quietly, and Griff nodded. Ro allowed her thoughts to linger for a moment more, but whatever had been there slipped away, and she nodded as well.

Griff counted, and as one they leaned forward. The flames shivered under their shared breath and then disappeared, there and then gone, and as they vanished Ro made the same wish she always made. The pale grey lines of smoke wound upwards and Ro watched them until they disappeared. She turned her head towards the hallway where she had caught the last glimpse of her son, and then slowly looked back to Griff and Della. Wordlessly, they all stepped away from the table. It was time to go to the memorial.

Chapter 32

Ro had expected they would be the first to arrive, but as Griff neared the track leading to the three houses she could see several cars already parked along the verge of the country road. Ann-Marie was there too, leaning against the old gatepost, and when she saw them she straightened and raised a hand.

She had taken down her usual tight ponytail, her hair splaying out dark and glossy against her shoulders, and she had swapped her jeans for a pair of navy trousers and a linen blouse. As Griff slowed, she indicated for him to pull over into the empty space she'd been guarding.

'We kept the closest spot clear for you,' she said as he wound down his window, then looked past him and Della, her eyes settling on Ro. 'Listen, quick warning, Heather's already up there and desperate to have a word. I told her now's maybe not the time, but . . .' Ann-Marie gave a shrug of defeat. 'Just so you're not completely ambushed.'

'Thanks. Good to know,' Ro said as Ann-Marie moved back to let them park.

Heather was indeed watching out for them, Ro could see as they walked up to the fork in the track, but she was not the only one. The Buckleys, who Ro hadn't realised were still in town, were among the handful of people milling about, and she was surprised to spot David Dower, who had volunteered as a maths tutor at the school until it closed. Beside the fence stood Jacob and Darcy, close together and with their heads bowed in deep conversation. Ro had the faint impression they were arguing about something, but whatever it was, they stopped as they saw her approaching along with Della and Griff.

Heather jogged a few steps down the track to meet them, her face anxious.

'Ro, listen, I know you won't want to hear this now, and I'm very aware this isn't really appropriate, but I am so embarrassed and ashamed about the medical centre damage and –'

She sounded so upset that Ro immediately felt guilty. They had been friends since they were in their twenties. Ro should have made the effort to return Heather's calls and put her mind at rest.

'It's okay, Heather, honestly, I –'

'No! My God.' Heather's voice was high and tight. 'It's absolutely not okay. For Zach and Kyle to do something like that at all, and then put you in that position? Jesus. Finding them and having to bring them home? I'm just so sorry. And *furious*, obviously. Noel is as well. We knew they were – not *knew*, of course, don't think for a second we were happy with it, I mean –'

'Heather, it's all ri–'

'They really want to apologise. To you, in person.' Heather glanced towards her younger sons, who were loitering some distance behind her, sombrely flanked on either side by Noel and Bernie. They did look fairly regretful, if not quite as though an apology was desperately tugging at their lips. But Ro didn't want or need to hear that they were sorry. One day, the medical centre – the whole town in fact, every building, every brick, and everyone who had ever lived in it – would be gone and forgotten, and that day was closer than any of them liked to think. She felt unable to match Heather's horror at the incident. What she mostly felt was tired and sad.

'If you're willing to hear it from them,' Heather misread her silence, 'which frankly I wouldn't blame you –'

'Yes.' Ro cut her off gently. 'I mean, I'm happy to hear and accept an apology, although it's really not – but yes,' she confirmed hastily, as Heather drew breath again. 'Maybe afterwards, though.'

'Of course.' Heather nodded, relieved. 'Absolutely. Thank you, Ro. Really. Sylvie's opening the pub apparently, so we can chat – oh, here she comes.'

Ro turned to see Sylvie, dressed in her customary black, making her way up the track. Her face looked stripped and old, as though she'd been crying again, and she barely returned eye contact as Ann-Marie went over to greet her.

Ro took the opportunity to move closer to Della, who was standing on her own by the fence post where Sam's car had been found, dry-eyed and very still.

'How are you?' Ro whispered.

'Holding up. Be good to get this over with.' Della paused, her eyes drifting over the small crowd. 'I know they mean well, but . . .' She gave a tired shrug. 'I feel like this meant more when it was just you, me and Dad.'

'Yeah. I know,' Ro agreed, and she knew Griff did too. 'You sure you don't want to say anything?'

'No, not this year. Will you?'

'No.' Ro had spoken last year and the year before but had found the experience draining rather than cathartic. 'If you change your mind . . .'

'I won't,' Della replied as Griff ended his conversation with Damien and came over to join them.

'Should we get this going?' he murmured, and as they nodded he cleared his throat. 'All right,' he called, and waited a moment as the voices quietened down and faces turned his way. 'Firstly, thanks everyone for coming. We're here, as you know, to remember Sam. Everyone knows the story, so I won't go into that again, but it means a lot to me and Ro and Della that you've come along.'

The mine moaned and creaked in the distance and a gust of wind sent clothes flapping as the dust lifted around their heels.

'You know, Sam was just a great kid,' Griff started, then stopped almost immediately as his voice caught. He shoved his hands in his pockets and drew a breath as he tried again. 'Best son I could have asked for, and I know Ro would say the same. Sam was always there for Della. He made us laugh. Made us proud. All that good stuff you hope for when you have kids, he brought it all. As does Della, obviously.' He looked at his daughter, who returned his small smile. 'And Sam –'

Griff's voice cracked again.

'I mean, when I think about him now –'

He swallowed hard, the muscles in his throat and neck moving and for a minute the only sound was the far-off rumbling. Every person ignored it, simply waiting patiently for Griff to continue. The silence stretched on, the industrial groans filling the space.

'We loved Sam,' Ro heard herself saying. She put a hand on Griff's arm and sensed him relax in gratitude. She took half a step forward, raising her voice over the distant noise. 'Losing him doesn't get any easier, honestly. I'd like to tell you it does, but in some ways it's harder now than it used to be because now I worry a lot about forgetting him.'

It was a constant fear, at times keeping Ro awake at night as she stared into the dark, recounting long lists of all the things she could recall about Sam. She hated doing it, hated the way it made genuine memories feel fabricated and unreal, like a word recited so many times that it lost meaning. Usually she'd end up convinced that her list was growing shorter and that scared her more than anything, the sensation of her irreplaceable memories slipping away.

'I actually don't talk about Sam that much anymore in my day-to-day life,' Ro went on, looking at the assembled faces as she spoke. 'Hardly ever, really. Mainly because most people in my day-to-day life now never knew him. They'd sympathise, obviously, and they'd mean it, but they don't know what Sam was really like, or know all the good things that made him who he was, or how much he's missed. And I don't always like to talk about my memories of Sam now because they've started to feel a bit . . .' She considered. 'I don't know. Fragile, I suppose.'

They seemed to become more delicate every year, wearing translucent and paper-thin in places. Once vibrant and robust, they had become almost too precious to unwrap and examine, as though they might disintegrate if exposed to light and air.

'But then, being back here in Carralon, with all of you,' Ro continued, 'it actually makes my memories of Sam grow stronger again. It helps me to be around other people who knew him, and who miss him as well. You remind me of things I'd forgotten, and that makes the stories I do remember feel clearer. When I'm here, with all of you, it makes Sam feel real again.'

That was true, Ro realised as she spoke. Her child's pres-ence was woven through every tree and paddock and brick and building and it was that, as much as anything, that drew her back year after year.

'Memories of Sam are all we have now and they're so important to us,' she finished, a little self-consciously. 'So thank you for helping us keep them alive.'

There was a soft murmur of appreciation as Ro stepped back, and she wondered if she should attempt to bring things to a close there. She was surprised to feel a rustle by her side as Della moved forward.

'Thanks, Mum, and on the back of that, I actually have a memory that I think is very much worth keeping alive.' Della's eyes held a gently amused light. 'It was Sam's – I think eleventh? We'll say eleventh anyway – birthday party, which many of us will remember well as the year he talked Dad into building him a homemade waterslide. And look, I know it was agreed at the time that we'd never speak of it again . . .'

Ro heard a few soft chuckles as Della spoke. Ann–Marie clearly remembered and even Darcy raised a half-smile as Della painted a picture of a slide that had been strong but also steep enough to send the town's kids skimming across the damp lawn with only the fence and bushes to break their momentum. That had been a good birthday, Ro thought as she listened to her daughter. A good day, full stop. And they'd had so many, really. She had been lucky. Without thinking about it, she reached over and took Griff's hand, and felt him squeeze back.

She looked around the small crowd as Della spoke. Heather was focused closely on her two younger sons, watching them with a sad look on her face. The boys were not making any trouble as they listened quietly. They appeared a little bored, if anything, which wasn't surprising, Ro thought. They were far too young to remember Sam's eleventh birthday, and in fact too young to have really known him at all, other than as a friend of their older brother's.

The thought of Darcy made Ro look over to where he was standing now between his dad and his grandfather. He was frowning at the ground, but Ro felt with a sudden instinctive certainty that just a moment earlier, he'd been watching her. His eyes stayed down, and he had an odd look on his face, as though debating something. Ro stared for a minute longer, trying without success to read him.

A movement at the corner of the group pulled her gaze and she looked over reluctantly to see Sylvie attempting to tug a tissue from the pocket of her tight jeans. She was crying silently, Ro realised with a small jolt, the tears sliding down her face. She had her back firmly to the Hillary house, seemingly unable to even look at the home she'd shared with Warren. With a final wrench, the tissue emerged in tatters and Sylvie stared at the pieces, mutely distraught. Damien sidled up and subtly handed her a clean one from his own jacket which she accepted with watery, whispered thanks.

'. . . it's meant a lot to all of us over the years.' Della was wrapping up. 'So thank you, and I think my dad might want to –'

She glanced over to Griff who nodded, his face calmer and his breathing returned to normal.

'Yeah, thanks Della and Ro, and all of you. For coming along, and for the way you've supported us, been good friends to us. You don't get that in every community but we've always found it here. And however difficult the recent past has been, and I know it's been tough for everyone, we – the three of us – are grateful for that. Sam was a fantastic kid, we loved him a lot. We wish he was here with us now, but he's not, so we appreciate you all being with us instead. And with that,' he glanced at Ro and

Della, 'that's probably about it, unless anyone else has something they'd –'

'Yeah, actually, I would.'

The voice was unexpected and Ro, along with everyone else, turned to look at Darcy. He shifted his weight under their collective surprise. 'If that's okay.'

'Sure. Yeah, I . . .' Griff flicked his eyes to Ro, who gave a tiny shrug. She couldn't guess what he wanted to add either. 'Yes. Go ahead, Darcy, mate.'

'Okay, well –' he began, then immediately faltered. Ro saw Heather and Noel exchange a glance. They seemed as taken aback as anyone, and watched with uncertainty as their eldest son gathered his thoughts.

'So, look, Sam was one of my best mates for most of my life.' Darcy tried again, better this time. 'We'd grown apart a bit, after he left for uni, but he was a good bloke. And a few things have happened recently that made me kind of look back on when he was here, and then listening now to his mum – to Ro –' He gestured awkwardly in her direction. 'What she was saying about how sometimes you can forget things but then you're around people and you remember them, and . . .' Darcy's eyes moved to his parents. 'The thing is, I know that most people here, my mum and dad and granddad included, have given up a lot to try to save this place, and I know there are strong memories attached, but . . .' He rolled his tongue over his teeth, uneasy, then sighed. 'Maybe it's time to just stop.'

The silence was absolute. Darcy's parents simply stared.

'Sam was the one who really got me thinking about it,' he carried on, speaking a little faster now, as though afraid to lose momentum. 'First, when he actually left here for uni, and then again when he came back. I could see that his life was better for leaving. He didn't rub it in or anything, but it was so obvious. And honestly . . .' Darcy shrugged. 'I was a bit jealous. Because he'd actually got out. And then later, that last time Sam was here, when he was interviewing us all for his research, he asked me about it. Asked why *I* was still around –'

Ro remembered that section of the notes. Darcy had said he enjoyed working outdoors.

'– and whatever I told him, I can't even remember now, but if you want to know the real reason I stay here in Carralon, it's because I feel like I owe it to other people.' Darcy sounded a little worried now, but he didn't stop. 'Owe it to my family, I suppose. Because I know how hard you've all tried to save this place, and I know it's important to you. And I understand that. Granddad?' He met Bernie's eye. 'I really do. And I love you. But this isn't the place it was. I'm sorry, but that's the truth. And I guess what I'm asking is –' His voice took on a new note, the sadness undercut with a hint of anger. 'How long are we all going to cling on to the idea of something that's not even real anymore? I mean, come on.' Darcy nodded to his younger brothers, who were watching with their mouths slightly agape. 'They're fifteen and sixteen.'

He turned back to his mother and father.

'You get pissed off with them for messing about, but what else are they supposed to do around here? I'm asking seriously. Because they're only trying to stop themselves from going crazy on their own. And yeah, okay, smashing things up –'

Ro saw Heather's face spasm with shame, but Darcy ploughed on.

'It's not what you'd want them to do, of course not, but you can't pretend you don't understand. Can you? Because *I* understand. I remember what it was like, and Jacob does and Sam did, and I know the three of us did things that . . .' His words stumbled briefly as he glanced at Sylvie and Damien, who were watching him with interest, then slid his gaze over to the Hillary house before quickly looking away. 'We did some things we wish we hadn't. But when Sam asked me why I was still here, it was a bloody good question, and it's one maybe we could all do with asking ourselves.' Darcy sighed heavily as he turned back to his family. 'And be honest about it. Because there's no prize for being the last one out. Anyway –'

He gave his head a hard shake as though waking up from a strange dream.

'I'm sorry. I know it's a complicated situation. And I don't want to hurt anybody. Really. But seeing as I'm saying stuff, this is also probably a good time to tell you all that Jacob and I are leaving. Next month. He's got a job in Blenheim – good on you, Jacob –'

He glanced over at his friend, who gave a shy half-nod in response.

'And yeah.' Darcy shrugged. 'I'm going to go with him. And I'll just have to work something out when I get there.'

Ann-Marie looked bewildered as she dragged her eyes away from Darcy and to her son standing beside her. She looked up at Jacob for a minute, then gently placed her hand on his back. She tilted her chin up and murmured something Ro couldn't hear, but Jacob's face seemed to relax.

Across the track, Noel had not moved throughout his son's speech and his face was heavy now as he stared down at the ground. When he finally lifted his eyes, they came to rest on his father, not his son. Bernie didn't react, his own gaze fixed on his old house in the distance, but behind them both, Ro caught Heather's mouth lifting a little at the corners.

'So, yeah, that's it.' Darcy patted the fence post beside him. 'I guess I'll just finish by saying thanks, Sam, mate, for asking the question. It was a good one, worth thinking about.'

Chapter 33

Sylvie smoothed over the abrupt end to the memorial in the best way possible, by declaring the pub would be opening in ten minutes' time.

'Thank you,' Ro mouthed as she passed.

'Least I can do,' Sylvie replied with a shaky smile as she led the exodus down the track.

Ro looked over to Della, who had somehow found herself cornered near the fence by Jacob and Darcy. The pair were talking fast and seemed animated and lighter in themselves in the wake of Darcy's announcement. Their words were tumbling over each other while Della nodded vaguely, a little bewildered as she looked from one to the other. They appeared to be asking her something, and Ro could see her occasionally trying and failing to edge in an answer. Ro managed to catch her eye, and Della seized the excuse to extract herself from the conversation.

'Listen, you and Dad are definitely coming along to the pub, aren't you?' she muttered as she came over. 'Because Darcy and Jacob want to pick my brains about going to university.'

'Really?' Ro was both surprised and not.

'Yeah, they're looking at doing some courses remotely and want to chat about the workload and things.' Della shrugged. 'Not that I have a clue what a degree in land management entails, but I guess . . .'

'It's good that they're interested.'

'Yeah. They seem enthusiastic, anyway. They're driving over to the pub now and have said to jump in with them, but –' She gripped Ro's arm. 'I do not want to be stuck with them for the whole evening. I know you and Dad like to hang around here for a little while afterwards, but you'd better be on your way.'

'We will be. Won't we, Griff?' Ro said as he came over.

'What's that?'

'On our way to the pub soon. Della's going ahead.'

'Della. My beautiful, wonderful daughter.' Griff wrapped his arms around her and rested his chin on her shiny hair. 'Just for you, light of my life, I will come for a drink at the pub.'

'Yeah, okay.' Della pulled away, grinning. She nodded to Darcy and Jacob, who were waiting for her a short way along the track, then raised a hand to her parents. 'See you both there. *Soon.*'

Ro could hear the roar of cars starting up along the road and looked over to the last two people still with them.

Bernie had moved over to the fence and was staring out towards his boarded-up home. The look on his face was pure grief. Noel simply waited nearby, his arms folded across his chest.

'Are you all right, Bernie?' Ro asked gently. He opened his mouth to respond, but paused at the sound of Darcy's car completing a U-turn on the road. Ro turned to look. Della was visible in the passenger seat and a shadow that could only be Jacob was sitting in the back, his bike strapped to the roof. None of the four watching from the track said anything as they drove off.

'Maybe Darcy has a point.' Bernie was the first to speak as the noise of the engine faded away. He sounded tired.

'Well, maybe.' Noel sighed. 'Yeah. I dunno, Dad. Look, it's complicated, isn't it? And Darcy knows that too, so –'

'He's right, though. Isn't he?' Bernie turned to Noel with real sadness in his eyes. 'Should he and his brothers really have to pay for our decisions?'

Noel didn't reply and Bernie took a final look at the land that had once been his, before walking over to Ro and Griff. He seemed older than Ro had ever seen him as he stretched out a hand to them both.

'It's people like you and your family who always made this town worth fighting for.' Bernie's eyes were watery and he blinked hard. 'I'm grateful to you for that, and I am truly sorry for your dreadful loss.'

'Thank you, Bernie,' Griff said. The older man nodded and dropped his hand, then gestured to his son as he turned and began making his way slowly back to the road. Noel paused beside Ro and Griff.

'See you both at the pub?' He sounded as sad as his father.

Griff nodded. 'Yes, mate. See you down there.'

Noel looked tempted for a moment to add something more, but then closed his mouth and trudged off in his dad's wake.

Ro watched the pair until they were gone, then wandered across the empty track. It felt big and wide now everyone had left. She felt curiously unsettled, and spent a minute trying without luck to pinpoint exactly why. It was likely just the grief and the high emotion of the gathering, she knew, but this uneasiness had a slightly unusual quality. It seemed to almost hover, whisper quiet, somewhere out of sight.

'God, what a day. Hey, thanks for helping me out earlier,' Griff said, as he leaned back heavily against a fence post. 'I know you weren't planning to say anything this year.'

'No worries, it was fine. I feel better for having spoken,' Ro said truthfully. 'I think Della probably does too.'

'And Darcy, I reckon.' Griff looked faintly amused for a moment before his eyes clouded again. 'I didn't want to get into all that with Bernie, but I reckon he was right, you know? Darcy has a point.'

'You think so?'

'Yeah. Don't you?' Griff said. 'Too many of us are here for the wrong reasons. It might have been for the love of the place at the start, but for most people it hasn't been that for a long time. Looking at it now, I'm guessing Sylvie's only stayed because she feels bad about putting pressure on Warren, and Damien definitely has.' He fell quiet for a minute. 'I would've said I stayed for Sam, but it wasn't even just for him.'

'What else?' Ro asked, surprised. She ran her eyes across his face. He looked exhausted as he shrugged.

'I think I wanted to punish myself. For not having done enough to find him at the time. And for blaming you, and for standing by and letting our marriage collapse –'

'No. Griff –' she started, gently.

'No, I know.' He gave her a sad smile. 'But it's hard when I think about how much it cost me. Us, actually. I put my own shame ahead of you, ahead of Della and our family – whatever it looked like now with just the three of us.' He shook his head. 'It was the guilt pushing me, you know? To a place where I was without you, without Della. Keeping me stuck somewhere that I didn't even want to be anymore.'

Deep in Ro's mind, something shuddered as though waking up. She waited, very still, but it didn't move again. Griff was watching her, and she went to him, reaching for his hand. His fingers closed around hers, his palm warm and dry.

'Look, you did your best in a situation no-one would ever want to be in, Griff,' Ro said. 'We both did. We can't change it, but we can learn from it. Make our peace with it. Decide what to do next, I guess.'

'Yeah.' He smiled at her. 'Thanks. And you're right.'

'But listen.' Ro smiled back. 'That's a whole discussion maybe best left for another time. Because for now, in the interests of keeping on Della's good side . . .'

Griff laughed. 'The pub?'

'That's my suggestion.'

'Sounds like a plan.'

Griff let go of her hand and walked to the side of the track, to the place where they'd found Sam's car. Ro watched as he crouched, putting his palms flat on the ground and touching the place where they had stood five years earlier, in those first alarming hours when they still thought they would find their son. Ro joined him, kneeling too and placing her hands on the ground beside his.

'Goodbye, mate.' Griff ran his fingers through the dust, letting it coat his skin. 'Love you.'

Ro felt the rough warmth of the earth where Sam had stood, and let herself soak it in, her hands creating a pattern as she gently swept them across the surface. She drew a breath to say something herself, but then stopped.

The words in her head were lost as, without warning, the slippery thought she had been chasing slid out from its hiding spot. It solidified as it took on a pattern of its own, shifting and shaping itself into an image that Ro recognised, taking on colour and texture and depth. She was momentarily surprised as she gazed at it in her mind's eye.

This was not something she had dreamed or imagined or remembered from years ago. This was something she had seen for herself, recently, and thought little of. So why was she thinking of it now?

The question drifted for a moment, and as if in answer, loose thoughts began rearranging themselves, weaving together to form a different idea. It had a disquieting familiarity, and Ro sensed it had been there for days, buried somewhere below the grief and confusion and sadness. She had not been aware of it, hadn't even noticed it, but she could see it clearly now as it loomed large, casting a strange shadow over everything.

Ro stood abruptly, pushing herself up from the ground, her breath shallow. She could feel Griff watching her as she rubbed her hands together, brushing the dirt from her palms. Under his gaze, she moved quickly to the side of the track and grabbed her bag, rummaging through until she drew out her keys. With fumbling fingers, she found the only one she was looking for and pulled it free, letting the daylight catch it as it dangled from its cockatoo key ring. She turned it over in her hands, the small metal shape she and Griff had discovered, lonely and forgotten, stuck between the stained floorboards at Warren's house. Griff got to his feet and Ro moved towards him. They stood in front of each other, listening to the groaning from the mine and the howl of the wind whipping through the empty houses, and suddenly, here in the place where they had lost their son, Ro knew which door this key would open.

Chapter 34

Eight years earlier

*W*arren had been barely a minute into the conversation when it dawned on him that he'd badly misread the situation with Sylvie. He sat on his verandah in the warm night air, gazing over the darkened back paddocks of his property as he held the phone to his ear, listening to her grow angrier on the other end of the line. He had expected it, to some degree, and knew he probably deserved it. But she was also crying, which to be honest was rare for Sylvie. Warren hadn't seen that coming, and hearing it made him feel sad for her and infuriated with himself.

'Sylvie, love,' he tried again to interject, 'I'm sorry —'

She wasn't listening yet, he could tell and he fell silent once more, staring out into the night at the distant unearthly glow of the mine. Part of him — clearly the slow, naive part — had expected Sylvie would actually be happy when he'd told her of his decision. She had asked him to sell the Hillary house, and now he would. It was what she wanted,

Warren had thought, but as she blew her nose and launched into a recap of the worrying phone call she'd received from her mother's nurse that morning, he felt a trickle of fear. He'd thought making the decision itself would be the difficult part and he was well aware he'd put it off, leaving it all pretty bloody late. Too late? This was supposed to fix things.

'Yeah, Sylvie, you're right. I should've —'

She cut him off and Warren let her. He loved her. The six years since they met had been among the happiest he could remember. He hadn't even really wanted to go to that loud, overpriced resort in Bali but he'd been feeling low and had hoped a change of scenery would help. And surprise, surprise, it actually had, because from the moment he'd first clapped eyes on Sylvie in her black bikini at the swim-up bar, Warren's life had taken a sharp turn for the better. And it had stayed that way, until Lentzer moved in.

Warren watched the distant industrial light blaze on the horizon, and felt the bile churn in his gut. Unable to sit there and look at it any longer, he swapped the phone to his other hand and hauled himself up from his chair, exhaustion washing over him. It had felt like a long day, and a long year. He crossed the verandah, the boards creaking under his feet. Some of the planks were a little loose, he'd noticed lately. He'd try to get around to nailing them down next time he had a minute. Or maybe, he realised with a painful jolt, he didn't need to bother with jobs like that anymore.

He'd left the back door open and glanced inside as he passed, checking the front one hadn't blown shut. But no, he could see all the way down the hall to where the yellow front door was still propped ajar. It had been a humid, stuffy day and the evening wind had brought with it a welcome cool change. It was worth airing out the house before he went to sleep, but he'd have to shut the doors soon. Leave them open too long nowadays and the place ended up covered with coal dust in no time.

'Sylvie —' Warren sensed a break and tried again, but she'd merely been drawing breath. He picked up his spatula from the outdoor table

and checked the barbecue, turning the sausages one by one. They were nearly done; he'd have to take them off the grill in a minute or so. He'd messed up the timing with this phone call, but to be fair, he hadn't actually expected to be talking for quite so long. Another error of judgement on his part, but at least this one was repairable. For Sylvie, his dinner could wait on a plate.

Warren leaned back against the railing and reached for his beer bottle, lifting it to his mouth and taking a deep swallow, but quietly. He didn't want her to think he wasn't paying attention, because he was. He was hearing everything she was saying and to be fair, he didn't disagree.

What he should've done, he was only now realising, was insist they have this discussion in person. Face to face surely would've gone better and it would have meant more to be able to look Sylvie in the eye when he said he was sorry. But his mistake – another one – had been trying to catch her at the pub that afternoon when she wasn't expecting him. He should have arranged a time to talk, when she had an hour to sit down and have a drink and chat properly. Warren had been too impatient, though, he'd known it even at the time. He'd really wanted to tell her, though.

The decision to sell his family's house had been the most troubling of Warren's life, but he had made his choice, finally. He'd made it for Sylvie – true – but also for himself. Perhaps for better, perhaps for worse, but either way, he had picked his path and with it a weight had tumbled from his shoulders. He'd felt instantly lighter and more optimistic than he could remember feeling in a very long time. Sylvie needed to know as well, he'd thought urgently, right that very moment, with no more time to waste, and against the whisper of his better judgement, Warren had climbed into his truck and driven to the pub, keen for her, too, to experience the burden being lifted and see the future brighten before her eyes.

Sylvie had not wanted to talk to him. She'd refused to stop work, noisily dragging crates across the floor and clinking bottles. Still, Warren *had tried until eventually, realising he was getting exactly nowhere, he'd slunk away after extracting a promise from her that she'd answer her phone if he called later during her break. He'd driven home feeling flat.*

He was right to sell, he'd tried to reassure himself on the journey home, repeating the words silently under his breath. Selling was the right thing to do. But by the time he'd pulled up outside the Hillary house, the first seed of doubt had already taken root. He had gone inside, wandering through the rooms he'd lived in since he was a child, running his hand over his mother's furniture, and remembering the various improvements and repairs his father and then he himself had made over the years. Surrounded by decades' worth of memories, Warren had felt a hot pressure building behind his eyes. He was right to sell, he repeated like a silent mantra, but he could feel that his conviction had weakened. The decision continued to bubble inside him as the day wore on, taking on the uncomfortable, corrosive quality of a shameful secret and by the time evening crept in, Warren was desperate to let it out. He needed to tell someone. Say it out loud to make it real enough that he couldn't back out.

Warren would have preferred that person to be Sylvie, but as he felt the cool night change rush over him, he reminded himself there were other people he legitimately could, and perhaps should, inform of his choice.

He wrestled with the idea only briefly before he buckled and rang Damien, as both his brother and property co-owner. As Warren dialled, he imagined his brother sitting in the bar of a Sydney conference hotel. They had argued, badly, when Damien had come to visit a few days earlier, hurling harsh words at each other about this very issue until eventually Damien had grabbed the overnight bag he hadn't yet unpacked and thrown it in his car. Even as he'd begun to drive away, Warren had wondered if he should stop him. He wished now that he had tried at least.

The ring tone trilled down the line. If Damien answered, Warren decided, he would open the conversation with an apology. Damien had always been the type who not only needed to be in the right, but also enjoyed hearing it. Warren was still planning his peace offering as the call clicked through to voicemail.

Damien had not answered.

Warren kept the phone to his ear for a moment, considering. He could believe Damien was busy because he so often was. But part of Warren could also believe his brother was sitting in the hotel bar, simply watching Warren's name flash up and then disappear from the screen before signalling for the bartender to pour him another glass of red. Warren lowered the phone and hung up without leaving a message.

What was the time? Still too early to try Sylvie. Warren felt his decision churning uncomfortably in his gut and so, hoping to hear a more reliably friendly voice, he'd tapped the button to call his cousin Griff.

He remembered Ro's father's funeral the second the voicemail kicked in. Griff had been tight-faced as he'd loaded up the car last week, thanking Warren for agreeing to water Ro's garden while the family was in Berowra. Warren felt stupid for forgetting and frustration made him curt.

'Sorry. Forgot where you were. Never mind.'

He hung up again. Having tried and failed to reach both his brother and cousin, Warren sat alone on his verandah and wished he'd called neither. Eventually, though, he hauled himself up, filling the long minutes until he could ring Sylvie by tidying the kitchen and then heating the outside grill, preparing it for his dinner. By the time he had finished, he felt a little better.

Warren needed to make things right with Sylvie; that was the thing to focus on, he reminded himself. He would tell her that, openly and honestly, because among Sylvie's many good qualities was the fact that she knew Warren well enough to recognise when he was telling the truth. Sylvie was his priority and yeah, he'd lost sight of that for a while. He'd let what they had together slip away, and that had been a bad decision on his part. But he had a chance now to make a better choice, and as he listened to Sylvie, so upset on the other end of the phone line, he only hoped he was still able to put things right.

'Sylvie,' he persisted and this time she fell quiet. Warren drew in a breath of relief but then held it, catching it in his lungs. He'd heard a noise. Not down the phone. Something on his end, somewhere nearby. He released the air silently as he stared out into the night, scanning the darkened land in front of him. Nothing moved out there.

'What, Warren?' Sylvie sounded both tearful and annoyed, and it was enough to pull his full attention back to her. She was listening now. Still not ready to talk properly, he could tell, but she might at least be ready to hear him. Warren put his beer aside and moved away from the grill, walking down the verandah steps until his feet hit the earth. He stood there in the still evening, looking not at the mine or even at his land, but tilting his face upwards until he could see the thick blanket of stars above.

'I want you to know that I love you, Sylvie. And I'm so sorry. I really am. You don't have to forgive me, but I hope you do, because you were right. About the house, and everything else. It just took me a while to get there. Too long, I know that, but I got there in the end. And I know you don't fully believe me, but I've made the decision so it's going to happen. I can promise you that, Sylvie, love. I'm selling the house because it's the right thing to do for us. For me and for you. I'll call Lentzer tomorrow and accept the offer. I can let you know when it's done, if you want.'

'Why, though?' She was crying again. 'Why now?'

'Because I can't carry on like this, Sylvie, love. I miss you too much.'

For a long moment, he could hear only her breathing.

'Sylv–?'

The line went dead and it felt like a blow to the chest. Warren dropped his hand, looking at the blank screen, then squeezed his eyes shut tight for a moment. It was a noise behind him that made him flick them open again. He twisted back to look at the house, starting a little as *he realised he was no longer alone. He squinted up at the figure standing on the verandah. It was silhouetted against the bright light from the hallway and, as Warren watched, slowly lifted a hand in greeting.*

    'Your front door was wide open. Did you know?'

Chapter 35

Ro stared unseeing through the streaked car window as the familiar scenery flashed by, the three houses falling into the distance behind them. Griff's hands were clenched against the steering wheel.

It felt to Ro as though they were surrounded by nothingness on that empty road, the land stretching out in every direction. In the growing dark, listening to the sound of their breathing and the lonely rumble of the tyres, she had a creeping sensation that perhaps she and Griff really were completely alone out there. The last ones left.

Ro tried to push the thought away but it lingered, anchored by a whisper of truth. One day, soon probably, someone would be the only one still here in Carralon Ridge. And then they would leave and there would be no-one. It was only a matter of time now before the emptiness permanently swallowed the whole town, settling over it like a weighted shroud. Ro said nothing of this out loud, simply returning her gaze to the window as Griff drove on.

Neither spoke until they neared the crossroads in the centre of town, deserted as ever in both directions. There were some signs of life, though, that evening at least. Light and music were floating from the pub, creating a single oasis in the shadows.

Griff slowed the car as they approached. 'What do we do about Della?'

Ro hesitated. Through the brightly lit window, she could see their daughter at the bar, surrounded by faces she had known for years. 'I think she's better off in there.'

'I do too.'

'Is everyone still inside?'

A pause as Griff studied the scene. 'Looks like it.'

Ro nodded. 'Okay, then.'

'Yeah. Okay.'

They both kept their eyes on Della as they slid past, letting the music and light and life slip into the twilight behind them. They lapsed into silence again, until eventually the stark beams of the headlights illuminated a junction they both knew well, and there Ro heard Griff exhale softly. He said nothing as he made the turn. They had arrived.

He pulled to a stop and killed the engine. The headlights died and the evening suddenly seemed very dark outside. Ro did not move and neither did Griff. They sat side by side and looked out at the stillness.

'Jesus. Maybe I'm wrong,' Ro said, finally.

Griff glanced over to her, then back out at the night. 'Come on.' He undid his seatbelt. 'Let's find out.'

Chapter 36

Five years earlier

*S*am Crowley caught the flash of movement out of the corner of his eye and immediately wondered if he'd imagined it.

He craned his neck back, looking up as he walked the last few paces to his rental car, still waiting where he'd left it by the side of the track. He almost leant against the driver's door then immediately thought better of it, the metal searing hot after more than an hour parked in the full afternoon sun. Instead, he straightened and squinted upwards, his eyes watering a little against the brightness. The sky looked empty, but the position of the sun made it hard to see and Sam felt fairly sure the drone was out there somewhere. He watched for a moment more, the new shirt he'd received for his birthday that morning sticking uncomfortably to his back in the cloying air. Finally, he gave up and pulled the car keys from his pocket.

He glanced back towards the three houses. The tracks had been even *worse than he'd expected and Sam was glad he'd made the effort to walk rather than drive up to the properties. The thought prompted him to crouch and check the car's red paintwork again. Not great. At least by walking he'd avoided adding any more dings in the past hour, he noted grimly, so that was something. Still had to get home, though, and the roads around his parents' house were rougher every time he visited. He'd have to take it slow, but that was fine. There was still plenty of time before his birthday dinner.*

The faint noise caught his attention, a persistent high whining that Sam always associated with Darcy's drone, and once more he turned his face upwards, peering into the sky. He listened closely, but it was hard to be sure what he'd heard with the mine grumbling so loudly in the west. Still, Darcy had mentioned he might go out flying today, getting some fresh photos of the mine. He'd been vague on the details, though, maybe because he was planning to fly closer to the mine than was legal. Or possibly, Sam suspected, because he'd already invited Jacob along and Sam could tell they were more comfortable now when it was just the two of them rather than three.

Sam wasn't sure exactly when he'd realised that their trio had become a pair, but somewhat to his surprise, he'd found he wasn't bothered about it in the way he might have been a few years earlier. It was still good to catch up with them, and he was looking forward to having a few drinks with them at the pub after his family birthday meal, but the once intense friendship had gradually dissolved into something lighter and more casual. It suited Sam better, and he was fairly sure that both Darcy and Jacob felt the same.

A hot gust of wind blew over the track, hurling grit at his skin. Sam unlocked the car door and reached into the back seat, fishing out his water bottle from where it had landed in the footwell. He straightened, undoing the cap before taking a deep swallow. He grimaced. The temperature reminded him of bathwater but still he gulped it down. He hastily screwed the lid closed again before tossing it back where he'd found it because, as Sam had tilted his head back to drink, this time he had spotted the drone.

It took him a moment to find it again, shielding his eyes against the sun, but suddenly it came into sight. High up and far away now. He didn't know exactly where it was in relation to the mine but he could tell it must be close to the boundary. Probably too close, knowing Darcy, and Sam tried to work out where he and Jacob would likely be positioned. He wondered if Jacob was happy enough to be there, watching on or maybe even taking a turn of the controls himself. Or whether he was glancing around, the way he always used to, growing increasingly anxious while Darcy either ignored him or told him to relax.

Sam felt a sudden surge of gratitude that those days were behind him. Darcy and Jacob might have grown apart from Sam since he went to uni, but Sam had also grown apart from them. He let his gaze drift away from the drone and back along the track to where the three houses sat quietly in the distance, and felt the faint familiar stirring of guilt. He was sorry for every one of those stupid stunts that the three of them had carried out, and not only the ones that had impacted Warren. They had struck him as genuinely funny back then, but now Sam wasn't sure how he could ever have seen them as amusing or even acceptable. For the first time, though, Sam felt his shame diluted a little with something closer to relief.

Damien had given Sam a gift without even knowing it during their interview earlier that day. Sam hadn't seen it coming, and had almost missed it himself after he'd made the mistake of touching briefly on Damien's decision to work remotely from Carralon Ridge. Damien's monologue on the lack of opportunities for both work and leisure in the town had been typically lengthy and one-sided, and Sam had barely been listening by the time Damien had mentioned that even when he was growing up himself, he'd had to scrabble around for ways to keep busy. While Damien himself had kept productively occupied with his studies and a part-time job folding the merchandise at Greeves & Son, many others had not. Warren, for example, had mostly amused himself with a pocketknife and a spot of light vandalism.

'Wait, sorry. Those carved faces are Warren's, are they?' Sam had asked when Damien paused for breath. He knew exactly which ones Damien meant. Sam had seen them hidden here and there all around the three houses over the years. He'd always liked the fun of discovering a new one unexpectedly, spotting the tiny face grinning out at him with its zigzag mouth that Sam only now realised was in fact a letter 'W'.

'Yep, all him. Which is exactly why . . .'

Sam had tried to focus once more as Damien launched seamlessly into an explanation of how poor future planning had cost the town both in the education and business stakes. It was another twenty minutes before Sam finally managed to wrap up the interview. Dodging the Hewett grandkids on their bikes as he said goodbye to Damien on the street, Sam had climbed into his rental car and immediately driven over to the three houses.

Sam had felt bad for years about what he and Darcy and Jacob had done to Warren and the others. He didn't even like to think about it too closely, hastily re-burying the thoughts whenever they arose. But he'd made himself exhume them as he'd walked up to each of the three houses in turn, holding the memories up to the light. He wandered slowly around the outside of the sealed stone bungalow, down the green-tinged hall of the ivy cottage, and through the large, abandoned rooms of the Hillary house. In every place he saw the evidence of Warren's own low-level teenage defiance, grinning out from hidden corners and crevices.

And although Sam knew it might not be his place to forgive himself, as he stepped out of the Hillary house and back into the sun, those little carved faces seemed to all be whispering the same simple message: Bored kids do stupid stuff. Warren would have understood.

Sam stood beside his car now and lowered his face from the sky, not searching for the drone anymore, just thinking. He felt better for having come out here, and he was glad that he had. He was reaching for the driver's door when he heard a mechanical noise and he automatically glanced up again, immediately realising his mistake. The sky was clear and empty. It wasn't the drone he was hearing, it was a distant engine.

Sam turned to look along the length of the country road that stretched out in the distance in both directions from the bottom of the track. A lone car was approaching from the east, and in the moment it took the vehicle to draw a little closer, Sam had recognised it. The driver had seen him too and as Sam watched, he could make out a hand lifted in greeting behind the glare of the windshield. He raised his own hand in return.

The car began to slow. It was stopping for him, Sam realised, and with a light inwards sigh, he slammed his own door shut again, clicking the lock automatically. He made his way down the track, reaching the end as the other vehicle came to a stop. It idled for a moment in the middle of the deserted road, the engine ticking over loudly. Then the driver's window wound down and a voice called out.

'What are you up to out here?'

Sam walked over.

Chapter 37

The grinding and groaning from the mine seemed to rattle around in Ro's head as she and Griff climbed out of the car. The sound carried on the wind, hitting her in waves as they made their way together towards the door they had come for.

As it came into sight they both slowed a little, reluctant to approach, but neither stopped until they reached the threshold. Ro let her eyes run over the details, muted in the dark. She'd seen this door many times before but had never once looked at it closely. It stood before her now, plain and solid and largely unremarkable. A scratch here and there on the paintwork, a tarnished brass knocker in the centre. The doorhandle to the left, and above that, a keyhole.

It was the right type, Ro could see immediately. The right size. But that meant nothing in itself. She had tried dozens similar over the past days without success.

Still, her hands were shaking as she reached into her pocket and drew out the key. She raised it, fumbling as she placed the pieces together, and for a single glorious moment she thought that *no*, it wasn't right, and it wouldn't fit, and she had been absolutely wrong, but then Griff's hand covered hers. He held it there, his palm on her fingers, and Ro felt the heat and the weight of him, each steadying the other as together they put the key to the lock.

Metal against metal, it slipped home and turned.

The air left Ro's lungs and sparks danced in front of her eyes. In that instant she felt as though she had left herself entirely, that she wasn't really there and instead was somewhere high above, detached and distant, not seeing and not feeling as she watched this door creak open in front of her.

It was the sudden silence of the mine that brought Ro snapping back, crashing down into her body, as the distant wailing abruptly flared and then dropped clean away, leaving a sharp pocket of nothing. And in that moment, as the huge industrial beast paused for a breath, Ro heard something. A soft sound, barely audible in the tiny hiccup of quiet before the mechanical shrieking started again. But Griff had caught it too; Ro felt it in the pulse of his hand. His grip tightened against hers and together they turned away from the open door and looked back to where they had both heard the low crunch of approaching footsteps.

Chapter 38

The musty odour of the relics and artefacts that crowded every inch of the Last Chance Saloon floated around Ro as she stood in the open doorway beside Griff. They watched, unmoving, as Noel crossed the paddock towards them.

The man raised his hand, something flitting across his face as he saw the pair of them standing in the entrance to his strange museum of memories. Something cautious and low. Ro had caught it the other day too, when she'd been in here with Noel to install the mirror. She'd mistaken the look at the time for some combination of stress and regret, but it was neither of those things, she realised now. It was a careful wariness.

'G'day. Everything all right?' Noel bared his teeth in a smile as he drew near. He jerked his head back in the direction of the main house, where Ro could see a smaller, frailer figure waiting at the edge of the paddock. 'Dad was finding the pub too much, so I brought him home. Was a bit surprised to see your car, though. I mean, obviously you're always welcome, but –'

Noel's eyes landed on the key in Ro's hand, then dropped to the large key ring he was dangling in his own fist and finally to the small painted ceramic frog that concealed the spare hidden on the deck.

'No. We didn't use the spare,' Ro said, and Noel's eyes flicked back up. She held out the key that had let them inside, the metal glinting in the moonlight. 'We got in with this. We found it jammed between the boards on Warren's porch.'

Noel didn't reply, but something in his face altered a fraction as his eyes rested on the small object in her hand.

'There was old blood, mate.' Griff spoke for the first time. 'On the boards out at Warren's place.' He sounded almost hopeful, looking to Noel as though he might provide an easy explanation. Ro couldn't blame him; the two men had been friends since they were boys. 'Do you know about that?' A note of desperation crept in. 'About the blood, Noel? How it got there?'

The groaning from the mine filled the air.

'That sounds like something you should probably ask Sylvie.' Noel tried for light curiosity but fell well short.

'We already did.' Ro kept her eyes fixed on him.

Noel blinked and she could almost see his thoughts spooling out rapidly. Beyond him, at the edge of the paddock, Ro caught a shadow of movement as the figure watching them began to make his way closer.

'So now I've got a better idea, Noel,' she said, quietly. 'How about we ask your dad when he gets over here? Find out what he can tell us.' She reached above the lock she had just opened and ran her hand across the panel of blue-painted wood. 'Seeing as this is his old door.'

Chapter 39

Eight years ago

'Your front door was wide open. Did you know?'

'Yep.' *Warren looked up at Bernie silhouetted against the back doorway and supressed a sigh. He liked Bernie, broadly, but he really didn't have the energy for him right now. The man was a good neighbour to the degree that Warren considered him a friend, but he hadn't been himself lately. Quick to get riled up about something or other, and from the look on his face, tonight was no exception. Warren nodded at the back door.* 'I was airing the place out.'

He glanced at his phone screen, on the off-chance that Sylvie had had a change of heart and called back. She had not, it seemed, so Warren ran his thumb over the screen and fired off a quick text.

I'm sorry, Sylvie. Never wanted to hurt you, *he wrote.* Just want you to know that I love you.

It was only as Warren slipped the phone into his pocket that an unwelcome thought struck him. He slid his eyes towards Bernie and wondered just how long the man had been standing there.

'Anyway, what can I do for you, mate?' Warren forced a levity he did not feel into his tone. 'I've finished with your power saw, thanks again for that. It's in the shed. Do you need a lift home? I'll chuck it in the car and drive you back along the track.'

'No.' Bernie had never been a man to be easily distracted and he waved a hand impatiently. 'It's fine. Noel's out the front, on the phone to Heather about the boys, but – listen, wait a minute.' He came down the verandah steps and stopped between Warren and the shed, just close enough that out of courtesy, Warren paused. 'Forget the power saw for now. Who were you talking to?'

'When?'

'When? On the phone, mate. Just now.'

'No-one. Sylvie.'

'About what?'

'Nothing. Few bits and pieces.'

'No.' Bernie fixed on Warren so intently that he couldn't look away. 'That wasn't nothing. Not from what I heard. You were talking about this house.' His voice dropped to a whisper of disbelief. 'Are you selling, Warren, mate?'

Warren considered denying it. But the lie didn't come to him easily and the truth had been eating away at him all day and in the second it cost him to decide, the moment had come and gone.

'You are.' Bernie's tone soared abruptly. 'Aren't you? You're bloody –'

'What's up?' Noel appeared from around the side of the house, frowning distractedly at his phone. He glanced over at Warren. 'G'day. Everything all right?'

Bernie raised an accusing finger, shaking slightly as he pointed. 'He's selling.'

'No, Dad.' Noel looked up properly at that, put his phone away. His voice was weary and a touch patronising and Warren suspected they'd had this same conversation about various people in town several times already. 'Warren's not selling this place. Sorry, mate.' Noel shot him an apologetic look. 'Dad's started on this new medication which is a bit of a nightmare. Isn't it, Dad? Makes you quite —'

'Jesus, Noel. It's nothing to do with the bloody meds! He is selling. I heard him.' Bernie's insistence had an air of truth to it. 'Telling Sylvie just then on the phone.'

'No. He's not selling out.' But a note of doubt had slipped into Noel's voice as he looked to Warren for reassurance. 'You're not, are you, mate?'

Warren hesitated, and he knew instantly that that was an answer in itself. He watched the dismay creep over the two men's faces until he couldn't bear it anymore.

'Listen, come on up,' he said finally, moving past them and climbing the steps to the verandah. 'Grab a seat. You want a beer? We'll talk.'

'I don't want a bloody beer.' Bernie was right behind him, practically breathing down his neck. 'I want you to tell me to my face that I've got it wrong, and you're not selling out.'

A faint smoke was filling the air. Warren's sausages needing turning on the barbecue, he could see. He was tempted to reach out and switch the heat off but Bernie was standing between him and the grill and Warren could tell it would only make things worse if he looked like he wasn't taking this seriously. Let the food spoil. He wouldn't be eating for a while at this rate, anyway.

'Take a seat, Bernie,' he tried again.

'No.'

Warren could see the shine of tears in the older man's eyes and a stab of guilt made him abrupt. 'All right, then. Don't, mate.'

'Warren.' Noel was still at the foot of the verandah, looking up at them both. 'What's going on here? You can't really —?'

'Yeah. I am.' Any relief Warren had enjoyed earlier in the wake of his decision was swiftly evaporating into the sky with the barbecue smoke. 'And, look, I am sorry about it.' He tried to be calm, but he could feel a *pulse of tension pounding in his head. He'd always known this conversation wouldn't go well, whenever it happened. He'd expected there to be a lot of anger and hurt, but he'd thought at least he'd have some time to prepare. As it was, Warren felt like his feet had been pulled out from under him.* 'And I'm also sorry you found out like this. If it helps at all, I haven't been sitting on it for ages. I only decided today, so I haven't even had a chance to tell Griff or Damien –'

'It's Damien who's talked you into this, is it?' *Bernie's words slid out, vicious in a way Warren had never heard him before.* 'That little English bast–'

'No, actually, Bernie. And look, leave him out of it, okay? He's only trying to help.'

'So, it's Sylvie, then? Or is it all about the money, full stop? Got dollar signs in your eyes now and can't turn away. You should be ashamed –'

'Yeah, all right, mate. Calm down.'

'If you sell –' *The older man's finger shook as he pointed in the direction of his stone bungalow. Warren could picture the familiar sight, the blue paint of the front door catching the last glow of the dying light as the sun sank in the west.* 'I'll lose my home too, I –'

'No. No, Bernie. You don't have to sell.' *Warren couldn't bring himself to meet the man's eyes because they both knew the lie when they heard it. The smoke from the grill was growing thicker, but Bernie leaned in, his voice softening as the tears spilled over.*

'I will. I bloody will have to sell. As you well know. And my place'll be worth nothing, if they've already got yours. Nothing. A bloody pittance, that's what they'll offer, and – no, shut it, Warren. Don't you dare try to pretend you don't know all this, because you do. And if I don't accept whatever bloody pathetic sum those bastards over at Lentzer offer me, they'll come onto this land, your land, and they'll run their noisy machinery and block my access and make my home unliveable, and Ann-Marie's, too, they'll make sure of that, they'll –'

'No.' Guilt made Warren deny it. 'There's every chance they'll be happy with just this parcel of land.'

Noel laughed at that, suddenly, loudly. He'd been listening from the foot of the verandah and now gave a dry, humourless bark. 'For God's sake, lie to us if you must, Warren, but don't lie to yourself.'

'And what about everyone else?' Bernie's pitch was rising. 'What about the rest of the town? This is a bloody domino property, Warren. You know that. They get this one and the expansion's on, no stopping it. All of us . . .'

'No. Not necessarily,' Warren repeated, helplessly.

'Yes. Yes, necessarily. Yes, absolutely.'

Warren could feel himself skirting around the truth. 'They might not –'

'They will!' Bernie roared. He fished in his pocket, pulled out his keys and wrenched one from the ring with shaking hands. 'They will, so –' He slammed it down on the table so hard that the legs shook. 'Here! Take it! Key to my house. Go on then, Warren. Bloody take it. You may as well, mate. You're pulling my house from under me, you selfish, disloyal –'

'Jesus, Bernie.' Warren was shouting back now. 'Don't be so bloody dramatic.'

It was the sheer shame of it all lashing out in his words and Warren could feel them burning his throat. Because Bernie may be ill and angry, but he was only saying what Warren himself had been thinking for the past year, and for a second, Warren felt his determination wobble. He caught it, though, made himself grab it as with a flash of clarity, he thought of Sylvie, and the unhappiness he'd caused her and the loneliness he'd felt since she'd left. Warren made himself focus on how much this sale meant for their shared future, and his resolve toughened once more.

'Listen,' he looked from father to son, his voice cold, 'this is getting us nowhere. And I don't think this is the right time or place to talk things *through properly so maybe it'd be best if you both get going. It's been a bloody long day and frankly I've had enough of –'*

'Don't sell.' Bernie was suddenly quiet. He was begging, Warren realised in shock. 'Please. Please don't.'

'Bernie.' He had to drop his eyes. This was unbearable. 'Don't do this. Mate? I am selling. Okay? I have to.'

'You don't have to. Please. I love that house. My own dad built it. My children were born there, my wife died there. Please, Warren. Please. If you sell, I won't be able to hold it. Plea–'

'Bernie, for God's sake.' The guilt flared, hot and exquisitely painful. This had to stop. Warren turned his back so he couldn't see Bernie's desperation. 'Mate, enough.' His voice was sharp. 'I don't want to hear it. I've made my decision. It's done now. So complain all you want, but I don't bloody care.'

It wasn't true. It wasn't even close to true. Warren cared deeply, he cared enormously. The decision may have been made, but it had cost him too, he wanted to scream out loud. It had cost him sleep, it had cost him peace of mind, and he knew it would cost him friends that he had held close his entire life. And it wasn't even that he felt sure it was a good decision, it was merely the faintly better of two bad options. Of course Warren didn't want Bernie to lose his place, of course he didn't. Nor Ann-Marie, for that matter. Why did Bernie think he'd held out for as long as he had?

But in holding out, Warren had stood by and watched his relationship collapse and his days grow miserable and he missed Sylvie, okay? He missed what they'd had, and he had known deep down for a while that she was right about it all. When it came down to it, she was more important to him than his friends and neighbours. And she was definitely more important than bricks and mortar. Warren's loyalty lay with her, but it didn't mean he wasn't filled with regret. Because he was, how could he not be? And he was already opening his mouth to apologise and to say all of this, already half turning to Bernie, when the blow from behind connected with a sickening thud.

Warren was falling. He was on his way down before he knew it was happening, knocked sideways by the force of the very man who had taught Warren himself how to tackle on the rugby field. Shown him how to throw his whole weight into an attack on an opponent in his way. How to mean it and how to make it count.

Warren grunted as he lost his balance, instinctively flinging an arm out and grabbing for the table to save himself. His hand slipped clear and it was his head that caught the edge. His skull smacked into the side with a crack that made Warren feel like he might vomit and then, curiously, he felt almost nothing at all.

He crashed to the floor, hearing the impact rather than enduring it, and was only vaguely aware that his head seemed wet and slippery and his eyes were so heavy that he could barely keep them open. As he landed with a dull thud, he blinked slowly and saw the silver of the key tumble from the table and bounce off his chest before disappearing out of sight.

Warren lay very still, smelling the smoke from the barbecue, and he knew he really should get up and turn it off because everything would be burned to a crisp and then what would he have for dinner? But then again, maybe that could wait, because for now all he wanted to do was lie on his own deck beneath the inky sky and the bright stars, feeling the dust brush softly against his skin as the warm night wind breathed across his land. He let his eyes close. And as the blackness washed over him, Warren heard a voice both muffled and urgent and maybe even a little scared, mutter: 'Oh, Jesus, Dad.'

Chapter 40

'It was my fault.' Bernie's voice had been quiet as he'd joined them on the deck of the saloon. 'So I'll tell you.'

Noel had made a strangled sound as though to object, but Bernie had simply rested a hand on his arm for a moment before beckoning for them all to follow him into the cabin. Bernie had picked his way through the bric-a-brac before lowering himself heavily into the green corduroy chair by the window. He'd motioned for Ro and Griff to take a seat too, but they'd both ignored him, remaining standing while they listened to him speak.

His story finished, he peered up at them, his face lined and weary. Noel stood unmoving in the doorway, eyes on the ground.

'Who drove him to the mine?' Griff's voice was low.

'I did.' Noel's words were barely audible. 'While Dad cleaned up the verandah.'

'You cut the hole in the fence. Threw Warren's body over?'

Noel uncrossed his arms and stared down at his large hands. 'Yeah. Left his truck there. Walked back.'

Griff gave no reaction at all for a drawn-out beat, then he abruptly twisted away, moving to the nearest window. He placed both hands firmly and deliberately on the sill and looked out, blinking hard at the shadowy land. Ro watched him for a moment, then pulled her attention back to the room.

'You couldn't find this?' She held out the key still clutched in her hand.

'No. We looked, but no,' Bernie said as Noel shook his head. The men's eyes met and a faint, dark connection seemed to pass between them at the memory. 'I scrubbed those boards. By the next morning the dust had covered them again. You know what it's like around here. Couldn't even tell they'd been cleaned. But we never found the key. Decided in the end it didn't matter on a practical level. I had a spare, Noel did too. It was lost under the house so we thought it'd stay there.' Bernie's eyes slid to the blue door that had been salvaged from his own bungalow. 'How did you know to try this one?'

Ro hesitated, debating silently with herself. She didn't owe either of them an explanation and she wasn't sure that the truth would be welcomed. It had been the flames of the birthday cake candles that had paved the way, their flickering lights gently rewinding her thoughts to the previous day, when she had seen Bernie on the deck of this saloon using a lighter to strip wire. Ro sat down beside him, right in front of a door that she had not checked, but should have. Bernie's own, which had stood a stone's throw from Warren's house for decades.

There had been more, though, and Ro let her eyes rest on Noel for a moment before speaking. 'It was what Darcy said at the memorial.'

'You listen here —' Noel was instantly on the attack. 'Darcy knows nothing of this. Nothing, right? He didn't have any —'

'No.' Ro cut him off. 'I realise that.'

Darcy probably hadn't known, she could believe that, but it had been his frank, impromptu outpouring that had spun the fragile but real thread in her mind all the way from Warren's bloodied boards to Bernie's blue front door. *Why have you all stayed?* he had asked, mystified. It had been a good question.

'What if it's guilt?' Ro had whispered to Griff as they had stood alone on the track, the last mourners at their son's memorial. The three houses had looked on silently, the wind swirling all around. 'Of everyone, I always thought Bernie and Noel stayed for the love of this place, but is that really enough? After all this time? Bernie knows end-of-life care will be a horrible experience here. Heather's miserable. The boys all hate it, the youngest two are smashing the place up they're so desperate to leave. And Noel's aware of all this but still . . .'

'Still, they stay.' Griff had looked at her, a new grim knowledge forming in his face. 'Year after year, they stay.'

Ro looked very sad as she caught sight of her own reflection now in the mirror she had contributed, just one more addition to the saloon's shabby collection. The place no longer offered any of the whimsy she'd once loved, or a sense of stepping into a treasure trove. Now it just looked to Ro like a sad, worn-out wreckage, collected by someone clinging on to an old fantasy.

'What a sacrifice.' She turned back to Bernie and Noel. 'Is that what you both told yourselves? That you'd confronted Warren for the good of the town? For your love of the community? It must have been hard later, though. Seeing the younger boys acting up and Heather so unhappy. But what choice did you both have, really? If you've literally killed for a place, it's not so easy to get up and leave like everyone else. So you stay, I suppose. But that's not commitment, is it? That's a penance.'

Neither man would meet her eyes so Ro walked over to where Griff stood by the window, unnervingly quiet. He had turned back to face the room and was now watching his old friend closely with an odd look on his face.

'Are you okay, Griff?' Ro asked gently and after a long moment, he slowly shook his head.

'No,' he said. 'Tell us the rest, Noel.'

Noel was very still but Bernie looked up sharply, his eyes quick and dark in the gloom. The silence stretched on until at last Noel shrugged, the movement forced and unnatural.

'The rest of what?'

'You know what. Noel? You know.' Griff made a distraught noise in his throat. 'Where is Sam?'

'No.' Noel shook his head once, a sharp jerking snap. 'No, I –'

'Yes,' Griff insisted, his voice frightening and low. 'Because I've been thinking about something while I've been standing over here, listening to this. And Ro's right about the guilt, isn't she? Makes you do strange things.' Griff began moving, looming large in the confined space as he stepped around tables and lamps and ornaments, ignoring them all. 'Been a few years since you stopped working on this place, mate. The boys not interested, you reckon? Even though they're bored out of their minds?'

Ro stared at Noel, who was motionless other than his eyes, which were following Griff around the room.

'But how long has it actually been since you stopped work in here, Noel?' Griff was watching him closely. 'Off the top of my head I'd have guessed roughly four or five years. But now I'm standing here, discovering what you're really capable of, and I'm

thinking very hard now, mate. Is it *roughly* four or five years?'
Griff's voice cracked. He took a final step and stopped right in
front of his friend. 'Or is it *exactly* five years?'

Whether Noel tried to respond or not, Ro didn't know,
because suddenly she was no longer looking at him. She was
staring past him, deep into the saloon. Past Bernie, past the
clutter and the junk and the battered furniture and the paintings,
past her own coloured glass mirror, her gaze pulled instead to
the very back, to the small, empty corner where nothing hung
on the walls and nothing stood on the floor.

She felt Noel's eyes on her and heard the catch of his breath
as she took a single step towards that lonely spot.

And Ro had never, ever believed that she had a sixth sense
and she didn't believe it now, but as she stared at that quiet,
forgotten space, she felt something wake in her bones, in her
blood, in her heart. In the five years since Sam had left her life,
if he had ever once been near, ever once been close, it was now,
in this room, in this corner. He was here, and he was crying out
for her.

Chapter 41

Five years earlier

Noel saw the bright red paint of the rental car flash in the sun as soon as he crested the rise. It was parked on the track that led to the three houses. Sam Crowley's car, he knew straight away. He'd seen it in his own driveway the other day when the kid had come to visit Darcy, and Noel had wondered then how the little city motor was coping with the uneven roads. Sure enough, as he drew nearer, he spotted Sam beside the driver's door, and Noel raised his hand in greeting. He wasn't sure if the boy could see him through the windshield, but as he watched, Sam gave a wave in return. Noel touched the brakes, slowing as he approached, and after a moment Sam began to walk down the track. They reached the road at the same time. Noel came to a stop and wound down his window.

'What are you up to out here?' he called with a grin as Sam came over and rested a hand on the car roof. 'Thought you'd be out flying the drone with Darcy and Jacob.'

Something knowing flickered in Sam's expression and Noel suddenly wondered if he'd put his foot in it. The three boys didn't seem as close as they used to be, now he thought about it.

'No.' Sam's smile recovered as he nodded back towards the houses. 'I just stopped by to have a look around.'

'For your research?' Noel asked, with genuine interest. He was keen to support anything that might help put the boot into Lentzer and strengthen the town's position, and Sam had always been a smart kid. His studies might yield something useful, you never knew.

'Yeah,' Sam replied a little vaguely. 'That's right.'

'All right, well, watch yourself in there, mate. It's not too safe out here on your own these days. There's some structural damage to the houses now, and bits of rusty metal and all sorts lying about.'

'Yeah, thanks. I know. I'll be careful,' Sam said, but he wasn't really listening, Noel could tell. Like Darcy, they were at an age where they felt invincible. Still, they'd both learn eventually, he supposed, he just hoped it wasn't the hard way. A thought occurred to Noel.

'Hey, I found those old maps I was telling you about. For your project.'

'Oh, that's great.' Sam's enthusiasm seemed real. 'I was actually thinking about them last night. Thanks for digging them out. When's a good time to grab them?'

'Now?' Noel shrugged. 'If you want?'

'Yeah, sure. Thanks.' He glanced back towards his own car. 'I'll follow you home.'

Noel looked past the boy to the small red city model and hesitated. 'I'll tell you what, jump in.' He nodded to the passenger side. 'I laid some fresh gravel on the drive the other day, it'll chew up your paintwork if you take that thing along there. I'll run you up to get the maps and drop you back.'

'Actually, that would be great.' Sam looked relieved. 'Thanks, Noel.'

He moved around to the passenger side and climbed in. Noel waited for him to fasten his seatbelt, then turned the wheel and together they headed away down the deserted country road, the red rental car winking alone in the sun behind them.

★

Heather had taken Bernie for a hospital appointment in Blenheim, and Kyle and Zach jumped at any chance for a change of scenery these days, so there was no-one home when Noel pulled up in front of his house.

He climbed out of the driver's door, letting Sam tell him all about uni life as they made their way around the eastern side of the house and over the paddock to the Last Chance Saloon. As they got closer, Noel felt a sting of irritation. Darcy had gone out yet again without fixing the outside railing that Noel had asked him to look at. And the younger two were supposed to have run the vacuum over some of the old chairs and soft furnishings over the weekend too, but Noel knew without checking that they wouldn't have done that either.

He sighed as he reached the deck and fished underneath the ceramic frog for the spare key. He grasped it and rose, his hand unsteady for only the briefest moment as he fitted the key into the familiar lock in Bernie's blue front door.

The door had been destined for the scrap heap on the day they'd boarded up his dad's bungalow, and Noel would have been very happy to see it go. But a group of Bernie's old mates had come over to give them a hand, and they'd insisted on easing the door out of its hinges before lovingly wrapping it in a sheet and driving it over to Noel's place. They had presented it to Bernie like a gift and neither Noel nor his father had been able to think of a good reason not to accept. And so here stood the door, at the front of the saloon, snagging Noel's gaze whenever he passed and sending his thoughts stumbling a little each time he stepped through it.

What Noel really wanted, as he turned the key in the lock, was a stiff drink but instead he gathered himself and let Sam into the cabin.

He edged past the boy and moved through the cramped room to the scratched pine writing desk where he'd stored the maps.

'Feel free to poke around,' he called to Sam. 'Just mind that back corner.'

'No worries.' Sam wandered over to the small space Noel had marked off with tape. A section of the floorboards had been removed, exposing the dark ground beneath. A damp smell wafted from the hole. 'What's going on here?'

'Touch of subsidence, I think.' Noel carefully laid the maps flat on the desktop, counting to see if he had them all. 'Need to get underneath and put in a new support stump.'

'Right.' Sam had already lost interest and was roaming around, examining the older pieces and new additions. 'Is that from the Ainsleys' house?' He pointed to a poor watercolour painting of the town hall in spring.

'Yeah, and that one, the summer scene.' Noel joined him in the middle of the floor, the maps neatly rolled and fastened with an elastic band. He held them out. 'All yours, mate. Have fun.'

'Excellent. Thanks, Noel.'

'No worries.' He nodded, a little distracted as he caught a glimpse of what could only be a crumpled sandwich wrapper shoved behind a sofa. Annoyance surged in his gut. If the boys had been messing around in here, he'd be having words. He turned back to Sam and gestured to the maps. 'Let me know if you have any trouble reading them, or if there's anything else I can help with.' He was already moving towards the door when he sensed Sam pause.

'Yeah, actually, Noel . . .'

He looked back. Sam swapped the maps from one hand to the other, suddenly a little uncomfortable.

'There was something. About Bernie.'

'About Dad?' Noel had trained himself well over the last three years and he could now keep his voice perfectly steady when talking about his *father, in any context and to anyone. His expression remained neutral and placid, even as the reflexive response flared in his chest, a bright, burning twin flame of anger and fear. Because although Noel was fairly sure that he hated his father for putting him in an unforgivable position three years earlier, he used to love his dad a lot. Still loved him a lot, unfortunately, even though it hurt now in a way it never had before. Noel felt all that and more, before shoving it down deep as he simply looked at Sam across the saloon and asked: 'What about Dad?'*

'Yeah. Look, it's a bit awkward,' Sam said, but carried on. 'When I interviewed Bernie the other day, he started talking a lot about the people who'd sold out over the years.'

'Right. Can't say I'm too surprised.' Noel gave the boy a dry smile, even as an ominous prickle ran across the back of his neck. He had been very against his father taking part in Sam's project. Bernie had been adamant, though. His memories were valuable, he'd insisted, and he deserved a chance to share them. 'One of his favourite topics at the moment, that.'

'Yeah, it did seem to be.' Sam's own smile flashed and then faded quickly. 'But he was going through all these names and he mentioned Warren as one of them.'

'Warren.' Noel frowned, resting his hand on the edge of the blue front door. 'That'd just be a mistake.'

'Right.' Sam nodded. 'I know it was.'

'And Dad's not too well at the moment. Did Heather tell you? They've got him on this trial treatment that's not agreeing with some of the other stuff he takes. Leaves him a bit out of it sometimes.'

'No. I know. Heather did say that. And Bernie was bringing up a lot of people, so I think he got confused. But the way he was talking –' Sam looked troubled. 'He made it sound like Warren had told Sylvie that he was willing to sell to Lentzer. Before he killed himself.'

'Ah. Right.'

'So,' Sam frowned as if Noel were being deliberately slow, 'I realise Bernie's not himself at the moment, but could you please ask him not

to go saying that to anyone else? Because people around here love to talk, and something like that . . .' He shrugged. 'It's the kind of thing that sticks.'

Maybe it was Sam's faint righteousness or maybe the hint of an order that rubbed Noel the wrong way because he felt himself bristle. It sat badly with him – the implication that Warren, before his death, was obviously in the right, and Bernie, who had done a bloody huge amount for this community, was so clearly in the wrong.

'For Warren's sake, I mean,' Sam was going on. 'And Sylvie's, I suppose. Because it's not like it's true.'

Noel should simply agree. Offer the easiest and smoothest response. He knew that. Of course he knew it. But even as he was reaching for the lie, it took him a fraction of a moment longer to find it than he'd expected. Barely a heartbeat, no time at all. But his pause seemed to stretch out, long and deformed, and in that strange, tiny moment, he sensed a window of opportunity snap closed.

'I know for sure it's not true.' Sam was watching him now. 'Because I asked Sylvie.'

'Yeah, well.' Noel felt a faint swell of bitterness at the mention of the woman, and forced himself to swallow it down, just as he did every time he saw her. It always burned his throat, though, because Noel had often reflected that if not for Sylvie in the background, whispering her plans for the future into Warren's ear, a lot of things wouldn't have played out the way they had. 'I suppose Sylvie would say that, wouldn't she?'

'Yeah, of course she would.' Sam was struggling to hide his annoyance. It was written all over his smooth, young face. 'Because Warren was a good bloke and he'd never have sold out. Ever. So whether Bernie's got mixed up or what, Warren doesn't deserve to have him –'

'Yep. All right, mate.' Noel had suddenly had enough. His head was beginning to hurt and his heart was already aching. He needed to get out of the saloon and into the daylight. And he really needed a drink, that's what he very much needed right now. 'I'll tell Dad not to say it.'

'Stop thinking it as well, ideally.' Sam's tone was blunt.

'Well, he can think what he likes, mate. As can you. But don't fool yourself. Warren was no better than the rest of them. And Sylvie.'

'Better than the rest of who?' Sam stared. 'The ones who sold out?'

'Yeah.'

'No, that's not the case. Sylvie told me.'

'It is the bloody case, mate. And Sylvie knows what he said.'

A pause. So slim and fine that it would have been easy to miss. 'How can you know that?'

Something changed in Sam's face, and Noel felt his innards begin to slither, cold and uneasy. He bought himself a moment by offering a light shrug.

'Yeah, fair enough,' he said. Did that response sound normal? Unbothered? He couldn't tell. 'Look, it's all water under the bridge now. Come on, I'll drive you back.'

In the small silence that followed, Noel had the dizzying sensation of being right on the edge of a cliff. He could almost feel the line with his toes, where it switched from solid ground to open air and he could imagine himself tipping forward. A sudden, breathless free-fall, the wind rushing past him at horrifying speed as his fingers scrabbled desperately for a handhold that would stop his plunge and let him drag himself back to safety.

For just a second, he wondered what it would be like to throw himself over, willingly. To make the choice to embrace both the terrible plummet and the hard smash into the ground. It would be agony, there was no question, but at least it would be over and in that there had to be some relief. It was tempting. And Noel had been tempted many times over the past three years. Desperate to split himself wide open and let his secret slide out, putrid and rotten and black, for the world to see.

However.

The thing that stopped him was always the same. Noel's secret was not Noel's alone. It was also his father's.

Noel's thoughts centred around Bernie these days with a frequency that felt like obsession. Not Bernie as he was now, old and unwell and complicated, but as he had been for most of Noel's life. Noel could remember intimately the feel of his dad's large, reassuring hand on his back. It had been there any time Noel had attempted to tackle something difficult and scary – riding a bike, working out a maths problem, asking a pretty teenage girl called Heather to come with him to the school's fundraising fete, trying to buy his own parcel of land, becoming a father himself, three times over.

'It'll be all right, mate,' Bernie had said, his comforting palm always right there, firm and solid. 'Trust me. We'll work this out.'

And so three years ago, when faced with a horrendous choice, Noel had walked across a darkened yard to his sick, scared father, who was kneeling in tears on his neighbour's bloodstained porch. He had put his own hand on his dad's back and he had made the same promise. 'We'll work this out.'

The afternoon light danced across the floor of the saloon as Noel stood opposite Sam and thought about his father and that promise, gifted back and forth between them and, slowly but deliberately, Noel mentally stepped back from the cliff edge. Their shared secret would not be smashed open today.

'Look, mate,' Noel tried. Sam was still watching him and at some point while they'd been talking, he had swapped the rolled-up maps to his left hand. In his right hand, he now held his phone. It hung casually by his side, the screen still dark. 'I overheard Warren and Sylvie talking about plans for the house.'

'Oh. Right.'

'So that's how I knew.'

'Okay. Yeah.' Sam's thumb moved, just a fraction, and the screen lit up. He didn't look down, and Noel had to force himself not to either.

'They were talking in the pub.' Noel didn't sound convincing even to himself, he was suddenly, devastatingly aware. He wondered why he was

still bothering and realised with a roll of nausea that he was simply trying to delay what was to come.

'Yeah.' Any trace of antagonism in Sam had vanished now. His attention was fixed fully on Noel, as he gazed over, clear-eyed, willing to please, his face carefully neutral. He was even nodding, his dark hair catching the thin rays of sunlight leaking in through the windows. Sam still thought there was a chance, Noel realised, and that alone made his throat close up and his eyes sting. Sam's thumb shifted against his phone screen as he agreed: 'That makes sense.'

But it didn't, did it? That was the thing. Sadly. So bloody sadly. It didn't make sense at all, Noel knew, as the blood roared in his ears and his stomach swooped and a resolute voice whispered awful instructions in his ear. And it would make even less sense when Sam had had time to sit down and think about it, and go back to Sylvie and work through the timeline logically, which he would, of course, because that was Sam Crowley for you and he had always been like that, ever since he was a little boy. Clever like his mum and thorough like his dad, and unfortunately just a bit too bloody clever and too bloody thorough this time, because now Sam had trapped both himself and Noel in a place that Noel had dreaded. He had feared finding himself here every day for three whole years because, in this place, there was no escape for either of them. No way out, because Sam was already nearly at the right answer anyway, even if he didn't quite know it. His fingertips were grasping at the truth. Noel could see it, right there in front of him.

And even before it was done, part of Noel already wanted to tell his dad exactly how far he had gone for him. Again. Look what you made me do now, he already wanted to scream in Bernie's face, knowing he never would. Noel would not burden his father in the way his father had burdened him. Noel would work this out himself. He would make things all right, one more time, for both of them. And he would carry this alone, the secrecy forming part of the gift.

Noel forced his raging mind to focus. He would not think about Sam, or Sam's parents, or Bernie. He did not even think about himself as he slowly raised his large fist and with a single, swift blow sent the phone spinning from Sam's hand. The shock of what he had become took his breath away.

Chapter 42

From high up on the ridge, through the hazy filter of distance, the town of Carralon looked almost unchanged as it shimmered under the glare of the afternoon light.

That the community could appear unscathed seemed simply unreal to Ro as she sat a little way back from the ridge's edge on a rough woollen blanket Griff and Della had dragged from the boot of the car. Griff sat beside Ro now, with the town spread out below them. It felt to Ro as though the whole place should by rights have spent the last thirty-six hours burning to the ground in a cloud of smoke and ash, or perhaps willingly turning itself over in surrender to the mercy of the mine, begging to be swallowed whole in a fit of self-destruction.

Instead, the patchwork pattern of bushland and paddocks and long winding roads remained as familiar as it had always been, the daylight colours shifting under shadows cast by the high white clouds that moved gently on the wind. In the west, the mine thundered low and continuous, its progress unimpeded by anything happening in the small community on the outskirts of its commercial boundaries. Amid the deep rumbling, Ro could hear a single bird call from the bushland behind them, the hidden cry lonely and plaintive.

The town might appear much the same from the height of the ridge, but there was movement happening down there, Ro was very aware. She would be able to see it herself, if she were to go to the edge and look. She chose not to, keeping her gaze focused instead on the distant horizon, where the blue sky met the long undulating line of the land, whispering its reassurance that there were other places out there, with different people living different lives. Something better, far away.

Ro felt Griff's body shift beside her, the heat from his shoulder warm against her own. His shoulders shook when he cried, which he had been doing without warning all day, pressing his knuckles to his face, his chest and back heaving with muffled gasps. Whenever that happened, Ro simply went to him and waited, resting a soothing hand on his knee or arm.

Griff's eyes were dry at that moment, though, as he sat with his head tilted back, his gaze following the sway of the trees against the sky. Ro followed his lead, raising her own face upwards to watch the shattered pattern of the branches against the light. She felt mostly numb, which she welcomed. Almost pleasantly dazed in a temporary cocoon of artificial calm, but already she could feel the security of it beginning to slip. The comforting layer was shredding in places, exposing ragged holes of blackness that she knew she would eventually have to face. At some point. For now, Ro carefully returned her eyes to the horizon and that distant promise of something else.

Della had been frighteningly efficient. Her natural response to heightened fear or stress had always been to grasp for some form of control and she had responded accordingly over the past day and a half. Her phone had been glued to her ear and her palm as she set about informing those who needed to be told in appropriate detail and gathering necessary information from the relevant authorities. Through Della's network of colleagues, she had secured the services of an experienced and well-respected lawyer who was now representing their interests. Ro was unsure exactly what her interests were at this surreal time, but she was yet again reminded how profoundly lucky she was to have Della by her side and in her life. She felt newly and deeply grateful for every single thing about their clever, stoic, kind daughter, who had weathered so much. Ro would make sure Della knew it, she promised herself, as she looked over at her now.

Della was standing near the ridge's edge with a pair of binoculars raised as she surveyed the town below. Perhaps feeling her mother's eyes on her, she turned and lowered the glasses. She held them out to Ro, who shook her head at the offer. Ro studied her daughter for a moment longer, then pulled herself to her feet and walked over to her.

Della gently reached out and took Ro's hand as she drew nearer. 'Watch with me for a while.'

Ro nodded, but felt her eyes closing in protest. She let herself stand there for a minute, cloaked in the bright red–blackness behind her eyelids, listening to the soft rhythm of her daughter's breathing, inhaling the fresh scent of her skin and sensing the tiny vital movements of her youngest child's body close to hers. She inhaled and exhaled, long and slow, before she heard a rustle behind her and then the soft tread of footfall. She felt Griff at her other side and at that, Ro opened her eyes and looked over to meet his. They were swollen and bloodshot, but his palm was large and solid as he took her free hand. They turned, together, and finally looked down.

Noel had called the police himself. He had walked out of
the saloon and away into the inky shadows of the east paddock
to make the call and as he'd done so, it had crossed Ro's mind
that he might disappear into the night and not come back.
Noel wouldn't run, she felt somehow sure of that, but she had
wondered if the next time he was seen it would be hanging from
a tree or with a shotgun wound through his head. Griff was
wondering the same, Ro had suspected. She could see her own
dark, conflicting thoughts mirrored in his face.

Bernie had said nothing. He hadn't tried to stop his son as he'd
walked away, but Ro had caught the flash of complicated relief
in his expression when Noel had finally returned. Noel had not
spoken, instead lowering himself down heavily on the top step of
the deck, beside his father. Ro and Griff had looked at each other,
and then in wordless unity had gone inside to be with their son.

Shaking, Ro had picked her way through the junk and sat
down on the floor beside Griff in that bare corner of the saloon,
neither of them saying anything or doing anything other than
simply being there. Occasionally, she could hear a soft creak of
the deck, but mostly all was quiet as the two men sat outside,
waiting, just like them.

Ro couldn't guess how long the four of them had stayed there,
suspended together in their shared horror, but it had felt like a
lifetime. Only when the first blue lights appeared through the
window on the distant road did someone finally speak.

'Ro? Griff? Dad didn't know about Sam.' Noel's bleak words
were hard to hear over the screech and growl of the mine. 'I
never told him. That's the truth.'

There was a long pause and Ro could make out the sound of
soft crying.

'You never told me.' Bernie's voice cracked. 'But it doesn't
mean I didn't know. Of course I knew.'

Ro had looked through the darkness at Griff, and against the grimy floorboard he had tightened his grip on her hand. At long last, at the very least, they knew too. Ro expected that later she would feel differently, would want to hear and learn much more. But right at that moment, sitting in the still night with her husband and son, simply knowing had been almost enough.

'There's someone leaving,' Della said softly, lifting the binoculars now to look down from the ridge, her head turned in the direction of Noel's family farm. Ro made herself follow her daughter's gaze. The hill to the east blocked the farm from sight, and Ro felt desperately thankful for that natural gift. She did not want to see the official work being carried out on that property today. Della was right, though, a vehicle was in motion. A large marked police van moved smoothly along the road that led from the hidden house. Ro did not let herself speculate on what the van might be carrying, but simply watched its journey as it drove on.

Only when the van reached the town centre did Ro let it go and allow her gaze to linger.

'Busy down there,' she said quietly.

Griff nodded slowly beside her. 'Haven't seen it like that in a long time.'

They all stared down at the crossroads, which had become something of a hub once more. The pub car park was full, every space taken by a police or media vehicle, and the various cars approaching the junction were forced to give way to each other for the first time in years. Outside the general store, a handful of people had gathered. Their heads were close, their bodies turned in towards each other as they spoke. Ro was too far away to make out the faces of the few remaining locals beneath their hats but she could see their shock reflected in their stooped postures, the distress in the comforting touch of a hand on a back or shoulder.

Ro watched the hive of activity with a sense of detached curiosity. It was like stepping back in time. It would all disappear in a matter of days, she knew, the car park emptying out and the roads falling silent once more. For now though, however briefly, the town seemed alive again.

'Sylvie should have opened the pub,' Griff said drily. 'For coffee at least. Be making a bloody fortune.'

Della gave a small smile. 'She's not even inside. Over there. See?'

She pointed and Ro's eyes followed, down to the three houses. The Hillary place, the ivy cottage and the stone bungalow stood dotted innocently among their surrounding paddocks. They looked like doll's houses from that distance, the winding track that connected them nothing more than a thin brown line. Outside Warren's house, a blue and white police car glinted in the sunlight beside a van painted with official markings that Ro couldn't discern. As she watched, two small uniformed figures emerged from Warren's back verandah and made their way around to the front of the house. Ro followed their progress up to the van then let her eyes continue on, down the winding trail until she had left the three houses behind.

Another police car was parked where the end of the track met the country road, and Ro saw that Della's attention was focused a little further along, towards the entrance of the bushland hiking route. Three cars were parked on the side of the road there, end to end. Even from that height, Ro recognised Sylvie's bright red Capri immediately, looking brilliantly garish between Damien's understated sedan and Ann-Marie's battered four-wheel drive.

'They've all been there for over an hour,' Della said, lifting the binoculars again to look at the trio. Ro watched them too. The three were leaning against an old fence, side by side with their heads turned towards the Hillary house.

'What've they been doing for an hour?' Ro asked.

'Nothing, really. Pretty much just that,' Della said as Sylvie leaned towards her companions. She appeared to say something and Damien and Ann-Marie both nodded. 'Talking mostly. Looking at Warren's place. They've all left more messages, by the way. Yesterday and again this morning. Keen to speak to you both whenever you're ready.' She paused. 'I think Damien was crying earlier, and Sylvie definitely was, but . . .' She adjusted the binoculars. 'I don't know. They seem a little better now. Maybe not Ann-Marie. She still looks a bit unsteady. I heard Jacob left for Blenheim this morning.'

'Already?' Ro asked.

'Apparently.' Della sighed. 'I can understand it, though. Not wanting to be around this.'

Ro felt Griff nod beside her. She could understand it, too.

'I wonder what Ann-Marie will do without him,' Della said quietly. 'Darcy'll miss him as well.' She hesitated, shot a glance at her parents. 'I know it's not my job to care about that family. At all. I just know that he and Jacob were pretty excited to go to Blenheim together. Start their new lives or whatever. I dunno. I kind of hope it still happens for them.'

Ro said nothing, but if she'd been forced to offer an opinion, she suspected a tiny part of her hoped it would too. She had been awake well before dawn that morning, sitting alone in the kitchen and watching the black sky lift to a gunmetal grey when she had caught the soft crunch of footsteps outside. She had listened as they approached the front door, waiting for a knock that never came. Instead, the footsteps had immediately retreated again. Ro had stayed at the table, her coffee cooling in the weak light until the sound had fully faded away. Only when she heard the faint purr of an engine disappearing down the road did she drag herself to her feet and go to the door.

The envelope was waiting on the mat, the whiteness of the paper glowing in the early gloom. Ro had stood on the deck, the wooden boards cold against her bare feet as she stared at it. Finally she bent and picked up the envelope, but did not go back inside. She sat on the top step in her dressing-gown, the high-pitched calls of the dawn birdsong cutting through the low grumbling of the mine as she carefully opened the seal. Inside, she found a short note.

We've been told we're not allowed to contact you. Ro had read the words slowly. She had not seen this handwriting since the days of shared homework and scrawled birthday cards. It hadn't changed very much at all over the years. *But I can't say nothing. I hope you understand. Sam was my best mate and I am so sorry. I had no idea, I swear that's the truth, and neither did my mum or brothers. We want you to know that. We will never forget Sam or Warren, or forget what's happened.*

There was something else in the envelope and Ro slipped it out. A photograph, she could tell immediately.

I've had this for a while, the words on the back read. *I thought you might want it instead.*

Ro turned the image over. It was of Sam, as she'd expected, but it was a picture that she'd never seen before. He was standing in an anonymous paddock, the clear early-evening sky glowing pink above him and the long grass shining and golden as it caught the last of the low sun. Ro could tell from her son's hair and clothes that the picture had been taken in one of those last few days, during his final visit to Carralon Ridge. It was clear from the angle that the image had been captured on a drone. Sam was grinning into the lens, his face tilted up, his smile broad and eyes crinkling against the light. Ro had sat on the step for a long time and gently held this picture of her child.

Now, she found herself thinking about it again on the top

of the ridge, beside her daughter and husband. She didn't know exactly when the photo had been taken, but in that moment, Sam had been smiling, back in the town that he still considered his own. He had been spending time with his parents and sister, and he had been catching up with his friends. He would have woken that morning and gone to sleep that night in his old bed in his childhood room. His birthday was around the corner. He was pursuing work he felt was meaningful. He was enjoying himself. And he was loved, very much.

Ro stood with her family, looking down at the town and picturing her son, and for the first time felt a quiet, calm gratitude for something she realised she had already known for a long time. In the last days of his life, Sam had been home and he had been happy.

Chapter 43

One year later

The end of summer was on its way and the new garden was
making the most of the last few weeks of sunshine. It had
done well, Ro thought as she surveyed the plants, gleaming full
and lush in the evening light. And this was only its first year. She
looked forward to seeing what the future held.

The three houses that stood at the end of that shared, winding
track had all been demolished over winter in the space of less
than a week. The Hillary house, the ivy cottage and the stone
bungalow were each ripped apart, brick by brick; the debris
removed and the ground evened out until there was no sign they
had stood there at all. The mine had used its newly cleared land
to build a wide access road leading to its eastern boundary. The
homes were farewelled by no-one from Carralon Ridge.

Heather had taken her two teenage sons and found a job in a

busy clinic in the centre of Sydney. She and Zach and Kyle lived in an apartment in the very heart of the city, surrounded each day from dawn until the early hours by activity and movement and comings and goings. The boys were apparently doing well in their large new school.

Ro knew all this only from other people. She and Heather were not in touch. Ro had seen the woman only once more in the few short weeks before both had left Carralon for good. Ro had been driving along the empty road towards the rubbish dump with what she hoped was one of the last loads from the final shed to be cleared when she had seen a car approaching from the other direction. She had recognised it straight away. Unsure what to do, Ro had found herself slowing. The oncoming vehicle had done the same. They'd come to a halt, perfectly side by side on the deserted road, and Ro had looked through the window at the other driver. Heather stared back. She had clearly been crying that morning, but then again, so had Ro.

Without thinking about it, Ro had reached for the doorhandle and climbed out as the other woman did too and, wordlessly, Ro put her arms out and found Heather's. She and her oldest friend had hugged, tight and long, on that vacant road that stretched empty in both directions. Heather had murmured something, her face damp against Ro's hair. *I'm sorry*, it sounded like, but Ro hadn't asked her to repeat it. Heather owed her nothing, had nothing to apologise for herself. Still, as they had parted, climbing back into their cars without another word and pulling away in opposite directions, Ro knew with a deep certainty it was the last time they would see each other. She had driven away and not looked back.

Darcy had eventually followed Jacob to Blenheim where they now shared a house. Darcy was studying online, reportedly focusing hard, staying in. He had resisted Jacob's urging to join the town's drinking and dating scene, seemingly preferring to live quietly and keep mostly to himself. He had, however, agreed to join Jacob in starting a small agricultural services business, with help from their key investor, Damien.

Damien had finally parted ways with his UK firm and instead secured a position with a financial institution that operated on Australian Eastern Standard time. He had moved to Sydney, working daylight hours and sleeping at night, and seemed all the better for it.

The entire proceeds from the sale of Warren's house and contents were fully intact in an interest-bearing account, Damien told Ro and Griff during dinner one night at a restaurant over-looking Sydney Harbour. He hadn't yet spent a cent of it.

'I've been waiting for something that felt right for the money, you know?' Damien said as he topped up their wineglasses. Behind him, the bridge and Opera House were lit up against the night. 'After everything that was said between me and Warren, I felt I owed it to him to get the best out of the estate that I could, but then I wanted to use it for something he would've approved of. I think this is it. Helping Jacob get a new start. It feels like a good use.'

'Setting up a community-based business run by locals?' Griff had smiled. 'Yeah, I reckon Warren would've been happy to back that. You think Jacob and Darcy can make a go of it?'

Damien had shrugged. 'I can afford to take the risk; I never needed the money from that place anyway. But yeah.' He'd nodded, with a gleam of something in his eyes that Ro could only describe as parental pride. 'I believe in them. I think they can do it well.'

He had been right so far, Ro knew, and Damien had kept a keen eye on his investment, driving out to Blenheim a couple of times a month to take Jacob out for a beer and a meal. It had become a ritual they both enjoyed, and for old times' sake they made sure they were always served by Sylvie, who now managed the bar at one of the nicer pubs in town, only a few kilometres away from her mother's care home.

Ann-Marie also showed her face in Blenheim, but only occasionally, having made sure Jacob was settled in his new life before taking the chance to seek out an adventure of her own. She had joined the Royal Flying Doctor Service as a registered nurse, treating remote communities in Queensland. During her time off, she was reportedly enjoying a liaison with a divorced surgeon in Brisbane and a fling with a younger builder in Adelaide and jetted over to see them each as she pleased.

Della had returned to her life in Sydney a little softer and more reflective, Ro had been aware. She moved through her days more slowly and deliberately, and had told Ro she was considering a career change. Change to what, Della wasn't yet sure. Something that meant more to her than the investment bank. While she considered, she had joined a weekend beach clean-up crew where she had met a fellow volunteer called Matthew, who was kind and earnest and asked after one clean-up session if he could buy her a coffee from the kiosk on the edge of the sand. He taught maths in a high school and laughed at Della's jokes. Coffee had turned into dinner and now Della seemed to spend nearly as much time at his apartment as she did at her own. Matthew was saving up in hopes of travelling a little next year, getting away to see something of the world. Della insisted she hadn't decided yet whether to join him, but Ro couldn't help but notice that she'd renewed her passport anyway.

Della had been happy and only the tiniest bit smug when Ro and Griff told her they were formally back together and looking for somewhere new to live.

Not in Carralon Ridge, though.

Sam's remains had been recovered from the earth beneath the floorboards in the bare corner of the saloon. His skull had signs of fracture, but the rest of his bones showed few defensive injuries. Ro chose to believe that meant when the end had come, it had come quickly for their son. Ro and Griff had taken possession of their child's ashes, and wondered for quite a long time what Sam would have wanted them to do.

Ro saw Griff coming across the lawn now, and smiled. He grinned back, and as he drew near she slipped her hand around his waist and he rested his arm across her shoulders.

'That jasmine's looking good,' he said, nodding to their wedding arch that was nestled in the centre of the new garden. The green tendrils and fragrant white flowers had wound their way through the wrought-iron metalwork, bringing it back to life.

'Yeah,' Ro agreed. 'It's coming in well.'

They had looked for a new home with an open mind, and before long the answer had presented itself. Not in Carralon Ridge and not in Sydney either, but somewhere in between. A cottage in a beautiful country town, midway between the two. Medium-sized in every way that mattered, their new community had tall trees and green paddocks and local shops and a medical centre and roads where Ro had to look both ways before she crossed and a pub that was open any night of the week that she and Griff felt like dropping in for a drink and a chat with their new neighbours.

Before they had left Carralon for the final time, Ro and Griff had carefully considered whether to scatter Sam's ashes there, perhaps in the small reclaimed garden along with his sunflower seeds. In the end, they had not. They would never be back, they both knew, and neither wanted to leave any part of themselves behind.

So they had waited, and when the right moment had come it

had been both unexpected and not. Ro had been sitting beside Griff in deckchairs on the back lawn of their new house, a few odd boxes still left to unpack but the place already feeling a lot like home. The sun had been low as Ro looked out over the back paddock, the early-evening breeze warm on her skin, the grass thick and soft against her bare feet. Ro could hear the gentle click of insects and late song of the birds. Della was visiting and was cooking in the kitchen, light music from the radio mingling with the sizzle and clang from the pans. Whatever she was making, it smelled good.

'What about here?' Ro said quietly. She had turned her head and looked over at Griff, who lifted his hat from his eyes. He didn't need to ask what she meant.

'Yeah.' He gave her a small smile. 'Feels about right.'

'It does.'

So they had fetched Della and the three of them had walked in the late sun out to the back paddock. This place didn't mean anything to Sam, Ro knew. He'd never been there. But she could tell it would come to mean something special to her and Griff and Della. And as they scattered Sam's ashes, Ro felt a sense of peace as she felt her son returning, not just to his family but to the world, to become part of the trees and the land and the air. He had always been one to explore.

As the first stars appeared overhead, Ro felt Griff take her hand, and she in turn put her arm around Della and together they turned back to their new house. There were only a few things Ro needed to feel like she was home, and that night, she had them all.

Acknowledgements

A huge thank you, first and foremost, to you for reading this book. Time is precious and there are a lot of books out there, so whether this is our sixth time around together or the first time you've picked up one of my novels, I'm grateful to you for choosing to come along for this story. I really loved writing this one, so I hope you enjoyed it too.

On the subject of writing, it takes a lot more work than you'd think from a surprisingly large number of people to take a badly formatted word document and guide it through all the necessary processes to become a beautifully finished book. From editorial guidance, to cover designs, to marketing and publicity and all the thousands of tasks in between, I'm so grateful to the many talented people who have worked so hard to bring this book to readers. Among them:

Claire Craig, Clare Keighery and Danielle Walker at Pan Macmillan Australia, along with the entire team, including

Tracey Cheetham, Brianne Collins, Katie Crawford, Tom Evans, Maria Fassoulas, Praveen Naidoo and Charlotte Ree; Christine Kopprasch at Pine & Cedar Books, as well as Kate Lucas, Marlena Bittner, Cat Kenney, Megan Lynch, Malati Chavali, Kate Keating, Katherine Turro and the whole Pine & Cedar Books team; Alex Saunders, Lucy Hale, Francesca Pathak, Laura Sherlock and all at Pan Macmillan UK.

My deep appreciation as always to my agents: Fiona Inglis at Curtis Brown Australia; Gordon Wise, Liz Dennis and Georgia Williams at Curtis Brown UK; Daniel Lazar at Writers House; and Leslie Conliffe at the Intellectual Property Group. I remain indebted to the late Jerry Kalajian, who was instrumental in bringing three of my novels to the screen.

This novel is dedicated to all the passionate and highly knowledgeable librarians and booksellers who have helped not only me, but so many of us, develop a love of reading over the years. Personal thanks to Monica Dullard at the Port Phillip Library Service for entertaining both me and my son, Ted, at your truly wonderful kids' storytimes at the Albert Park branch. Your sessions are inspiring for children and adults alike, and were a highlight of our week.

Out of the library and into the sports halls, thank you to Debby Reynolds for the sidelines book chat and recommendations at basketball. Go Dolphins!

My gratitude once again to my parents and early proofreaders, Helen and Mike Harper. Thank you for pointing out that 'chunder' has only one specific meaning. The word I wanted was in fact 'chunter', you were quite right.

Thanks to my siblings and their families for their ongoing support for the books: Michael Harper, Susan Davenport and Ivy, Ava and Isabel Harper; Ellie Harper and Jenia Tsenter, and a warm welcome to Ethan Tsenter.

To my husband Peter Strachan, thank you for coming up with the excellent title for this book, along with all the many other ways you've supported it. And lots of love to my wonderful children, Charlotte and Ted Strachan. I know it takes me longer than Andy and Terry to write a whole book, thank you for your understanding and patience regardless.

MORE BESTSELLING FICTION BY JANE HARPER

Exiles

Aaron Falk returns in the masterful novel of intrigue

At a busy festival site on a warm spring night, a baby lies alone in her pram, her mother having vanished into the crowds.

A year on, Kim Gillespie's absence casts a long shadow as her friends and loved ones gather deep in the heart of South Australian wine country to welcome a new addition to the family.

Aaron Falk, federal investigator, is joining the celebrations. But as he soaks up life in the lush valley, he begins to suspect this tight-knit group may be more fractured than it seems. As hidden truths slowly emerge, Falk faces the darkest of questions.

WINNER OF THE NED KELLY AWARD FOR BEST CRIME FICTION 2023

'You'll find yourself immediately hooked' *THE AGE*

'A thoroughly enjoyable rural mystery' *CANBERRA WEEKLY*

'*Exiles* is another heart-pounding mystery from Aussie crime-writing royalty' *NEW IDEA*

'A beautifully observed crime novel' *SATURDAY AGE*

'An evocative and suspenseful mystery' *MARIE CLAIRE*

'The queen of "outback noir"' *SYDNEY MORNING HERALD*

The Survivors

NOW A NETFLIX TV SERIES

Even the deepest secrets rise to the surface . . .

Kieran Elliott's life changed forever on the day a reckless mistake led to devastating consequences.

The guilt that still haunts him resurfaces when Kieran and his young family visit his parents in the small coastal community he once called home. Between them all is his absent brother, Finn.

When a body is discovered on the beach, long-held secrets threaten to emerge. A sunken wreck, a missing girl, and questions that have never washed away . . .

'It's now clear Harper has a gift . . . every book has a distinct landscape that plays a central part in the plot made possible by her uncanny knack of bringing scenery to life' *DAILY TELEGRAPH*

'Another suspenseful thriller . . . unearthing dark secrets, hidden guilt and simmering social tensions' *HERALD SUN*

'A crime-writing force of nature' *ADELAIDE ADVERTISER*

'Jane Harper creates an impressive landscape that serves to illustrate how the experience of place inevitably shapes the lives of those who live there. You may find it hard to leave behind' *SYDNEY MORNING HERALD*

The Lost Man

'The man lay still in the centre of a dusty grave under a monstrous sky.'

Two brothers meet at the border of their vast cattle properties under the unrelenting sun of outback Queensland.

They are at the stockman's grave, a landmark so old, no one can remember who is buried there. But today, the scant shadow it casts was the last chance for their middle brother, Cameron.

The Bright family's quiet existence is thrown into grief and anguish. Something had been troubling Cameron. Did he lose hope and walk to his death? Because if he didn't, the isolation of the outback leaves few suspects . . .

For readers who loved *The Dry* and *Force of Nature*, Jane Harper has once again created a powerful story of suspense, set against a dazzling landscape.

WINNER OF THE NED KELLY BEST FICTION AWARD 2019
WINNER OF THE DAVITT READER'S CHOICE AWARD 2019
WINNER OF THE ITW THRILLER AWARDS BEST PAPERBACK NOVEL 2019

'I absolutely loved *The Lost Man*. I devoured it in a day. Her best yet!'
LIANE MORIARTY

'Harper's books succeed in part because she conveys how even now, geography can be fate. Book by book, she's creating her own vivid and complex account of the outback.' *NEW YORK TIMES*

'In *The Lost Man*, as in Harper's previous two novels, place is paramount, a multifaceted character that's in turns brutal and breathtaking.'
WASHINGTON POST

'Harper adroitly blends the tension and brisk pace of a thriller with the psychological acuity and stylish prose of literary fiction.'
IRISH INDEPENDENT

Force of Nature

NOW A MAJOR MOTION PICTURE STARRING ERIC BANA AS AARON FALK

Five women go on a hike. Only four return.

When a group of colleagues are forced to participate in a team-building exercise in the Giralang Ranges, they reluctantly start walking down the muddy track.

But Alice Russell doesn't appear at the other end. Her last phone call was to Federal Police Agent Aaron Falk.

Alice is the whistleblower in his latest corporate fraud case and as he pursues the investigation, Falk uncovers a tangled web of suspicion and betrayal.

How well do we know the people we work with?

WINNER OF THE READERS' CHOICE DAVITT AWARD 2018

'Once again, Harper manages to touch on something mythic in the Australian experience of the land.' *SATURDAY AGE*

'There are echoes of *Picnic at Hanging Rock* and *Lord of the Flies* as any appearance of civility slips away and the women lose direction in a hostile landscape . . . The novel delivers and Harper writes like a dream.' *SATURDAY PAPER*

The Dry

NOW A MAJOR MOTION PICTURE STARRING ERIC BANA AS AARON FALK

Who really killed the Hadler family?

It hasn't rained in Kiewarra for two years. Tensions in the farming community become unbearable when three members of the Hadler family are discovered shot to death on their property. Everyone assumes Luke Hadler committed suicide after slaughtering his wife and six-year-old son.

Federal Police investigator Aaron Falk returns to his hometown for the funerals and is unwillingly drawn into the investigation. As suspicion spreads through the town, Falk is forced to confront the community that rejected him twenty years earlier. Because Falk and his childhood friend Luke Hadler shared a secret, one which Luke's death threatens to unearth . . .

WINNER ABIA BOOK OF THE YEAR 2017
WINNER ABIA GENERAL FICTION BOOK OF THE YEAR 2017
WINNER INDIE BOOK AWARDS DEBUT FICTION 2017
WINNER DAVITT AWARDS ADULT FICTION 2017
WINNER DAVITT AWARDS READERS CHOICE 2017
WINNER NED KELLY AWARD BEST FIRST FICTION 2017

'One of the most stunning debuts I've ever read . . . Read it!'
DAVID BALDACCI

'Every now and then an Australian crime novel comes along to stop your breath and haunt your dreams' *SYDNEY MORNING HERALD*

'This is a story about heroism, the sins of the past, and the struggle to atone. But let's not forget the redbacks, the huntsmen, the rabbit scourge and all that makes this quintessential Australian story beautifully told'
THE AGE

'Try to set aside one sitting to indulge in journalists Jane Harper's page-turning debut novel. The pace never falters' *DAILY TELEGRAPH*

'There is about *The Dry* something mythic and valiant'
CANBERRA TIMES